Dear Reader

When Harp[...]
three of my [...]
cause it meant I had an opportunity to not only
revisit old friends like the delicious Raphael (and
his alluring tattoo), but also to answer a couple of
questions about the Dark Ones mythology and
explain the basics.

My vampires are always male and come in two
forms: Dark Ones, who are either born of an
unredeemed (i.e., soulless) father or who have
been cursed to that state via a demon lord, and
Moravians, males who possess their souls but
still require blood to exist. There are also female
Moravians, immortals who, unlike their male
counterparts, can exist without consuming blood.

Does that sound sexist to have only the males be
the true vampires? In a way it is, but in truth, my
mythos has its basis in the biblical notion of the
sins of the father being visited upon the sons. That
idea stuck with me when I was thinking of writing a vampire series, mostly because of the unjust
nature of it—which gave me a perfect opportunity
to create dark, tortured men who, through no
fault of their own, are damned to wander around
without a soul, hope, or love . . . until, of course,
the heroine enters the scene.

A Girl's Guide to Vampires serves as an introduction to the sometimes complicated mythology
of Moravian Dark Ones and their Beloveds. I hope
you enjoy dipping your toes into their world!

Katie MacAlister

By Katie MacAlister

The Dark Ones Series

A Girl's Guide to Vampires
Sex and the Single Vampire
Sex, Lies, and Vampires
Even Vampires Get the Blues
Just One Sip
Last of the Red-Hot Vampires
Zen and the Art of Vampires
Crouching Vampire, Hidden Fang
In the Company of Vampires

KATIE MacALISTER

A GIRL'S GUIDE TO VAMPIRES

AVON

An Imprint of HarperCollins Publishers

This book was originally published in Great Britain in 2007 by Hodder & Stoughton, a division of Hodder Headline.

AVON BOOKS
An Imprint of HarperCollins*Publishers*
10 East 53rd Street
New York, New York 10022-5299

I offer my profound thanks and gratitude to Christine Feehan, not only for taking my vampire virginity in a way that left me her most devoted fan, but for her friendship and support, both of which mean worlds to me (especially since they survived a dicey rune stone reading). Big smoochy kisses go, as ever, to my critique partner Vance (who thinks up the best titles), my agent Michelle (who is just all around fabulous), my editor Kate Seaver (who sends me notes to "write funny"), and my husband (who puts up with me).

Chapter One

"Gin makes me brilliant."

"No, Joy, you just *think* gin makes you brilliant. Gin makes you sotted. Chocolate makes you brilliant."

I looked at the reflection in the French door of the dark-haired woman sitting next to me in a circle of lit candles, and shook my head with a solemnity that I hoped belied the aforementioned sottedness. My reflection shook her head as if to warn me. I decided to heed the warning, and carefully set down my glass. "Chocolate has many powers, most notably in the area of adding heft to my hips, but gin, in fact, makes me brilliant."

Our companion drifted around the room lighting more scented candles, pausing to raise her eyebrows at the sight of our mutual friend snorting with laughter into her vodka martini.

"No more libations of a vodka nature for you, Roxanne," Miranda warned before lighting one last candle and dropping down onto a taupe and green leaf print rug across from us. "The Goddess doesn't grant her blessings upon those who are soused. Joy, what is it you are being brilliant about?"

I plucked the lime wedge from my gin and tonic and sucked the gin-soaked meaty pulp from it, mentally bemoaning my Amazonian stature, as Miranda, with the grace of a gazelle who had been taking ballet lessons since birth, pulled her long, slender legs into a lotus position. I gave a moment over to damning the Viking genes that left me towering over most women, and many men. "This plan of Roxy's to find us a pair of dishy guys. I've decided, after much due consideration and many, many brilliant gin-inspired thoughts, to allow you to make my case before your Goddess. If she'd like to point me in the direction of a guy who is the perfect embodiment of everything manly and good, well then, it behooves me to listen. There, in a nutshell, is my brilliance."

Roxanne snorted into her drink again. "In other words, you've broken up with Bradley again."

I shrugged. My on-again, off-again boyfriend had lots of good points, qualities like faithfulness, devotion, patience, and a sunny, optimistic nature. "The problem with Bradley is that he's just not the one—the man who makes my heart race just by being near him, the man who makes me believe in wonderful things like falling in love at first sight. He's just . . . Bradley."

"That's just my point, Joy! You're so stuck in your ways that you can't even be bothered to look for a man you deserve, not old stick-in-the-mud Bradley Barlow, who wouldn't know excitement if it bit him dead center on the ass."

I couldn't help but bristle at the judgmental tone in her voice. I've known Roxy since we were in kindergarten, but that didn't mean she could get away with every snide comment she felt like launching in my direction. "You should

2

speak, Miss Still a Virgin at Twenty-four. What you know about relationships with men could be written on the head of a vibrator."

She spewed martini out her nose.

"Can't take you anywhere, can I?" I said, mopping up the spewed vodka. It had sprayed out all over her jeans and the lovely hardwood floor we were sitting on.

"Geez Louise," she gasped, hacking and wheezing and blowing her nose. She took the cloth Miranda silently offered, mopping up her T-shirt before glaring at me with red-rimmed eyes. "Don't do that to me again!"

"Sorry. It was the gin talking. Told you it makes me brilliant."

"So *that's* what you call it?"

I stuck my tongue out at her.

She turned her glare up a notch. "As for what I was saying when you so rudely brought up the subject of sexual aids— which, just for the record, I don't have, need, or ever expect to use, unlike some people I could mention. Anyway, I'd like to point out that with regards to men, I have the good taste to save myself for someone really meaningful." She paused to blow her nose again. "I hope you notice the contrast between my actions—responsible yet hopeful realism regarding the man destined to be my future husband—and yourself, who has settled for a guy who can't give you anything more than a good fu—"

"Ladies!" Miranda shrieked, cutting Roxy off cold. We both looked at her. She glared back at us. "I refuse to help you if you argue with each other. Honestly, how you two can call each other best friend is beyond me, but regardless of that, I won't have dissension in my house. The Goddess is not in charity with feelings of pettiness and ill will, Roxanne, and since you asked for the Goddess's help, you should be prepared to approach her in a penitential manner with a pure heart and unblemished soul."

I directed a smug smile at Roxy. She ignored me and fought to wipe the stubborn-as-a-mule look from her face. "Sorry," she mumbled, clasping her hands and staring down at them in a close approximation of demureness and penitence.

"The same goes for you, as well," Miranda frowned at me. I widened my eyes and tried to look innocent of all wrongdoing, but it was hard to even think of muddying the truth when Miranda's eerie light gray eyes settled on me.

"I didn't come here desperate for you to find me a man," I pointed out with as much dignity as possible. "Roxy begged me to come."

"I did not!" she snapped, her expression no longer demure. "I simply said that if Bradley was the best you could do for yourself, it wouldn't hurt to have the Goddess look around and see if she couldn't find someone a little better. That's hardly begging. Lord above, I'd think you'd be grateful for this chance to find what most people don't ever have a chance to find—their true soul mate."

I opened my mouth to dispute her statement, but caught sight of an extremely fat black cat with white whiskers and one white paw who was uncurling himself from an adjacent cushioned wicker chair. I held out a lime-scented hand, but the cat, with disdain that would do a king proud, gave me the equivalent to a cat sneer and waddled over to plop himself down before Miranda.

"Whatever," I shrugged off my friend's comments, figuring the evening would go faster if I kept my skepticism to myself. I didn't really believe in all of the hocus-pocus that Miranda claimed to tap into with her spells and invocations to the Goddess, but then, there were a few things that had happened in her presence that I couldn't easily explain. Roxy swallowed it all, though, and despite what she said, she *had* asked me to sit with her for support. I figured it was the least I could do for someone who'd been with me through good times and bad. "Miranda, don't you think it's time to put Davide on a diet? He's almost as big as the Rottweiler that lives down the street from me."

"We are ready to begin." Miranda glared me into silence, sent Roxy a warning look to keep her quiet as well, then closed her eyes and began to breathe deeply, humming a soft little tuneless hum. A gentle breeze swept in through a nearby window, pushing before it the familiar scent of the herbs Miranda used in her invocation candles. A bit guiltily, I remembered that I was supposed to be making my mind open and responsive, and spent a few moments doing a spot of breathing and humming myself, until I got tired of squashing all the little thoughts that kept popping into my head when it was supposed to be an unpainted canvas just waiting for fate's bold brushstrokes. Or whatever it was that Roxy had read from Miranda's instructions. I couldn't quite remember, that part of the conversation being in the pre-gin-and-tonic part of the evening. Instead I looked back at Davide, now engaged in doing a hearty round of personal hygiene on his rear legs.

"It really is funny that you should have a black cat."

Roxy, who had been emulating Miranda, cracked an eye open and rolled it toward Davide. "Why is it funny she has a black cat?"

Miranda continued a soft hum of indistinguishable words, swaying slightly from side to side as her voice rose and fell fluidly in the evening air. I raised my voice a little so I could be heard over the Call to the Goddess. "Because she's a witch, idiot. I wouldn't think most witches would want a black cat, but you have to admit Davide fits the role of familiar perfectly."

The hum became a bit more pronounced, although Miranda kept her eyes firmly closed.

Roxy sent a worried little glance to her, then leaned close to me and whispered, "I don't think they like the word

5

'witch' anymore, Joy. *Wiccan* is what you're supposed to call them now."

I whispered back to her, "Why? What's wrong with 'witch'?"

She sat up straight again and closed her eyes. "Not PC," she hissed out of the side of her mouth. "Besides, Wiccans are more in touch with nature. Can't you feel the power in her Summoning?"

I looked at the Circle of Knowledge Miranda had laid out around the two of us, and felt a little shiver of excitement ripple down my back. I may be a skeptic, but I wasn't a boob. There was something in the air, an electric charge that had the fine hairs on my arms waving around. I reminded myself that it wasn't everyone Miranda practiced her magic for, and tried to look grateful.

"It's a bit nerve-wracking, this," I muttered a few minutes later to Roxy in a soft voice so as not to disturb Miranda as she was Communing with the Goddess. I fished out a piece of ice from my drink and popped it in my mouth. "Not that I think it'll work with me, but still, it is a bit nervy just sitting here waiting for a spirit on high to flash me the curriculum vitae of the love of my life."

"It's time you got a little proactive with your love life," Roxy muttered back at me. "I may still be a virgin, but at least I'm trying to find Mr. Wonderful. You don't even go on any dates. How do you expect to find the heavenly bliss of the man nature created just for you if you won't even look for him?"

"Well," I said around the crunching of ice, "there *is* Bradley."

"That's not heavenly bliss, Joyful." Roxy smiled, taking the sting out of her comment with the use of my childhood nickname. "That's purgatory."

"You have a point," I conceded, grimacing at the sight of Davide as he turned his attention to his rectal area. I fervently hoped it wasn't a comment on the success of Miranda's foreseeing. "Although it's not like I haven't tried or anything, God knows I have, but you've experienced the single scene out there—it's blood tests and background checks and references and 'Please pee in this cup before we go on a date' screenings, all clinical and stripped bare of any romance."

"True," Roxy nodded.

"Whatever happened to good old fashioned falling in love at first sight? That's all I ask for, a little romance and candlelight and staring meaningfully into each other's eyes, knowing you've met your perfect mate the second you see him."

"Too many creeps out there these days," Roxy replied. "Love at first sight has been replaced by a comprehensive credit check."

Miranda's soft hum took on a decidedly strident tone. I listened for a moment to the murmured words, but could make nothing of them.

"Shhh." I pinched Roxy. "You're going to blow your chances with the Goddess if you keep flapping your lips when you're supposed to be concentrating."

"You're the one who's supposed to be concentrating." Roxy pinched me back. "I already know what qualities I want in my perfect man. I bet you haven't thought about what you want in a man at all."

"Both of you are supposed to be concentrating," Miranda intoned between hums.

Roxy and I looked guiltily at one another.

"It really is sweet of you to spend your evening on this, since you had to close your shop for the ritual cleansing and all," Roxy smiled.

I nodded.

"You're a true friend, Miranda," Roxy went on. "I hope you know I wouldn't have asked you to go to all this work if it hadn't been an emergency, but what with that date last night with Mr. Octopus Hands, well, a girl just has to do something when she hits the 250th date mark with nary a boyfriend in sight to show for her trouble. And, of course, Joy needs all the help she can get."

"Hey!" I glared at Roxy. She just grinned back at me.

"In fact, I've been worried about her for some time. She's got a dead-end job, an ex-boyfriend who could bore an ice cube, and no interests outside the library. If we don't take matters into our own hands, she'll end up single and chaste the rest of her life, living in a small pink house with thirty-seven cats all named Kevin, with no one to talk to but her successful, happy, catless friends."

"You're delusional," I said with great dignity. "And for the record, you have the same dead-end job I have."

"So if you don't see her soul mate in the immediate future," Roxy continued, ignoring my interruption, "I for one would appreciate it if you would lie and say you did. She's desperate, if you know what I mean."

And lonely. I was willing to admit that. Very lonely. I swirled the ice in my glass around and reflected on my loneliness. "I'm not desperate, Rox, I'm just . . . available."

"Well, there's always Germany if we can't find nice American men."

Miranda opened her eyes to shoot a questioning look at Roxy.

"Germany," I reminded her. "Roxy and I are part of the team going to the Frankfurt Book Festival. I have to admit, I wouldn't mind one of those dishy blond German men. You think some of them might be wearing lederhosen? Hubba hubba!"

Miranda opened her mouth to say something, thought better of it, and shook her head. She continued the soft chanting, a prayer, according to the cheat sheet Roxy had

given me earlier, to the Goddess for strength and enlight-
enment.

I flicked ice chips at Davide for a few minutes until Miranda opened her eyes and pinned me back with a look that
could strip the stripes off a tiger. "Now is the time for both
of you to focus your attention on envisioning your ideal
man. You must open yourself to the image engraved on your
heart and your soul. Focus on that image, allowing it to fill
your awareness, narrowing your thoughts until they are
made up only of him."

"Oooh, goody, fantasy time!" I rubbed my hands together
and thought of the ideal man made up of the better parts
of Colin Firth, Alan Rickman, and Oded Fehr, all rolled into
one luscious, droolworthy package.

"Dibs I go first!" Roxy said quickly. I made mean eyes at
her. When Miranda sighed and nodded, Roxy sat up as tall
as a person who barely tops five feet could, closed her eyes,
and started ticking items off her fingers. "OK, here's my order: someone not too tall, that is important point number
one. Lord knows I've been on enough dates with tall men.
Do you know how disconcerting it is to find yourself staring
a man straight in the nipples? I'd like someone of medium
height, please. And just to make things easier on you, I won't
be picky about hair color or eye color, or even how handsome the man is, as long as he has really nice hands, knows
how to cook, and wants lots and lots of children."

Miranda smiled as she got to her feet and began sprin-
kling rose petals around the Circle, still chanting, pausing
to make gestures of protection to the four compass points.

"And he's got to have a good sense of humor. I'm afraid
that is a must-have; I'll have to return any prospects who
turn out to be humorless. Life is simply too short to be stuck
with a guy who can't be silly once in a while."

"I understand. Joy?"

I glared at my friend. "Geez, Rox, leave something for the rest of us to work with, will you?"

She smirked at me. Miranda cocked an eyebrow in such a manner that I immediately cleared my mind and tried to picture the perfect man.

"Um, well, tall, dark, and handsome goes without saying. Roxy was right about one thing, a sense of humor is good, I'd prefer a man who likes to laugh."

Roxy rolled her eyes.

"And . . . um . . . well . . . I'd . . . um . . . like someone who's nice to animals."

"Bo-ring!"

"And one who likes to read."

"So in other words, you want Beaver Cleaver's dad?"

I ignored Roxy's comments, deciding if I was going to do this, I might as well do it right. I thought for a long moment about what I wanted in a man, what I really wanted, what secret desires were hidden deep within me. Slowly, out of the everyday confusion of my mind, an image wavered before me, growing solid as the gentle herb-scented night breeze washed over me. With the brightening image came the words, hesitant and charged with a strange emotion, as if it weren't really me speaking. "He will send shivers of delight down my spine with the dark cloak of intrigue wrapped around him. He will captivate me, fascinate me, fold me into the air of mystery and adventure that surrounds him, making my blood sing with desire. He will need me, depend on me, trust me where he has trusted no other. He will light my dark hours, and his love will shine as a beacon that will guide me through the most twisted of paths. He is my strength, my faith, and I will not really begin to live until I know his heart is mine."

"Ooooh," Roxy breathed. "That is so romantic. You should write that down."

I blinked as the image in my mind turned to mist and

evaporated. I felt a bit dizzy, like I'd been turning somersaults down a long hill. I was more than a little bit weirded out by the whole thing until I remembered the gin and tonics I'd been sipping on. Although alcohol had never triggered that sort of a vision before, there was a first time for everything.

"I want all that on my list, too!"

"Too late, it's mine," I told Roxy with a dazed grin. She punched me in the arm.

"Is that all?" Miranda asked us both, completing the circle and returning to her spot.

"It is for me, since old greedy-guts there won't share the good stuff on her list," Roxy said huffily.

I ran down my mental checklist. Yup, it was all there, all but for one last item. . . .

"I have one more request," I said.

Miranda paused in the act of lighting the large candle sitting before her.

"Big private parts," I told them. "That's important, don't you think? I mean, size does matter, no matter what they say, right? And since we are talking *the* man for me, my soul mate, he'll be the only one I sleep with for the rest of my life, so I think he should have really nice personal equipment. Something memorable. The phrase 'hung like a horse' comes to mind."

"Joy Martine Randall!" Roxy choked.

I made an innocent little moue at her. "What's wrong? Mad you didn't think of it first?"

Her hazel eyes flashed a warning at me. I cackled. She *was* mad I had beaten her to big genitals.

Miranda gave me a look of martyrdom that had me biting back my cackle to a more seemly giggle. "OK, you don't have to include that last item on the official request list. I can live with a man with a regular set of dangly bits as long

11

as the rest of the items are there. If he meets the other requirements, I'll be happy."

Miranda sighed and shook her head. "You're so flippant, both of you, I don't know how you expect me to help you find the man you are searching for if all you're thinking of is the size of his crotch and whether or not he's likely to laugh at your jokes. This is serious; the power of the Goddess is nothing to be taken lightly. You should be reaching out with your heart and soul to find this man, not parroting the silly ideas you've soaked up from those romances you both read."

Roxy and I instantly united in a solid front against her condemnation of our beloved romances.

"They aren't silly or horrible; romances are upbeat and fun to read," my bosom buddy protested.

"Yeah," I added, flipping another ice chip at Davide. He gave me an open-mouthed silent hiss that raised the hairs on the back of my neck. Skeptic I might be, but there was no reason to be stupid and tempt powers I wasn't sure didn't exist.

Miranda stilled. "What about those vampire books you are both addicted to?"

Something in the air between us thickened. I wondered if an electrical storm was on its way. "What about them?" I asked.

"They're dangerous."

"Dangerous? How can books be dangerous? They're just a series of stories about heroes who happen to be vampires, Miranda. It's not like they advocate the drinking of blood or anything."

"Some people," she said to me, without taking her gaze off Roxy, "believe them to be a guide to their fate."

I looked between her and Roxy. The latter was sitting quietly, picking at the leather thong on her sandal, not meeting our eyes.

"Some people believe every word written in them to be the truth."

I shook my head. "No one really believes in the *Book of Secrets'* Dark Ones," I told Miranda. "They're just really dark, broody heroes that turn a lot of women on, myself included, I'm not too horribly embarrassed to say. Just because we like the stories doesn't mean we believe that vampires really exist."

"I do," came a soft voice.

I stared at my friend of nineteen years.

"I do," she said louder, with more confidence, an obstinate set to her jaw that I knew well. "I believe they really exist. C. J. Dante, the author of the *Book of Secrets* series has done extensive research in the Moravian Highlands, the area where the Dark Ones live. He even moved there so he could be closer to them, so he could study them and learn their ways. I believe they exist."

She must have felt the weight of two sets of disbelieving eyes, because she hiked her chin up even higher. "Well, I do!"

"Roxy . . ." I shook my head. "Honey, I know it's a tempting thought to believe that such things really exist, but come on! Vampires? Men who drink blood and burn up in the sun and wander around all tormented and angsting because they haven't found the right woman to save their soul? I'll admit some of the guys you've dated might meet a few of those qualifications, but we're going to have to have a long, long talk if you're going to start believing in ghosties and goulies and things that go bump in the night."

I had forgotten in whose house I was sitting.

" 'There are more things in heaven and earth, Horatio, than are dreamt of in your philosophy'," Miranda said quietly.

"Yeah, but I don't think Shakespeare had Moravian Dark Ones in mind when he wrote that," I argued.

She just looked at me with light gray eyes that reminded me of a full moon at its brightest. Her belief in things that I doubted made me uncomfortably aware of just what I was doing sitting in a circle of candles. "Look, why don't we get on with this? Dr. Miller wants me to re-catalog the entire biology collection before we leave for Germany, and I'd like to get some sleep before I face a bunch of books on fungi and spores and mildew in the morning."

"No," Roxy said stubbornly. "I want to hear why Miranda believes in the good powers she uses, but won't admit the possibility of a darker side of the same power."

Miranda shook her head, her red curls a riot of crimson and gold in the candlelight. "I never said I don't believe in a dark power, Roxanne. I do, most profoundly. There are things I have seen that I hope I never see again, but that type of danger is not what I'm speaking about. I'm talking about the power of persuasion, the intent of the author who includes in his fiction ideas dangerous to your soul."

"Dante writes them as fiction, true," Roxy argued, "but all of his followers know the stories are based on truths he has uncovered during his research. You should see the websites devoted to the genealogies of the people Dante has written about—"

"They're romances for the masses, glorifying the cult of bloodsucking killers."

"Oh!" Roxy stormed, leaping up. I reached out to grab the back of her leg, but she sidestepped quickly until she was almost out of the circle. "Bloodsucking killers? I'll have you know that every single Dark One is tormented, very, very tormented by the horrible truth of his life, and none of them kill people. They just borrow a little blood now and again. I don't see what's so wrong about that!"

"Roxanne, if you don't sit back down, you will break the Circle of Truth, and the Invocation will be useless."

She sat down with a hrmph. "Take it back, Miranda."

"This Dante is guilty of brainwashing you, of seducing innocents like yourself into thinking the darkness found in men's souls is something to be tampered with . . ."

"Luke, beware the dark side," I intoned in my best Obi Wan Kenobi voice.

Both women turned astonished faces at me. I gave them a weak smile and held up my hands. "Sorry, I thought it was funny. You know, Miranda, I don't mean to be picky, but some of what you believe could be thought to be a bit . . . well, out there."

She raised an eyebrow. "My beliefs are not the point—it is the silliness of these books, these novels that you and others insist on believing are real that I'm concerned about."

"I don't believe they're real," I said at the same time Roxy muttered, "They're a lot more real than some things I can name."

"Only the foolish meddle in the darkness in men's souls," Miranda warned.

"Dark Ones are not evil, they just appear that way at first!" Roxy snapped back.

They glared at each other until I decided to mellow them both out.

"Would you two lighten up a bit? You're giving me the creeps with all this talk about the dark power of men's souls and stuff."

Miranda was shaking her head again, even before I stopped speaking. "The dark power within each of us is nothing to joke about, Joy."

"Right. Sorry. So why don't we agree to disagree?" I asked, gesturing between the two of them. "Roxy will continue to believe that there are actual Moravian Dark Ones wandering around looking for women to save their souls, and you'll continue to believe that famed author C. J. Dante is a nutball bent on world domination by brainwashing millions of frustrated housewives. K? Are we all happy now?"

"I won't be until she takes back what she said about the Dark Ones!"

Miranda sighed as she made sweeping gestures with her hands to reinforce the bounds of the circle. "Very well, I take it back. They're harmless little books that give you and millions of others pleasure, and as long as you realize they are fiction, complete fiction, and not a guidebook to exploring the dark forces within, I will withdraw my objections."

I figured that was as much of an apology as she was going to give. Roxy evidently decided the same, because she nodded.

"I want to warn you both, though," Miranda added as she shook a long, elegant finger at us, "that those who play with fire should expect to be consumed by it."

"Consumed by the fire of passion." I grinned at her as I fingered the remaining ice in my glass. "Sounds like something from one of Dante's books! I'm willing to bet there are worse ways to go, huh?"

Davide gave me another silent hiss.

Chapter Two

"You think she's mad at us?"

Roxy rolled her eyes and shifted into third, a quick flip of her wrist sending her ancient MG hurtling into what looked like a four-foot space between two semis. Once I stopped screaming and peeled my hands from my eyes, I turned to glare at her.

"No, I don't think Miranda is mad at us."

"Oh, good." If there's one rule I try to live my life by, it's not to make a witch angry.

"I think she's mad at *you.*"

"She is not," I said indignantly, trying to adjust my legs. In the tiny car, my knees were pretty much jammed under my chin. It's been my experience that people who are six feet tall and built like a brick house don't fit well into tiny sports cars. "You're the one who had to go babbling on and on about how you believe in the Dark Ones."

"Well, I do. You do, too."

"I do not."

17

"Ha! Just last week when you finished *Book of Secrets XII* you said that Xavier was the hunkiest Moravian yet, and that if you had been around, he never would have had to face The Decision by himself because you would have been there to save him before he became that desperate. Go on, tell me you didn't say that. Tell me you didn't call dibs on him before I could."

"Fwah! I don't believe in any of that hocus-pocus, and you know it."

"If you don't believe, why do you read rune stones for people, hmmm?"

I gave her a jaded smile. "Because they're pretty. You know full well it's just a party trick, nothing more."

"Ha! A party trick doesn't explain—"

"LOOK OUT! Dammit, Roxy, will you watch where you're going? You almost gave me a heart attack!"

She honked and waved at the semi truck driver as we swerved around it, zooming down the long, curving highway so characteristic of the wild, untamed back roads of Oregon. I read her the riot act on trying to kill us through careless driving, which she responded to with injured silence. I took advantage of the quiet to think over the events of the evening. Evidently, Roxy was doing the same.

"Joy?"

"What?"

She said nothing for a minute. "You know, you don't have to go to Czechoslovakia with me."

"It's the Czech Republic now."

"Oh." An owl flirted with the car's high beams, a flash of ghostly white wing catching my peripheral vision before it melted into the darkness. "Whatever they're calling it now, I appreciate the offer to come with me, but given what Miranda said . . ."

I swallowed hard and gnawed on my lip, trying to remind myself that I didn't believe in any of the things Miranda said she could do, or see, or manifest. Most were coincidences that would have happened regardless of whether or not she was seeking the advice of some greater being. I was a sensible person. I didn't believe in Bigfoot, or ghosts, or vampires, or even the powers held by white witches.

". . . Well, I just want you to know that I won't hold you to your offer. Of keeping me out of trouble after the Book Fair, that is. You can spend your two-week holiday tooling around Europe and seeing Paris like you had originally planned. I'm sure I won't have any trouble getting to the Czech Republic by myself." She offered me a weak grin. I bared my teeth in what I hoped was a semblance of a smile, and returned to staring out the window at the passing night and trying to rub the goose bumps from my arms.

Roxy's session with Miranda had gone just fine, no surprise to me since everyone liked Roxy. She was petite, had curly black hair and blue eyes that made her look like an elf or pixie or one of those cute little munchkin people. Men generally feel all masculine and protective of her, and erroneously assume she's shy and delicate despite the fact that she has the constitution and willpower of an ox. She was to have it all, the Goddess told her through Miranda. She was to meet her perfect man before the moon rose and set again; she would give her heart and receive one in return; she would fulfill the destiny laid before her feet. I could practically hear the Disney chorus of woodland creatures breaking into song, what with all the sweetness and light that filled Miranda's living room . . . until she'd scried *my* future.

The wind seemed to forespell my doom as it gusted into the room, blowing out half the candles in the circle, and sending the spray of rose petals around us dancing into the far corners of the room. Roxy leaped up to close the French doors as Miranda quickly relit the candles. Once settled, she waved at me to begin reciting my part of the Invocation. I felt a bit like an idiot, but knew there was no way Roxy would let me out of there without giving the Goddess a shot at me.

> *"Power of earth to move his feet*
> *Across the mountains, here to me.*
> *Water's power to plumb the depths*
> *Of the storm-toss'd briny sea.*
> *True love's image, I invoke*
> *Powers of air, and red-hot fire;*
> *One to burn him with my glance,*
> *One to stoke my heart's desire.*
> *Seven knots I double-tie*
> *Moon and candles light the way,*
> *Seven knots for me and love.*
> *Entangled heart in heart to stay."*

"So, what do you see?" I asked impatiently a few minutes later as Miranda stared sightlessly into a bowl of water. "Do you see Mr. Right? Is he cute? Does he look like he's really loaded in the groinal region?"

"Joy!"

I made a face at Roxy and turned back to Miranda. Her eyes had lost their focus as they did when she scried Roxy's future, but there was something different about her bearing now, something tense and unyielding that was in direct contrast to the relaxed posture she had with Roxy. Davide rose to his feet and started to stalk toward me, the hair on his back rising as he approached me.

"Jeezumcrow, that's a little creepy," I muttered, getting a serious case of the willies as the cat stopped about six feet in front of me, his yellow eyes never wavering from me. Miranda started to speak, so low both of us leaned forward in order to hear her better. Her low monotone, so different from her normally warm voice, added to the eerie atmosphere, and it took a few minutes before I could understand her words. Outside, the wind suddenly picked up, slamming into the house, tiny ticks and thumps indicating that debris and pinecones were being kicked around in the wind.

"All this needs is some lightning and a ghostly figure with a red-stained butcher knife suddenly appearing in the window," I said in an undertone to Roxy. What I had intended to be a light, joking tone came off as pregnant with foreboding. She looked at me with large, serious eyes.

A shiver went down my spine suddenly, the old *someone stepping on your grave* feeling my grandmother used to talk about. My arms were goose-bumped all the way up to my shoulders despite the warm night. If only the cat would stop staring at me like I was a three-headed Hydra, I'd be OK.

Miranda's voice strengthened, but she didn't seem to be speaking in English. I glanced back at Davide. He appeared to have been turned into a stone statue that sat staring at me.

"Aren't cats supposed to see ghosts?" I asked Roxy.

She nodded, one hand reaching over to grasp mine. I tried to tell myself to relax, that this was all in fun, that I was simply humoring a friend, but the air inside the room was almost blue with static electricity. When the hairs on my arm all suddenly stood on end, I decided skepticism was for the dogs, and I was ready and willing to believe whatever it took to get me safely out of this situation.

"You will take a trip."

The words, clearly spoken in the quiet of the room, made us both jump. Miranda was still staring at her bowl of water, her face pale and drawn. As her words sank in, I relaxed and disengaged my hand from Roxy's, giving her a little pat in the process.

"Yes, that's right. I told you we were going to Germany."

"You will take a trip unlike any other you have taken."

21

I relaxed even more, a faint burble of relieved laughter building inside. After this weird setup, all I was going to get was the standard "cross my palms with silver" fortune reading? No problem! I'd play along. "Two for two, I've never been to Europe before."

"You will travel by water, held firmly in the Goddess's womb, protected but not protected, in danger but not in danger."

"Um . . . OK." I tried to remember if there were any boat trips needed to get to Frankfurt. There were none that I could think of. And what was all that about being held in the Goddess's womb? It didn't sound like a particularly enjoyable or comfortable way to travel unless there was lots of legroom inside.

"A child of darkness will cross your path."

My jaw dropped as Roxy sat bolt upright next to me, clutching my hand again. A child of darkness? Was Miranda talking about a Moravian? A Dark One? No, she couldn't be, she didn't believe they existed . . . or did she? She never really came right out and said they didn't exist, she just went off about how dangerous it was to toy with the darkness within, and all that business. She couldn't really be saying what I thought she was saying, could she? I slid a glance over to Roxy. Her eyes were hollowed as she looked back at me and mouthed, "Vampire."

"The child of darkness will hold your fate in his hands, but you must not be blinded by his unholy attraction, for down that path lies eternal night."

Well, *that* didn't sound good!

"Um." My voice came out a squeak deep in my throat. I cleared it, glancing nervously at Davide. He continued his stare-a-thon. "When you say 'child of darkness,' what exactly do you mean?"

"His soul is a well of despair. A great wind howls within

22

him, but you must not be tempted to save his soul, for his is a path you cannot take."

"Oh my God," Roxy whispered, her fingernails digging into my arm. "Oh my God, Joy, do you know what she's saying?"

Oh, sure, I knew what she was saying. I was about to walk straight into the arms of some axe-murdering maniac.

"This child of darkness that you see," Roxy asked, loosening her grip when I tried to pry her fingers off my wrist. "Is this the man who is Joy's soul mate? Is this the man you see as part of her future?"

Oh my Lord, what a horrible thought! I had a quick flash of me standing in an antiseptic prison room marrying a man with tattoos all over his head.

"The one filled with despair is part of it, but he is separate, holding himself aside. There is a second man, a shadow, who stands behind the child of darkness."

Great! Two axe murderers! I'd get to commit bigamy with two homicidal maniacs. Oh, lucky, lucky me!

"Gark," I said.

Roxy hushed me. "Be quiet or you'll have to leave. I'm trying to figure this out for you. Miranda, or whoever is talking through you right now, could you please be a little more specific about these two men you see? I don't quite understand how they can be her future and yet be such a threat to her."

Miranda shook her head slowly, her eyes roaming blindly around the room as if she were seeking something but not finding it. Her gaze settled on me as she reached for the crystal hanging from her neck. "I cannot see clearly, the vision is fogged. It could be that the child of darkness is trying to create an illusion, or it could be the shadow cast by the second one that is tainting the image. All that is clear to me is danger, mortal danger to your soul when you are in the child of darkness's presence. You must be careful which man you choose, for to decide unwisely between the two will cast your soul into eternal night."

Suddenly Miranda's eyes focused and color rushed back to her face. The weight of her gray-eyed gaze left me feeling as if she had brushed her fingers against my flesh. She blinked a couple of times and looked between the two of us. "Why are you both staring at me with your mouths hanging open?"

"Oh, no reason," I said in a tight, choked voice. "No reason at all, unless you count your prediction that I'll end up a soulless, tormented who-knows-what living the life of the undead in eternal night a reason."

Miranda looked at Roxy. "Did I say that?"

She nodded, slowly relaxing her grip on my hand. "You weren't too clear, though; what you said was pretty vague. I couldn't understand if it was the Moravian who is Joy's perfect man, or the someone evil behind him."

"Either way, it sounds like if I hook up with either one of the two guys you mentioned, I'm sure to end up a zombie-woman, roaming the earth forever in search of a soul. That's not exactly what was on my list of required elements of my perfect mate, eh?"

Miranda opened her mouth, then snapped it shut again. She looked drained, exhausted, and suddenly I was overcome with guilt at making light of something she took seriously, especially when she was trying to do us a favor.

"I'm sorry, I didn't mean that to sound so flip. I truly wouldn't want you to think I wasn't taking this seriously, or was wasting your talents. I can see this type of ceremony takes a lot out of you. We both owe you for this, big-time."

"Speak for yourself," Roxy snapped, sounding more like herself as she started blowing out the candles still burning around us. "I'm not the ungrateful beast you are. I gave Miranda that old Herbal I found at the estate sale."

"Ah." I thought for a moment of a way to repay Miranda

without involving money, something I knew she felt was taboo. I snapped my fingers as an idea occurred to me. "I know! I'll donate my time at the next Womyn's Magyck Festival. I could set up a booth and cast rune stones again. . . ."

"Goddess help us, no!"

I blinked at the outburst. Miranda's auburn curls stood out in agitation as if she had been running both hands through them. Her pale gray eyes glistened with strong emotion as she leaned forward and, avoiding the flames of the candles still burning in front of me, carefully took both of my hands in her own. I peered over her shoulder. Roxy was nodding sanctimoniously and petting Davide.

"Promise me . . . no, *swear* to me that you won't ever cast your rune stones in public again! Not after the last time!"

I looked back at the witch. "But—"

"Swear!"

"Miranda, that was just a fluke. It could never happen again—"

"SWEAR!"

"I'm not the least bit psychic, remember? You told me that everyone had some sort of psychic ability, even if it was buried deep where the person wouldn't recognize it. Everyone but me, that is. You *told* me that! You said I hadn't even an atom of psychic ability, so you can't possibly blame the . . . the . . . happenings on me and my innocent little rune stones!"

"Swear you won't cast them again or I will ask the Goddess to remove her protection! Without her blessing, you will not be successful at any task you undertake."

I pulled my hands from hers. "Well, I don't think that's very nice of you, and I just bet your Goddess doesn't like to be used like a revolving door. Besides, I don't know what you're complaining about. That earthquake had nothing to do with my casting. It was just a very odd coincidence that the stones suggested Lydia would bring down the wrath of

Odin if she continued to ignore the warnings sent her."

"You said the earth would tremble with Odin's wrath if she didn't heed the warnings," Roxy piped up. I frowned at her.

"You are not helping matters, missy. What I told Lydia was standard rune stone–reading talk. Everyone says stuff like that. It's in all of the books."

"Joy, you predicted that Lydia's courage would be shaken if she didn't alter her course; you didn't say the earth would tremble under the entire northern California coast!" Miranda looked grim.

"Well . . . Odin was very strong. I guess his wrath just kind of spilled out . . ."

"And the fire? What about the fire? Miranda, ask her about the fire!"

I raised one eyebrow and ignored both of them to look out the window in silent contemplation of the blue-black clouds racing across the face of the silver crescent of moon. There were times when it was simply best to say nothing at all.

"Loreena," Roxy nudged Miranda. I sent her a silent cease-and-desist semaphore with my eyebrows that she summarily ignored.

"I haven't forgotten that," Miranda said slowly, her gaze holding mine. "That was your first reading, wasn't it? You predicted that Loreena Bronze would be cleansed and re-born just as the phoenix was . . . rising from the ashes."

I couldn't help myself. I pursed my lips and twisted my fingers together. It *had* been an odd coincidence that I had seen fire in the leader of Miranda's coven's future. Still . . . "Stranger things have been known to happen."

Miranda took a calming deep breath, stretching her arms to the side as she inhaled, crossing her wrists gracefully over one another as she exhaled. Roxy plopped a pillow down on the floor next to her and dropped onto it. "Don't forget

26

the rainstorm, the one that struck the North Shore. You *do* remember that nice couple who you predicted would be taking a long journey by water?"

"Well, they did." I stared at my fingers. They suddenly looked fascinating. There was a whole world of entertainment to be found in cuticle gazing.

"Their house slid off the cliff into the ocean!"

"That's a journey by water in my book. How either of you can blame a rainstorm on my rune stone reading—"

"Joy, you cast your stones for eleven people that day, and of those eleven castings you saw disaster in ten, four of which involved natural disasters that manifested within three weeks," Miranda said firmly. "The Womyn's Magyck Festival Council has forbidden you ever to cast your stones within their domain. They would have banned you completely except they knew how much you help out at the Shoppe."

"And how much *you* donate each year in support of the Council," I muttered darkly.

Miranda waved a hand. "Exactly. So no rune stones! I might have been a little hasty in suggesting you don't have any psychic ability. You do seem to have one."

I looked up from cuticle watch, shooting a smug glance at Roxy to make sure she was listening. "Oh? What do I have? Precognition? Clairvoyance? The ability to leap tall buildings in a single bound?"

She ignored my attempt at humor. "No. I think you're cataclysient."

Huh? "Cataclysient? Is that a word?"

"What does it mean?" Roxy asked.

Miranda closed her eyes, breathed in deeply the scent of the herbs bound into the invocation candles, and traced an ancient symbol of protection in my general direction. "It means when you cast your rune stones you have the dangerous and uncontrolled ability to call down cataclysmic disasters."

Roxy snickered. I was stunned by Miranda's outrageous, and patently false, claim. I stood up, saying, "You're making that up. There is no such word as cataclysient, and even if there was, I'm not it. I'm just a simple woman trying to do you a favor, and I resent the fact that you can think something so ridiculous about me. Sheesh!"

"Oh, I don't know," Roxy started to say. I mouthed that I'd get her later. She just grinned and continued on. "There's just something about you that shrieks cataclysmic disaster. I think Miranda's dead on."

"You would."

"Ladies!"

We stopped sniping and looked at our friend. She shook her Invocation candle at us. "I don't know what exactly the Goddess chose to reveal to your eyes, but I do know this— you are taking her gift far too lightly. There is purpose behind everything she reveals, and if you do not take careful heed of her warnings, you will suffer."

"Are you trying to scare us?" I asked.

"If she is, she's doing a good job," Roxy muttered sotto voce. I agreed wholeheartedly.

"Yes, I am, if that's what it will take to bring you to your senses. The Goddess did not share her vision of your future with me, Joy, but this I sense: If you continue down the path you have started, you place your life, your very soul, at risk. Please keep the Goddess's words close to your heart, and make no foolish decisions."

It wasn't so much Miranda's words, but the almost tangible sense of fear surrounding her that remained with me, still palpable almost an hour later as we drove through the winding roads toward the small town on the southern Oregon coast where we lived.

"What are you going to do?" Roxy asked.

"About what?"

She shot a fast glance at me out of the corner of her eye as she turned down the street where I lived in a tiny studio apartment. "About our trip. I know you think I'm an idiot to spend my two weeks in Europe hunting down a Dark One, but I *was* hoping you'd come with me because I think we'd have a lot of fun. Now . . . well, now you have a really good reason to go to Paris instead."

I shrugged. "You know, I like Miranda a lot, she's a very kind and giving person, but I have to tell you—it just rankles when someone tells me not to do something. It makes me all that much more determined to do it. And this whole business with the 'child of darkness,' and a soulless wonder—well, you have to admit it sounds like it's straight out of a book. And not a very well-written one, either."

Roxy pulled into the driveway leading to my apartment. "So you're going to come with me, then? You'll help me find a Moravian Dark One?"

"No." I levered myself out of her car, making yet another mental promise that I'd never ride in that car again without first losing twenty pounds. "I won't help you find a make-believe being that doesn't exist anywhere but in the world of fiction; however, I will go with you to the Czech Republic, but only because it's an historic area that sounds interesting, and because you have absolutely no ability with foreign languages. I'd never be able to live with myself if you ended up in some Czech prison because you inadvertently propositioned some policeman rather than asking him where the nearest toilet was. I'll come with you, but don't expect me to pander to your idiocy over vampires and others of their ilk."

She grinned, her eyes shadowed in the flat glow of the overhead light. "Dante's castle is next door to the town I'm going to, you know. You said you want to see some castles while we're in Europe, and if we hang around Dante's long enough, we might get a glimpse of him. I'm going to take all my books just in case we can corner him."

"That poor man," I said in mock sorrow, shaking my head as I retrieved my purse from the back seat.

"Why is he a poor man?"

"I'm sure the last thing he envisioned when he started writing books was the hordes of ravening women who would turn stalker just to get his autograph." I flashed her a quick grin before I closed the door on her outraged protests.

I waved and toddled up the stairs to my attic apartment, a vague uneasy feeling still gripping me despite my determination to pooh-pooh the evening's events.

Miranda's predictions weren't real, couldn't be real, I told myself. At least, they weren't real in any sense a normal, feet-on-the-ground woman of moderate intelligence would recognize.

So why did I feel like I was being dragged slowly, but inexorably, to the edge of a black chasm from which there was no return?

Chapter Three

"So, what do you recommend as the sights to see around Blansko?"

"Oh, there are many magnificent tourist sights," the tall man sitting across from us answered, pushing his glasses higher up on his nose. "There are the karst, of course: Catherine Cave, Sloupsko-Šošůvské Cave, and Balcarka Cave are some of the better-known examples. And the Macocha Abyss is not to be missed; it is 138 meters deep, you know."

I didn't know, as a matter of fact, which was why, when I found an English-speaking ex-Czech national on the train heading north of Brno returning to his homeland for a brother's wedding, I pumped him for information on the area.

Roxy looked up from one of the *Book of Secrets* novels that I had secretly reread before the trip—secretly because I didn't want Roxy thinking I was reading it less as fiction and more as a guidebook to the area, as she was. "An abyss? There's an abyss? Is it dark and mysterious and bottomless?

Are there things lurking in its hidden depths, things that no man has lived to tell about?"

"Ignore her," I told the man and his companion. "She refuses to read guidebooks, preferring to be surprised instead." I pulled out my own guidebook and flipped through it until I found the item mentioned.

"The Macocha Abyss is a famous geological formation," I told Roxy, "and the picture shows it's not in the least bit dark or mysterious. There's a trail you can take to walk down into it, to the Punkevní cave."

"Oh," she said, clearly disappointed. She glanced out the window at the scenery—heavily forested land, rising in elevation as we headed into the Moravian Highlands and the small town of Blansko. I knew from my glance at the map that Drahanská Castle, cuddled up close to Blansko, sat hidden in the forests of the eastern edge of Bohemia.

"Caves sound cool, but what is that other thing you mentioned?" I asked. The man looked confused by my question.

"I think she's asking what a karst is, Martin."

I nodded to Martin's wife, a lively blond American named Holly. "On the nose. I haven't a clue what a karst is."

"Ah," Martin answered, smiling and rubbing his hands. It turned out I was asking the right man, since Martin was a geophysical expert who told me more than I ever wanted to know about the canyons, gorges, and more than four hundred large and small caves that honeycombed the surrounding area. Even Roxy pulled her nose out of her book and paid attention once he described some of the more spectacular caves, ones that had underground rivers running through them. I rustled through my guidebook looking for information on the ones that were open to the public.

"Sounds cool." I smiled, trying to cut off the flow of information about the biochemical makeup of the limestone and the effect it had on the surrounding water table.

"What about the castle?" Roxy wanted to know.

"Oh, yes, the castle. Drahanská is the name. Very impressive, but not open to the public as it's privately owned, but the grounds are very fine and open year round. You should visit them; the sculptures were by Schweigl."

I made an impressed "No! Not Schweigl himself!" face, and nodded, hoping our source of unbounded information wouldn't go into detail on the chemical composition of the soil in the Schweigl-decorated gardens.

"The castle itself is limestone, of course."

"Of course," I agreed, and hurried another question forward before Martin continued that particular thread of conversation. "My friend is interested in some of the folklore which I understand is particularly rich in this area."

"Yes, it is," Holly answered for Martin. "Very rich. Moravia was a separate state for centuries, you know, and they have a fascinating history. Much of their folklore has been carved from the dark roots of their past."

She must have noticed the look Roxy and I slid each other because she gave a little laugh and explained, "I have a degree in Eastern European history. That's how I met Martin—I was studying at Ostrava University when he was finishing up his metallurgical degree. This area is a veritable hotbed of folklore, everything from heroic tales of knights to more traditional examples of what we think of as a standard fairy tale involving princesses and enchantments."

"Fascinating," Roxy said, leaning forward. "Tell us more. These dark roots you mention sound thrilling—you mean like horror tales? Burning witches and all that?"

"Oh no, much darker than that," laughed Holly. "Supposedly—this is just folklore, mind you—this area is second only to Transylvania for its population of supernatural beings. Vampires and necromancers, secret societies practicing blood sacrifices, shape-shifters, cursed families, centuries-old feuds between families with seemingly unholy powers—that sort of thing."

"Foolishness," snorted Martin, pulling out a Prague newspaper. "I grew up not more than thirty kilometers from this area, and those stories were only used to keep small children from wandering the forests alone at night."

"Yes, of course, foolishness." I smiled brightly, pinching Roxy on the wrist to keep her from disputing the statement. She glared at me and angrily rubbed her arm, but didn't say anything more when I turned the conversation to less interesting topics.

An hour later we arrived at our destination, the "bustling market town of Blansko" as the guidebook called it. I looked up from the book and peered around me.

"Not much bustle," Roxy commented sourly, slinging the strap of one bag over her shoulder while grabbing the two other pieces. "More like a limp, if you ask me. There's not even a porter or someone to bribe into carrying our bags. What sort of place is this?"

"Exactly what you wanted, missy, so stop your whining. If you hadn't insisted on bringing three bags, you wouldn't need anyone to carry your stuff."

Luckily for my peace of mind, there was a taxi in the small town, but it was off running someone else to their destination. I chatted with the stationmaster in my high school German for a few minutes, then went over to where Roxy sat camped out on her mound of luggage next to the taxi stop. She got up and wandered over to the station wall to read all the bills posted announcing local bands playing taverns, housecleaning services, tour times to the various caves, et cetera.

"Hans the stationmeister says the taxi guy should be back in fifteen minutes, so if we sit tight, we won't have to haul all your luggage up that hill. Brrr, kind of cold out here, isn't—"

"OHMIGOD, Joy, c'mere!"

"What?"

She jumped up and down in place, her breath puffing white in front of her as she beckoned me over to a spot on the wall. "You're not going to believe this! Look! Just look! Just stand right there in front of me and read that, and tell me that Miranda didn't foresee this!"

"What?" I asked again, warily this time as I approached a large black and red poster. "It doesn't have anything to do with axe-murdering maniacs, does it?"

"Stop being such a poop and read it! Oh, what a glorious, glorious time we're going to have!" She hugged herself with happiness, and whirled around until the fringe on her jacket spun out.

"I *knew* it, I *knew* it," she chanted to herself. I looked around quickly, hoping no one could see us in the gathering darkness of the late afternoon. I was ready to disavow her if she was going to stand in a foreign country and act like an idiot.

"Read it!" she demanded, pointing a finger at the poster.

"Stop acting like a boob, and I might."

"Read it!"

I read it. The sign was printed in English, German, and French. GOTHFAIRE! it proclaimed in bold, red letters: TAKE A JOURNEY TO THE DARKNESS THAT DWELLS WITHIN US ALL, EXPERIENCE DARK PASSIONS AND DARKER SINS. INDULGE IN YOUR DEEPEST, MOST SECRET GOTHIC DESIRES AS YOU PLUNGE INTO A WORLD FILLED WITH THE MACABRE, THE BIZARRE, THE ENDLESS NIGHT. TICKETS AVAILABLE BEGINNING 24 OCTOBER. "Sounds like a carnival or something like one of those Renaissance fairs, only this one is devoted to the Goth scene. What about it? You don't plan on going to it, do you?"

"Look at the bottom," Roxy chanted, dancing a grapevine dance past the luggage. "Look at the bottom, look at the bottom."

"You need serious medication," I muttered before bending over almost double and squinting at the tiny red print.

GOTHFAIRE IS PROUD TO SPONSOR THE ALL HALLOW'S EVE FES-
TIVAL OF THE DARK, 31 OCTOBER AT DRAHANSKÁ CASTLE, BLANSKO,
CZECH REPUBLIC. TICKETS TO THE FESTIVAL WILL BE AVAILABLE AF-
TER . . .

"Oh, Lord." Just what I needed, a big party celebrating a
fictional cult of vampires. It wasn't bad enough that Roxy
had planned for us to spend every evening scouring the area
for any possible Dark Ones who might be roaming the
streets in search of prey; no, now she would drag me to a
week-long fair and festival with a bunch of pimply teens
who were heavily into the Goth scene. "No, no, no," I
groaned.

"Yes, yes, yes," Roxy sang as she danced by me. "You see?
Now do you believe in Miranda's powers? She said you'd
meet a Dark One, and just look! There will be a whole fair
full of them! Not to mention the ones we'll find at the Festival!"

"Oh, for heaven's sake, Rox, there are no such things as
vampires!"

My words fell on deaf ears, but before I could shake some
sense into her, a small, beat-up blue Peugeot that looked
like it had been through a couple of wars squealed to a halt
beside us. I grabbed Roxy and shoved her toward the car.
"Taxi's here. Grab your luggage while I tell the driver what
hotel we're staying at. And for God's sake, stop dancing! You
want everyone to think Americans are lunatics?"

The Hotel Dukla wasn't really that far from the train station, but it was up a steep hill, and off the main square on
the edge of the town. Within half an hour of arriving in
Blansko, we had checked in, hauled our luggage up the
three flights of twisting, uneven stairs to the loft rooms assigned us, and quickly changed out of wrinkled travel
clothes to something a little more decorous. Roxy beat me
to the communal bathroom, so I had to wait until she was
finished before I could wash up.

"See you in the bar," she called out to me a few minutes later as she skipped down the stairs. I grimaced at the careless way she raced down, hoping she wouldn't break her neck on the steps' uneven tread, and set about making myself presentable to the local populace. I had this Audrey Hepburn image in my head of how I wanted to appear: sophisticated, elegant, and unmussed. I carefully unpacked my long black velvet dress that made me look thinner, pinned up my plain brown hair that a stylist once kindly referred to as chestnut, and dabbed on a little perfume.

"You're a long way from Audrey Hepburn." I wrinkled my nose at the reflection in the tiny mirror over an oak bureau. "But you'll do."

I don't quite know whom I had pictured as the patrons in the hotel's bar, the most popular in the city according to the proud hotel owner, but the sight that met my eyes was not it. I imagined people in tweed hats and dirndls and such, but what I saw was a room with a low ceiling made of dark, smoky beams crossing in a herringbone pattern. The few people already in the bar were for the most part in jeans and sweaters, and there was nary a dirndl to be seen. At the opposite end of the room, two large windows ran ceiling to floor, overlooking a balcony that opened to a grassy meadow that brushed up against the darker purple rise of the Moravian mountains. Peeking through the dark trees, I could see a part of a turret of Drahanská Castle. The sky above it was deepening into an indigo that matched the soft lines of the mountains nestled against the town. There was something about the rich shades of blues, blacks, and purples that struck a chord deep within me, but before I could wander over to the window to look out at the scenery, I was hallooed.

Roxy called out from a long table that hugged one of the side walls. She sat in the middle of the table with two women on either side of her. At least I guessed they were women; they could have been men in drag. It was hard to tell, what with the layers of pancake and kohl and the crimson lipstick that slashed their mouths into hard, unbending lines. They were dressed similarly, both in black vinyl lace-up bodices over red chiffon blouses. Although their lower halves were hidden by the thick polished plank that served as a table, I assumed they also had spiky, high-heeled black leather boots, and probably micro miniskirts with the visible garter belts that so many young women thought looked sexy.

"Damn. She's found herself some Goths," I swore to myself, looking around the room for an escape. There was none, so I slapped a pleasant smile on my face and wound my way through the chairs and tables to where Roxy was waving vigorously at me.

"There you are. I thought you'd never get here. Joy, this is Arielle and Tanya. They're both witches."

My smile frayed a bit around the edges as I held out my hand to Tanya, sitting nearest me. She examined my hand as if it might have leprosy, then gave me a sour look and dismissed me as unworthy of her time. Goths—the poseurs of the underworld. Where would we be without them?

"Actually, I'm apprenticed to Tanya," the woman named Arielle said as she stood up and leaned over the table to shake my hand. She had a faint Slavic accent mixed in with heavy French. Her friendly washed-out blue eyes were a nice counterpoint to her friend's hostile glare. "I'm not a witch yet, but I hope to be as powerful as my sister in a few years."

"Your sister?" I asked, pulling out a chair across from Roxy.

"They're sisters," Roxy said helpfully, smiling at Tanya. She ignored both of us, her eyes darting around the room, glancing frequently between the long windows and the door opposite. "I got you a beer. I hope you don't mind if it's dark. That's all they seem to drink here."

Roxy pushed a huge mug toward me. I figured the Czechs must have bladders of iron if they were able to drink that much on a regular basis.

"You'll never guess where Tanya and Arielle work! The GothFaire! Isn't that great? Arielle says they have all sort of attractions like palm readers, and tarot card readers and a medium, a magician, and lots and lots of vampires."

I choked on the tentative sip I was taking of the dark brown beer, just barely keeping it from taking the passage north to my nose.

"I *beg* your pardon?" I asked, licking the foam from my upper lip.

"Vampires," Roxy said happily. "Loads of them. Isn't that thrilling?"

"Loads of them," I repeated, looking from Roxy to Tanya to Arielle. "How many is *loads?*"

Although I was curious about the so-called vampires connected with the fair, I wasn't entirely surprised to hear they were present. I had a friend who had flirted briefly with the Goth society in San Francisco, and she told me that vampirism, in its pretense form, was very popular amongst the set. Some of them really got into the image, with cosmetically enhanced canine teeth, drinking animal blood obtained from slaughterhouses (something that was more common than I cared to think about), and living, in general, the vampire life without actually being undead.

"Dominic and Milos, the owners of GothFaire, are *Vampyr,*" Tanya answered in a husky, heavily accented voice. She pronounced the word *vampire* in the affected, artsy-fartsy way that never failed to make my teeth itch.

"Are they? How very interesting," I said brightly. "And how enterprising of them to own a business. I wouldn't imagine vampires had much need for money, but I suppose the price of capes and dental care has gone up."

Tanya's kohl-laden eyelids lifted to pierce me with a gaze that would have had more impact on me if her pupils hadn't been dilated. *Drugs, no doubt,* I thought to myself. I'd heard that hallucinogenic drugs were particularly popular with the Goth groups, since they were felt to enhance the user's abilities to have visions. Duh, said I.

"There's almost twenty of us with the Faire," Arielle said quickly. "We travel all over Europe, and Dominic pays us a share of the profits, keeping none for himself or Milos."

"Ah," I nodded, willing to let the subject go. I was conscious of a slight feeling of edginess, which I put down to being in a strange country with some extremely strange people. I glanced out the window again, my eyes drawn to the line of ebony mountain silhouetted against the now dark sky. Something didn't feel right, but I couldn't decide what it was. After being in Frankfurt for a week, both Roxy and I had adjusted to the time difference, so that wasn't the problem. . . .

Roxy glanced at her watch and asked Arielle when the fair opened.

"One hour after sunset," she said with a shy little smile. She really was cute; it was just too bad that someone had talked her into dying her hair a flat, dull black, and slathering on way too much makeup. I pegged her at about seventeen, and hoped this was an experimental phase she would grow out of quickly.

"Good. We'll go just as soon as we've had dinner, right, Joyful?"

My sense of unease grew. I glanced again at the mountains. What was it they were trying to tell me? "Hmm? Sure, if you like. We can take in the sights. Have our palms read, and watch the magic show, and stake a vampire or two through the heart."

"Joy!"

Tanya's eyes snapped open at my words, her nostrils flaring in a manner that reminded me of a horse, an observation I wisely kept to myself. Her fingernails were long, sharply pointed, and painted black. It was entirely possible she'd dipped the tips in poison.

"Sorry." I offered a cheesy smile as a token of friendship. Tanya dismissed it with an impatient snort. Once again her gaze shot to the door.

I decided to offer my olive branch to Arielle. "So, are you guys only here for a drink before the show opens, or would you like to have dinner with us? The owner said the pub grub was supposed to be pretty good."

"Pub grub?" Arielle looked confused.

"The food they serve here in the bar," Roxy said soothingly, shooting me an admonishing glance. "You're welcome to join us; we'd love to find out all about the fair and what you do there, and of course, what it's like to work with two vampires. I mean, *Vampyrs*."

I rolled my eyes.

"We've already had supper," Arielle said quickly, darting a nervous glance to her sister. "We're just here waiting for the men. We always gather in a public location before we open the fair. Dominic says it impresses people and makes them curious about the fair."

"I imagine it also serves as sort of a cattle call, too." At Arielle's blank look, I elaborated. "You know, it lets them look over the available stock of blood donors. Heh heh heh."

She shot another look at Tanya, and gave me a worried little feeble laugh. Roxy paused in smiling at her long enough to shoot me a warning look that I ignored. She chatted happily with Arielle about the sights at the fair, what her role was (she read tarot cards), and how she enjoyed traveling all over Europe, all the while I sat and fidgeted. The uncomfortable feeling of something portentous heading my way was growing steadily stronger. I had a momentary image in my mind of a shadow stalking through the woods, the scent of pine so strong it almost tickled my nose. I blinked the sensation aside and rubbed the back of my neck as I tried to focus my attention on what Arielle was saying.

". . . was very nice, but just after we arrived there, someone was horribly murdered in the adjacent town, and the Heidelberg police closed all the roads for a day, so we were late for a show in Aufsdajm."

"Oooh, a murder," Roxy cooed. "How thrilling. Did the police grill you?"

A wave of foreboding crashed over me, almost making me gasp with the intensity of it. I looked around the room, trying to decide if it was someone staring at me that was having the affect on me, but no one was looking our way. Maybe I was just tired from a day spent on the train.

"Grill? They wanted to know if we'd seen the woman who was killed." Arielle's voice trailed away as she fretted with the stem of her glass of beer.

"And had you?" Roxy asked, ever curious.

Arielle swallowed hard, her gaze glued on the tabletop. "Yes, I had. She came to the fair a few days before. I read the cards for her."

"A great many people came to the fair that week, Arielle," Tanya snapped. "I have told you before that you have nothing to feel guilty about."

"But I didn't see the danger," Arielle all but wailed, her pale blue eyes swimming with sudden tears. "I did not see it. I saw nothing. I let her go without warning her at all!"

Tanya leaned forward across Roxy, who plastered herself against the high back of the wooden chair in an attempt to get out of the way. "You . . . did . . . nothing . . . wrong." The words came out hard and short, distracting me for a moment from the gathering blackness I could feel approaching.

"I know you say that, but I should have seen, I should have known . . ." Arielle grabbed for her napkin and wiped at the tears spilling from her eyes.

Tanya spat something out in a language I didn't understand. Whatever it was, it was effective. Arielle nodded, mumbling an apology to us while she mopped up. Roxy went immediately into comfort mode, putting her arm around the young woman and patting her shoulder.

"It's not every day you meet someone who's read tarot cards for a murder victim," I commented chattily, receiving for my efforts identical glares from both Roxy and Tanya.

"It wasn't just the one," Arielle said, blowing her nose delicately. "There was another woman murdered in Le Havre just after we left, and one in Bordeaux three months ago—do you remember, Tanya? She bought a love spell from you the week before. We saw her picture in the paper. She was the latest victim, until Heidelberg."

The room spun into a gray swirl of confusion as the image of a man burst with startling clarity into my mind. He was in black, his features shadowed, silhouetted against the night, walking with long, tireless strides. The wind brushed against him as he moved through the woods, driven by a need I couldn't begin to understand. I was pulled toward him, merged with him until I could feel the blood moving through his veins and the breath on his lips as he approached the town, stalking through the night with an arrogance that bespoke centuries of existence. Through his eyes I saw the lights of the town as they flickered through the pine boughs; when his breath quickened as he inhaled deeply to catch the scents of the town, so did mine. The images in his mind filled mine, thoughts of humans, warm and alive, their blood singing a sweet siren song he couldn't resist. He leaped over a drainage ditch, moving swiftly and powerfully up a hill to the outskirts of town, muscles and sinews and tendons working with graceful efficiency. The scent of blood was strong in our nostrils now; the taste of it made our mouths water. I knew from our memory that the feel of it was like nothing I'd ever known, hot and sweet, flowing down my throat—

"JOY!"

I jumped as the horrible sensations faded, leaving me nauseated and shaking, clutching the table as the room dipped and spun around me. It was like the experience I'd had a few weeks prior at Miranda's, but a hundred times more intense, a thousand times more terrible. I hadn't just seen a man this time, I'd merged with him, become part of him, joined with him as he stalked his prey. My mind was screaming out demands for information and warnings with equal confusion, and yet in all the chaos, one question repeated itself again and again until it consumed me.

What the hell was happening to me?

Chapter Four

"Are you all right? You look like you're a million miles away, and you're breathing funny. Is it your asthma? You want me to go get your inhaler?" Roxy's voice was tight with worry.

I shook my head to clear the remnants of the . . . there was no other word for it but *vision* . . . and pushed the glass of beer away from me with a shaky hand. I still felt sick and dizzy, but it was fading. "Sorry. No, I'm fine. Just spaced out there for a few minutes. I guess I'm not meant to be drinking alcohol anymore."

Roxy shot me a curious look, part concern, part exasperation, but said nothing further about it. She chatted to Arielle while I tried to pull myself together, tried to analyze what games my mind was playing on me. It had to be the beer, I've never been the type of person to experience anything creepy like that. Not even the ill-fated rune stone reading at the Womyn's Magick Festival had made me feel as if I were a pawn to a force I didn't understand, let alone believe. Either I was having some sort of reaction to the beer, or I was going insane. Maybe that was it, maybe I was going mad. That seemed almost a preferable fate than to thinking the vision I had was real. I licked my dry lips. I could still taste the metallic bite of blood as it flowed over my tongue and down my throat.

"What did you mean, 'latest victim'?" The words were out of my mouth before I realized it. All three women stared at me. Something Arielle had said suddenly seemed to be important. "You mentioned a couple of other women who had been to your fair, women who died afterwards, and you said one was the latest victim. What did you mean?"

"Nothing," Tanya spat. "She meant nothing. There is no connection, as the German police have proven to their satisfaction, so your accusations will serve no purpose."

I pushed the worry of my potential insanity aside, surprised by the intensity of Tanya's verbal attack. "Look, Tanya, I'm sorry if you think I'm accusing you of anything, but I'm not. I'm just curious about what Arielle said about there being more than one murder victim."

"Arielle said nothing of interest," Tanya said sullenly and stared into her beer. I pursed my lips and looked at Roxy. She shrugged. I sat back, ignoring the darkness creeping into my mind to concentrate on the bit of information Arielle had presented. I've always loved murder mysteries, and this seemed like the ideal thing to occupy my mind while I waited for the guys in the white suits to show up and take me away.

"So . . . there was more than one body?" I asked Arielle. As soon as the words left my lips, my mind was flooded with the immense satisfaction found in acts of dominance and conquest, the heat of another's body pressed tightly against mine, the scent of her shampoo, the silk of her skin against my mouth, warmth trickling through me, filling the icy regions, quieting the beast that howled within . . . I snapped

46

my eyes open, coughing and choking to clear my mouth of the horrible substance. Blood.

He was feeding.

It was too much for me. I half stood, clutching the table for support. "I think . . . I think I . . ." A red pit opened before me. I clawed at the table to keep from falling into it.

"Joy?"

Roxy was there in an instant, her arms around me, pushing me back into the chair. "Put your head down between your knees. It'll pass in a minute."

I did as she ordered, unable to stop the trembling that racked me. My mind was shrieking, screaming with the need to know what was going on, what was wrong with me, why I was suddenly seeing things I had no desire to see, let alone believe in.

Vampire, whispered the wind. I shook my head vehemently, banging the back of my head against the underside of the table. I clutched at the sensation, welcoming the pain since it was real, not imagined. Real—I desperately needed something real.

"Joyful, you OK?"

I opened my eyes and lifted my head cautiously. Roxy was squatting next to me, applying a cold wet cloth to the back of my neck. "Geez, you scared the crap out of me. Your face went absolutely pale, and your eyes were empty like there was nothing there. Don't ever do that to me again, OK?"

"OK," I agreed, mustering a ghost of a smile.

She hugged me tightly for a moment, whispering, "Don't make me get tough with you, sister," before she pulled back.

I gave a shaky little laugh at her order as I sat up slowly. Arielle stood on my other side holding out a glass of water, the bartender next to her speaking rapidly in Czech. I swallowed a bit of the water and in German assured the man I was just fine.

47

"Delayed jet lag," Roxy told him. "Jet . . . lag. Delayed. Looong time," she repeated louder in that weird pidgin form of English so many Americans abroad adopt.

"He's Czech, Rox, not deaf," I pointed out, wiping my face with the wet cloth before handing it back to the bartender. I sipped a bit more water while everyone drifted back to where they were sitting, just as if nothing earth-shattering had happened. I rubbed my forehead and wondered why my mind had chosen that moment to snap, and what I was going to do about piecing it back together. What I needed was some time to myself with a big gallon jug of brain super glue.

"I think you should go lie down rather than go to the GothFaire," Roxy pronounced, evidently reading what remained of my mind. "You look like death warmed over."

"Thanks a lot." I struggled to block out the feeling of danger that surged within me until it howled like the wind in a storm. I gritted my teeth as Roxy chatted on, unwilling to give in to the sensation, clutching the arms of the chair in an attempt to focus on what was real, not what my mind was generating. The wood, that was real. It was hard and smooth from years of polishing, the intricate scroll carving on the arms was deep, the edges blunted with use. I fought to control my breathing, denying the need to pant as the blackness drew closer.

He is coming, a voice whispered in my head.

There is no one! I yelled back at it. I wondered if somehow Tanya hadn't slipped me one of her hallucinogenic drugs. Maybe she put it in my beer before I came, intending on pulling a little prank. If so, I didn't appreciate it, but at least it served to comfort me in an odd way. If I was suffering the effects of a drug, I wasn't going insane. Or worse.

I grabbed at the water glass and choked back a swallow, unable to hear the conversation around me for the howling of the wind. I was surprised no one else commented on it, but a slow glance around the room confirmed that every-thing was normal. People chatted, laughed, smoked, and drank just as if they weren't caught in the middle of hurricane-force winds. A pleasant-faced dark-haired man in a suede coat walked through the door, pausing to greet the bartender and several of the men clumped together before accepting a glass of wine and joining a lively group. A bar-maid wandered through the crowd with a tray of beers. Someone brought out a pack of cards. It was all utterly nor-mal.

The wind rose to an unbearable volume, shrieking and screaming out words of torment and pain, but just when I thought I was going to scream myself, just when the red pit opened up before me again, all was suddenly quiet.

He had come.

"Joy? Did you hear what Arielle said? Their rune reader up and quit last week."

"Huh?" I turned my head slowly, my gaze touching each person in the room as I turned to look at the door. No one looked out of the ordinary. How could it be that no one else could feel the danger that sparked through the air?

"She says Dominic is looking for someone to take her place. You could ask him about taking on the job for a few days while they're here in Blansko. That would be so cool!"

"Dominic? Runes?"

"She's great at predicting natural disasters," Roxy bragged to Arielle.

The door burst open as she spoke, the blackness of the hall beyond untouched by the lights within the room. I froze, my breath a solid lump in my chest as I waited to see him, waited to see what horrible creature my mind had con-jured up. Would he be a hunchback? Would he be twisted and maimed, with flesh hanging off him in rancid strips? Would it be something worse?

With a swirl of black material, a man stepped through the

door, pausing dramatically to survey the room before saun-
tering forward. He had dark blond hair that curled back
from a pronounced widow's peak, dark eyes, and a face so
handsome it would make an angel weep. He was followed
by another man, taller than the first, probably topping me
a good four or five inches, also dressed in black. He wasn't
particularly handsome, and he was certainly more conven-
tionally dressed than the first, but there was something
about him that held my gaze.

"There's Dominic now," Arielle said happily.

"What?" Roxy asked, her head swiveling around quickly.
"Where? Oh my God, is that him, the guy in the cape? God
almighty!"

I sat silent in my chair, my head reeling with the sudden
absence of sound, my skin prickling with anticipation.

"Yes, that's him," Arielle confirmed. Tanya rose and
started for the two men. My gaze went back to the first man.
He had waited until all eyes were on him, then plucked the
black cape from his shoulders, tossing it onto a coat tree
before turning to smile at everyone in the room. His canines
were elongated, pointed, and looked very sharp.

And they were as phony as he was, I was as sure of that
as I was of my own name. Surer. Which meant, if I wasn't
going mad and I hadn't been given any drugs. . . . My eyes
turned to the tall man standing in the shadow of the doorway. His face was set in grim lines, all harsh angles and
planes, his eyes a curious light brown color—amber, I'd
guess, although it was difficult to be sure all the way across
the room. But what captivated me was the aura of quiet
power and confidence that he seemed to wear as naturally
as he wore his dark leather jacket and black jeans.

Vampire, the voice whispered again in my head.

"Who is the second man? Is that the other owner?" Roxy
asked in an excited whisper that barely penetrated the
tangle of my thoughts.

50

Vampire. The word was as soft as down in my mind, brushing at the edges. I tried to squelch that insidious little voice once and for all, but the problem was, he looked just like I'd always imagined one of Dante's Dark Ones: masculine, elegant, arrogant, and so sexy I wanted to rip his clothing off and do wanton things to him with a pair of chopsticks and a large bottle of olives. My thoughts snapped back from where they were wandering with an annoyed exclamation. *What was I thinking?* A vampire? A real vampire? He wasn't any more a vampire than his friend with the bonded teeth and phony actor's smile.

"No, Milos is away on business. He has many ventures. GothFaire is just one of them. That's Raphael. Dominic hired him after Le Havre. He's in charge of our security."

The man named Raphael watched with an unmoving face as Tanya greeted his employer. Slowly he moved forward, nodding his head when the bartender called out a greeting, accepting a large glass of beer.

Vampire.

"You can just get stuffed, because I'm not listening to you," I muttered to the voice.

"What? Did you say something?" Roxy asked.

"No."

She cocked an eyebrow at me, but quickly turned back to the two men who were dominating the room with their very presence. Or rather one man; Dominic was clearly not up to Raphael's snuff.

"So, this Raphael . . . is he a vampire, too?" Roxy asked Arielle.

Arielle worried her beer stein. "I'm not sure. I don't think he is, but he moves very quietly, and sometimes I have the feeling he is watching me. . . ."

Was he or wasn't he? Only his hairdresser knows for sure. I smiled a grim little smile at my feeble joke, and tried to decide once and for all if I was A) going mad, B) having a hallucinogenic experience, or C) in the presence of something I didn't believe existed, but given my experiences of the evening, who was I to make any sort of assessment of what was real and what wasn't? I glanced back at Raphael. He was leaning against the wall next to a tall potted palm, nodding his head as the bartender chattered away. When the man moved off for a minute to fill an order, Raphael shifted, accidentally spilling half his beer into the plant. I thinned my lips. No one likes a soused vampire!

"Oh, God, he's sooo gorgeous! I just knew they'd look like that! Joy, are you looking at him?"

I mumbled that I was. Dominic and Tanya were still playing to the crowd, she simpering as he pawed her in a manner I'm sure he thought was shocking and erotic, but was really only faintly tawdry as he nibbled with those doctored teeth on her long white neck, generally hamming it up. I dismissed them as uninspiring and focused my attention on the man who had moved farther along the bar to resume his conversation with the bartender. Raphael had taken off his jacket, and the long line of his back held me spellbound as he leaned forward to speak in the bartender's ear. Like Dominic, he was also in black, but on him it looked elegant and intriguing and . . .

"Virile," I breathed.

"You can say that again," Roxy agreed, her eyes on Dominic.

Everyone's attention was on the show Dominic and Tanya were presenting as he suddenly whirled her into a waltz around the room, his skin paper-white in comparison to the black of his pants and silk shirt, carelessly unbuttoned to expose half his chest.

"Probably uses pancake as well. And shaves his chest," I said softly.

"You think?" Roxy asked, her eyes alight as the couple swept past us, Dominic's teeth bared for full effect. She gave a lustful sigh. "It sure does look good on him. I wonder if Miranda couldn't have got the Goddess's messages mixed up, and I was supposed to find a Dark One as my perfect man. I could go for a man like that!"

It was on the tip of my tongue to say Dominic wasn't even as remotely intriguing as his companion, let alone a vampire, but as my eyes turned back to Raphael, I was stunned to find him watching me. He held a drink nonchalantly in one hand, his head still bent to the bartender, but his strangely colored eyes were on me. Our gazes met and locked. Instantly I was swamped with emotion: rage, stifled but still an awesome force to deal with; loneliness, such great loneliness that tears came to my eyes in sympathetic response; and finally despair, great waves of it that rolled over me and sucked me under. Almost as soon as the emotion washed over me, it was gone, leaving me feeling curiously bereft if extremely confused.

"Oh, God, I'm in trouble, serious trouble," I moaned, dragging my eyes away from the man who was everything Miranda warned, and so much more. My skin tingled and burned where it was exposed, as if just his gaze had the power to scorch me.

"What's wrong? You feeling faint again?" Roxy studied me with a worried eye.

I shook my head. "No. Just suffering delusional episodes. Nothing to write home about."

She frowned. "What are you babbling about now? Are you feeling OK or aren't you? If you want me to help you up to your room, just let me know."

"I'm fine," I reassured her and flashed Arielle what was bound to be a frighteningly insane smile. "Maybe just a bit tired, but OK. Just ignore me while I have my breakdown."

She leaned back against her chair and gave me a "wait till I get you later" look. Her attention was quickly pulled to other, more interesting things when Dominic strutted over with Tanya on his arm. I wanted to turn my head to see if Raphael was coming our way, but I couldn't bring myself to do it. I didn't need any more episodes of the sympathetic whatever-it-was I felt around him.

"Roxy," I leaned across the table and hissed through my teeth as Dominic made a production of sweeping Tanya's chair with (what else) a black handkerchief.

"Huh?" She turned reluctantly to look at me. "What?"

"Is he heading this way?"

Her eyes wandered over to Dominic, who had turned to answer a question from someone at a nearby table.

"No, not him, the other one. The big one." I almost said *the real one*, but stopped myself in time. I did *not* believe in vampires.

Roxy's gaze swept the room, then settled on me. "Why do you ask?"

I tried to shrug, but my skin still felt burned. "No particular reason."

"He's tall."

"So?"

"You're tall, too."

"Did you take *all* your medication this morning?" I asked snidely.

She grinned. "I was just asking. I thought maybe you might have a thing for him."

Me? With a possible bloodsucking monster? "Not on your tintype, Nelly! I don't even know the guy!"

Her grin widened. "Awfully vehement, aren't you?"

"Stop it."

"OK."

She kept smiling at me. I glared at her.

"Hey, Joy?"

I decided to ignore her. I'd take just a peek, one little itty-bitty peek and see if he was still staring at me. If the burn on my skin was any sign, he was.

He wasn't. He wasn't at the bar counter, he wasn't anywhere I could see at all. Damn.

"Joy?"

I casually turned to look in the other direction. Dominic was handing out flyers to the tables nearest us, but there was no sign of a big, dark man who could potentially, if I wasn't insane or drugged, be a vampire. *Vampire*, my mind echoed in an extremely annoying fashion.

I decided insanity was the better choice.

"Joy!"

"What?" I snapped, looking back at her.

"He's right behind you."

I jumped back so fast I knocked the chair over, myself with it, cracking my head on the floor in the process. The last thing I remember before sinking into an inky black pool of oblivion was the group of people who gathered around to look down at me. One pair of eyes stood out from all the rest; they were amber—clear, brilliant amber.

"Unearthly," I sighed, and let the blackness claim me.

Oblivion wasn't nearly what it was cut out to be, so I made the visit a short one and regained my wits as soon as possible. Once I realized where I was, I felt a pang of homesickness for the state of unconsciousness. I did a quick survey of my body, and discovered I was sitting on the cold floor, propped up against something hard and warm. Something that breathed. Slowly I turned my head to look at who it was. Raphael's amber eyes met mine.

Vampire.

I closed my eyes, leaning into the shoulder that supported me, unable to keep from breathing in his scent. It was a heady mixture of the spicy tang of a healthy male and the faint, lingering scent of soap. Vampire or not, I couldn't help but be thankful he wasn't one of those men who liked to douse themselves in cologne and aftershave.

"Joy? Her eyes were open, weren't they?" Roxy asked.

Reluctantly I started to pull away from the warm body behind me. An arm locked around my waist kept me from leaving him. The gesture warmed my heart in an odd fashion.

"Oh, good, she's awake. Arielle, you can put down that bucket of water; she's awake now."

The faces peering concernedly at me spun around until I thought I was going to throw up all over everyone.

"Uh-oh, you're turning green. That's not good."

"She looks ill. Should I fetch her more water?"

"Heinrich, call the doctor. We don't want her to blame us for this accident."

"It's time to go, Dominic. Surely you can't want to stay?"

The voices clamored loudly in my ears, spinning me in and out of the warm, cloying darkness that hovered over me, increasing the nausea until I was sure I was going to vomit. The arm holding me securely around my waist tightened as I clutched at it, clinging desperately to it in the hopes that the room—and my stomach—would settle down.

"I think perhaps we should give the lady some air."

I turned toward the voice that cut through my nightmare. The faces around me pulled back until one came into focus. It was one of the bar patrons, a nice-looking man with high cheekbones, and dark, fathomless eyes. A wave of bile choked me as I struggled to keep it contained. I tightened my grip on the arm holding me up.

"You will feel better in a moment." The man smiled and brushed his hand across my forehead. His voice was beautiful, pitched low, but velvety in its smoothness. It wrapped around me like a soft warm cloak, comfortable and reassuring. Instantly the nausea receded and the room slowed its spinning. "You are not used to our beer. Strangers often find it too strong for their palates. I would advise you next time to try our wine."

I'd only had a sip of the beer, so I knew full well that it wasn't what was affecting me, but I found myself oddly re-luctant to dispute anything the man said. I gingerly felt at the back of my head, locating a lump the size of a runty plum.

"You have a small swelling," the man reassured me, his fingers flicking lightly over the painful bump. Behind me, Raphael shifted slightly.

"Are you a doctor?" I asked the man with the silky voice.

His eyes grew black with sorrow for a moment. I wanted to reach out and take him in my arms, to comfort him and ease his pain. "I am not a doctor, although I've had some training in the healing arts. Your injury is not serious and should not trouble you beyond this night."

The pain that had been blossoming in the back of my head eased, fading with the nausea. I'd never been one to have much faith in alternative medical techniques, but I had to admit this man had an extremely soothing way about him.

"Who are you?" I couldn't help but ask. His eyes were intriguing, so expressive and full of emotion, I found myself wanting to draw closer to him, to look deeper into those eyes.

"My name is Christian," he answered, another smile teas-ing his lips as the voices around us rose in approbation.

Didn't anyone around here believe in using his or her surname?

"I believe it would be best if we got you off the floor and into bed," a voice rumbled in my ear. I stiffened in response. Where Christian's voice was as smooth as water sliding over sand, Raphael's was deep, slightly roughened, and set up a most amazing resonance deep within me. Weren't vampires supposed to be able to work magic with their voices and eyes? Before I could mull this over, I was hoisted up. Raphael released me, then grabbed me quickly when the room started spinning again.

"Well, at least she's not green anymore," Roxy muttered, wringing her hands. "I think you're right about getting her into bed. We're on the top floor, though, and she looks a bit shaky to me."

Raphael didn't answer, just put an arm behind my knees and scooped me up.

"Um," I said, turning my head and flinching just a bit as a hall light hit me square in the eyes. My nose brushed his cheek. I couldn't believe he was carrying me up three flights of awkwardly steep stairs, and he wasn't even breathing heavily. If it hadn't been likely he was a bloodthirsty member of the undead, I would have kissed the man.

One glossy chocolate eyebrow rose as he glanced down at me. "Um?"

"You're carrying me," I said, feeling it necessary to say something intelligent, but lacking the wits to actually pull intelligent things out of my scrambled brains. First insanity, then drugging—now I was in the arms of a man who might be a vampire, and all I could think of was how nice he smelled and how warm he was.

Of course he's warm, he just fed.

I squashed that inner voice down flat and met his amber eyes without flinching. Much.

"Yes," he agreed, his voice thrumming inside me. He had an English accent, giving his voice a richness that reminded me of antique mahogany. It was very sexy. I liked it. *A lot.*

"Up the stairs."

"Your room's at the top," he replied.

"But you're not puffing or straining or breaking out into a sweat."

Both eyebrows went up at that. "Should I be?"

"I'm not an inconsiderable weight," I pointed out. "Most

men would balk at hefting me across a room, not to mention up three flights of stairs."

"I am not most men," he stated, turning on the first landing.

You can say that again, trembled at the edge of my tongue, but I bit it back, saying instead, "Regardless of your obviously fit state, I'm too heavy. I'll give you a hernia. If you put me down, I'll be happy to walk the rest of the way."

"You're not too heavy."

I looked at him as if he had an extra toe growing out of his ear. "What planet are you from? In case it escaped your notice, I'm six feet tall and built like a brick oven, as my mother used to say."

"I happen to think a woman's shape looks better with curves," he said blithely, looking me up and down. "Yours look good on you."

Well, stap my vitals! A man who had enough muscles to haul me around and still managed to say nice things about my overabundance of curves? If only he wasn't the walking dead, I would have proposed marriage on the spot. But the probability was that if I wasn't insane, he was what he shouldn't be, so marriage was out. Which was a shame, really, because the closer I got to him, the better he looked. He was about four inches taller than me, was broad in all those areas that men look good being broad in, had a hard, angular face and dark curly hair, but it was those eyes that snagged and held my attention. Amber, deep amber, pure and clear and flecked with gold and brown. He started up the second flight of stairs

Vampires can mesmerize with their eyes.

"Um."

"Are we back to that again?"

I tried to look down my nose at him, not an easy thing to do when you're being carried. "I apologize for the lamentable lack of scintillating conversation, sir, but I have recently been unconscious and I find some allowances are going to have to be made."

"I see."

"For example, we haven't been introduced."

He rounded the last landing, looking faintly startled by my words. "I thought introductions went the way of eight-track tapes and laser disks."

"They're not entirely extinct," I answered. "I'm Joy Randall."

He hauled me up the last few stairs, stopping at the top to look into my eyes. "Raphael."

"Just Raphael?"

He shrugged.

"Most people have two or more names."

"Do they?"

"Yes." I waited. He looked at me with those beautiful eyes as if he were memorizing my face. I got tired of waiting for him, and decided to give him a nudge in the right direction. You'd have thought someone who'd lived for centuries would have picked up a few social skills along the way. "My middle name is Martine. I was named for my grandmother. Joy Martine Randall."

Abruptly a smile quirked at the corner of his lips. "I was named for my great-grandfather."

"Great-grandpa Raphael?"

"Griffin. My name is Raphael Griffin St. John."

"Nice to meet you, Raphael." I hazarded a smile before I realized what I was doing. Flirting with a vampire! What was next for me—French kissing a werewolf? Dirty dancing with a zombie? "For the record, I think your parents did the right thing."

I loved his eyebrows. I loved the way they zoomed up and down and were so expressive without saying a word. "Your name," I told the eyebrow arched in question. "It's different. I've never known a Raphael before. It's very romantic. Dramatic, too. I like it."

I mentally groaned to myself as the words left my lips. I was babbling. I was clinging to a man who just possibly might be undead, and I was babbling about how much I liked his name.

"It is a family tradition. All the men in our family are named either Raphael or Griffin."

"And you got both."

"Yes."

"Fun tradition," I commented. He made a little moue of distaste.

"It's on par with the other family tradition."

"Really? What's that? It doesn't involve webbed toes, does it? 'Cause if it does, I don't want to know about it."

His eyebrow arched even higher. "No webbed toes, thank you for asking. The family tradition to which I am referring is much more disconcerting: A St. John man knows the woman he will marry the first time he meets her."

I blinked at him. "Oh. That's a bit different. Men don't usually fall in love at first sight. Still, Raphael is a cool name, so I guess your family traditions aren't all bad."

"I, on the other hand, dislike the name intensely and would much prefer it if everyone just called me Bob."

"Bob?" A vampire named Bob? Was that allowed? "Bob? Why Bob?"

His shoulders moved in an elegant shrug despite the fact that he was still holding me. "Why not Bob?"

He had me there. "But Raphael's a nice name. It's exotic. It's unusual. It—"

"Sounds like it belongs to a male prostitute," he interrupted.

"Well, I think it suits you," I said as he walked down the short hallway.

He looked at me out of the corner of one of those delicious eyes. "You think I look like a man who takes money to pleasure women?"

"I think a lot of women would pay you money to give them pleasure," I said. "I know I certainly would if I had some spare cash lying around."

He stopped before my door, giving me a curious look. "I don't know whether to be flattered or insulted. Are you saying you'd like to have sex with me?"

"Well, it's not written in stone, but I have to admit that right now, with you holding me and all, it's on my list, although I should warn you that I just discovered my mind is pretty much shot, so perhaps I'm not the best judge."

He carefully set me on my feet, holding on to my waist while I waited to see if the room would stop spinning. It did.

"I believe the best course will be for me to take that statement as a compliment." His hands were warm on my waist, his fingers doing a little caressing thing that had my knees melting.

"Now I've offended you. I'm sorry. It's just that the women in my family tend to call the shots as they see them. I forget that not everyone is thrilled to hear my opinions."

His eyes glittered brightly into mine. I wanted to dive into their amber depths and bask in the warmth contained within them. "On the contrary, I find myself strangely compelled to encourage you to share your opinions."

If he weren't so damned sexy I'd have been OK, but he stood there positively smoldering with sensuality. I fought the unseemly urge to throw myself into his arms, and stepped back. "I think you'd better go. I'm liable to launch myself at your head if you don't, and you don't look like the kind of a guy who likes to be rushed into a kiss."

His eyes deepened into a look so wicked it took my breath away. "You'd be surprised at what I like."

Oh man, oh man, oh man! I stared open-mouthed at him. Fortunately, he didn't wait for a reply and took pity on my scattered wits. "Do you have your room key?" he asked, holding out his hand.

"I have it," a cheerful voice piped up behind him. "Boy, these stairs are tough on the toes. Here I come, everyone hold tight. Joy, the hotel owner wants to know if you want him to call a doctor. At least, I think that's what he said. Jeezumcrow!" Roxy stopped on the other side of Raphael and gave me the eye. "You really have taken a beating today, haven't you? You look awful. Thanks a lot, Raphael, I'll tuck her into bed. You don't mind my calling you Raphael, do you? Will you be at the fair tomorrow?"

A surge of annoyance welled up at the sight of my best friend batting her eyelashes at what was probably the only person in existence who could carry me up three flights of stairs, and still tell me he liked my curves.

I smiled my best shark smile at him, and reached behind Roxy to pinch the back of her arm.

She yelped and jerked her arm away, glaring at me. "So it's like that, is it?"

"No."

"Hrmph." She rubbed her arm as she unlocked my door. "Thank you, Bob," I said graciously to Raphael.

"My pleasure," he replied, his eyes glittering dangerously at me.

"Bob? I thought his name was Raphael?" I allowed Roxy to drag me into my room and fuss over me, putting an ice compress against the lump that no longer ached. I lay back on the bed and let her lecture me about being more careful when we were in a country where the health care might be dicey, not to mention my stupidity in literally falling head over heels for the first dishy guy I saw.

The last bit made me sit up. "What? Are you nuts? I fell over, Roxy, I didn't go throwing myself on the man. You make it sound like I was instantly enamored of him the minute he stepped into the room."

I ignored the voice inside me that said her accusation was closer to the truth than I was willing to admit, especially if the world as I knew it had turned upside down and he was a . . . I clapped a mental gag over my brain and wouldn't let it say the word.

"Well, you have to admit you were interested in him. And he certainly isn't bad looking, once you get past those weird eyes."

"They aren't weird, they're beautiful," I snapped, pulling off the ice bag. "No, I don't need any aspirin; my head feels much better now."

"Fine. You rest and you'll feel shipshape in the morning. You want something to eat?" Roxy tidied up my clothes and brought me a glass of water and the book I'd tucked away in my luggage.

"No, thanks. You'd better get something, though. You get manic if your blood sugar drops too low." I sank back into the down featherbed and gave myself up to the luxury of being pampered.

"Yes, Mom. Go to sleep. We'll talk in the morning."

"About what?" I asked, frowning at her as she stood in the open doorway. "If you're going to harp at me about that guy—"

"His name is Raphael," she said with obnoxious coyness.

"—you can think again because there's nothing to discuss."

"Go to sleep," she repeated with a knowing smile. "You have a big day ahead of you tomorrow."

I decided to try out one of Raphael's eyebrow moves just to see how well it worked for me.

"The fair," she answered my silent question. "You want to look your best for the fair! You're going to meet your Dark One there!"

What if I already had? "Like hell I am!"

"The man whose soul you'll save!"

"You really take the cake, you know that?"

"He'll clasp you to his manly chest, and look deep into your eyes, and tell you that you are his and his alone, and not even *you* can want him to do that if you look like you do now!"

"I hereby declare you certifiable. I'll have the plaque made up in the morning."

"And then he'll complete the ritual of the Joining, and you will live happily ever after with your vampire lover, just like in Dante's books."

I took a deep breath. "THERE'S NO SUCH THING AS A VAMPIRE!"

She grinned. "Nighty-night, don't let the bedbugs bite. You'll want to save that treat for *him*."

The ice bag missed her, but it made a very satisfying bang as it hit the door.

Chapter Five

"It's just too bad Raphael isn't a Dark One," Roxy announced the following afternoon as we dragged ourselves up the three flights of stairs to our rooms. A day spent wandering the Macocha Abyss had left us both with tired legs and the need for a long soak in the tub. "If he were, then you'd know it was him Miranda was talking about."

I glared at her.

"Look at your watch," she answered my unspoken accusation. "It's after three. I waited a whole extra four minutes."

"How fast time flies when you're not talking about mythical, pretend, made-up, utterly fictional creatures," I muttered as I pulled out my room key and unlocked my door. Roxy followed me into my room since it was bigger than hers and had an extra chair.

"Don't think I'm going to let you put a moratorium on things I want to talk about every day. The only reason I agreed not to mention the Dark Ones until we got back was because you looked so awful this morning."

66

Strangely enough, I hadn't *felt* awful. My head was only slightly tender around the area I'd banged, and my mind was strangely calm. That was due wholly to the little pep talk I'd given myself during a quick morning bath. Although I'm not normally one for deep introspection, this, I felt, was necessary. It was that or sign myself up for electroshock therapy.

"The human mind is a strange and wondrous place," I had told my bath sponge as I lathered it up with my favorite jasmine soap. "It is highly susceptible to suggestion, and can easily be fooled into perceiving something that really is not present. Stress, in particular, can do weird things to the brain, causing it to defend itself by releasing tension in the form of vivid dreams and visions."

The sponge declined the opportunity to comment on my theory, so I put it to use as I reasoned out the rest of the argument. The episode with Miranda, brought on by the couple of gin and tonics I'd imbibed, had obviously burned itself into my then-impressionable mind. Once I arrived in an area purported to contain elements of fantasy that had been mentioned at Miranda's, my brain decided to relieve a bit of the tension of being halfway around the world in a foreign land by dredging up related images and presenting them as reality.

I ignored the little voice that pointed out I wasn't particularly stressed out about anything, least of all my vacation in a long-dreamed-about Europe, nodding my head as I got out of the tub and reached for a towel. The episode at Miranda's could be explained by drink, while the previous evening's fireworks were due to illusion and a little innocent delusion on the part of my mind. It made sense, and had the added bonus of being entirely reasonable. Far more reasonable, my cynical self piped up, than the thought that I could have been whisked away like Dorothy and plopped down in my own personal paranormal version of Oz.

A newly restored calm mind and a day spent exploring the amazing geological phenomena of the area had done much to restore my good humor. A couple of times during the day I thought of bringing up the subject of the strange delusions I had experienced the night before, but was reluctant to tell even my closest friend about them. They were just too . . . personal. Once we returned to the hotel, I decided that since Roxy had refrained from mentioning her vampires all day, it was only fair to let her have a turn. I'd play devil's advocate for her; she always enjoyed that, and now that I had things settled in my mind, it wouldn't hurt me in the least to play along.

"OK, I'll bite. How do you know Raphael isn't a vampire?" I asked as I peeled off a dirty sweatshirt and grabbed my bathrobe.

"Hmm? Oh. Easy. He was drinking."

"What?"

She nodded and started unlacing her hiking boots. "In the bar last night. He had a beer. Everyone and their Aunt Fanny knows Dark Ones don't drink anything but blood. You've read the books—you know that it's only after the Joining that they can ingest something other than blood."

"You are entirely too conversant with those books for my peace of mind." I pulled off my jeans and grabbed fresh underwear from the tiny bureau drawer.

She smiled and kicked a boot off. "You have to understand the habits of the prey you are hunting, don't you? Besides, you shouldn't complain. All my knowledge is going to come in handy to you when we find you your Moravian. You . . . er . . . don't think it's Dominic, do you?"

I let her comment about finding me a vampire go, and shuddered over the idea of having anything to do with poseur Dominic. "Ick. No. I doubt seriously if he's any sort of vampire, Roxy, except in his own mind. Those teeth are definitely fake." I kept a tight rein on my mind as the shared memory of fangs biting into flesh shimmered through it. Imagination—it was all just my fertile imagination, nothing more. I stripped out of my underwear and slipped into my bathrobe.

"Oh, you're just prejudiced. Promise me you'll keep an open mind tonight at the fair."

I didn't want to have an open mind. Open minds led to visions, and that was definitely not good for one's sanity. Still, I'd always prided myself on my ability to judge impartially all the facts in a situation, so I supposed it would only be fair to not be too judgmental before weighing all the evidence and finding that there were, in fact, no such things as vampires.

Besides, I pointed out to myself, I knew I was right and she was wrong, so it wouldn't hurt me in the least to have an open mind. If everyone at the fair was like Dominic, there was nothing to worry about. I grabbed my bath things and turned to face Roxy. "Fine, I'll have an open mind."

"Promise you won't pick on Dominic."

I held my hand up. "I won't pick on Dominic."

"And you'll be nice to any vampires you meet."

"Sure. You want the tub first?"

"No." She pulled off her other boot and hobbled toward the door. "You look like you need it more than me. I'll see you downstairs at six for dinner, and then we can go to the fair after that. Don't forget to take a nap! You always get cranky if you're up late without a nap, and I want to see everything in the GothFaire. I can't wait to see that Dominic again. He's just so dashing!"

And well he knew it. "Rox, a word of warning."

She paused at the door, her head cocked. "What?"

"Tanya looked awfully possessive of him. I wouldn't suggest you tangle with her. She doesn't look like the type to tolerate encroachment on her domain."

She smiled one of her patented "men fall for me like trees

under an axe" smiles. "Don't worry about me. Go take your bath. Oh, and Joy? Wear something sexy. Even if Raphael isn't the man of your dreams, he's the only one I know who could carry you up three flights of stairs without having to take a rest stop. You might want to check him out a bit. It's just too bad he isn't a vampire. . . ." She drifted out of the room.

I watched the door as it closed behind her, seeing not it but the bar below. The image was fresh in my mind: Raphael standing at the end of the bar, talking to the bartender, his eyes on me as he held a stein of beer in his hands.

If I took a huge mental pinch of salt and was willing to admit the possibility that such a thing as vampires existed and were bounded by the laws set forth in Dante's books, wouldn't self-preservation necessitate the pretense that they fit in to human society?

It seemed to me that if a vampire truly wanted to keep his secret, he might go to a bar and order a drink, and then give the appearance of having drunk part of it by, oh, say accidentally spilling half of it in a place that no one would notice.

Like a potted palm.

I had my bath and took a brief snooze. It pains me to admit that Roxy was right about me not being a night person, and since the GothFaire was open until two A.M. each night, I knew there was no way I could last through it without having a nap ahead of time. I got up two hours later and pulled on a pair of brown wool pants and a bulky fisherman's sweater, adamantly refusing to dress in anything that could be mistaken for sexy. Raphael, I was sure, was a very nice man—in addition to being an exceptionally strong one—but despite all of Roxy's hopes and plans for me, I wasn't really on the prowl for a man.

Well, OK, maybe I was a little interested, but I didn't really have the time to start something, so it was for the best that I stick to the ogle-but-don't-touch plan.

As I started down the winding stairs, I heard a door close behind her. There were two rooms and a bathroom on the upper floor, so Roxy and I pretty much had the bathroom to ourselves. Out of curiosity I paused on the curve of the landing and waited to see who had invaded the top floor.

A pair of thick-soled, chunky black boots came into view, followed by black and white striped tights visible through the poofy black net skirt that brushed on the stair treads behind her, crowned by a red and black strapped velvet top and . . . Tanya's head. She stopped when she saw me.

I blinked at her hair. "I don't think I've ever seen anyone with hair that's actually crimson. Nice color. Matches your top. I had no idea you were staying here. I assumed everyone connected with the fair lived in the trailers parked around it."

"We do live there," she said in her husky, thickly accented voice. Her eyes shone brightly, her face painted white, her lips set off by the dramatic black lipstick so dear to the Goth heart.

"Oh? Just checking out the view from up this high?"

She started toward me. The staircase, as I have mentioned, is narrow, winding, and due to its age, has uneven steps. Tanya left me no choice but to turn around and descend in front of her.

"I was looking for the toilet," she said to my back.

"Oh, really?" I paused a moment as I reached the second landing. "There's one on the ground floor, you know, quite handy to the bar."

The way her eyes glittered in the dimly lit staircase reminded me of a snake that's just spotted a particularly juicy mouse. I decided not to stand around waiting to see if she'd pounce, and started down the next flight, holding on to the wall for support. When you are six feet tall you tend to have big feet, and big feet in a building with three-hundred-year-old staircases can mean trouble.

"The toilet was occupied." The words were clipped and pointed. I was willing to bet she was spitting them at me, but with my back to her, I couldn't tell.

"As far as I know," I called out over my shoulder, "there is also a toilet on the second floor."

"It, too, was occupied."

"Ah." Why didn't I believe her? Maybe because she rubbed me the wrong way? Maybe because she was ruining Arielle by making her over into a copy of herself? Or could it be because the only other rooms on the upper floor were Roxy's and mine, and that meant dear little Tanya might have been snooping around?

"You know, I've heard the Czech prisons aren't terribly nice places to be in."

"Why are you telling me this?" She must smoke five packs a day to get that grating tone honed to razor-sharp roughness.

"Oh, no reason. I was just thinking how terrible it would be for anyone caught stealing, especially someone who wasn't a Czech citizen. Tourism is a god in this area. If, for instance, someone broke into a hotel room and messed with a tourist's belongings, I imagine the police would prosecute that person to the fullest."

I stumbled on a particularly warped tread as I started down the last flight, and clutched the wall more diligently.

"You should be careful how you are marching down these stairs," Tanya growled behind me in a sickening parody of sweetness. "If you fell, you could break your neck, and that would be so tragic."

I glanced back at her and bared my teeth in a smile. She bared hers in return. As I rounded the last curve, something slammed into the back of my knee, knocking my leg out from under me. I shrieked and went down, slamming first into the wall of the staircase, then rebounding off it and hurtling straight for the hardwood floor of the narrow hall.

I didn't end up on the floor, although it felt like I hit a brick wall. Just as I went sailing off the stairs, Raphael loomed up out of the darkness and grabbed me, pulling me against his body as he did an impressive half-twist so it was his back rather than mine that crashed into the oak-paneled wall. I leaned drunkenly against him, clinging to his coat and panting with shock, my heart racing madly from the rush of adrenaline. I got my feet under me and stood up slowly, looking up to find his amber eyes dark with concern.

"Boy, do you have fast reflexes. Are you all right?" I asked.

One glossy chocolate eyebrow rose, just as I knew it would. "I was about to ask you the same. You should be more careful on the stairs. These old buildings can be dangerous if you aren't watching where you step."

His arms were still wrapped around me, but I wasn't complaining—he might have felt as hard as steel when I crashed into him, but I was thankful he was there. He was also extremely warm, had that same enticing scent of soap and man that I noticed the night before, and was close enough that I could see the pulse beating in his neck.

I wanted to swoon into him but managed instead to push myself back, out of his embrace. "As a matter of fact, I *was* watching where I was going—that's the problem. I couldn't see the steps and the she-devil behind me at the same time."

"*Chérie!* You are not accusing Tanya of foul deeds?" asked a voice from the left. Dominic stood in front of the door to the bar, Tanya cuddled up against him with such a smug look on her face, I wanted to pull her blood-red hair out by the roots, paste it on with glue, and pull it off again.

"You bet I'm accusing her! She pushed me down the stairs because I threatened her with the police when I found her where she had no right to be."

"She lies," Tanya cooed in Dominic's ear.

"Like hell I do! You kicked me on the back of my leg. I bet I'll have a huge bruise there from those monster shoes you're wearing."

"Monster shoes!" Tanya's eyes spoke volumes, and they were all about methods of disembowelment. "You Americans know nothing about that which is fashionable—"

"Enough!" Dominic shouted, and shoved Tanya away. He sauntered over to where Raphael and I stood, eyeing me up and down in a manner that set my hackles rising.

"Dominic!" Tanya looked mad enough to spit fire, but Dominic paid her little heed. He made a pretty pout and tsked as he saw me rubbing the sting out of my wrist where I bashed it against the wall. He took my wrist in his hand, pushing away my other hand to rub little circles on the wrist bone.

"But you have hurt yourself!" he said in a syrupy voice. He had surprisingly short fingers for a man who seemed long and lean otherwise, something I noticed when he bent over my wrist, licking his lips as he brought it up for inspection. "This does not seem to be a day which brings you great luck. *Yet.*"

"Let her be, Dominic." Raphael looked bored as sin leaning against the wall, but there was plenty of command in his voice, and his eyes were blazing with something I hoped Dominic found threatening.

"Yeah, let me be, Dominic."

Tanya nudged his arm, but he ignored her to give me a fanged grin. "And if I cannot, little one?"

Little one? I stood almost eye-to-eye with him. Who was he kidding?

"What agonies would you suffer if I withdrew my attention from you?" With his free hand he cupped my chin and tipped my head back, his fingers lingering on my neck. I jerked my head out of his grasp, but his hand clamped down tight on my wrist. Pain shot up through my arm.

"Let go of me, you fake-toothed creep!"

"Dominic!" Tanya was tugging on his arm, trying to get his attention, but he hissed and pushed her aside, reeling me in by my wrist.

"Let her go, Dominic." Raphael's voice was low and deep and rumbled around the narrow hallway. Something warm and pleasant inside me started to hum in response to it. He was still leaning against the wall, looking more bored, if possible.

The grateful look I was about to send him dried up. I glared at him instead. "Are you going to just stand there and hold up the wall, or are you going to help me?"

"Raphael is in my employ," Dominic purred as he pulled my wrist up to his mouth, parting his lips and baring his pseudo fangs. "He knows well the dark forces I can command if he tries my temper."

I felt like I was in the middle of a badly written Gothic soap opera, something along the lines of *Dark Shadows Meets The Munsters*.

"You are the hammiest actor I've ever met," I told Dominic. A muscle in his eyelid twitched.

"Dominic, I insist you stop this at once!" Tanya was a veritable blaze of fury, but she backed down immediately when her lover spun around—jerking my sore wrist in the process—and spat out a string of invectives in French.

"So help me God, if you don't let go of me, I'm going to sue you for assault up one side and down another!" I tugged on my wrist. "And don't think I can't do it, either! My mother is an attorney!"

His fingers tightened painfully around my wrist. "*Chérie!* So impatient! I like a woman who is demanding. I also like one who has spirit. Fight me, *mon petit chat.* It pleases me to see you struggle."

I stared at him for a moment in utter disbelief, then turned to glower at Raphael. "Dammit, he's your employer—*do something*"

He shrugged and straightened up. "What would you have me do?"

"Is castration out of the question?"

"You will be mine tonight, *mon ange*," Dominic promised, pulling me closer and making sure I saw him lick his fangs. "But I think you need a little lesson in manners first." As he spoke, he pulled my hand to his lips.

"Raphael!" I swear his eyes glowed bright for a moment in response to my demanding plea.

Just as Dominic's tongue snaked out to lick my pulse point, I made a fist with my free hand and prepared to knee him in the happy sacks, but before I could, all hell broke loose. A wordless cry of fury echoed in my head as the door to the outside crashed open in a sudden gust of wind, rattling the windows and sending a blast of cold air and a flurry of dead leaves in through the open door. At the same time as Raphael lunged for Dominic, Roxy and Christian, the man with the nice voice I'd seen the night before, came racing out of the bar. Dominic screamed as if he'd been struck, and released my hand as he staggered backwards. Tanya howled and headed for me with her claws bared, leaping past Roxy, who clutched Christian and bravely shouted, *"Aidez-moi! Aidez-moi!"* in the worst French accent I'd ever heard.

"Aidez-moi?" I asked her as I avoided impalement on Tanya's fingernails. "You want someone to help *you?* What about *me?*"

With a movement too fast for me to follow, Raphael grabbed Dominic by the fancy ruffled poet shirt he wore and slammed him against the bar wall. Tanya came at me again with a frustrated shriek, but I grabbed both her arms and held her off.

"Remember your position!" Dominic screamed as Raphael snarled and lifted him off the floor with one hand. Christian jumped in and wrestled Tanya away from me, pulling her away and holding her until she calmed down.

"Remember who I am, St. John! You will have nothing without me, nothing! I can break you with just a word!"

Brave words, considering it was Raphael who was holding Dominic impotent with only one hand, but to my immense disappointment, the words seemed effective. Slowly Raphael let Dominic slide down the wall until he was once again on his feet. Dominic smiled a completely repulsive smile full of gloating, and with exaggerated gestures straightened his shirt and striped vest.

"It is a wise man who knows when he has met his master," Dominic crowed, turning to retrieve a furious Tanya from Christian.

Employer or no employer, I hoped Raphael would punch him, but other than flexing his fingers, he did nothing. His face was tight and expressionless, and grudgingly I gave him full marks for control.

Dominic's gaze settled on me as I stood next to Roxy. He smiled and dropped his eyelids in what I'm sure he thought was an extremely sexy look, but which really just made him look dopey. "And you, *mon ange*—I will *see* you later tonight, eh? I promise you, I will fulfill all your darkest fantasies, no matter how extreme."

Tanya made a wordless noise of protest.

"Oh, goody," I said with irony that I doubted he would appreciate. "It's been eons since I saw a really quality vampire-staking. So glad you've volunteered."

The muscle over his eye twitched again, but he held on to his leer. With a showy bow to me, he flashed his canines at everyone and stalked to the door.

"Raphael!" Dominic paused at the door, but did not bother with the courtesy of turning around and facing Raphael when he spoke to him. "I expect you to be on the grounds before opening."

"I'll be there," Raphael answered, crossing his arms over his broad chest and sending Dominic a look I hoped to heaven no one would ever point at me. Dominic swirled his cape over his shoulder and swept out the door with a grand flourish, Tanya following sullenly behind.

"Bet he learned that in Dramatic Exits 101," I murmured to Roxy. She snickered in return. I gave Raphael a grateful smile. "Looks like I owe you one."

His jaw tightened. He didn't smile in return. In fact, he looked mad as hell. "Looks like you do," he acknowledged with a terse little nod of his head.

I thinned my lips at him, all thoughts of thanking him evaporating under the glare of those wicked amber eyes. "Let's not be overly gracious about this, shall we?"

He took a step forward—a long step forward; the man had legs that went up to his armpits—and frowned down on me. I have to admit he made a very intimidating figure, but I refuse to let anyone intimidate me with nothing but a bunch of muscles, a handsome face, and eyes that could drop a horse at ten paces.

"I could have lost my job because you insisted on flirting with Dominic. Isn't there an expression that says if you can't stand the heat, stay out of the kitchen?"

My jaw dropped. I looked at Roxy to see if she was hearing the same outrageous accusation I was. She didn't seem to, since she had a hand clapped over her mouth and was clearly trying not to laugh. Christian's dark eyes were bright with interest on me, but he didn't seem to be appalled either. I raised my chin, spun around to face Raphael, and let him have it with both barrels.

"Flirting? Heat? *Kitchen?* Are you mad? Crashing against the wall like that must have scrambled your brains, mister, because there is no way on God's green earth anyone could claim I was flirting with old fang-tooth!"

Raphael took another step forward until we were toe to toe, nose to chin. "You allowed him to hold your hand, and I noticed you weren't fighting too hard to get away. Not to mention you repeatedly batted your eyelashes at me in an obvious attempt to make him jealous. In other words, you showed every sign of a woman who was desirous of a man's attention by putting on a show of indifference to pique his interest. That, Joy Martine Randall, is flirting. I'd appreciate it if you could leave me out of your plans the next time you want to play your little sex games."

"Oh!" I huffed, unable to believe how wrong I'd been about him. I liked him better as the blood-sucking undead than I did as the self-centered, stuffy, righteous, PRIGGISH male he was. "For your information, Mr. So-Stuck-on-Yourself-You-Probably-Attract-Flies, I was not flirting! I do not play games! And I most certainly was *not* batting my eyelashes at you, so you can get that idea right out of the pudding that passes for your brain!"

"Pudding?" he bellowed at me, outrage bristling from every pore.

"Vanilla. With lumps in it!" I bellowed back.

He took a deep breath, his fingers flexing as he struggled to keep control of himself. Oddly enough, the fact that he was bigger and stronger than me wasn't threatening. Somehow I knew that, try him though I might, he was not the type of man who would hurt me.

"You are the most exasperating woman I've ever met," he growled through clenched teeth. His eyes were things of beauty to behold, but I wasn't about to tell him that, nosiree, not me. A compliment would be the last thing out of my mouth to a man who was so pigheaded he could be served at a luau. "I wouldn't doubt for a moment that you planned this whole fiasco just so I'd lose my job. I had you marked as trouble the moment I saw you fawning all over *him.*" He pointed at Christian.

I stared at Christian in open-mouthed surprise, so flabbergasted I couldn't think of anything to say. Christian gave Raphael an odd look that mingled surprise with anger. I wondered briefly what he had to be angry about; it wasn't him being slandered in such an atrocious manner. My flabbergastedness lasted about three seconds.

"You great big tottyhead! First I'm flirting with Dominic and then I'm fawning on Christian? Is that what you think? Because if you do, you're deranged, you're just one hundred percent deranged! You've got some sort of sex obsession, that's your problem!"

"Unlike a woman who has thrown herself at three men she's met in the space of a single day, I do *not* have an obsession with sex."

"Three? *Three?*" I steamed at him.

"I'm the third. Have you forgotten last night?"

"That was different. I have long since changed my mind," I argued, poking him in the chest and tipping my head back so I could glare at him better. "I know your type, all strong and silent and sexy as hell, and believing every woman within a five-mile radius has the hots for you. I bet you even think *I'm* attracted to you."

"You are the one who said you'd pay me to have sex with you."

"Joy!" Roxy gasped.

"It was a joke," I told her, lying through my teeth. I turned back to Raphael. "I'd just hit my head. I obviously wasn't myself."

His eyes glittered wickedly at me as he dropped his head so he could glower into my eyes. "Very well, we'll forget last night, but that doesn't explain the fact that you're attracted to me now."

"I am not!" I said, outraged at such an idea, refusing to

admit that my body was thrumming like a plucked string in reaction to his nearness.

"You are. You're practically begging me to kiss you. If that's not being attracted to me, I don't know what is."

His breath feathered across my face, distracting me for a moment. I bathed in the light of his heated eyes, feeling warm and feminine and very, very aroused.

Damn him.

"If I wanted you to kiss me, *Bob*, I'd be checking your tonsils right now."

"Is that so?"

He was so close to me, I could feel the heat of his chest as it brushed against me. His eyes burned into mine, our mouths just a fraction of an inch apart as I acknowledged that he was right, I did want him to kiss me, more than anything else I could think of.

"Yes, it's so. I think *you're* the one who wants to kiss *me*. Why don't you just give in and say it?"

"You say it first."

"Never."

"I don't give in," he warned just before his mouth brushed against mine.

I drowned in his eyes and parted my lips, preparing for full surrender, but was rudely dragged back to reality when Roxy loudly cleared her throat and said, "Um, guys, you're not actually going to have sex—paid for or otherwise—here in the hallway, are you? 'Cause it sure looks to me like that's where you're headed, and for one thing, I don't want to see it, and for another, I doubt if it would prove to be the experience you want it to be, what with all the people going in and out of the bar."

With an effort I wrenched my lips away from Raphael's and swallowed. Hard. I refused to look at him and turned to give Roxy and Christian a shaky smile. "I'm sorry, Christian, I'm sure you didn't enjoy seeing that, but as you are aware, he started it."

"You're the one who's thrown herself on me. *Twice,*" Raphael rumbled behind me.

"What I see is something that requires a little investigation," Christian replied neutrally, his voice silky with comfort. "I suggest we adjourn to the dining room. Roxanne has very kindly invited me to join you, and perhaps this gentleman would like to do so as well?"

"I've already eaten," Raphael answered, picking up my bag from where it had fallen when Tanya sent me flying. He brushed it off and handed it to me.

I was still charged up, and although I'm ashamed to admit it, didn't want him to leave. So I did the only thing I could. "Afraid you won't be able to keep your hands off me if you have dinner with us?"

I swear steam just about boiled out the top of his head. "Are you trying to bait me?"

I smiled.

"Fine," he snapped, his eyes narrowing. "Since you can't bear to be parted from me"—I made an outraged "Oh!" of protest to that—"I will accede to your feeble woman's ploy and join you, although I have, as I already mentioned, already dined."

"That's OK," Roxy said, taking his arm and steering him toward the dining room. "You can sit and watch us eat. If you stare at Joy long enough, she's bound to spill something on herself. That's always entertaining."

I watched them disappear into the seldom-used tiny dining room (most of the hotel patrons preferring to take their meals in the bar), and looked at Christian. "Have you *ever* seen anything like that aggravating man?"

"Never," he replied, taking my hand and gently massaging my wrist. A vague sense of warmth and comfort filled me at his touch. I smiled into his dark brown eyes, but he didn't

82

smile back. He just held my gaze captured in his for a moment, then lifted my hand to kiss it. I'd never had a man kiss my hand before, and had always thought it a pretty silly gesture, but with his dark-eyed gaze holding me prisoner, the brush of his lips against my knuckles was anything but silly. Slowly he turned my hand over, his mouth a hairsbreadth from my pulse point.

The room suddenly went gray as a wave of bone-deep hunger slammed into me, sucking at me, pulling me down into its icy hold. I was gripped by it, possessed by it, drowning in a need I couldn't begin to understand. Just as abruptly as it started, it ended, leaving me gasping at Christian as he placed a chaste kiss on my wrist. I pulled my hand back, wanting to scream, wanting to know what was happening to me, needing to understand why my mind was suddenly doing things it shouldn't be doing. *Something is wrong with you,* a frightened voice in my head cried out. I whirled around, desperate to run away, wild to escape the imaginings of my fractured mind.

Raphael stood in the doorway to the dining room watching Christian. His eyes were hooded, glowing with unspoken emotion, hard and glinting and so full of anger the hairs on the back of my neck stood on end. Slowly he moved his gaze to me, then gestured to the dining room and held out his hand for me. "Shall we?"

I stood sick at heart with the knowledge that I must truly be going mad, and struggled to control my beating heart. Inside my head I was shrieking and screaming and pleading for someone to explain to me what was happening, but outside I stood silent, unable to move lest the stillness break and the madness descend upon me again.

You see visions of vampires. Something is wrong with you.

"Joy? You look like you need to eat. Come, let us have dinner."

Christian's voice was an oasis of calm, but it didn't stand

a chance in the wild turbulence that filled my mind. He, too, held out his hand to me. I stared at it, unable to move.

Vampires or insanity—which did I want as an explanation? My mind fractured a little more trying to decide. I put my hands up to my head, wanting to hold it together, terrified that I would lose control over everything important to me. Vampires or insanity? Which was real, and which was my imagination? How would I know which was which? Could I trust myself to recognize reality anymore, and if I couldn't, who would help me?

Your mind can't recognize what's real and what's not, the voice in my head whispered. *Something is wrong with you.*

"Joy."

Raphael's voice glowed like a beacon in the maelstrom of my whirling thoughts. I fought to control the swelling panic that gripped me, tried to focus my thoughts so they didn't drag me down with them, drowning in a sea of confusion and fear. Desperately I clung to the thought that if I could just have a little time, I could figure things out and make sense of all the disorder.

There is no hope. SOMETHING IS WRONG WITH YOU!

"Joy."

"There is nothing wrong with me!" I yelled at Raphael. "So I have a few visions? So what? Who doesn't? I REFUSE TO GO MAD!"

The words echoed in the long, narrow hallway, disturbed only by the muffled hum of noise from the bar. Shocked that I had yelled out loud, I stared wordlessly at Raphael.

He pursed his lips. "I think you're going to be more trouble than I first anticipated."

Chapter Six

Dinner was a trial. Despite my bellowed statement that I would not allow myself to go mad, I was worried about the disintegration of a formerly sound, if not terribly brilliant, mind. As I saw it, life was offering me two paths: Either I could believe in vampires and live happily ever after, or I could go not-so-quietly insane and have myself locked up. Given those choices, there was really no contest. I took a deep mental breath and told my skeptical self that I was only doing this for sanity's sake.

I would believe in vampires.

During dinner neither Christian nor Raphael made mention of the episode in the hall, a fact that left me wondering uneasily if they were humoring me in order to keep me from going off the deep end again.

I did not like the feeling.

"Oh, come on, have a little din-din. Tell you what, it'll be my treat," Roxy pleaded with Raphael a few minutes later.

"No, thank you. I told you I've already eaten."

85

"Yeah, but surely you could put away a little something extra? You're a big guy, I'm sure there's room in there for a little pork and sauerkraut, eh?" Roxy grinned at him, nudging me under the table with her toes. I gave her the one-eyebrow "Yes? You wanted something?" lift, as perfected by the man sitting across the table from me.

"No, thank you."

"How about dessert? The strudel here is really good."

"No, thank you. I don't want anything."

"Roxy, leave him alone."

"Appetizer?"

"No."

"Glass of wine?"

"I don't drink wine."

"Roxy!"

"I can't sit here and eat my stuffed pork and dumplings if he's not going to eat anything!" Roxy declared, frowning at Christian in a meaningful manner until he obediently transferred his attention to the menu. She turned back to Raphael and was going to bait him further, but I made the squinty eyes to end all squinty eyes at her, and for what was probably the first time in her life, she backed off.

"Geez, you guys don't have to look at me like that, I was just expressing a polite interest. Wasn't I expressing a polite interest, Joy?"

"No, you were being obnoxious and pushy. You deserve to be snapped at."

"Oh, sure, you take *his* side. No surprise there, considering you almost had your tongue down his throat a few minutes ago."

"ROXY!"

"Good, here comes the waitress. Has everyone but Stretch here decided what they want?"

I prayed for an earthquake to open the earth up at my feet and swallow me whole. From the martyred look on

Raphael's face, he was praying the same thing.

"So, do you live around here?" Roxy asked Christian once we had placed our orders.

He nodded, his fingers tracing the rim of his wineglass. "I do. About a kilometer west of here."

"Really? What do you do?"

"Roxanne!" I slapped at her hand as she was about to snag the last bit of bread.

"What?"

"It's not polite to grill people. I told you almost everyone but Americans find it invasive to question them about their life."

She grinned her pixie grin at him. "Sorry; didn't mean to be rude."

He smiled as he took the piece of bread she offered. Roxy turned to me with her eyebrows lowered. "Am I allowed to talk about myself, or is that also rude?"

I shot Raphael a "what can I do with her?" look. He lifted both eyebrows in return in a manner that seemed to suggest a gag might be effective. I was forced to agree he had a point.

Christian laughed at Roxy's question, the warm sound rolling around the room and covering everything in a soft blanket of silk. "I'm not in the least bit offended by your questions, although I would much rather hear about what brings two such lovely women to a small corner of the Czech Republic."

"A wild goose chase," I muttered.

Roxy ignored me. "Have you ever heard of a local author named Dante?" she asked Raphael and Christian. The former shook his head.

Christian frowned slightly as he toyed with his bread, rubbing crumbs off the crust. "Yes, I have."

"I thought you might; he lives in this area," Roxy continued, digging through her sizeable purse for a copy of the book she was reading. "He writes the most delicious books about Moravians—vampires, you know—and we're dying to meet him. The books are fabulous, utterly, utterly fabulous, with mysterious, dark, brooding heroes to die for. You really should read them—not that you'd find the heroes to die for, since you're men, not unless you're . . ." She glanced up at Christian and Raphael, then back down into her purse. "You really should read them. There are twelve books out now, and there's supposed to be another one in a few months. Drat, I must have left the book in my room."

Christian's brows rose as he looked from Roxy to myself. I gave him a five for effort—he was good, but he couldn't hold a candle to the Browmaster sitting opposite me. Raphael was leaning back in his chair, his arms crossed, a pained expression on his face. I couldn't figure out if he was bored with the conversation or the company. He certainly wasn't contributing much to the conversation. I wondered why, if he was so unhappy, he'd agreed to sit with us; then I wondered why I cared. Just because I was the teensiest bit attracted to the man didn't mean I had to like him.

I shot a look at him from under my lashes. He watched me through half-closed eyes, his expression making blood rush to all sorts of interesting spots on my body. My question as to why he was bothering with us was answered by the interest that flared deep within the glittering slivers of amber.

Christian listened as Roxy recapped the plot of the latest book, continuing to toy with what remained of his bread, looking a bit askance at Roxy's enthusiasm. Raphael glanced at his watch, which prompted me to shut Roxy up and turn the conversation to something that might interest him.

"I really don't think they care about the books, Rox."

"On the contrary," Raphael spoke up. "I'm finding it a

fascinating look at what women feel are missing from their lives."

"Missing? What do you mean, missing?" I asked.

He rubbed a finger along his jaw, his lips donning an insufferably smug look. "From what Roxy says, women are the primary readers of these books."

"Yeah, so?"

"And they feature male characters who are dominant and aggressive, especially toward women?"

"They're called alpha males, and what of it?"

A slight smile quirked his lips. "You needn't get so defensive; I was merely pointing out that books whose readership is predominantly female, featuring aggressive male characters and including what I assume are numerous scenes of a licentious nature—"

"Licentious?" I gasped. How dare he say that about Dante's fabulous, romantic, sensual, *erotic* books?

"I bet you're one of those men who likes to feel superior to women," Roxy said suspiciously.

Christian turned a laugh into a cough. Raphael and I ignored both of them.

"—can only indicate that the books strike a chord with their readers, fulfilling a need, if you will, unmet in their everyday lives."

"Well, look who has a psychology degree," I snorted, and damning the calories, slathered fresh butter on my piece of bread.

"Bristol University, 1992," he agreed.

"Oh. Sorry." I ate crow in the form of my bread.

"I'm not." Roxy shot him a squinty eyed glare. "I think he's one of the alpha males he's so quick to damn."

"You tell me, then," Raphael offered, leaning backward on the back legs of the chair, his hands locked behind his head, "what it is you both find so attractive in these books."

89

I looked between him and Christian, wondering if they were just humoring me again.

"Please," the latter said, brushing bread crumbs from his shirt, and giving me an encouraging grin. I thought something flashed in his eyes, but it was quickly gone. "I am just as interested as Raphael. Are the men such as you described the type to interest you, personally?"

"A man like one of Dante's heroes?" Roxy asked.

He nodded.

"Ooooh," she squealed, "yes! Yes!"

"Not on your life," I answered at the same time. "They're fun in fiction, but I imagine real alpha males are the absolute pits to live with. They've got all those arrogance and domination issues, not to mention being obstinate, pigheaded, and determined to rule everyone's lives. Alpha males are not what women are looking for in a man." I smiled pointedly at Raphael.

"Don't listen to her, she's got no spirit. You have to understand, these heroes aren't just alpha males, they're Moravians. Dark Ones. *Vampires.*"

Raphael rolled his eyes. Christian smiled, waiting until the waitress set down our meals before continuing. "I would have thought most people would find vampirism an experience they would not wish to explore in any depth, let alone consider it an asset in a mate."

"You're dead wrong there," Raphael said before Roxy could dispute Christian. "I've been with the GothFaire only four weeks, but they've made a small fortune at each of their stops. Some people come for the bands they hire, others come for the novelty of a traveling fair, but most are young people who want to be a part of the Goth community."

"Goth?" Christian asked him.

"It stands for Gothic, supposedly a society devoted to the dark side of life. Vampires, necromancers, morbid poetry and loud, grating music . . . anything that can be classified as strange and unusual. From what I've seen, the stranger and more unusual a person or thing, the more successful it'll be at the fair."

"Poseurs," Roxy said.

"Dominic," I offered.

"Exactly," he agreed with both of us.

"You do not believe that Dominic and company are what they claim, then?" Christian asked.

Raphael snorted in the negative, and sat upright again, glancing at his watch.

"And how about you?" Christian asked Roxy and me.

Roxy watched Raphael closely for a minute. "Well . . . Dominic might not be a vampire, but I do believe they exist. I'm quite certain that Dante couldn't have made up the whole race of Moravians based on just a little folklore. There has to be some truth in it."

"Ah. And the lady who refuses to be mad? Are you a skeptic or a believer?"

A blush crept up my cheeks as I told myself not to be annoyed. I had wanted them to stop pussyfooting around me, and Christian had done just that. I met his dark gaze and shrugged, unwilling to commit myself verbally. Despite the decision to do whatever it took to keep my mind from slipping away, I was having difficulty admitting out loud that I believed in something so extreme as vampires.

"Some people might consider it foolish to view a vampire, these Dark Ones, as a source of entertainment," Christian commented to Roxy.

"And if vampires really existed, they'd be right," Raphael interrupted. "You don't believe that Dominic is a real vampire, do you?"

Christian's eyes darkened. I wondered if it was easy to do. I made a mental note to practice in front of a mirror to see if I could do it. "No. I believe he is merely playacting a role."

"And not doing a very convincing job of it, either," I said wryly.

"I agree, but I'm afraid others are not so clear-sighted. You have not seen the north meadow today?"

"The north meadow? Oh, you mean the big open area beyond the hotel? No, we were off in the other direction today. Why? What's going on there?" Roxy asked.

"People come to this area every year at this time. The Harvest Festival draws some of them to Brno, others come here for an All Hallow's Eve celebration."

"Oh, we heard about that. The GothFaire is sponsoring a festival at Drahanská Castle." She turned to Raphael for confirmation.

He glanced at his watch again. "It's a festival to celebrate the cult of the dead, as demonstrated by particularly loud forms of music, the overconsumption of alcohol, and the more popular attractions from the fair, all of it amounting to a security nightmare. And speaking of that, I must leave. We are expecting a significant increase in attendees tonight, and as you heard, my presence has been requested."

He stood up, nodded to us, and grabbing his jacket, headed out the door without a look back.

"Well!" Roxy sniffed, then gave me a sympathetic look. "I think you can do better, Joyful."

I resisted the urge to roll my eyes again. "Will you give it up?"

She grinned, then asked Christian if he wanted to join us at the fair that evening. "It should be fun. There'll be lots of vampires to look at!"

"Will there?" he asked with a wry twist to his lips.

"Sure there will. You *do* believe in vampires, don't you?"

We both looked at him. He was poking at his goulash, but he looked up and gave us another of his nice smiles. " 'There are more things in heaven and earth, Horatio—' "

"Too weird!" Roxy interrupted. "Oh, I'm sorry, I didn't

mean to cut you off, but someone said that to Joy just a few weeks ago, and it seems odd you should repeat it now. Almost like it was a sign!" She sent me a look that spoke volumes.

I sent her one that told her she was writing the wrong book. "Yes, how very strange that an obscure and unknown author like Shakespeare might be quoted twice in a month. Just let me make a note of the date and time. I'll want to include mention of this rare phenomenon in my diary."

"I would be happy to join you at the fair tonight," Christian cut in before Roxy could respond.

"Fabulous!" she crowed. "Now, let me tell you the basic storylines of the twelve *Book of Secrets* volumes, so you'll know what to look for in Dark Ones when we're at the fair. First of all, vampires are always men."

He raised his eyebrows at that. "Really? How interesting. Why is that?"

Roxy shrugged and stuffed a forkful of pork and cabbage in her mouth. "Something to do with the manner of their punishment, I think," she said indistinctly. "Anyway, they can't eat or drink anything but blood—it doesn't have to be human, though—they can't tolerate sunlight, of course, and they have great powers of mesmerism. They can also change their forms into animals, and are difficult to kill or wound. A Dark One can't ever become human again, but once he has completed the Joining with his Beloved, the woman who is his soul mate, he can do a lot more stuff like tolerate a little bit of sunlight. But the best part is that they're all, without exception, fantastic lovers."

I stopped frowning at my salad and gave her an exasperated look. "Oh, for heaven's sake, Roxy—"

"Well, they are!"

"Dark Ones are fictional characters—"

"Damned sexy fictional characters!"

"What is this Joining of which you spoke?" Christian

asked, mostly, I suspected, to keep the peace between Roxy and me.

She waved her fork at him as she chewed. "That's really cool. There are seven steps to a successful Joining."

I glanced at the small wooden clock on a shelf near the door. "Roxy, it's almost six. We really should be going if you want to have maximum play time at the fair."

"This won't take a minute. Christian's interested, aren't you?"

"Fascinated," he said, pushing his plate aside. I frowned at it for a minute. It was bare of all except a few pieces of garnish. He ate even faster than Roxy, and if she wasn't awarded the world's fastest eater title by the record-keeping people, it wasn't for lack of trying.

"The seven steps are this: First, the Dark One marks the heroine as his own; second, he protects her from afar; third, he conducts the first exchange—"

"Of body fluids," I interrupted. "Such as blood, saliva, that sort of thing. I know it sounds icky, but I have to admit, the way Dante writes it, it's really not. Usually the first exchange is a really steamy kiss."

"—followed by the fourth step, where he entrusts the heroine with his life by giving her the means to destroy him; then there's the second exchange." Roxy wiggled her eyebrows at him. "I'll let you guess what sorts of bodily fluids are exchanged there. The sixth step has the Dark One seeking the heroine's assistance to overcome his darker self, and finally, the last step is the ultimate exchange—their lifeblood. The heroine redeems his dark soul by offering herself as a sacrifice so he can live. He doesn't let her die, of course, but it's all very romantic!"

"And utterly fictional," I muttered. Roxy didn't hear me, but Christian did. "That's it, Rox, you're done. Eat your dumpling and let's get a move on. The fair is about to start, and you're boring Christian to tears."

"Mmmm," Roxy said with a knowing smile, scarfing down the last of her dumpling. "The fact that a certain hottie guy will be hanging around there has nothing to do with your desire to check it out, huh?"

I stood up and grabbed my dearest friend in the whole wide world and muttered dire threats in her ear if she continued with that thread of conversation. She just stuck her nose in the air, and graciously allowed Christian to pay for our dinner.

We ran upstairs to collect our coats since the nights were starting to get cold. As I locked my hotel room behind me, I came to a fast decision.

"Rox," I said as she toddled out of her room. "I want to tell you something, but I don't want you to freak out."

She stared at me for a moment. "Well, I've seen you naked so I know you're not really a man. What's the problem?"

I cleared my throat nervously and tried to think of how to say it without sounding any more deranged than I was feeling. "You remember last night in the bar, when I got dizzy?"

She nodded, looking impatiently toward the stairs, taking my arm and trying to tug me in that direction. "Yeah. You said it was because of the beer, not that you had a lot of it."

"Well," I said, reminding myself that she was my oldest and dearest friend, and if she wouldn't be understanding and supportive in my time of need, no one would, "that wasn't exactly the truth."

Her eyes widened and she stopped trying to shove me toward the stairs. "Oh my God! You don't mean . . . Joy, why didn't you tell me?"

"I didn't know quite how," I said miserably, playing with the buttons on my coat. "It's not quite something I want everyone to know."

"I'll say! Geez, this puts a whole new light on things, huh? When are you due?"

"Due?"

"The baby. When's it due? And what are you going to say to Bradley?"

I smacked her on her arm. "I'm not pregnant, you boob!"

"Oh." She looked a bit disappointed. "If it's not a baby that made you feel faint, what was it?"

I took a peek down the stairs to make sure no one was hovering just out of sight. "I'm having, for lack of a better word, visions."

"Visions?"

"Yeah. You ever had them?"

"You mean visions of the Virgin Mary, that kind of vision?"

"No, not that. My visions are about . . . a man."

"Ooooh, now that sounds like my kind of vision! Is he naked? Are you? Are you touching each other? Does he have a really big package?"

"Will you drag your mind from the gutter for a moment while I'm explaining to you how I'm going stark, raving mad? Do you think you could do me the common courtesy of being WORRIED about the fact that I'm having visions?"

"Why?" she asked, her head tipped in question.

"Why?" I gawked at her in disbelief. "Why? WHY? You ask *why?*"

"One why, not four."

I grabbed her ear and peered in it. She tried to squirm away. "What are you doing?"

I released her earlobe. "Looking to see if I can see through to the other side. Did you not hear me? I'm seeing visions! *Visions!* Strange, unexplained phenomena whereby I'm possessed by the emotions and feelings and sights of someone else. In this case, I'm feeling things from someone who's . . ."

I couldn't bring myself to say it.

"Someone who's what?"

"A vampire," I mumbled, wishing now I hadn't brought

the subject up. It was far better to go quietly insane on my own than to suffer the embarrassment of admitting I was being used by a creature whose existence I had long and vociferously denied.

"What? I couldn't hear you."

"A vampire," I said a bit more loudly, peeking at her from under lowered lashes.

She blinked at me. Twice. "OK."

I made scrunched-up lips at her. "OK? Is that it? I tell you—that's me we're talking about, the skeptical one—that I'm having visions coming from a real, honest-to-goodness, card-carrying vampire, and all you can say is OK? You're not going to laugh or make fun of me or tell me I must be imagining it?"

"Idiot!" she said fondly, grabbing my sleeve and pulling me toward the stairs. "It's because I know you that I know you must be going through hell experiencing something that's way beyond your control. Come on, Christian's waited long enough. Let's go see if we can't find the Dark One who's giving you all the trouble."

"Wait a minute! You're not even going to question whether or not I'm really having visions? I thought I was going insane before I decided to believe in them! The least you can do is appreciate how hard this is for me!"

"Oh, I know it's hard for you. I know you must be wigging out at it, and squirming with embarrassment because now you have to admit that I was right about vampires all along, but I'll save my gloating for later."

"How grateful I am for your tender mercies. That aside, how do you know that the one who is affecting me will be at the fair?" I asked, following her down the stairs, more than a little befuddled by her quick acceptance of something that still gave me the willies to think about.

"Has to be," she called back over her shoulder. "He's marked you. That's the first step in the Joining, and everyone knows they can't Join with you unless they're physically close."

I looked down at my hands as we descended the second flight of stairs. "I'm not marked."

"That's what the visions are—his mark. If they're like what's described in the books, you're experiencing things that he sees and feels, basically all his strong emotions. Dark Ones can only do that with their true soul mate, so if he's projecting to you, that must mean he's marking you as his."

Instantly I thought of Raphael.

"How many visions have you had?" she asked as we rounded the landing.

"Hmm?" I pulled my mind from the thoughts it was pursuing. "Well, the one at Miranda's was due to the gin, I'm sure, so that leaves me a couple last night in the bar, and one just before we had dinner."

She paused and turned around to face me. "You had one before dinner? When?"

"When I was standing in the hall with Christian."

"Christian?" She thought for a minute, then shook her head. "Nope, can't be; we've seen him eat and drink. Hey!"

Her eyes met mine. A chill rippled down my back. I swallowed. "Raphael."

She nodded.

"The last vision happened when Christian was kissing my hand. Raphael was standing in the doorway, watching us."

"Cool!" she breathed.

"It is not," I snapped, pushing her to get her going. She stood where she was.

"When the first visions in the bar came, where was Raphael?"

The sensation of blood flowing down my throat, subduing the hunger howling inside me flashed into mind. "He was . . . uh . . . feeding."

Her eyes widened until I thought they'd pop out. "Oh, that

is so cool! He shared his feeding with you? Wow! What did it feel like? What did he do? Could you see everything?"

I closed my eyes for a minute and took a couple of deep breaths to rid myself of the remembered images. "Yes, and I'd really like not to remember it, if you don't mind."

"OK." She thought for a moment. "So you had a vision *before* Raphael came into the bar? Just before?"

I nodded.

"Well, then, there's your answer!" She started back down the stairs.

"Wait a minute!" I hurried after her. Christian was waiting for us at the door. "Roxy, wait up—what do you mean, there's my answer? What answer?"

"Sorry, Joy's having a bit of vampire trouble," she told Christian in a confidential tone that made me want to die right there on the spot.

Not surprisingly, he looked astonished by the news. "Is she indeed?"

"Do you have to tell everyone?" I hissed, pinching her arm, flashing a reassuring smile at Christian. He just looked at me with a faintly puzzled frown between his brows, no doubt trying to calculate how much trouble it would be to bundle me away to the local loony bin.

"That's OK, Christian believes in vampires. Remember the 'more things in heaven and Earth, Horatio'? Joy's having visions," she added. "She's been marked by a Moravian. I was just explaining to her that it must be Raphael, since he refused to eat in front of us."

"Wait a minute," I said, remembering something she'd said that morning. "You said just this morning that he couldn't be one because he had a beer at the bar."

"Ah," she said cannily, throwing open the door and charging out into the night. "But did you actually see him *drink* the beer? Let's shake a leg, people. I want to examine Raphael up close. Imagine sitting next to him and not even knowing what he was!"

I grabbed Christian by the hand and hauled him with me as I ran after Roxy. "But what did you mean when you said something was the answer to my visions?"

She stopped just beyond the stretch of graveled area that served as the hotel's parking lot. "Think about it. You have visions seeing Raphael approaching the bar—"

"A man. I didn't see his face. It could be anyone."

She gave me a condescending look. "Hardly. OK, so you see this man approaching the bar, projecting his thoughts and feelings to you as he gets closer, right?"

I shot a quick glance at Christian, realized I was still holding his hand, and dropped it with an apologetic moue. "You must really think I'm nuts."

"On the contrary, I find this fascinating" he said. "Who knew there were such dark depths to Raphael? He seemed like a perfectly ordinary man to me."

That set my hackles to rising a bit. "He's anything but ordinary."

His eyebrows went up. "Indeed."

"Do you want to hear this or not?" Roxy interrupted. I nodded. "Where was I? Oh, that's right. So, you're having these visions of what Raphael or whoever is seeing and doing as he approaches. Did it get worse just before he came in?"

I nodded again, my skin prickling with the remembered sensation of danger approaching. I frowned for a moment, examining that thought. Why was it that when Raphael approached the bar I felt danger drawing closer, but when he was angry with me earlier tonight I felt perfectly safe with him? I asked Roxy.

"Easy," she said, making an impatient gesture with her hands. "He wasn't aware of you before he saw you, but he was afterwards. A Dark One would never harm their Beloved, you know that as well as I do. To get back to your visions—once he entered the bar and saw you, he must have recognized you for his soul mate, seen that you were picking up this thoughts, and closed them off to keep from distressing you further."

I twisted my hands together as I thought it over.

"Makes sense, doesn't it?" Roxy asked Christian.

"It would appear to, yes."

"But this evening . . ." She shot an appraising glance at Christian. "Dark Ones are notoriously jealous about their soul mates. I'd suggest that in the future you keep your flirting with Joy to a minimum, unless you want to tangle with a really pissed-off vampire."

He gave her a faint smile. "That would, I admit, be a unique experience."

She nodded. "Any more questions? No? Good. Let's go, I want to check out the fair and see how many other vampires are there, and then we'll corner Raphael and get all the dirt from him."

"We will do nothing of the kind," I said firmly as I stalked behind her, Christian at my side. "I'm willing to concede, since the only other explanation is that I'm going quite, quite mad, that I'm having visions, and the visions' source is a vampire, but we don't know if it is Raphael or not. The poor man could simply be in the wrong place at the wrong time."

"Hrmph," she snorted, slowing down until she was walking on the other side of Christian. "How likely is it that there's another Dark One lurking about that you haven't seen? You said yourself that Dominic is fake, and he's the only other guy around here who fits the bill, right?"

"Maybe. Regardless, I don't want you saying anything to Raphael."

"Now you're being stubborn. There's no other explanation that fits. What do you think?" she asked Christian.

He raised both hands in a gesture of neutrality. "I believe I will leave this discussion to the experts."

"I'll give you some of the *Book of Secrets* novels in the morning," she said. "You read them. You'll see I'm right. I'm always right when it comes to Dark Ones!"

Fifteen minutes' walk away from the hotel was a wide, open meadow. The north end of it was given over to the Goth-Faire, a circle-shaped collection of trailers, small tents and wooden booths, and one large main tent structure at one end where the bands performed. It was strongly reminiscent of a small traveling circus, right down to the smell of stale smoke and popcorn. The south end of the field, empty when we had seen it the morning before, was starting to fill with individuals' tents, trucks, cars, and portable toilets. Beyond the tent city rose a dark line of trees marking the edge of a forest, through which a turret of Drahanská Castle could be seen, the rest hidden by the trees.

"What's the game plan, Rox?"

"Tarot card readings, Kirlian aura photos, palm and rune-stone readings—Arielle is doing those since their palm/rune-stone reader left—spells and incantations . . ."

"It sounds like one of those psychic fairs they set up down at the bingo hall," I protested.

"This is better. The GothFaire is run by real vampires, so you know everyone working for them must be the real thing, too."

"Why settle for imitation vampires when you can have the real thing?" I teased, looking to Christian for sympathy. He just shrugged.

I ignored Roxy's frown. "OK, let's start at the top of your list. Who's doing the tarot card readings?"

"Tanya."

"Thanks for warning me. I'll stay away from that booth. What about the aura photos?"

A GIRL'S GUIDE TO VAMPIRES

"Done by a couple named Reynaldo and Demeter," she answered, reading the fair pamphlet that was pushed in our hands after we paid the admittance fee. "Bet Reynaldo's a vampire. Oh, this sounds interesting! There's a woman who does past-life regressions. At eight, Dominic is doing his Magique Macabre show, and then at ten, the music starts. Tonight there's two bands—Six Inches of Slime is first, followed at eleven-thirty by a local band named Rychlovka." She looked up at Christian. "What's that mean?"

He choked.

"That bad, huh?"

"I fear so."

"Really?" I asked as Christian grabbed my elbow and steered me around a group of teenagers dripping in narrow chains, clunky shoes, and more black vinyl than you could shake a stick at. "Is it a swear word? If I get really annoyed with Roxy, can I snap out *'rychlovka'* at her?"

He laughed. "It is not a word of swearing, no. It means to engage in a quick sexual act."

"Rats. I guess I'll just have to make do with *do prdele*."

He choked again. I grinned and looked when Roxy pointed to a small black tent with a crowd gathered around it. "What's over there?"

The crowd parted as we approached. One of the vinyl-clad teens was doubled over a bucket. I glanced up to a sign hanging on the tent behind them. "Piercings. Remind me to avoid this tent."

"You and me both, sister," Roxy said with a dark look at the ralphing teen. She turned her attention back to the pamphlet. "Hey, this sounds like it'll be right up our alley—a Dungeon Room! Interesting, huh?"

I made a face at her suggestion and continued what I'd been doing ever since we had arrived—scanning the crowds for a tall, handsome man with unnatural amber

103

eyes, and what I feared were even more unnatural dining habits.

"Dungeons, I have found," Christian spoke up in a voice that was as smooth as milk chocolate, "do not in general meet the expectations one has of them. What do you suppose is the attraction in this particular dungeon room?"

"Um . . . let me see if it tells." Roxy flipped over the pamphlet. "It just says 'Enter the Shadoworld and fulfill your dark destiny.' What do you think that means?"

I stopped peering around the crowds long enough to grin at her. "I think it means you'd better stay away from it unless you want to experience the sting of the lash on your tender little flesh."

"You have bondage on the brain." She tucked the flyer away and clutched Christian's arm, giving him one of her impish grins. "I bet Christian isn't afraid of a little dark destiny. You'll go with me to the dungeon room, won't you? Joy, as you can plainly see, is too much of a poop to have a little fun in a dungeon."

"Sure, go ahead." I shooed them toward the blood-red tent that loomed ahead of us. "I'll go have Arielle read the runes for me while you're frolicking in the Merry Widow."

Roxy rolled her eyes and pulled Christian toward the red tent. "That's Iron Maiden."

"I will not frolic in an Iron Maiden," Christian protested. "In it there will be no room for the dancing or the Maypole."

Roxy stopped and stared at him for a minute. I giggled. He smiled.

She turned back to me. "Just remember that you can't let Raphael take the third step of Joining until I'm there to watch."

"The third step?" What was she talking about? "What happened to the second step?"

She dropped Christian's hand and with a big, exaggerated sigh hurried over to where I stood, counting on her fingers as she said, "The first step is the mark, right?"

"Right. You say that's the visions."

"And who knows Dante's books better than anyone else on this whole planet?"

"You do," I acknowledged.

"Right. Trust me, the visions are his mark, the first step. The second step is—"

"Protection from afar."

"Exactly. And who was it who grabbed Dominic and slammed him up against the wall with one hand when he was about to bite your wrist?"

"Well—that wasn't protection from *afar*, though."

"Afar, a-near, same difference," she shrugged. "It was protection, and that's all that matters. And if I hadn't interrupted you, he'd probably have taken the third step."

The memory of his body pressed against mine was not one I'd dismissed. I'd carried it around, tucked away in a corner of my mind like a little treasure, something I could bring out and examine in private. I said nothing.

"Just promise me he doesn't lock lips with you until I'm around to see it, OK?"

"Go. Away."

She grinned and dashed back to Christian, grabbing his hand and hauling him to the Dungeon Room tent. He sent me a pitiful look over his shoulder. I blew him a kiss.

Chapter Seven

Because the real moneymaking attraction of the evening—
the Goth bands—wasn't slated to start until later, the people
who were present during the early hours of the fair were
almost normal looking. Yes, there was PVC and vinyl and
thick, clunky-looking shoes, and black, black, black everywhere, but there were also a lot of couples, young people
in small groups walking around giggling and pointing out
the oddities to each other, and even some families, although
I noticed that admittance to several of the more question-
able attractions was limited to those over the age of twelve.

Czech, German, and French were the predominant languages heard, with a smattering of English here and there,
giving truth to what Christian had said earlier about people
traveling to the area from all over Europe for the All Hallow's
Eve celebration.

I worked my way through the thickening crowd, heading
for the booth with a sign painted with a big blue hand gar-
nished with a gilt Mannaz, one of the rune symbols used in

divination. Happily for me, the next-door booth—Tanya's tarot card booth—was vacant. Although I had no qualms about facing her again, I didn't particularly want to encourage another scene like the one we'd been through earlier. I figured Tanya must be off casting spells and grinding up warts for love potions, which suited me just fine.

Arielle was seated at a low table covered with the standard moon-and-stars cloth you see at a lot of occult shops, cupping a blond twenty-something's hands in hers as her fingers traced lines on the woman's palm.

"Your life line is very long and very strong. This is always a good sign," she told the woman in German. She gave a shy smile to the man standing behind the woman's shoulder. "You have only one marriage line."

The blond woman tittered and turned to shoot coy looks from under her lashes to her companion.

"Your heart line joins your line of head, so in relationships, your head very much controls your heart."

The woman dimpled at her, pleased. I waved at Arielle and got in line behind the couple. So far what I'd heard was pretty standard fare—generalizations and vague concepts that were meant to send the customer away with a warm, happy glow.

"You have only one infinitesimal line of fate. This means that fate will not play too much of a role in your life. This is good, you understand? It means you are in control of your life."

"Oh, yes, very good," the woman agreed, starting to get into the reading. "I like to be in control."

Her companion snorted in obvious agreement. She ignored him, peering into her palm as Arielle pointed out a bump. "Your inner Mount of Mars indicates aggressiveness, but your outer Mount of Mars indicates self-control, so sometimes you find yourself wanting to push everyone out of your way, but you hold yourself in check."

The woman was nodding at everything Arielle said, her brows drawn together as she watched Arielle point to her fingertips and describe how they indicated she was a creative, artistic person. Five minutes later, Arielle concluded that the woman would have two children, travel extensively, and have intermittent luck throughout her long life. The German woman, all smiles after the reading, handed over the reading fee, slipping Arielle an extra couple hundred koruna as a tip before heading off to have something on her boyfriend pierced (Nostrils? Nipples? My German wasn't up to anatomical piercing dialogue).

"Good evening, Joy," Arielle greeted me in her softly accented English. "How is your head feeling?"

"Much better. I'd like you to read the runes for me, but first . . ." I gnawed on my lower lip and looked around us. Since the fair had just opened, there weren't a lot of people lining up for readings yet, and we were fairly private at the end of the row of booths. "I was wondering if you could tell me where Raphael might be."

She gave me a conspiratorial wink. "He is very handsome, yes?"

My cheeks started to pink up. I just hoped that in the washed-out light of the bulbs overhead, she wouldn't see me blushing like a virgin. "Um . . . I guess. Do you know where he is?"

She gave one of those eloquent shrugs that only the French seem to know how to make. "I do not. He generally checks in to see how I am doing before Dominic's show, when he watches the crowds in the main tent. Otherwise, he promenades the fair and keeps control of the people."

"Ah. OK. I'll just keep my eyes peeled for him promenading." I waved at a velvet cloth bag sitting at the end of the table. "Would you do a reading for me?"

"With pleasure," she answered, pulling out a casting cloth of garishly colored red and gold, "although I am very new to it, and the readings are not very strong within me yet."

"No problem. To tell you the truth, I'm just killing a bit of time until Roxy and Christian get tired of playing on the rack."

She paused as she reached into the bag. "The rack?"

"Nothing. Go ahead, I didn't mean to interrupt you."

She scattered glossy black hematite stones painted with gold runes on the cloth, and asked me in her professional, chatty voice if I was familiar with rune stones, then suddenly caught herself and said in her normal voice, "Oh, but Roxy said you read runes. Please forgive me, I didn't mean to insult."

"You didn't in the least," I assured her.

She put her professional face back on and started her patter back up, instructing me to think of a question or issue for which I sought an answer.

"When you have your question firmly fixed in your mind, please select five stones that call out to you."

I looked at the stones scattered on the casting cloth. I'd never done a reading in that manner, but I figured it was good to learn new things, so I closed my eyes and picked out five stones.

"Very good," she said, scooping up the remainder and slipping them into the bag, then placing the five chosen stones in a cross arrangement. "I do the Cross of Thor spread for you now."

I nodded. I prefer the nine-stone Odin's hammer layout myself, feeling that bigger is better, but I figured maybe the rule at the fair was to give the customer a quick, easily generalized reading and send them on their way.

"The first stone is Dagaz, and it is the rune for the present. Dagaz means daylight or the light of divinity. It is the rune of dawn or midday, and is symbolic of illumination."

"Ah. Illumination." I felt anything but illuminated by her vague interpretation of the stone, but before I could ask her what she thought the illumination indicated, she was on to the next stone.

She went through the rest of the reading in quick order, giving me predictions for the obstacles and assistance I'd find, as well as my past and future, all in relationship to my question. It was all very positive, very generic, and completely uninspired. When she was finished, I hesitated for a moment before glancing behind me to be sure no one was waiting for a reading, then turned back to Arielle.

"I hope you won't be offended by what I'm going to say, but I couldn't help noticing that you're using the standard interpretation of the runes."

"Yes," she acknowledged, her face a picture of misery. "I'm sorry, but I am not very good at it. Claude, our palmist, used to read the runes as well. He was good, very good. He taught me to read palms, but I hadn't learned the runes when he left, and yet they are very popular, so . . ." She gave another little shrug.

"You're not bad at all," I reassured her, not wishing to hurt her feelings. "And I'm far from an expert on the subject, but the rune stone book I read said if you were going to do a reading for someone, you should make it personal. It said that anyone, even a computer, can give a standard interpretation, but the real power in a reading—this is the book talking, not me, because I don't really believe in stuff like . . . er . . . never mind—the book said the real power in a reading came from the person interpreting the reading."

"Ah, yes, I see." Arielle looked confused. "What do you mean by personal? I do not ask the people I'm reading for to tell me their question, so I don't understand how I can make it personal."

I thought for a minute. "Well, the couple of times I've done readings, I've tried to look beyond the standard interpretations, using the stones' meanings as a sort of self-help tool. For instance, the first stone here, Dagaz—that's not just the stone of daylight and illumination, it's a stone indicating a breakthrough, a great change, an awakening, if you will. In its position of the present, it indicates that the person you're reading for is standing on a point of no return. The illumination part comes in because the light banishes the darkness, completely wiping it away with a brilliant light. Taken with the other stones"—I waved my hand over the cross—"I would suggest to the readee that they are starting a new chapter in their life, and although the pages are blank, they alone dictate what will be written on them. In other words, it's kind of positive reinforcement to take the bull by the horns and make the most out of their life."

"That is very interesting. What do you make of this stone?" She tapped the stone indicating the forces acting against me, one whose definition she had particularly stumbled over.

"Mannaz reversed—not a good stone in this position, eh?" I grinned at her.

She gave me a feeble smile in return.

"OK, well, I'd read this rune as a warning against becoming too self-focused and oblivious to others' feelings. This stone says to me that pretty much everyone is lining up to take a swing at you. It says that the very passions and opinions that make you who you are are rubbing some people the wrong way. So in the position of obstacle, it acts as a reminder that it's important to take responsibility for your own actions and not indulge in contempt for those around you who you think are inferior, because underestimating them will bring you down in the end."

"Oh, that's so true," she said breathily, her eyes wide with amazement. "You are very good at this. Have you done this for a long time?"

I laughed and scooped up the five cold hematite stones, handing them back to her. "I've done readings in public exactly one time, and that didn't turn out terribly well."

"You should read them professionally," she insisted. "You have the strength within you, I can see. You have the true gift. It is not everyone who is so blessed."

"Well," I said modestly, not wanting her to get started on Roxy's half-baked and thankfully stunted idea of me reading the runes for the fair while it was in town, "I can't see anyone wanting to pay me to read the runes. To tell you the truth, I don't hold a lot of belief in their power as anything but a tool to self-awareness, and truly, I really don't know that much about them."

"That is quite obvious," a snotty voice growled behind me.

"Hello, Tanya." I stood and smiled at the woman who scowled fiercely at me in return. "Run out of cattle to scare barren, did you?"

I could see her working through the insult, and when it finally sank in, she curled her lip and spat at me. Literally. I had to jump aside to avoid being hit.

"Such ladylike manners," I scolded, glancing over her shoulder. Roxy and Christian were strolling toward us, but upon sighting Tanya, Roxy took off like a gazelle, Christian following at a more decorous pace. "Spitting, brawling in public, kicking people down the stairs . . . tsk, tsk. Whatever will be next? Picking your nose? Scratching your crotch in public?"

Arielle hurried around the table and grabbed her sister's arm. She said something to her in a low, intense voice. It didn't seem to have much effect on her, though, because Tanya pushed her away and faced me with clenched hands and blazing eyes. Arielle took one look at those eyes and hustled off. I just hoped it was to find help, and was not ashamed to admit I prayed it came in the form of a six-foot-four man with wicked amber eyes.

"You are not welcome here."

I pulled out my ticket stub and showed it to her. "This says I am."

"You try my patience once too often, *connasse.*"

My French wasn't terribly good, but even I knew what that word meant, and it wasn't in the least bit complimentary. My smile frayed a bit around the edges, but gamely I held on to it. I'd be damned if I let her drag me into another scene. Once she realized she wouldn't get a response from me, I was sure she'd leave.

"You think you are safe from me, but you are not. Dominic's protection of you will be withdrawn as soon as he has seen you as I have, and as for the other you attempt to arouse"—she tossed her head and snapped her fingers—"he is nothing, a stupid man hired to keep people like you away from us."

"What*ever*," I pretended to yawn as Roxy dashed up to us, Christian on her heels. "Much as I appreciate you painting me as some sort of *femme fatale* bent on seducing every man she sees, the truth is I'm not trying to arouse anyone. I'm just here to see the fair with my friends."

"Yeah," Roxy confirmed. "We're just here to see the fair, not arouse anyone, although that's not entirely out of the question if it was the right person."

"You're not helping matters," I hissed to her. "If you'll excuse us, Tanya, we'll just be on our merry way."

"You push and push your way to his attention," she snarled at me, stepping to the side to block my exit, "but this I tell you—none of your tricks will work. I will cast a protection spell for Dominic to keep him safe from you."

Fine. She wanted to snap and snarl, she could do it by herself.

"Have fun at the dungeon, did you?" I ignored the furious woman in front of me to ask Roxy.

"Loads. Christian wanted to buy some fur-lined handcuffs, but I told him that was just gross."

"The handcuffs?"

"The fur."

I looked at Christian with speculation in my eye. He gave me one of his warm smiles in return. "I thought it might add an unexpected depth to certain experiences."

Who would have thought? I was about to mull on the deep waters that stirred Christian, but it was brought to my attention that Tanya didn't like being ignored

"You will not turn away from me! You will not brush me off like the stinging bee!" She gave me a shove in my shoulder as she spoke. Roxy whistled low and grabbed my arm. I bit back the desire to kick Tanya in the shins, determined not to let her get to me.

"I will speak and you will listen. Your plan to push yourself into the fair as a reader of the rune stones will fail. You do not have the skill, no matter how big you make yourself appear."

I frowned over that puzzling sentence until I shrugged it off, figuring that not only was Tanya obsessed with Dominic and paranoid about me having whatever plan she was convinced I was plotting, she also was losing her grasp on English the angrier she became.

"You are nothing, you are insignificant to Dominic! You will not succeed."

I tried to walk away, I really did. I smiled, said, "You're repeating yourself. It's been lovely talking to you, Tanya, really it has, and don't let anyone convince you otherwise," and took Roxy by the arm and tried to walk away, but Tanya wouldn't let me.

"*Salope!*" she sneered after me, proving that if nothing else, she had an excellent grasp of gutter French. "Crawl away, that is good. Your weak attempt to bring yourself to Dominic's attention has failed, for you have no talent for divination. Dominic seeks only those who have *true* abilities, not poseurs. Go back to your hotel and remember who has been victorious this night."

"Poseur? That's a bit ironic coming from you," I said slowly, turning back to Tanya. Roxy shouldered me aside, her eyes raging with indignation on my behalf. I grabbed the back of her jacket to keep her from tangling with the larger, meaner woman, but she just pulled away.

"Are you implying that my friend is making a play for Dominic? You're dead wrong, sister, if you are. She thinks he's a creep, a big old creep. And you know what? So do I! So you can just put *that* in your pipe and smoke it!"

"Roxy, stop. Don't lower yourself to her level."

"You are just as bad as she is," Tanya snapped at Roxy, her hands fisted. "You seek the favor of Dominic's eye as well, but you will not have it either. I will cast a spell against you both!"

Roxy made a disgusted noise and deliberately misunderstood Tanya. "As if I wanted his eye! You're nutso, lady, you know that? And another thing—don't call my friend a poseur. She's very good at reading rune stones, something I'm willing to bet you can't do. If you didn't have your head stuck so far up your butt, you'd be down on your knees begging her to help you guys out."

"Roxy," I said uneasily. Christian appeared at my shoulder, his eyes narrowed as he watched Tanya with an intensity that made my skin itch.

"I would rather die than ask that *vache* to join the fair," she snarled.

Cow? She called me a cow? Well! I searched my mind for French obscenities. The worst I could come up with was the phrase telling her that her speech was worse than that of a female fishmonger. I figured it would do in a pinch.

"Good! There's no way I would ever consider working alongside you," I said, moving forward and gently pushing Roxy aside. "Not in this or any other lifetime."

"La putain de ta mère," she hurled at me.

"Right back atcha, babe!" I answered, incensed enough by her continuing attack on me, not to mention the slur on my mother, to go a few rounds with her.

"Do you both plan to make your arguments a regular part of the evening's entertainment?" a voice asked from behind me. "If so, I wish you'd tell me. I have a slot before the magic show and after the poetry reading that might suit. Perhaps we could even add wagering on the outcome."

Arielle was directly behind Raphael as he rounded the corner of the tent at a fast walk. My heart did an unpleasant little flip-flop when I spotted him, much like a fish does when it's been yanked from the water. A sudden overwhelming need washed over me, making me want to stand close to him, to smell him, to slide my hands under his shirt and over the planes of his chest. It seemed so very important that I touch him, I actually took two steps toward him before I reminded myself that there were far more important things than my unseemly desires.

What, I couldn't remember, but I felt sure there was something more important.

Tanya turned to Raphael and went off in a flurry of a language I didn't know, pointing at me and no doubt vilifying me, my ancestors, and probably my descendants as well. I caught his eye and gave him a mildly apologetic "What could I do, I was just standing here and she walked up and started the fight, I am truly innocent of all things" smile. He quirked a brow, his eyes turning hot and seductive and mesmerizing, and once again I felt the need to touch him, to do any number of things that I was quite sure would raise his eyebrows—among other things—again and again.

"That's enough," Raphael ordered, holding up his hand to cut off the flow of Tanya's poison. "You are beginning to attract attention, and I doubt if it's the kind Dominic would be pleased to see you soliciting. Why aren't you at your booth?"

"She ran out of bats' testicles and hares' anuses," I piped up. A corner of his mouth twitched and my knees melted in response. I was just about to damn restraint and fling myself upon him when it suddenly occurred to me that he was cheating. He was pulling mind tricks on me, getting me all hot and bothered via long distance, seducing me with his vampire ability to merge his mind with mine, and dammit, I wasn't going to stand for that! I might have accepted the fact that the only guy who suited me was a soulless undead who lived in darkness and indulged in unorthodox beverage choices, but I'd be damned if I'd just let him waltz into my mind and make it look like *I* was the one with hot pants! No sir! If he wanted to seduce me, he'd have to do it the old fashioned way.

"Is it anuses or ani?" Roxy asked in an aside, looking perplexed. "You say octopi, don't you? Shouldn't more than one hare's anus be ani?"

"I ran out of nothing!" Tanya was saying. "I thought to check on Arielle, and found this evil one with her, puffing herself up like a stoat over the runes."

"That's a very good question," I answered Roxy, greatly enjoying the furious looks Tanya blasted at both of us. I turned to Christian. "Which do you favor, anuses or ani?"

He opened his mouth to answer, but Tanya cut him off with a shriek that could have curdled milk. "You mock me! You see how she mocks me? This I will not stand for! I insist that you remove her from the grounds immediately!"

"No," Raphael said, his eyes narrowed as he pinned her back with a hard, uncompromising look. "I suggest you return to your booth, and make an effort not to speak to her again." I shot Tanya a smug look until he turned the same look on me. "And *you* could help matters if you were to stay away from those members of the fair who seem to have a grudge against you."

"Perhaps it would be wise if we were to move on to the next attraction," Christian suggested, but before we could move, we were stopped by a polished voice.

"A grudge? Someone has a grudge against *mon ange*? This I cannot believe. Who could wish ill for Joy who has captured my heart?"

I rolled my eyes as Dominic oozed his way between Christian and Roxy, pausing to give the latter a quick fangy grin. A smaller dark-haired man with the flattest, most expressionless gray eyes I'd ever seen followed him. I gave him the once-over, wondering who he was until he turned those creepy serial-killer eyes on me.

"Dominic!" Tanya grabbed Dominic's arm and stared at him with eyes so bleak with pain, I wanted to flinch. "How can you abuse me so? How can you say such things in front of that *vache*?"

"You know," I said to no one in particular, "I'm really getting tired of being called a cow."

Raphael raised both eyebrows, giving me a look that could steam the wrinkles out of a prune. I contemplated ripping off all his clothes and molesting him on the spot before I remembered that such an act was sure to be an idea *he* planted in my head, not one of my own. I glared at him instead.

"You are angry with me," Tanya continued as if I hadn't spoken. "You cannot mean what you say. I will forgive you this once, but you must not allow yourself to be influenced by her attempts to arouse your interest."

Arouse—oh yes, what a very nice word that was. I looked at Raphael. He looked back at me. Several parts of me that weren't on public display brought out their pompoms and began cheering.

"I begin to find you tedious, *ma petite*," Dominic told

Tanya as he peeled her hand off his arm. He turned to his companion. "As I have no further use for her, she is yours if you want her, Milos."

So that was Dominic's missing partner? I filed away that fact as I took a step toward Raphael. His muscles bunched as if he wanted to move closer to me, but he wouldn't allow himself. I grabbed my hips and ordered my legs to stop listening to his silent siren call.

"Are you all right?" Christian asked in a low tone that felt like warm velvet brushing against my skin.

"Fine," I whispered back. "I'm just having a bit of a control issue with a vampire trying to get me into his pants. Nothing to worry about."

He looked startled. I smiled in reassurance.

"I do not take any man's leavings, my brother, not even yours." Milos looked over Tanya with an implacable face. "I doubt she would sufficiently interest me."

"*Connard!*" Tanya spat at him, and threw herself on Dominic. Milos didn't look at all fazed by her opinion on the marital status of his parents. In fact, he didn't look anything, not even bored. He was the most unexpressive, controlled person I'd ever seen. Raphael might put on an impassive face now and again, but I knew that it was just a mask covering a seething river of emotion. Unbidden, my gaze wandered back to admire his profile.

"What's wrong?" Roxy hissed in my ear. "You look funny all of a sudden."

"It's Raphael," I whispered back. "He's doing something to me. Something with his mind. He's evil."

Her eyes got big.

"Do not punish me this way," Tanya cried to Dominic, clinging to his cape. He snarled at her in another language and tugged his cape from her grasp.

"You mean he's merging with you? Right now? This instant?" Roxy whispered her question, one eye on the unfolding scene between the two men and Tanya, the other on Raphael. "What's he doing?"

I yanked my gaze away from Raphael, determined not to allow him to sway my mind without my permission, instead focusing my attention on Tanya's anguished face. Even knowing she'd tried to do me serious injury by kicking me on the stairs, I couldn't help but feel a twinge of sympathy for the horrible manner in which Dominic was treating her. It was a very small twinge, however.

"What is it you are whispering about?" Christian leaned in to ask us.

"It's Joy. Her Dark One is doing something to her mind."

"Really?" he asked, examining my face. "She doesn't look any different. What is the vampire doing to her?"

"It is all her fault!" Tanya screeched, mindless of the attention she was drawing to our little group. She spun around and pointed at me dramatically. "She has cast a spell upon you! You are doomed to fall under it unless I can reverse it. I, alone, have the power to save you from her!"

I waggled my fingers at her. "Boogedy-boogedy-boo!"

She turned red with fury.

"She's having visions like before, aren't you, Joy?" Roxy tugged at my sleeve, dragging my attention back to her.

"No, it's not like the visions," I whispered out the side of my mouth, too embarrassed to admit that Raphael could have such an effect on me with just a few lewd thoughts planted in my head.

"*Ma petite,* you go too far. *Mon ange* has not the evil presence in her soul. It takes one who knows evil to cast spells."

"You're not helping calm her down," Raphael told him at the same time I commented, "Ooooh, low blow, Dominic!"

Dominic just smiled at me and made a corny bow.

Raphael shook his head, raising his hands in defeat as he took a couple of steps toward me. I switched my attention to him, smiling victoriously as he moved closer. Two could play at this little mind-seduction game. I'd been willing him to come to me, and now he was.

"Then what is it he's doing?" Roxy whispered in my ear, so low I almost couldn't hear her over the shrieks of anger Tanya was emitting at regular intervals as she lambasted Dominic for his nasty comment. "Joy? What's Raphael doing to you?"

"Seducing me," I answered, taking a step forward and letting my eyes go all soft at Raphael. I thought he needed a little reward for giving in and coming to me once he realized I had an iron will that couldn't be swayed by a little mind-seduction. His amber eyes opened wide in response. I took a deep breath and inhaled that lovely Raphael scent that wrapped around him. The cheerleading team in my nether parts kicked into overdrive.

Raphael, with one last look at me that I was sure would turn all the bones in my body to oatmeal, turned back to Dominic. Tanya was on her knees before him, pleading with him to listen to her.

"If having a nightly catfight is a new attraction," Raphael told him, "you really should consider charging more for admittance." He nodded toward the people gathering behind Dominic and Milos. I turned to grab Roxy and Christian and make an escape while we could, but Christian had disappeared.

Dominic stiffened and gave Raphael one of his pseudo-haughty stares. "You will not speak about *mon ange* in that manner."

"Will you give it up?" I frowned at Dominic, interrupting the reply Raphael was about to make. "I'm not an angel, and I'm certainly not *your* angel. If I'm anyone's angel, I'm his." Of its own accord, my finger pointed at Raphael. I clapped a hand over my mouth a fraction of a second after the words left my lips. Raphael's eyebrows raised in an expression of sheer, unadulterated surprise.

"You're not playing fair!" I accused him. "You made me say that! You're making everyone think I'm the one who's wild about you! I'll thank you to stay out of my mind, and stop seducing me!"

"Seducing you?" he asked, ignoring Dominic as he frowned at me. "I am seducing you?"

"Yes, you are, and you needn't try to look so innocent, we both know who you are and what you're doing, so you can just wipe that 'I haven't the slightest clue what you're going on about' look off your face, and keep your mind to yourself! If you want me in your bed, you're going to have to do it properly, you got that?"

"Certainly. Perhaps you could tell me when and how you would prefer I seduce you? I would hate to catch you unaware at an inopportune time, or go about it in a manner that did not meet with your express approval."

"*Mon ange.*" Dominic separated himself from Tanya, taking my hand before I could stop him. "You are distressed and speaking in the heat of passion. What is this Tanya is babbling about rune stones?" He turned my hand over and pressed a red-lipped kiss to my palm. I made a fist.

"You want a knuckle sandwich, buster, just keep it up."

Dominic laughed and turned to Milos. "She is delightful, is she not? Do you not envy me my good fortune in finding her?"

"Oh, for God's sake, I'm going to plant one on him . . ." I thought about taking a swing at him, but decided I wouldn't just a nanosecond before Raphael grabbed my hand, my entire fist wrapped firmly in his. I shivered at the touch and tried to keep the cheerleading squad in my womanly parts from breaking out into back flips.

"She has spirit. She will be an excellent consort for me," Dominic continued, one hand holding Tanya down as she flailed at his feet, beating on his legs and screaming obscenities.

"That's not spirit, it's just gas," Roxy spoke up, her arms crossed. I glared at her. There were times when I really didn't need her help. "Which, if you think about it, is a rather fitting comment on her opinion of you, don't you think?"

"You will read the runes for me," Dominic said, releasing my hand when I jerked it hard enough to make him stagger forward a few steps. "No, no." He held up his hands when he saw me about to protest. "You must. Did you not hear Tanya? She has challenged you. You must avenge the insults she has made against your honor."

I grabbed Roxy by the arm. "Thanks, but no thanks. We'll be on our way now. I'll see you later," I said meaningfully to Raphael as I dragged Roxy past him.

He blinked. "Will you?"

Dominic called something out to me. Tanya shrieked in response. I ignored both of them to stare into the loveliest eyes I'd ever seen. "I assume so. We have unfinished business, don't we?"

He looked at my lips. I suddenly found myself wanting to lick his.

"Yes," he replied, his eyes going molten. My breath caught in my throat as he reached out and brushed a strand of hair where it had flown across my cheek. "I believe we do have unfinished business."

"Good," I gulped, suddenly one big mass of tingling body parts that wanted an immediate introduction to all of his body parts. I tried to slam down a mental barrier between his mind and mine, but it did no good. The cheerleaders in my groin were setting up fundraising car washes to finance a field trip to his groin.

"Hey! I don't want to leave yet! Just because you've got a witch all mad at you and a weirdo claiming you for his consort, not to mention a vampire just waiting to sink his fangs into you, doesn't mean I have to go back to the hotel room and twiddle my thumbs. I want to be where the action is!"

I released Roxy's coat. "No problem. You might go find Christian and apologize for how the evening turned out. Poor guy must think everyone around here is a lunatic."

"I'm sure he's in no doubt that some people are, at least," Raphael muttered. I squinted my eyes at him just in case he was talking about me. Was that any way for a Dark One to speak of his Beloved?

"Later." I nodded to him.

He made a slight bow to me, his rugged, manly lips quirked in an odd little smile.

I ignored Dominic's demand to stay where I was, and skipped off into the night. When I looked back, Raphael had a hold of Dominic, and was speaking vehemently in his ear.

I raced back to the hotel, in a bit of a swivet because of the dark promise Raphael had let me see in his eyes.

Chapter Eight

It was one thing to prepare for a date, I mused as I walked briskly by the people streaming into the fair, but another entirely when the date one was preparing for was a vampire, and quite likely to feel a bit peckish at some point in the proceedings. I tried to decide if I was the type of woman who allowed a first date to drink my blood, and after weighing visions of me appearing the following morning covered in bandages against the erotic descriptions of lovemaking in Dante's books, I decided I'd just wing it.

"I'm getting the hang of this believing-in-vampire stuff," I praised myself as I stomped up a grassy slope toward the hotel. "It's not so hard, really. You just have to carry around a really big grain of salt at all times."

By the time I arrived at my room I had my game plan well in mind. First, I'd have a long soak in the tub. I knew Raphael wouldn't be able to seduce me properly until after two A.M., since his duties at the fair would keep him busy until then, so soaking time was not an issue. Following that, I would don an extremely sexy bit of nightwear, and lounge on the bed practicing provocative poses and seductive looks until Raphael arrived.

An hour later, having had my bath, I paused as I was brushing my hair and stared into the mirror at my frowning face. Why hadn't the thought of Raphael's employment struck me before? Why hadn't I ever wondered why a vampire, a man who must be several hundred years old, was working for his living? Surely vampires were all independently wealthy. I knew the Dark Ones in Dante's books were. They never seemed to worry about money.

"Just my luck," I told my reflection as I brushed my hair until it crackled with static. "I get the only poor vampire in town. Eternity on a budget . . . oh, happy day."

If I have to admit to having one weakness in life—and in truth, I have many, my reaction to a certain amber-eyed Dracula for one—it's that I love slinky nightwear. I fully admit to being a negligee connoisseur; I must own more than a dozen of them, all silk and satin, with oodles of lace. I'd brought only two with me to Europe, however, so my decision of what to wear for Raphael was not difficult, but it still took time.

"Do I want the *Take Me I'm Yours* dusty rose with the rosebud ties that will make him think I'm shy and innocent, or the midnight blue *Touch Me And You'll Burn* that tells him I'll steam the wrinkles right out of his shorts? Oh, decisions, decisions."

Since I wasn't sure of what I wanted to have happen between us—certainly I wanted *something* to happen, I just wasn't sure how far I wanted it to go—I settled on the shy and innocent rose. I checked my hair, dabbed a little perfume behind my knees, and settled in bed with a murder mystery, figuring I'd read a bit before Raphael showed up.

What does he do with his fangs when he isn't using them?

that pesky voice in my head asked as I was reading. I ignored it and read on.

Where does he sleep? Is it in a coffin, like in the movies, or in a darkened chamber, like the Dark Ones in Dante's books use?

I ground my teeth and read each word with deliberate slowness.

If he sleeps in a coffin, does he have a coffin built for two?

I gave up and put my book down. Fine, I'd play a round of twenty questions with myself if that's what it took to settle my mind.

Question number one: Did I want to sleep in a coffin? I knew from Dante's books that although a Dark One's Beloved was made immortal, she was not vampire, so at least I wouldn't have to worry about drinking blood, but could I honestly say I wanted to spend the rest of my days sleeping in a coffin?

"Mmm . . . think that's a negative," I decided. *What about sex?* my inner self wanted to know. I knew that Dark Ones were fully capable of having children, which meant that any exchange of body fluids beyond the third step would have to be conducted while pertinent parts of him were clad in the appropriate scrap of latex. I made a mental note to buy a package of condoms the following day.

"Just to be on the safe side," I told my toes as they twitched with pleasure at the thought of Raphael's pertinent parts. "Not that I'm anticipating needing them soon—he may intrigue me and melt my knees and make me want to do wicked things to him with a pair of those fur-lined cuffs Roxy was going on about, but that doesn't mean I'm going to right away. I have *some* standards. I do not jump into bed with the first amber-eyed vampire who makes me go all girly inside!"

My toes didn't look like they believed me, which, I reflected with a sigh, was probably because my protestations weren't particularly convincing.

"Fine," I scowled at my toes, "I'm loose as a goose when it comes to Raphael. Are you happy you've shamed me into admitting it? Come to think of it, it's probably not even my fault. It's probably an aftereffect of *his* mind-seduction. I'm just an innocent bystander, caught up in his smutty imaginings!"

I shut up after that. It was a sad end when one was driven to defend one's virtue to one's toes, especially when neither toes nor self was buying the story. I fluffed up my hair, checked the clock, and propped my book up to read. Four hours was nothing. I'd just read until Raphael arrived to sweep me off my jaded toes.

Beloved, the voice echoed through my head. I woke up enough to realize I had been sleeping. My body was heavy, bathed in languid warmth so pleasant it seemed a shame to even try to move. A breeze rippled down my length, almost as if unseen hands were stroking and caressing the air above me.

A face shimmered, then solidified in my mind's eye. Raphael. He had come to me. I tried to open my eyes, tried to lift up my arms to greet him, but I felt pulled down into the softness of the feather bed, my body unwilling to respond to my demands.

Beloved, the voice repeated, the world trembling in anticipation of his arrival. I pictured him just beyond my door, dressed in his habitual black jeans and leather jacket, his muscled frame moving with the powerful elegance that sent shivers of delight down my spine. His pain filled my mind as he approached, drawing my awareness to his desperate need for me to soothe the blackness within him.

Raphael. I knew every angle and plane of his face, knew the power in his eyes. I felt him seep through the door into my room, charging the very air with his presence, turning my small room into a warm, intimate sanctuary. I struggled to open my eyes so I could gaze into his amber fire, but could not make my eyelids move. Forced to rely upon senses I did not know I possessed, I shivered a delicious shiver of anticipation as the blankets melted off me, leaving me exposed to his gaze.

Raphael. Warmth blanketed me as he hovered above, his long-fingered hands skimming me in a whisper of need. He opened his mind to me, filling me with images of stark longing and sexual need, erotic images mingling with the knowledge that I was created just for him. My body cried out for his touch. I turned blindly to catch the elusive essence that sank into my blood, but couldn't find it. A shadow crossed my mind as sudden hunger gripped him, a hunger for more than just sustenance, a hunger for my soul to merge with his, a blending of our life forces that would tie us together in a manner that could withstand the boundaries of time.

Raphael?

Give yourself to me. His demand rang in my head just as his mouth closed on mine, claiming me as his, urging me to surrender, swamping me with the rush of his hunger. A soulless voice cried out in my head with frightening intensity, making me call out in reply. Something was wrong; something was suddenly very wrong.

Give yourself to me. The shadow of his thought swirled around in my mind as I tried to struggle against him, panicking as the shadow grew and took form. Peril. I was in deadly peril.

"Raphael! *Stop!*" I screamed the plea at him, but he did not hear. His mouth moved over my neck, heading straight for where my pulse was strongest. I knew what he was going to do, and instinctively I knew he must not, that to do so would damn us both. I struggled in earnest, trying to bring my body back to my command so I could call out a denial.

His eyes were, I was certain, blazing with a fire hotter than any in hell itself. I could almost feel the touch of his gaze as I could his mouth. I struggled harder, fighting to push him from me, desperate to open my eyes so I could plead with him.

I must do this. His words were meant to be comforting, but I was in full panic mode, screaming silent screams of frustration and terror. I felt his lips part over the pulse in my neck, his breath hot on my skin as he prepared to take what was not mine to give him.

"Raphael!" I screamed, pleading one last time for him to stop, but the scream sounded to my ears like a weak sob of prayer.

His breath remained where it was for a moment; then suddenly it was gone, leaving me cold and shaking, dizzy with fear, but safe. I felt sick to my stomach just as I had when the visions had struck before, but more than that, I was sick at heart. Why did Raphael want to harm me? Why was I certain with every molecule in my body that I was in deadly danger with him? Why did he want to harm me if I was his Beloved?

Awareness slowly crept back to my limbs, my eyes opening to find myself alone in the room, the bedside lamp shedding a soft golden glow over the bed.

"What the hell?" I asked, pulling the blankets up over my goose-bumped arms. I stayed that way for a good hour, shaking with cold and starting at every noise in the old building, my mind chasing around and around as it tried to analyze the threat Raphael posed to me.

I fell asleep with the light on, not because I expected him to return, but because I succumbed to the childish fear of the darkness.

The soft knock at my door woke me with my heart in my mouth. I swallowed it back down, and croaked to Roxy that I'd be there in a second, glancing at the clock as I slid out of bed. It was just ten minutes after two. She must have stayed for the bands.

"You must be out of your mind," I said as I opened the door, intent on lecturing her for staying out so late dancing with a bunch of pierced teens.

"Probably," Raphael replied, filling the doorway. "But I *was* invited." His eyes widened as they traveled from my face down to my toes, and back up again. His Adam's apple bobbed a couple of times. He had a slightly stunned look around his eyes that would have pleased the feminine me excessively if, a few hours before, he hadn't been poised to damn me to eternal hell with his bloodthirsty desires.

"You stay away from me," I warned, stepping backward and making the sign of the cross with my fingers. "I don't care how much you want to seduce me and do all those wild, erotic things you were thinking about doing with me— and as I'm on the subject, I have to tell you that some of them are just not physically possible, although I must admit that one or two struck me as particularly interesting—still, you're not going to! You're bad! You're a bad, bad, bad man, and I've changed my mind about you."

Raphael stood in the doorway for a moment, then stepped into the room, leaving the door open. I reached behind me to find something to protect myself against him, but stopped when he held up both hands. There was something . . . different. *He* was different. There I was, trapped— helplessly—in a small room with a man who a couple of hours before had scared the bejeepers out of me, a man who wanted to take my soul and suck my blood, and yet he felt . . . right. Good. *Desirable*.

Maybe it was just all a nightmare? Maybe I had conjured up Evil Raphael to assuage the guilt I felt about falling madly in love with a man I didn't know? Maybe I really had gone insane, but the man who stood before me now, watching me with concerned amber eyes, was not a man who wanted to do me harm. I rubbed my forehead, too confused to fig-ure it out, knowing only one thing: I trusted him. Despite the warning vision, despite the possibility that he was a vam-pire, I trusted him.

"Well? What will it be? Should I leave?" he asked, one hand on the door.

"I . . . er . . ." I swallowed and took a couple of steps to-ward him, waiting to see if my inner warning system was going to go off. It didn't. The cheerleaders woke up, though. "I'm sorry. I had a . . . thing. You can come in."

He closed the door, a little frown pulling his brows to-gether. "I've never known a woman to run as hot and cold as you do. One moment you're stripping me with your eyes—"

"Oh!" I gasped, filled with outrage. "I never stripped you with my eyes! Well, OK, maybe just the once, but you were looking in the other direction, so don't tell me you could see me doing it!"

"—the next, you're recoiling like I'm a hair in your soup. Would you please just tell me what it is you want from me?" He ran a hand through his dark curls as he spoke. My fingers itched to do it for him, but I told my fingers to mind their own business.

"What do you mean, what do I want from you?"

He started to roll his eyes, but stopped himself, running his hand through his hair a second time. My fingers tingled in response. For that matter, so did the rest of my body. This definitely was not the same Raphael that appeared in my vision—this Raphael was tired, and a bit cranky, and sexy as hell. "It's not that difficult a question. You tell me you know who I am and what I'm doing, and invite me to your room in the dead of night. Since you're wearing a garment that molds to your body in a way that is illegal in three countries, I assume you want something from me."

"I don't know what you mean," I said with dignity,

crossing my arms under my breasts. That just served to act as a push-up bra, a fact Raphael noted, and expressed his appreciation of by allowing his eyes to wander freely over the large amount of exposed flesh.

He took a step toward me. I took a step back. He might not pose the threat to me he posed in the vision, but that didn't mean I was going to give in to my inner strumpet and throw myself on him the way my body was demanding.

"What's the matter with you?" He frowned as I continued backing up, suddenly lunging forward at me.

I squealed and jumped backwards, out of his reach, but he got to me first. He grasped my arms and pulled me forward slightly. "You were about to crash into the bureau," he explained, his fingers splayed wide on my arms. "Why are you backing away from me? I know it can't be because you don't feel the attraction between us—"

His hand brushed my cheek. I quivered in response. Attraction? Is that all he thought was going on? And here I was thinking it was a consuming inferno of need and want and desire, topped off by a healthy dollop of love. Hmm. Maybe giving in to my inner strumpet wouldn't be such a bad thing after all.

"—because it's apparent you feel the same thing I feel."

He tugged me toward him until I was flush against him, all my soft curves pressing against his hard planes. It was the moment of truth. Squished up against him, I couldn't help but remember the horrible feeling of danger he had triggered in the vision, but that feeling dissolved into a sense of rightness as I basked in the glorious desire that heated his eyes, breathing in the wonderful scent of him that set my blood to boiling.

"What is it you want from me?" he repeated, his lips almost touching mine. I leaned harder into him, noticed something, and looked down.

"Wow," I said, wishing I could touch but knowing I probably shouldn't. At least not until I was invited to. "At least Miranda got that part of the order correct."

"What?"

"Nothing; it doesn't matter. I've changed my mind, and since I don't feel like I'm in any danger, it appears we're on the same track together, so if you want to move ahead to the third step and kiss me, I won't object." I offered my lips up and slid my hands under his opened leather jacket to the black sweater he wore beneath. Even through it I could feel his marvelous heat.

"Ah," he answered, and sidestepped me to sit down in the armless chair next to the bureau. He crossed his legs, grimaced, and uncrossed them. "Perhaps before we get to the kissing stage, you might just tell me what it is you want from me in exchange for keeping your information to yourself."

What? He wanted to know what I wanted in exchange for keeping the fact that he was a vampire secret? Didn't he have any more faith in me than to know I'd never reveal who he was? Well, true, Roxy had blabbed the news to Christian, but I was sure he was trustworthy, and I'd warn Rox against telling anyone else. Beloveds did not turn their Dark Ones in. Surely he must be acquainted with how things work?

I decided the time for inner strumpeting was now. Raphael was clearly under the impression that what we had was just a minor little attraction. Being a woman—the one who was more in touch with emotions—it was obviously my duty to clear that point up for him, and since actions were louder than words, I threw myself into his lap to set a few things straight. He grunted as my thigh connected with his groin.

"Sorry," I apologized, sliding down his body just a bit. "Didn't mean to squash anything important. Big Jim and the twins OK? Good. Now, where were we?"

Before he could answer, I slid my hands through his curls

and grabbed his head, using him as an anchor as I let my tongue set sail in the wondrous sea of his mouth. He stiffened in surprise, and I thought for a moment he was going to protest my brazen action, but he relaxed back into the chair, groaning into my mouth as he grabbed my hips and pulled me forward.

I twisted my lower body away from him, my mouth still pressed to his, the taste and smell and feel of him making me feel light-headed as I resettled myself so I had his hips between my knees.

"Much better," I moaned, sucking his lower lip into my mouth so I could gnaw on it a bit.

"You're driving me mad," he answered, his hands digging into my hips as he pulled me up against his erection, then reclaimed possession of my mouth. I hoisted the surrender flag and welcomed the boarding party.

"You know that, don't you?" His hands released my hips and started pushing the filmy silk of my nightgown up my thighs, leaving trails of fire where his fingers danced on my flesh. "You're driving me barking mad. Everything about you pushes me to the edge. I've never met a woman like you, one who affects me this—"

I cut him off with a particularly effective tongue move. He rallied to my *en garde*, his tongue a lick of flame on mine as he parried, thrusted, and lunged in a manner that made my whole body want to stand up and shout, "Ahoy, matey!"

"Too much talking," I told him when I retrieved my tongue and paused to breathe for a second or two.

"Mmm," he agreed, one hand leaving my thigh to slide up my hip, toward my waist and the two breasts that were screaming for his touch.

I tugged on his hair until he tipped his head back, exposing a strong column of throat that desperately needed to be kissed. I nipped at that delicious spot just behind his ear, and started kissing my way down his neck. It was hard to keep my concentration on him, what with the inferno his fingers were starting as they weaved a path up my thigh, but I made an effort.

"If a thing is worth doing," I murmured as the pulse in his neck raced under my lips.

"—it's worth doing right," he answered, his hand sliding up to the center of my universe.

"Oh, God," I moaned, sucking on the tender flesh beneath his ear as his fingers stroked the silk of my underwear.

"Not God, heaven," he corrected, his other hand tightening around my breast.

"Sorry, my mistake," I said as I arched back under the flames his hands were creating. His fingers slid under my underwear, curling into me at the same time he pulled me up until he could capture a breast in his mouth, suckling through the silk until I was sure the sensations were going to make me pass out.

He kissed a path over to the valley between my breasts, his fingers below stroking and teasing, mimicking the motion of his hands on my breasts. His mouth was hot and wet and everything erotic, and the feel of it on my neck as he paused over my pulse made me frantic. He licked the wild beat of my pulse with a long, slow movement of his tongue. I tried to rally an objection to what he was going to do, but this time it was different, it was right. I was meant for him.

"Go ahead," I breathed, tilting my head back to give him better access to my neck. "Bite me. Feed from my blood. I want you to. Let me give you my life."

His fingers stilled as I waited breathlessly for the feel of his teeth piercing my flesh, erotic descriptions of the act from Dante's books melting in my mind and making me wild with desire.

He pulled back from me with deliberate slowness. I

looked down on him in surprise. His eyes, moments ago brilliant with desire, were now shuttered.

"I hadn't pegged you as someone who went in for that sort of thing," he said slowly.

"What sort of thing?" I asked, confused. Why wasn't he diving in like earlier? I was sure he was going to feed then; what was holding him back now?

"I'm not going to bite you."

I blinked at the disapproval in his eyes. "You're not?"

"No."

"Not even a little nibble? Just a light snack? *Dessert?*"

He just looked at me for a moment, his breath ragged as he withdrew his hands from the fun zones of my body and let them hang alongside the chair.

"Joy, I don't know what you want—"

I squirmed against his crotch.

"All right, I do know what you want, but I don't know why you want it, nor why you're holding whatever you have found out about me over my head, but I do know this."

My heart did a little dive to my feet. He wasn't going to bite me and make me his Beloved? Not even after I went through all the angst to believe in what he was, to trust him with myself despite the disturbing vision?

"I know that it's not going to be physically possible for me to remove you from your current position," he continued, his voice suddenly hoarse. It just added a new element of sexy to a man already at the top of the tingle-meter. "I thought I might be able to, but that was before you sucked the brains right out of my head with kisses so hot they could melt steel. My grandfather was right."

"Huh?"

"When he told me that a St. John man knows from the very first meeting who the woman is that he will spend his life with. He was right. I know."

I sat perfectly still as my heart did a happy somersault. "I don't think that sentence is grammatically correct, but it is hands down the loveliest thing anyone has ever said to me."

He twitched in response to my words. We both looked down at the twitching part. Raphael's adorable lips twisted into a grimacing smile. "You see? Even my body knows. And if just thinking about you has this effect on me, how am I supposed to make you remove those long, glorious thighs from where they're burning every inch of my legs, and walk away? It's just not possible." He shook his head for emphasis.

I disentangled my fingers from his hair and sat back on his thighs. He shuddered, and his fingers spasmed, but he didn't grab me.

I didn't quite understand what was going on here, but I was determined to figure it out. "Let me see if I have the sequence of events straight here."

He nodded, his eyes momentarily devouring the exposed parts of my breasts before he gulped back a big breath of air, and nodded again.

"First you came into my room and did weird things to the air, and then you kissed me and were about to feed on my blood when I begged you to stop."

"What?" he asked, his eyes narrowing. "What are you talking about?"

"You came into my room," I answered, a bit annoyed with this pretense he obviously insisted on maintaining. It wasn't necessary; he certainly had no need to fear I'd expose what he really was.

"You invited me," he protested. "You gave me come-hither looks, and you're wearing that flimsy little bit of nothing, and if that's not an invitation, then I'd certainly appreciate you telling me what it was."

"No, not just now; earlier. You nibbled my neck, and you were about to sink fang."

He stared at me, his jaw slack for a moment.

"Then, when I beat you back, you went away, only to return a couple of hours later and refuse to do what you wanted to earlier."

"Joy." Raphael put both hands on my thighs. He twitched again. "I want you to listen very carefully to what I say, because I'm not sure how much longer I can sit like this with you all warm and inviting and hotter than purgatory without actually going insane, but I did *not* come into your room earlier this evening."

I stopped staring at his crotch and blinked at him. "You didn't?"

His eyes held mine in a solemn gaze. "No, I didn't."

"Are you sure?"

"Absolutely."

"Maybe you forgot?" I really didn't want to think that my midnight visitor wasn't him.

"Joy—" I shifted on his lap and he groaned, his face tight with strain. "God help me, woman, stop tormenting me like that! I'll say this one more time, and then you're going to remove your luscious self from my lap and allow me to go back to my own bed. I did not come here earlier and touch you."

"You make it sound like touching me is something repugnant," I said indignantly, pulling back.

"Do I look like I'm repulsed by you?"

He didn't. Especially the bulgy parts of him. "Well, no—"

His eyes smoldered into mine as his fingers clutched my hips. "I am a man, just a man, but a man who has limits to what sort of torture he can stand, and if you wiggle just one more time, I'm going to die and then you'll have to explain to the police why you have a dead Englishman in your room."

I resisted the urge to move again. He really did look like he was at the end of his rope. I decided to leave the subject of who had visited me earlier and tackle something else he'd said. "What exactly did you mean when you asked what I knew about you? Did you mean to imply that I was blackmailing you about something? Do you have some deep, dark secret that you're not telling me?"

He grunted in pain as I leaned forward, the better to see into his shuttered eyes. "Forget I mentioned it. I was simply being overly cautious. It's of no matter."

I touched the frown wrinkling between his brows. "Are you in some sort of trouble?"

He caught my hand and looked at it for a moment before kissing the tips of my fingers, his tongue flicking against my suddenly sensitized skin.

"Joy, I want to make love to you, but I don't think now is the right time. You're obviously distressed about something that happened earlier, and . . . well, much as I would like to take you up on your offer, I don't think tonight is the best time for either of us. I think it would be better if I left."

I touched my fingers to his lips for a moment, disappointment warring with the knowledge that he was being wise when I was not. "You don't want me?"

He put my hand on his groin. The evidence there was indisputable.

"You *do* want me?"

"So much that I'm willing to wait until a time when I can show you that with us, lovemaking will be more profound than just sex, yes."

"We'll be profound together?" Gee, I was just brimming with questions.

He twined a strand of my hair around his finger. "Oh, yes, baby. We'll be *very* profound together."

I nodded and thought about what he said for a moment, then got off his lap. "Are you sure it wasn't you earlier?"

"Quite sure," he said, standing up, grimacing as he adjusted his pants.

I tried to piece the puzzle together—to see how the early Raphael and the present Raphael fit together—but they didn't mesh. I blinked a couple of times in an attempt to clear my mind. "Well, if it wasn't you who came calling, then who was it?"

That, as it turned out, was indeed the question.

Chapter Nine

"So who *did* go into your room earlier in the evening if it wasn't Raphael?" Roxy asked several hours later as we sat together in the pale sunlight of a late October morning.

"I don't know for sure."

"But you have an idea?"

"Possibly." I wanted to avoid my idea, actually. It was fairly unsavory.

"Well, we'll come back to that in a minute," Roxy said as she waved a roll slathered with butter and jam at me. I damned her metabolism for a moment before turning to my naked toast and fruit. "First I want to hear what happened to you."

I frowned. "What do you mean, what happened to me?"

"You know!" She scooped up another large spoon of preserves and coated her roll with it.

"You'll get diabetes doing that," I predicted sourly, nodding to the roll. She just grinned and licked her fingers. "Assume I don't know what it is you're talking about and fill me in with words of one syllable or less."

"I'm talking about what happened last night after Raphael told you he couldn't peel you off his lap. Did you . . . *you know* . . . or did you talk, or did you get up and cordially wish him a good night and spend the rest of the night touching yourself pretending it was him doing the touching?"

"Roxanne!" I choked, coughing and sputtering on my toast until I had tears in my eyes. I wheezed and snorted as I sipped a little coffee, trying to end the paroxysms.

"I didn't *say* you got your jollies off, I just asked if you did!"

I hadn't, but the thought had crossed my mind. "No, I did not—not, I might add, that it's any of your business. Nor is it any of your business *what* I might or might not have done with Raphael. You may rest assured I will tell you anything of importance."

"I can tell you didn't get any last night," she said sanctimoniously, licking the jam from the butter knife. "You're always surly in the morning when you're in a frustrated way."

I gave that statement all the attention it deserved—none.

"So if it wasn't Raphael about to do the blood thing with you earlier in the evening, who are your prime suspects?"

I poured myself another cup of coffee and leaned back in my chair, enjoying the warmth of the sunlight. This late in the morning, we were the only people in the tiny dining room.

"I don't know, Rox, that's the problem. It seems to me the field is narrowed down to just a couple of guys."

"Well, I still think it's Raphael," she sniffed, sipping noisily on her hot chocolate. She licked the whipped cream from her upper lip and added, "For some reason, he just doesn't want you to know it's him. We just have to figure out that reason, and then you can tell him to knock it off and get on with step four."

"That doesn't make sense," I said, poking at the remains of my breakfast. "Have you ever read about a Dark One lying to his Beloved?"

She frowned as she thought. "Mmm. You may have a point."

"No, I think . . ." I chewed on my lower lip as I pulled out the memories of the past evening. "I think Raphael's telling the truth. It didn't *feel* like him the first time."

"But you said you saw his eyes, saw him standing beyond the door before he melted through it—which I have to say is a totally awesome thing to see."

I was shaking my head before she finished. "No, I told you I couldn't move, couldn't even open up my eyelids. The stuff I saw—well, it could have just been my imagination. I could have *imagined* I saw Raphael there, that it was him touching me rather than whoever it really was."

"But then who was it really?" she asked for a third time. I just stared helplessly at her in return.

"OK, let's go about this systematically." She pulled out a tablet of paper and started writing. "One: you say the Dark One is not Raphael."

I nodded. "At least, the Dark One who came to my room last night wasn't Raphael. I thought it was until he kissed me; then I knew something was wrong, that it wasn't him."

"Check. Since it's impossible for more than one Dark One to claim a Beloved, that means the first batch of visions you were having were also from our mystery man, to wit, not Raphael."

I nodded, then shook my head, then nodded again.

"What?" she asked, sucking on the cap of the pen.

"I don't know—it seems to me that it was Raphael that first night. I felt him approaching, felt him feeding, and then, whammo! There he was with Dominic."

Roxy tapped the pen on her chin for a moment before making another note. "OK, that's point two: Who arrived with or just following Raphael?"

"Dominic," I said. "But he's not the vampire, I know that. I can *feel* that."

She grinned and tipped her head to the side. "You've sure come a long way in just a few days. Once it was 'Oh, no, Roxy, there's no such thing as Dark Ones,' and now you know with just a feeling if someone's a vampire or not. Next thing you know, you'll be believing in leprechauns and the Loch Ness Monster."

I didn't feel like laughing. It wasn't *her* neck that was attracting rogue vampires all over the place. "This is serious, Roxy."

"Nothing is so serious you can't have a bit of fun at your oldest friend's expense. So, if it's not Dominic, then who? Who've you met since we've been here?"

"Tanya and Arielle," I counted off on my fingers, "but they're women, so they don't enter into the picture. Then there was Dominic and Raphael, but we've already crossed them off the list."

"*You* have," Roxy said darkly. "I haven't until I see some solid proof."

I let that go. "Then Christian showed up—"

I looked up at her. She raised her eyebrows for a moment as she tapped her pen on her lips. "Naw, can't be," she shook her head. "He ate dinner with us, remember? And wasn't he in the bar much earlier, before Dominic and Raphael arrived?"

I closed my eyes so I could concentrate better on the memory of that night. "I think so—yes, I remember seeing him with a wineglass as he joined a table where some men were playing chess."

"Right. So Christian is off the list."

"Although he did disappear last night," I pointed out.

"Disappear? No, he just needed to go the bathroom. I ran into him just after you left. He went to move his car; then we hung out together until the bands got to him."

I made a face. I was not a devotee of music that was loud for the sake of being loud. "I don't blame him. Were the bands bad?"

"Ghastly," she answered, chewing on the pen. She looked down at her paper. "So who does that leave us with? Is there anyone else you met here that first night who could be a Dark One? The bartender?"

I shook my head, looking out the window and watching as some crows pecked at apples that were rotting on the tree. "Has it occurred to you that perhaps I did not actually see this Dark One directly after the visions? Maybe just being in relatively close proximity was enough to do it, without having to actually be physically near one another."

"Mmmm," Roxy hummed, considering that. "I suppose there's nothing that says he had to be at the same location as you. There are several instances in the books of Dark Ones who knew their Beloveds were approaching well before they did, so I guess that would make sense. But if that's the case, who is it?"

"There's one man we saw last night who, I'm extremely sorry to say, fits the bill of vampire awfully well."

She stared at me. "Who?"

"Milos."

"Milos? Oh, *Milos*. You think?"

I nodded. "I think. Have you seen his eyes? They're flat, absolutely flat, like there's nothing behind them but empty space. He gives me the willies in a way Dominic doesn't even come close to achieving."

"But, but—Joy, this is *your* Dark One we're talking about. The man made for you, the one Miranda predicted you'd find here. He's your soul mate, your other half."

"Well, I don't want him," I said with more than a little

146

petulance. "I want Raphael instead. He's . . . he's right. He smells right and he feels right, and Lord knows he tastes right."

She stared at me in horror. "You can't mean that! You barely know the man! How can you tell me he's the one you want when you just met him a couple of days ago?"

I waved the waitress over to clear the table. "You've been happy as a clam at the thought of me being a vampire's main squeeze; now you're telling me that because he's *not* one of the bloodsucking night walkers I'm rushing things?"

"Well, of course," she snorted. "Everyone knows that to be a Dark One's Beloved is forever, but a relationship with a mere human man . . . *that* can go belly up faster than an overfed goldfish."

"Someday I'm going to figure you out, Roxy, and then you'll be sorry."

She just grinned at me. "Right. So we have Milos as a *possible*, Christian as a *did not start*, and Dominic and Raphael as *possible but probably no-gos*. I believe the next step is to eliminate the possibles."

"How do we do that?" I asked suspiciously.

"Simple!" she said, standing up and stretching before reaching for her jacket. "We beard the lion in his den. Or in this case, the vampire in his lair."

"I feel stupid," I said a half hour later as Roxy and I skulked around the outside of the trailer Raphael lived in while he worked at the fair. "I know Raphael isn't a vampire; I don't need to see him sleeping to prove it."

"Yes, you do. There are still too many coincidences to make me happy." She tried the knob on the trailer door. It was locked. I sighed in relief.

"Like what?"

"For one, he sleeps during the day and is up all night."

"So does everyone else in the fair," I pointed out.

"For another, you said you saw him ditching his drink, and we've not seen him eating yet. Regular food, that is. One of us might have seen him feeding on something else," she added as she shot me a meaningful look. She rustled around in her oversized bag before pausing. "Um . . . you go circle around the trailer to make sure no one's watching us, OK?"

"Why?" I asked suspiciously. "The door's locked, we can't get in, so what's the use in staying? And what are you looking for in your bag?"

"Gum. Now go on. I don't want anyone to see us."

I muttered a choice comment about what I wanted, but gave in and slunk my way nervously around the trailer to verify that no one was watching. Other than several magpies flying overhead, there was nothing around us but blowing leaves and a few pieces of debris that had escaped the trash cans. The noise of a generator kicking in over at the tent city rumbled ominously in the background.

"Roxy, this is stupid." I whispered when I completed the circuit. "You're basing your supposition on two flimsy pieces of circumstantial evidence."

"There's more," she said as she stood with her hand on the door. "Remember Raphael's reaction when he caught you alone with Christian? You said he was in a rage."

I allowed the memory of the shared emotions to wash over me again. Rage was a pale word compared to what I had felt. I shrugged. "It's no different from the other visions the Dark One sent to me long distance. Maybe he could see stuff I saw, and he got angry at Christian. I don't know exactly how that happened, but I *do* know that we're wasting our time here. The door's locked, so let's leave."

She grinned as the latch to the trailer clicked open. "I must not have turned the handle hard enough."

I glared at her, whispering furiously so as not to wake the occupant of the trailer. "Roxanne Mathilda Benner, if I thought for one minute you brought your lock picks with you to a foreign country and picked Raphael's lock, I'd—"

"Now, now," she calmed me. "Picking Raphael's lock is reserved solely for you, if you know what I mean."

"I do, and that's not what I meant, as you well know. Breaking and entering is—"

"Shhh!" she hissed, pushing the door open and mounting the three metal steps so she could stick her head in the door. "Coast is clear," she whispered before disappearing into the trailer. "Come on!"

I debated staying where I was, standing firm for ethical reasons, but the thought that she'd be in the closed, womb-like confines of the trailer alone with Raphael was enough to spike my jealousy count off the chart. I climbed the steps as stealthily as I could, flinching when the trailer made the usual creaks and noises of someone moving around. It was dark inside, almost completely pitch-black except for the light coming from the opened door, which was extinguished as soon as I stepped into the trailer proper.

"Rox?" I froze where I was, unable to see anything once she shut the door.

"Right behind you," she whispered in my ear. "I think the bed is at the far end. Just walk in a straight line until you reach a door."

"Easier said than done," I muttered as I edged forward, my hands held out before me. I couldn't see anything but the faintest glow around what I assumed were blinds drawn tight over windows. I banged my shin on something hard, stopping to clutch my leg and swear profanely but silently until the worst of the pain was over, then hobbled forward.

"If Raphael doesn't have us arrested and thrown in jail for breaking and entering, I swear by all that's holy I'm going to get you for this, Roxy."

I could feel her grin even if I couldn't see it.

"Just remember that I get to be your maid of honor."

I limped my way past what felt like a small Formica table on the left, and a bank of cupboards and counters on the right.

"Kitchen area," I hissed back to her.

"Good. Bedroom door is straight ahead."

Four more steps and my searching fingers found the door. It was shut.

"If the door to his bedroom is shut, why can't we open up a blind and have a little light?" I asked.

She tsked. "What if he is a Dark One? The light'll fry him when you open the door! You want to take a chance on that?"

"No."

"I didn't think so. Are you at the door? Open it up and let's see if he's warm-blooded and breathing, or cold and lifeless."

I muttered an imprecation at her as I gently turned the knob, praying as I did that it would be locked.

It wasn't.

"Now what?" I said almost silently in what I assumed was Roxy's ear.

She shoved me forward, toward the bed. Unfortunately, neither of us realized that the bedroom consisted of space for the bed, and that's it. When she shoved me forward, my knees hit the end of the mattress, and I tumbled forward onto it, onto the legs that were currently occupying the space. At the same time, the lights in the tiny room clicked on, and I found myself lying across Raphael's shins, staring down the barrel of an extremely efficient looking gun.

"You two are the worst housebreakers I've ever encountered," he told us calmly, tucking the gun away under his pillow. I muttered an apology, my face hot and red, and pushed myself off the bed, hoping against hope I'd find a way to explain what we were doing there. That's when I noticed Roxy. She was standing in the doorway staring at him. I turned to see what made her eyes bug out like they did, and felt my jaw hit the ground.

Raphael was sprawled over his bed—there's just no word for the masculine grace he displayed as he lay there—totally, completely, utterly naked. I let my eyes go wild, feasting in an orgy of delight as I gazed at all that flesh, starting at his toes (nice long, narrow feet), working my way up muscular calves and heavily muscled thighs to pause for a long, long moment on that part of him that many parts of me were even now clamoring for. I swallowed back a good gallon or so of saliva that was threatening to issue forth as drool and forced my perusal upward to his stomach, where I stopped to admire a sunburst tattoo just below his belly button. It was about the size of a half dollar, and was made up of a sun with wavy rays emanating from it. I'd never seen anything like it, and although I wasn't a fan of tattoos, that one had me licking my lips. I tore my eyes from it and let my gaze continue up to a broad chest with insouciant nipples that screamed for attention, taking two side excursions to arms that were muscley without being obscenely big, stopping finally when my eyes met his.

"You are *so* lucky," Roxy said to me in a voice filled with awe.

I blinked.

"Would you like me to turn over so you can see my other side?" Raphael asked.

"Would you?" Roxy breathed hopefully.

"No, he would not," I snapped, shoving her out the door.

She pushed back to leer at Raphael as he started to get out of bed. "Nice seeing you! And I mean that literally!"

"Roxy!"

She craned her head around me again. "That's a really great tattoo, by the way. Sexy! Bet it drives the women wild."

"ROXY!"

"Sorry. I'll just go sit out here while you conduct the test."

"What test?" I asked in a low whisper.

She mimed pulling the blinds, then turned and disappeared into the blackness of the trailer.

I faced Raphael, now pulling on a pair of jeans. "I . . . um . . . suppose you'd like to know what we're doing here."

He scratched his chest and sat on the end of the bed. I wanted to shove his hand aside and scratch it for him, but the dark circles under his eyes reminded me that whatever he was, he'd only had a few hours sleep.

"I'm really sorry about this," I said, filled with remorse at allowing Roxy to drag me into the idiotic scheme. "It's just that last night . . ."

He covered his mouth as he yawned. "What about last night?"

"Well, last night . . . that is, I need to make sure that you're who you say you are." His back stiffened at my words. I hurried on to try to explain. "Not that I don't believe you, but as Roxy pointed out, it's better to be sure so I can eliminate you from the list, and . . . well . . . I can't do that unless you let me open the blinds."

He shook his head and rubbed a weary hand over his eyes. "I'm not following any of this, not the least of which is who you think I am, so if you could explain why it was so important that you go to the trouble of breaking into my trailer to talk to me, I'd appreciate it."

I sidled along the two-foot space at the end of the bed toward the window. "Can I just open this?"

He looked at the window. "Why? Do you have a camera crew out there? Are you part of one of those shows on the telly where they film people unawares? Is a man in a gorilla suit going to jump out of my closet?"

"No, no, honestly, it's nothing at all like that, I just want to open the blind. Is that OK?"

He rubbed his eyes again. "Please yourself."

I put my hand on the blind cords. "Are you sure? It won't . . . uh . . . hurt you in any way?"

He narrowed his eyes at me. "Hurt me? Woman, you are steadily going from confusing to incomprehensible."

I waited.

"No," he said. "It won't hurt me."

I yanked on the cord and let the pale sunlight wash into the tiny bedroom, covering him in a golden haze. He raised his eyebrows.

"Wahoo!" I shouted, jumping up and down and spinning around with the joy of it all. "You're not a vampire! You're a nice, normal man with nice, normal eating habits and no ability to merge your mind with mine!"

Raphael shook his adorable curls. "I think, for my sanity's sake, I'm going to stop trying to understand you and just go with the flow."

He grabbed me as I twirled around again, and pulled me down onto the bed, leaning over me so his chest was pressed against mine, his lips perfectly placed for kissing.

"Nice," I said, unable to keep from smiling as I stroked his chest. "I like a man with a hairy chest."

"Oddly enough," he grinned back at me, "I like a woman who likes a man with a hairy chest. And speaking of chests . . ." His head dipped as he nuzzled aside the lace collar of my blouse.

"Hey! You guys can't do that while I'm here! I can see everything, you know!"

"Rats. I forgot about Roxy."

He pulled his head up from my chest and put it back into kissing position. "I find it difficult to believe anyone could forget about Roxy."

"I heard that!"

I smiled at his smile and willingly gave myself up as he nipped at my mouth, parting my lips when his tongue demanded entrance. His skin was warm and soft as I stroked my hands down his chest, trailing my fingers over his ribs so I could wrap my arms around his back, pulling him on top of me. His tongue danced a tango for two, sending my senses whirling and dipping with each stroke. He groaned in the back of his throat as I suckled his tongue, twining my own around it as I attempted to merge myself with him. He tasted hot and exotic and male. My fingers danced over the muscles of his back, sweeping upward until they stroked along the contours of his shoulders.

His kisses were everything I wanted, but suddenly they weren't enough. I wanted more; I wanted all of him.

"You know, we hardly know one another at all," I gasped as his mouth left mine and did some exploring in the sensitive area beneath my ear.

"That's true," he said just before he sucked my earlobe in for a little quality time. His fingers splayed over my left breast, cupping it through the heavy wool of my sweater. "Your heart is racing."

"A lot of stuff on me is racing," I purred as he sucked a line down to my collarbone, while I slid my hands down the wonderful landscape of his back to the curve of his behind. Even in jeans it was a very nice behind. "But the truth is, we just met a few days ago, so someone might say that we were rushing things a bit."

"Mmm." He kissed up the opposite side of my neck, starting little fires of desire all over my body. "Do you think we're rushing things?"

"I do!" Roxy called from the other end of the trailer.

"Ignore her; she liked you better as a vampire."

He stopped kissing me, a faint line of puzzlement between the two delicious chocolate brows. I gave in to temptation and kissed along each one. He waited until I was through to say, "First things first. Am I rushing you?"

I smiled. "No. It's true we don't know each other awfully well, but that just adds a little zip to the whole thing, don't you think? Uncovering each other's likes and dislikes and finding out who we are and exposing secrets . . ."

He stiffened as I said the last word, pulling back from me, propping himself up on one elbow, a full-fledged frown on his face now. I reached my hand up to smooth away the lines, but he caught my fingers before I could touch him.

"That's the third time you've mentioned secrets to me. I can only assume that by your constant reference to that, you have some information you'd like to discuss with me."

"Information? What sort of information? You mean the secret you accused me of knowing last night? I know now you're not a Dark One, so that can't be it. What are you hiding?"

He stared at me for a second, then pushed himself up into a sitting position. I gave myself a moment to admire the sight of his back, then sat up as well.

"Don't try to confuse the issue with all this Dark One talk. What do you know about me, and what do you intend to do about it?"

He was looking irate now, not something that pleased either of us. *"I'm* confusing the issue? How about you? Raphael, I haven't the slightest idea what you're talking about when you accuse me of knowing something about you. Other than knowing you've obviously studied kissing with the best, and you have stupendous . . . um . . . physical endowments, I don't know anything about you other than I really like you and I want to be with you. There. I admitted it first. Are you happy now?"

His eyes searched my face; then he looked away and rubbed his jaw. "I must be mad—that's the only explanation for it. I've gone mad and no one bothered to tell me, and now I'm living a madman's life where beautiful women think I'm a vampire and speak in riddles and try to seduce me at every turn."

"Beautiful women?" I asked, pushing his arm. "What

women? I realize we just met and all, and it's not like I'm asking you to marry me or anything, but I must insist on exclusive rights. I never did learn to share my toys with others."

"I was talking about you," he said with an odd look to his eyes.

"Oh. Well, then, that's OK, although I would like to point out that I haven't tried to seduce you at every turn."

"No," he agreed, still looking at me oddly. "You haven't. I stand corrected." He hesitated a minute before making an embarrassed little grimace. "You really thought I was a vampire?"

It was my turn to look embarrassed. "It seemed like the only explanation at the time," I mumbled. He lifted my chin and leaned forward to look into my eyes.

"And that's why you asked me to bite you last night?"

I nodded, my face flaming. I was an idiot, truly an idiot not to have figured out the truth earlier, but Raphael was enough to make any girl's senses swim.

His lips twitched, then smiled a slow, sexy smile. "I thought you were just into deviant sexual practices."

I had a hard time pretending to scowl under the influence of that smile. "Me? You thought I was into the kinky stuff? Lord, no, I'm strictly a white-bread sort of girl when it comes to sex. Most of the time, anyway."

His lips brushed mine as the last words were spoken into his mouth.

"What are you hiding from, Raphael?"

He froze above me.

"Please," I whispered, stroking the line of his tight jaw. "It's obvious you're worried that someone is going to find out something about you. I want to help, if I can. You don't have to tell me your secret, just tell me if you're in danger of some sort."

His eyes went from liquid amber to hard, glittering stone.

"No danger," he said, his breath steaming my lips. "I . . . there is a situation with my last employer, Joy. I can't tell you anything about it, but as long as I'm here, all is well."

I nodded, understanding him better than he realized. There was something in his past that he feared would be exposed, something bad enough that he believed he would be blackmailed. I stroked my hands down his arms. His muscles were taut with tension, a sign that he wasn't trying to be offensive in accusing me of knowing his secret and using it against him—he clearly suspected everyone. I wondered what had happened on his last job that would drive him into burying himself in a wandering troupe of entertainers. Pushing him to open up would do me no good, so I did what I could to reassure him I was no threat. I teased the edges of his lips and moaned when he opened up for me, his tongue quickly assuming control and setting a rhythm that had me wishing Roxy had stayed back at the hotel.

"Are you guys starting that again? Look, Joy and I have things to do and people to see, so if you could wrap it up, I'd really appreciate it!"

"She's right," I murmured against his lips, giving him one last sweet kiss. "You need to get your sleep, and Roxy and I have to go do some things."

"What things?" he asked as I slipped off the bed and pulled my sweater down from where his wandering hands had slipped under it.

I had a strange suspicion that he wouldn't approve of us going to peek on Milos, so I made a dismissive gesture with my hands. "Oh, just stuff. I think we're going to the caves today, aren't we, Rox?"

She appeared in the doorway. "Caves. Yes. Caves. Right. Gotcha. Caves."

Raphael didn't look like he believed it for a moment. He snaked a hand around my waist and tugged me to him to lay his lips on me one last time. "Unfinished business," he reminded me of my words of the previous day.

"Unfinished business," I agreed, and with an effort I didn't think myself capable of, tore myself from the warm haven of his body and pushed a madly grinning Roxy ahead of me as we walked toward the outer door.

Raphael flipped on a light that illuminated the whole trailer, then leaned against the door frame to watch us as we left. I paused on my way out the door. "This thing that you're worried over . . . is it why you sleep with a gun under your pillow?"

For a moment he didn't answer, his eyes smoldering with a strange light as he nodded. "You never know who is going to come calling at all hours of the day . . . and night."

I nodded as well, then waved goodbye, closing the door quietly behind me.

"You OK?" Roxy asked me as I leaned against the door and caught the breath that had eluded me since I entered the trailer. "That was some kiss he was giving you, eh? Damn near curled my toes, and I wasn't even on the receiving end."

"Mmm," I said, thinking not about Raphael's kisses—wondrous and toe-curling as they were—but about the look in his eyes when he accused me of knowing a secret about him. What was I doing, practically promising myself to a man who could have any sort of secrets in his past? A man who kept a gun under his pillow when he slept? A man who was apparently well educated, and yet who worked for what were probably piddling wages with a small traveling fair?

I knew nothing about him, nothing, and yet here I was contemplating starting something serious with him, something important and meaningful. I couldn't conceive of what it would mean to uproot my life to stay with him, and yet that was exactly what I was thinking seriously about doing. Changing my life didn't bother me so much; it was the fact that although I was mad about Raphael, I didn't really know him.

Or did I? Maybe I knew him better than I thought I did. Then again . . . what was it Dominic had threatened him with the first night we arrived? *"I can break you with a word."* That sounded to me like Dominic had a hold on Raphael, and wasn't above using it to keep him in line.

Which made me more confused than ever.

"Joy? You're not having one of those visions again, are you?"

I shook away my questions and gave her a weak grin. "Nope. Just wondering how late Arielle sleeps in."

She looked a question at me.

"I want to ask her a few things," I said as I grabbed her arm and started off in the direction of the hotel at a fast walk.

"What sort of things?" Roxy asked worriedly.

"Things about Raphael. I think Dominic is blackmailing him, and in order to help him, we have to find out what his secret is. I'm hoping Arielle can shed some light on the subject." I started to trot. "Come on—if we hurry, we can catch a ride with that Canadian couple to Punkevní Cave."

"You want to go to a cave now? Now? When there's a vampire to find and a blackmailer to catch? Geez, I sound just like someone out of a really bad adventure book. Hey, wait up, I don't have giraffe legs like you do."

"No one at the fair will be up until this afternoon, and the cave is only a half hour away. We'll worry about the Dark One later. Right now I want to see that cave."

"OK, but when we get back, remind me to tell you something."

I stopped. "What?"

She sprinted past me. "Something to do with the fair."

I loped after her, cutting across the meadow, avoiding the tent city that was just starting to come to life.

"What?" I called out, getting a bit winded as I pounded up the hill to the hotel.

She picked up her speed and yelled something back at me that sounded like *rune stones*.

"What? What about rune stones? Roxy, will you stop running away from me and just tell me whatever it is!" I started to get a stitch in my side, and slowed down.

She had a good thirty-yard lead on me now, damn her "jog five miles every day, rain or shine" hide. She stopped and turned back to me, cupping her hands around her mouth and bellowing, "Rune stones! Tanya said you have no skill at reading runes, and I said you did, and somehow it ended up as a wager. I bet everything I have on you, so unless you want me to lose my entire life's savings, you're going to have to answer Tanya's challenge. I've set it all up with Dominic—you're going to do a reading tonight to prove we're right and she's wrong."

I staggered up the hill, my teeth bared. I was going to kill her.

"Don't look at me like that. I couldn't let her malign you—she was saying all sorts of nasty things about you. It'll just be a few readings, you can do that on your head. After that—well, Dominic said he'd be happy to offer you the position of rune-stone reader if you wanted to join the fair."

I clutched my side and tried to ignore the pain. I was really going to kill her.

"Of course, he said that meant you'd have to be his consort and all that, but I'm willing to bet that part is optional. You can probably negotiate that out of the contract."

"You're a dead woman," I yelled at her as she waved and spun around to dash up the rest of the hill like it was no more than a curb. "I know, because I'm going to be the one to murder you!"

"Hurry up or you'll miss the Canadians," she called as she rounded the hotel, heading for the lobby. "You think it's too late to change the bet to double or nothing? We could really clean up!"

"Make your will now, you're going to need it," I yelled.

Her words drifted back through the night air. "I wonder if I should warn the hotel owner to take out some extra insurance, just in case Miranda was right about you being a cataclysient."

I smiled a grim smile as I staggered my way up the hill, wondering if the Czech Republic had the death penalty for the murder of an American tourist.

Chapter Ten

Despite claiming the last thing she wanted to do was spend her day deep in the bowels of the earth, Roxy enjoyed the visit to the Punkevní Cave just as much as I did. Since we didn't have time to do the half-hour walk, we took the five-minute gondola ride down the Macocha Abyss past Drahanská Castle to the cave entrance. We walked through the cave for a bit on a well-lit path, admiring all the weird formations, then climbed aboard the red and white boats that took us on a half-hour ride deep into the cave via the Punkva River. The caves were pretty much what I expected—dark, damp, and humid—but these particular caves also had fantastic formations that looked like tall stone cones made of Cream of Wheat.

"Stalactites," Roxy said.

"Stalagmites," the guide corrected, pointing to the ceiling as we entered a large open area with wickedly sharp spikes dripping from above. "This is the Masaryk Dome. Those are stalactites."

Roxy clammed up after that, which for those of us who know her, indicated she was up to something. What, I didn't know, since I was officially not speaking to her. It wasn't until three hours later, when we arrived back at the hotel, that I lifted the no-speak moratorium. Our Canadian friends went off to ride bikes through the countryside, and Roxy and I staggered up the stairs to change our clothes into something that smelled a little less like damp cave and wet limestone.

"I hope you have used your meditation time well," I said to her as I unlocked the door to my room. "I hope you have crafted, honed, and polished your apology to me until it fair blinds the eye."

"Oh, you're speaking to me again? Good. I have lots to tell you. About Milos—I think I know of a way we can tell if he's a Dark One or not."

She followed me into my room. I raised a hand and stopped her before she could sit on the chair that Raphael and I had frolicked upon the past evening. "Wait just one minute, missy. Before you try to talk me into another one of your cracked plans, you can apologize."

"Oh, give it up," she scoffed, and sat down in the chair, pulling off her boots and wiggling her toes with relief. "You know it's not that big a deal! It's just a couple of rune readings, for pity's sake! Christian said he wouldn't miss it for the world."

"Oh, great, now you've arranged for a crowd to watch? You swore to me that all I'd have to do is a couple of quickie readings, and my pride—which I'd like to point out again was not the least bit affected by Tanya's nastiness—and your puny bank account would be salvaged. That's all I agreed to—just a couple of readings. Right?"

"Sure," she said, "just a couple of readings for one or two people. So! That was some boat ride, huh? Too bad you got seasick. I hope you barfing into the river won't damage some sort of delicate ecosystem."

I plopped down on my bed and glared at her. "Oh, no! You changed that subject too quickly for my taste. Which one or two people am I doing readings for?"

She avoided meeting my eye. "Christian volunteered to be one of your guinea pigs."

I made a face.

"What? You like him."

"Yes." I waved a hand and lay back on the bed, thankful the seasickness was short-lived. "Go on, who's the other one."

"It's two others, actually."

I sat up again. I had a nasty suspicion who the two were. "Don't tell me—Dominic and Milos?"

"You see!" she said as she jumped up from the chair and grabbed her boots, heading for the door. "You're positively psychic! You'll have no problem at all reading the stones for them."

"No," I agreed, "no problem at all."

She paused at the door and waited for me to finish.

"I won't have any problem because I won't be reading for them. Christian, yes. Arielle, sure. Raphael—you betcha. But not the gruesome twosome, nosiree."

"Joyful—"

I propped myself up enough to deliver a real quality glare. "NO!"

"OK, whatever, I'm sure we can work something out. Did you want to hear my idea about how to find out who the real Dark One is?"

I lay back down and flapped a languid hand at her. "Go ahead."

She grinned. "We're going to call in an expert."

"An expert," I repeated, closing my eyes and wondering if I had time for a short nap. I didn't get much sleep the night before, and if I had to stay up late reading runes at the fair, I'd need some time to catch a few Z's. "What sort of expert? A priest?"

"No, a real expert. The one person who knows more about Dark Ones than anyone else in the world except the Dark Ones themselves."

I mused on her words for a few seconds before I understood who she was talking about. I sat up. "You mean—"

"Yup, the man himself. I'll just give Dante a ring and see what time this afternoon is good for us to swing by."

I was too tired to even goggle at her. I contented myself with a grouchy glare. "Roxy, he's a big famous author! I'm sure he doesn't appreciate deranged fans like you calling him up. Oh, I don't know what I'm worrying about; you won't get through to him."

"That's what you think!" She smiled a particularly triumphant smile and waved a scrap of paper at me. "Got his private number! Turns out that Theresa the barmaid used to be a maid at the castle. Cost me a bundle to get it from her, but I'm sure it'll be worth it. I'll arrange with the hotel to have the taxi downstairs in, oh, say an hour. Get dressed in something nice. It's not every day you meet famed reclusive author C. J. Dante!"

I collapsed back onto the bed. Maybe Raphael had it right after all. Maybe we were all mad, and living in a madman's world.

As it turned out, it was a good thing I made Roxy call Dante's residence before we rode out to Drahanská castle.

"The housekeeper says he's out, but she'll leave a message for him," Roxy said as I emerged from a steamy, jasmine-scented bathroom a short while later. "She says he doesn't see many people, though, so our chances don't look too good to get a private audience with him."

"I don't blame him. If I had all sorts of women fans slavering over my studly heroes, I wouldn't want them knocking on my castle door, either," I said. "If we don't have to race off, I'm going to take a nap. I'm going to need one, since you volunteered me to be the evening's entertainment. Wake me up in time to go to the bar."

"Aha!" she leered, wiggling her eyebrows. "Going to hang out at the bar in hopes a certain hunky non-vampire puts in an appearance?"

"Well, of course I am. If you were me, wouldn't you?"

"Naw." She shook her head.

"You wouldn't?"

"Wouldn't need to wait for him, because if I had been you, I would have kicked me out of his trailer and spent the rest of the day riding him like a bucking bronco. Have a nice nap. Think I'll take one myself. I've got my eye on Henri, the guy who operates the dungeon room, and I'll have to get some sleep if I want to dance the night away with him."

Three hours later I woke up Roxy to tell her we'd received a phone message from the mysterious Mr. Dante.

"Go 'way," she mumbled, refusing to come out from under her sleep mask.

"Come on, Rox, you have to wake up! Dante's secretary called, and we've been invited to a late tea. If you don't get a move on, we'll be late!"

"Wha'? Dante? He called?"

I rustled around in her wardrobe, pulling out the one dress I'd insisted she bring with her for any fancy events we might attend. "Here, go wash your face and put this on. You want to look nice when you meet Dante, don't you?"

She lifted a corner of the mask and peered at me. "This wouldn't be a cruel joke, would it?"

I put my hands on my hips and glared at her. "Do I look like I'm joking?"

"No. You're wearing your good dress."

"Right. Now get dressed. The taxi will be here in fifteen minutes."

Thirty-five minutes later we drove past the gatehouse to Drahanská Castle and up a graveled road. Torches had been lit along the way—real torches, not electric lights. Roxy and I were impressed.

"Must be nice to have the servants necessary to keep torches lit," I mused.

Roxy grunted her agreement, her face pressed to the window of the taxi as she peered out into the falling darkness. I knew from my guidebook that along the front side of the castle were immaculately groomed lawns and what looked like a formal flower garden, where the GothFaire would hold their All Hallow's Eve festival. As the gravel drive curved around toward the back of the castle, we passed all sorts of black, bulky shapes that indicated outbuildings.

"Look at that," Roxy whispered, awe evident in her voice as we passed the family burial grounds. Torches blazed on a small, vaulted building made of stone. The light from the flames cast sharp focus on the intricate carvings engraved in the stone mantel that arched over the door, topped by two stone eagles with outspread wings and heads tipped back to shriek their eternal agony to the sky. "What do you think it is?"

"Mausoleum, by the looks of it," I answered back, annoyed to find I was also whispering. I cleared my throat. "If you think that's something, look up ahead."

She turned to look where I was pointing. The silhouette of the main part of the castle cut into the darkening indigo sky, the pointed spire of a turret on one side balancing off the gabled tower on the other. The whole place positively reeked of history, which wasn't surprising, since it had been the seat of the lords of Perstejn—a ruling family for several centuries—between the fourteenth and sixteenth centuries.

The windows, narrow and high, were framed in the local white stone that we saw everywhere.

"Glorioski," Roxy breathed as the taxi came to a halt before two dark doors recessed into the wall of the building, flanked on either side by lit torches. "What do you think it costs to keep all those torches lit?"

"Don't ask," I replied, craning my head back to try to see all the way up to the top floor.

Roxy handed the driver a handful of local currency, and we headed for the door. Before we could knock, it was opened by a small, tidy woman with sleek blond hair. "Miss Randall? Miss Benner?"

We nodded. She smiled a smile that didn't touch her eyes and moved back so we could enter the building. Roxy hoisted her bag—filled with all twelve *Book of Secrets* novels—higher and flashed me a grin.

"Remember your party manners," I hissed.

We were escorted down a bewildering maze of dark passages, lit with electric lights, I was glad to see, figuring that an old building like this would be a fire hazard. We climbed a black staircase and came out into what I assumed was the great hall of the castle, passing under vaulted wooden arches from which ragged banners swayed gently in the air. Wood paneled most of the walls, although occasionally I caught glimpses down dark stone passages that I guessed led to older, unremodeled sections of the castle. The woman told us as she took our coats that her name was Gertrud, and that she was Dante's housekeeper. "He will be with you in a short time," she informed us as we were ushered into a cozy room lined with mahogany-framed, glass-fronted bookcases.

I looked around with amazed interest. "Have you ever seen so many old books in your life?"

Roxy did a little spin and clutched her bag to herself. "I can't believe we're really here! I can't believe we're really going to meet him! I wonder what he's like, what he's really like. Do you think he's old or young? Do you think he likes American women, especially petite American women with curly dark hair and a beguiling manner?"

I laughed and bent over to peer in an environmentally controlled case at the open page of an illuminated manuscript.

"Honestly, Rox, I think he's a man like any other. If you just act like yourself and don't pester him with questions, I'm sure he'll like you well enough."

"Truer words have seldom been spoken," a lovely warm voice said from the doorway. Christian stood smiling at us, a small leather-bound volume in his hand.

"Christian?"

"Joy. You look lovely in that dress. Garnet suits you." He turned to Roxy. "And you are in a very attractive dress despite telling me you did not care for them."

"Are you here to meet Dante, too?" Roxy asked, confused.

The light bulb finally went on over my head.

"Your middle name wouldn't happen to be something starting with the letter J, would it?" I asked.

He set his book aside and came into the room, taking both my hands in his, kissing the backs of each. "It is Johann."

"Do you know Dante?" Roxy asked. "You could have told us you knew him. Geez, I would have told you if you were in my place!"

"Rox," I said, gently disentangling my hands from Christian's. "Meet Christian Johann Dante, famed recluse and author of the *Book of Secrets* novels."

Christian made a formal bow to Roxy, who stared at him in stunned silence for a minute, then flung her bag away, shrieked, and threw herself on him, wrapping her arms and legs around him as she babbled about what a fool she'd been. Christian looked upward to heaven when Roxy grabbed his face and started kissing his cheeks. I laughed at the look of consternation on his face as Roxy squealed again. He swung her around once, then gently set her on her feet.

"Ohmigod, ohmigod, ohmigod!" She jumped up and down for a moment, then grabbed her bag and flung herself at his feet, scrabbling for her books, muttering about finding a pen worthy of the great Dante's fingers.

I smiled one of my best patronizing smiles and patted her on the head. "So much for remembering your party manners."

It took Roxy a bit of time to calm down, but eventually she did, aided by some of Christian's aged brandy. He spent a goodly amount of time apologizing for misleading us as to his identity, but we both assured him we weren't in the least upset.

"As if we could be upset with *you*," Roxy said with worship in her eyes. She sat next to Christian on an embroidered settee, her body language that of an acolyte before an idol.

He laughed, the sound soft and pleasing as it echoed around the room. "Last night you told me I was a beast because I would not have your name tattooed on my buttock, and today I can do no wrong." He shook his head and grinned at me. "I believe I preferred being a beast."

I had a hard time dissuading Roxy from monopolizing the conversation by grilling him as to past and future books, but after another brandy, she finally allowed the conversation to be turned in the direction I wanted.

"Joy's giving me that look that says she's going to pinch me black and blue the minute your back is turned, so I suppose we'd better get to what we came to talk to you about."

"I am destroyed," he said mildly, looking anything but. "I assumed your enjoyment of my books was such that you merely wished to meet me in person, but now I find that is not true, that I am but a cog in a bigger wheel. Alas, how the mighty have fallen."

"You're almost as big a ham as Dominic," I told him.

His lips quirked, but he managed to keep a grin from forming as he placed a hand on his chest and gave us a little mock bow. "How can I be of assistance to my two favorite Americans?"

"It's Joy's vampire," Roxy said.

Christian settled back and crossed his legs, his elegant fingers tapping out a rhythm on his knee. "Ah, the admirable Mr. St. John."

"No," Roxy said. "Turns out he's not the Dark One. That's what we wanted to see you about. We need your help."

"Me?" he asked, his brow furrowed as he looked from Roxy to me. "How can I help?"

"Roxy's hoping your experience and research will help us figure out who the Dark One is," I said. "We know he must be close, because he's shared visions with me, and although I had assumed it was Raphael, it turns out I was wrong."

"Indeed? I had assumed you had a preference for the good Raphael. Am I to gather that something has gone amiss in your path to romance?"

Roxy snorted. "Not likely. They can hardly keep their hands off each other."

"Raphael is not the issue," I said with a bit of a red face at the thought of discussing my blossoming relationship with Raphael. I blush easily, a fact that annoys me more than a little, but I have yet to find a cure for it. "The point is that if the Dark One is not him, it must be someone else."

"We have a list," Roxy announced, digging through her purse. I remembered who was on the list and tried to catch her attention to dissuade her from reading it aloud, but wasn't in time. "Here it is. Let's see—Dominic is a no, you're a no, Raphael is a probably not, and Milos is the favorite."

My blush heated up a few notches as Christian gave me a cool, appraising look. "I didn't intend any offense," I explained. "More or less every man I've met has been on the list. We crossed you off it immediately."

"I am grateful for small mercies."

"However," Roxy cut in, "since you are the reigning king of the Dark Ones, we figure it should be a piece of cake for you to figure out who the man is who has marked Joy."

"According to Moravian lore," Christian said slowly, his finger rubbing his lower lip, "once a woman has been marked by a Dark One as his Beloved, she does not seek any other mate. Yet Joy seems unhappy with the thought of living her life with a man who will eternally worship her. I find this conflict intriguing."

"I doubt if you'd find it so intriguing if you were in my shoes," I answered. "I understand what you say about Moravian lore, but what I want to know is whether or not it's true. You say that each Dark One has one woman and one woman alone who is his soul mate. Has there never been an occurrence where the two don't get along, or there's two men for one woman, or vice versa?"

Christian shook his head. "Not that I am aware. It has always been one woman for one man."

"What happens if the one marked as Beloved does not wish to Join herself to the Dark One?"

Christian shrugged. "He continues on as he has done all the years before him. Darkness, eternal struggle, and damnation without the possibility of ever finding salvation—the torment simply continues. The Dark One can make the choice to end his torment by exposing himself to the sun, a drastic last step of desperation. It is not uncommon."

Roxy shivered. "Poor Dark One. I'd never leave him like that. Joy, you ought to be ashamed of yourself."

"I'm not saying I am abandoning this guy, whoever he is,"

I objected, feeling utterly guilty and lower than a worm's belly. What sort of woman was I to damn a man to a black eternity just because he didn't do things to me that an amber-eyed Lothario did? "But first I want to know who the Dark One is. Then I can figure something out. Maybe there's been a cosmic mixup or something, switching soul mates between two sets of people.

"I don't think that's possible. Do you, Christian?"

He eyed me with consideration. "I have never heard of it happening, no."

" 'There are more things in heaven and earth,' " I quoted softly to him.

He smiled. "Very true."

"So do you think you can pick out the Dark One at the fair tonight?" Roxy prompted him. "Joy's going to do the rune stone readings, and you get to be one of her victims."

"Thanks," I said dryly.

"I am not sure," he answered Roxy's question. "I have little knowledge of those connected with the fair."

"You met Milos last night," I pointed out. "Wouldn't you have known if he was a Moravian then?"

"Possibly," he allowed.

"So—was he? What did you think about Milos?" Roxy asked.

He looked at Roxy for a moment, then switched his attention to the fireplace that blazed with a bright fire. "I believe that Milos is a man who is dangerous to women who are unescorted. As to whether he is a Dark One or not . . . a second look would not be amiss."

"Dangerous, huh?" Roxy nodded her head and popped a lemon drop in her mouth. She offered the package around before tucking it back into the Black Hole of Calcutta that doubled as her bag. "I agree one hundred percent. He looks like the type who'd take advantage of a woman."

"I believe the danger he poses goes a bit deeper," Christian answered.

I glanced at the clock. "Well, dangerous or no, we're going to have to be going, since Roxy signed me up to be the evening's entertainment. Thank you for answering our questions," I said as I rose.

His lips curled into a smile, but his eyes were watchful and worried.

"I would be happy to escort you again, if you are not tired of my presence."

Roxy almost fainted at the thought, but I managed to revive her by promising she could sit next to him in the front seat of his car. We arrived at the fair a short while later, amazed to see how many people were gathering.

"All right, you blackmailed me into this, but if I'm going to do it, there are going to be some ground rules," I told Roxy as we lined up in the queue waiting to buy tickets.

She looked around us. "Boy, you weren't kidding when you said people would be streaming in all week," she told Christian. "There's got to be double the people who were here yesterday."

"Rox, can we force ourselves to stick to the issue at hand—namely, my happiness?"

"You're a selfish, selfish person," Roxy replied, then turned her back on me and smiled at Christian.

"The rules are these," I continued on, ignoring her ignoring me. "First, I have to have my own set of rune stones. I don't want to borrow the ones Arielle was using. They don't have a good feel to them."

"You wouldn't believe she was the biggest skeptic in all the world last week, would you?" Roxy asked Christian. "Boy, has she changed her tune!"

"Yes, now I believe six impossible things before breakfast," I replied, giving her a look that should have warned her. "It's that or go insane. I chose sanity. Second, I get to choose who I read for."

"Dominic said it has to be three readings."

"Fine," I said. "Then I'll read for Raphael, Christian, and Arielle."

The line shuffled forward a few steps. "Aye aye, *mon capitaine*," she answered, still smirking at Christian. He shot me a martyred look.

"And last but not least, I don't want a lot of people watching me. I get nervous before a crowd, and we all know what happened the last time I got nervous when I was reading the stones."

"What happened?" Christian asked.

"Earthquakes, floods, fires, you name it. She's a cataclysient—predicts natural disasters."

"I am not a cataclysient, there is no such thing as a cataclysient, so you can just stop telling everyone I am one. It was all just coincidence, Christian. A group of Wiccans has banned me from ever reading for them again, that's all. But still, having me do public readings probably isn't a terribly bright idea. I wouldn't want anything to go wrong."

We moved forward a yard or so. Roxy mouthed "cataclysient" to Christian.

"The most important thing is to find a set of rune stones," I decided. "Luckily, I saw some yesterday at one of the booths that sell crystals and stuff."

We paid our entrance fee and worked our way through the increasing crowds until we came to the merchant. I perused his limited selection of stones, trying to decide between the pink rose quartz and the deep purple of the amethyst. Once the merchant told me the amethysts were runes of joy (rose quartz were runes of love), the decision was made.

As I was handing over the money for the stones, the hair on the back of my neck stood on end and shrieked out a warning of danger. I spun around and met the cold, flat eyes of Milos. He nodded his head, gave Christian the same impersonal look, and turned to leave. He stiffened for a moment as he looked at something beyond the edge of the tent, then turned on his heel and walked in the opposite direction.

"That guy gives me the creeps," Roxy said from where she was busy trying on necklaces.

I glanced at Christian. He was watching Milos depart, his fingers absentmindedly stroking one of the rose quartz runes.

"You really shouldn't touch the stones," I warned him, tapping his fingers.

He looked down at his hand. "I shouldn't?"

"No. It's supposed to be bad for whoever reads them if someone else touches them. Imprints them or something. I was told to never let anyone touch my rune stones. Not that I ever really believed in that stuff, but . . ." I smiled lamely. "I guess if I can believe in vampires, I can believe in touchy rune stones."

He quickly put the stone down and smiled.

"Come on, beautiful," I called out to Roxy who was peering into a mirror admiring a crystal necklace on herself. "I want this over with as quickly as possible."

"You just want to be done so you can play a round of kissy-face with Raphael," she said, turning slightly to check out the side view.

"That isn't why I want to be done with it," I said indignantly, not in the least denying the truth in her statement.

"I'm sorry to hear that," Raphael said from just beyond the tent. "The thought of playing a round of kissy-face is one I hate to discard, but disappointed and slighted though I am, I will see my duty through as best I can. Your presence, madam, has been requested."

He held out his hand for me. I smiled and took it, reveling

in the warmth of his touch as his fingers closed around mine. "You'll notice, disappointed and slighted as you are, that I did not discount the idea of playing kissy-face."

"I noticed," he answered, his eyebrows giving me a slight wiggle.

Christian appeared at my side, giving Raphael a neutral look. "St. John," he said, glancing down to where Raphael held my hand. His lips tightened as he took my other hand and tucked it into the crook of his arm.

"Dante," Raphael nodded back, giving him a cool, assessing look. Something elemental and male passed between them, something I could sense but was not privy to. I was about to suggest they stop acting like cavemen when Roxy, her purchase complete, strolled past us and nailed the situation on the head.

"Reminds me of two dogs with their hackles up over the same bone," she called out over her shoulder. "You'd better be careful, Joy. Next thing you know, they'll start marking their territory, and you know what that means! They'll be peeing everywhere!"

To my surprise, Raphael—and Christian—did not escort me to Arielle's palm-reading tent. Instead we marched down the avenue lined with booths, heading straight for the main tent, the one used for the big events. I assumed Dominic didn't want to interrupt the flow of business at the palm-reading booth by having me do my demonstration there.

"How long have you known who Christian was?" I asked Raphael as we walked. "And why didn't you tell us? You could have saved Roxy and me from making fools of ourselves by telling Christian all about his books."

Christian murmured in his rich, silky voice that he would never think me a fool. Raphael just shrugged. "Last night. Someone in the bar told me. I thought he would have told you; you seem to spend enough time with him."

"Oh, stop it," I told Raphael as we wended our way through the crowds of people patronizing the line of tents. Arielle had a large group in front of hers, I was happy to note. Tanya, grim-faced and hollow-eyed, also had a sizeable crowd in front of her spell-casting booth. "You make it sound like Christian is interested in me in a romantic way, and he's not, he's just being polite. I've never understood why men get so territorial about a woman having a platonic relationship with another man."

Raphael stopped, pulling Christian and me to a halt as well. "You're serious, aren't you?"

"About what?" I asked him. "About men acting like boobs around other men? Yes, I'm serious. I've seen it before—"

"No, not that." His lovely amber gaze shifted until it rested on Christian. "You're serious about thinking he's not interested in you the same way I am, isn't that right?"

I glanced between the two men, the fingers of my right hand entwined with Raphael's, held strong and safe, my left hand tucked into Christian's arm. "Stop embarrassing me," I said in a low tone to Raphael. "Of course he's not interested in me in that way."

Raphael kept his eyes on Christian. "Tell her."

Christian pursed his lips, his gaze holding Raphael's. "In my own good time."

"Tell her now."

"Tell me what? Dammit, I hate feeling like everyone else at the party knows a joke and I don't. What does he want you to tell me?" I asked Christian. "I'm not completely stupid. I've dated guys before, I know all the signs one makes when he's looking for a little nookie, and you're not making them, so yes, please, just tell me whatever it is that Mr. Possessive here thinks you need to tell me."

"Very well," Christian said, placing his hand on top of mine. "If you insist."

With a move too fast to see, he pulled my hand from

Raphael's, wrapped both arms around me, and slammed me up against his chest just as his lips swooped down to capture mine. I stood for a moment in stunned surprise, then realized what he was doing and tried to shove myself off his chest.

"Let go of her," Raphael growled behind me.

Christian's arms held solid behind me, not giving an inch when I tried to squirm out of them. I was just starting to get panicky when he suddenly let me go. I stared at Christian in open-mouthed surprise. His eyes were black, solid black as if his pupils had dilated to consume his irises, black and glittering and full of something that made me shiver.

Raphael pushed in front of me, shoving me behind him as he growled directly into Christian's face. "Touch her again and you'll have to answer to me."

"Hey!" I said, nudging Raphael in the back. I didn't mind a little bit of a possessive attitude, but he was taking things a bit too far.

"What's the matter?" Roxy called from behind me, hurrying up. "Everyone is waiting in the main tent. What are you guys lollygagging for?"

"Hans and Franz here are duking it out."

"I answer to no man, St. John," Christian said in a silken voice that only magnified the menace inherent in it. "If Joy does not wish to receive my advances, she will tell me."

"Oooh! They're fighting over you? Cool! I figured it would take a couple more days before things escalated to that point."

"*I'm* telling you she doesn't want them," Raphael said, his voice dropping in pitch. While he wasn't as good with the unspoken menacing as Christian, I did not like the way the conversation was heading. It was all very flattering to think that they'd want to mix it up over me, but it was also extremely stupid. There was only one man present I wanted to get to know better.

"All right, both of you, stop it now," I said, pushing Raphael until I could squeeze between them. He didn't back up at all, which meant I was pressed up against a likewise unmoving Christian. I turned my head to Raphael. "Just so you know, you're standing so close my breasts are pressed up against him."

Raphael immediately backed up a couple of steps, but took me with him as he did so.

"Look, this is silly," I appealed to Christian. "I'm very flattered that you want to kiss me and everything, but the truth is that I'm just not quite with you on that. I assumed you knew that Raphael and I are, for lack of a better description, interested in one another."

"He knows that," Raphael grumbled behind me.

"So you can both just stop your posturing and growling and pretending I'm nothing more than a mindless, ditzy bit of fluff who will happily walk off with whoever wins this pissing contest, and get back to the job at hand."

Raphael's hands on my arms tightened painfully as Christian stepped forward, took my hand in his, and turned it over to kiss my palm. It was the same move that Dominic had pulled on me, but Christian didn't leave me with the desire to wash off my hand. "As you have asked, I will not press my suit. Yet."

"Fine. Now that we're all friends again, can we get these stupid readings over with so I can enjoy the rest of the evening?"

Christian smiled and tucked my hand back into the crook of his arm. Raphael grumbled to himself, but took my other hand.

"I feel like I should be singing 'We're Off to See the Wizard,' " I said as we headed for the main tent.

Neither man laughed, although Roxy, accepting Christian's offer to take his other arm, broke her silence with a comment that she'd like to know what perfume I was using to have three men slobbering over me the minute I arrived in the country.

"No one is slobbering over me," I told her with a look that promised a much more detailed chastisement in the near future. "You make me sound like nothing but a choice piece of meat. I'd like to just drop the subject, if we could. Did you tell Dominic that I wanted to pick the people I'd read for?"

"No. I thought you guys were right behind me, not standing in the middle of the fair having a testosterone contest."

I snickered. Raphael glowered. My snicker died when I got caught up in the snare of his eyes, the heat in them sending a wave of warmth through me that kindled a fiery reaction at several key points of my anatomy. The cheerleaders woke up and started rallying the crowd for the main event. If I had any before, the steamy, seductive look in Raphael's eyes left me in no doubt that tonight he would not be asking me to remove myself from his lap.

"Hooo," I sighed, and allowed him to hustle me off to the main tent.

Chapter Eleven

"No."

"Come on, Joy."

"No!"

"Mon ange—"

"You call me that one more time, and I swear I'll *mon ange* you so hard you'll walk funny for a week. And stop slobbering on my hand!"

"You are distraught, *mon ange—*"

"RAPHAEL!"

"Dominic!"

"Joyful—"

"All right, stop it, all of you!" I yanked my hand from Dominic's and glared at the assembled company. "This is starting to resemble a circus. You!" I pointed to Roxy. "Sit. You!" I pointed to Raphael. "Stop flexing your muscles at Christian and watch Dominic. You!" I pointed to Christian. "Stop glaring at Raphael, sit next to Roxy, and keep her in line. Feel free to sit on her if you need to. Now, as for you, Dominic,

182

I want it made perfectly clear that I am doing this against my better judgment, and *only* because my friend foolishly wagered every cent she has that I would. So I will read the runes for three people, and three people only: Raphael, Christian, and Arielle."

"No!" Tanya shrieked from where she was sitting sullen and angry behind Dominic. "That is not a fair test. She chooses three people who would lie for her, who would say that whatever she tells them is true!"

"Oh!" I gasped, outraged. "I would never ask anyone to lie for me, and certainly none of the three people I mentioned would think to do so!"

"Why not? You have slept with both of the men, and I saw the way you watched my sister. Even an innocent like her is not safe from your lustful appetite!"

"You witch!" I stormed, jumping up from my chair and heading off the stage to where Tanya sat.

She leaped up and headed for me. "That's right, I *am* a witch, and you'd do well to remember that for you I have created a spell most powerful. It will rid us of your unwanted presence . . . permanently!"

Raphael grabbed my arm and kept me from flinging myself down the three steps to the seats. Milos grabbed Tanya and pulled her backwards, none too gently I was pleased to see.

"*Joie.*" Dominic oiled over to me and took my hand again, tugging me back to the table he'd set up for the reading. "You make my heart ache when you insist on deranging yourself over such trivial matters. This wager, it is a minor matter, one that is better forgotten when compared to your happiness. I will wave it away and absolve your friend from her responsibility."

I eyed him warily. "You will? What's the catch?"

He moved closer to me, his eyelids at half mast as he leaned his head to mine. "If it is within my power to make you happy, *mon ange*, I will climb the highest mountain to see it so. I will swim the deepest ocean, I will move—"

"Yeah, yeah, yeah, get to the point. What do you want in return for calling this whole thing off?"

He leaned close enough to peer down my cleavage. "A night spent in the arms of *mon ange* is not too much to ask, I think."

"Think again," I snapped, and turned back to the table.

He grabbed my hand and hauled me up to his chest.

"Raphael!" I turned to him with a meaningful glare.

"Dominic—" he warned with a flash of his amber eyes, starting toward Dominic.

"*Mon ange*," Dominic pleaded, one eye on Raphael as he approached.

"There they go again," Roxy said to Christian. "Kind of like watching an episode of *The Waltons,* isn't it?"

He raised his brows at her. She fawned at him.

"This has gone far enough," Raphael said, pulling my fingers free from Dominic's, massaging the top of my hand with his thumb as he walked me back to my chair. I would have allowed the tingles his touch generated to sweep through my body, but given the present company, I figured it was better to keep all my wits present and accounted for. "Why don't we stop wasting time? Whom do you want her to read for, Dominic?"

Dominic looked peeved at having his toy taken out of his grasp, but he rubbed his hands together and gave me a leer that all but stripped off my lovely garnet dress. "Myself, of course, Milos, and Tanya. I believe the three of us will offer ample opportunity for Joie to prove beyond a shadow of a doubt that Tanya's claims are false."

"No, no, and over my dead body. I don't give a hoot what Tanya claims," I muttered. "The bet was *only* that I do three readings."

"I cannot allow her to stain your honor in such a manner,"

he answered. "Alas, it is my unfortunate duty to remind you that the wager said you would successfully conduct three readings. Thus you not only do the readings, but they must be accurate."

"You can't get fine accuracy with rune stones," I protested.

"Within reasonable doubt," he added.

"Fine," I said, unhappy but without many choices. "But there's no reason I have to read for you three. Arielle is certainly above suspicion of complicity, Christian is neutral, and Raphael is your own employee, for heaven's sake! There can be no objection to my reading for them."

Evidently there could. Tanya spat a flurry of unintelligible comments to Dominic, who shrugged and turned back to me. "You must read for three fair employees to satisfy Tanya, *mon ange*," he said with a hint of immovability.

I debated continuing the argument until I wore him down, but figured I might as well give in and get the blasted thing over with.

"Fine. I'll read for Raphael, Arielle, and Milos. Happy now?"

"With one slight adjustment—you will change Milos for Tanya."

I looked between the cold-eyed Milos and the raging Tanya and gave a mental shrug. One was bound to be as bad as the other. "Fine, but she's last. If my reading calls down any acts of God, I want to be able to leave quickly."

I ignored Dominic's hand and seated myself at the table, grimacing at the showy casting cloth set over the table. I yanked it off and yelled to Roxy, "Give me your red scarf, would you?" She brought it over and I smoothed it out until it lay flat on the table, then looked out at the people assembled. I was at the edge of one corner of the stage, sitting behind a small table, melting under the bright stage lights someone had turned on. Tanya and Milos dragged two chairs from the seating section to join the semicircle of people already sitting in front of me. The irony of the situation—having to prove something I didn't believe in—did not escape me. If this kept up, I'd be like Lewis Carroll's Alice, believing six impossible things before breakfast.

"Right. I'm ready. Let's have Arielle first."

Arielle, who had been sitting quietly next to Roxy, gave me a tentative look, shot a quick glance at her sister, and took the chair opposite me.

I smiled to reassure her. She was clearly ill at ease—that made two of us. "You know the routine, Arielle," I said in a voice that I hoped sounded confident. "I'd like you to think of a question and focus on it."

She wrung her hands and nodded.

"Good. In the Odin's Nine layout, the first rune stands for hidden influences on your past, the second for your present attitude on past events, the third for hidden influences on the present, the fourth for your attitude on the present, the fifth on delays or obstacles that may prevent the outcome you seek, the sixth is the outcome or result of your question, and the seventh through ninth stones indicate what you already have, or will need, to influence your past, present, and future respectively. Got all that?"

She nodded again.

"OK, here we go." I reached into the bag and started pulling out stones, laying them in the Odin's Nine layout, naming each stone as I did. "Uruz reversed. Raidho reversed. Gebo. Eihwaz. Isa. Sowulo. Nauthiz. Berkana. Pertho."

She shifted in her seat, eyeing the stones warily. "Since you know how to do this, I'll dispense with the explanations of what each stone means and get right to the juicy parts. The past influences on your question are indecision, impaired personal judgment, burdensome tasks, and low self-confidence."

She looked a bit startled by my stark appraisal of her past, but didn't disagree. I glanced over at Tanya, who sat smiling smugly at me as if she knew a secret and I didn't. Based on the fact that Arielle might have had a life away from the bad influence of her sister, I figured that so far my reading was dead on.

"The present influences on your question indicate that you are at a turning point in your life where you are about to enter into a partnership, but feel as if you are pulled in two directions. Be assured that this relationship will be one that flourishes."

"Oh," she said brightly, looking much more happy at the thought of her present. I mentally crossed my fingers that it would mean she'd find someone who would take her away from Tanya's influence. "That sounds very good. Please go on."

"The future influences indicate you must shed old habits and relationships gone sour in order to move forward with your life. With this shedding will come clarity and inner peace, the power to achieve what you want most. This last stone"—I tapped Pertho—"is one that says that although there will be obstacles in your path, all roads will lead you to where you want to go."

I sat back, pleased that the stones were cooperating and not making me look bad in front of everyone.

"This is ridiculous!" Tanya sputtered, leaping to her feet and pointing at me as she turned to shout at Dominic. "She is not doing the reading correctly! How can we judge if she has at all the powers of the mind?"

"Arielle," I asked gently. "Would you mind telling us what your question was?"

She blushed but unexpectedly raised her chin and looked her sister in the eye. "No, I do not mind. My question was about Paal, whether or not he would ask me to join him when he returns to Norway in the spring. Paal was *mon petit ami* since the last year, you understand, but my sister did not like him and convinced me that he was not true to me. Because of that I separated from him, but now all has been made clear. Tanya was wrong about Paal, and we are no longer separated," she added with a militant look in her eye. "I love him. I wish to be with him, and I will not allow you to drive him from me again."

"Go, Arielle!" I said softly, then louder as Tanya was about to say something scathing to her sister, "So that's impaired judgment and indecision in the past when Tanya was trying to break you up with Paal, a new relationship and turning point in the present, and a future that can be achieved happily only if you shed the sludge from your life." I looked pointedly at Tanya. "Well, that looks like three out of three for Team Joy."

"Yay!" Roxy cheered.

Tanya snarled an obscenity and sat down, but not before sending her sister a look that did not bode well for her. Arielle sat as far away from Tanya as she could get. I made a mental note to have a talk with Raphael about watching out for her in the future.

"Next?" I tipped my head at Raphael. He rolled his eyes upward as if he were praying for patience, but took the seat before me readily enough. Tanya was whispering vehemently in Dominic's ear, but he seemed to be ignoring her. He gave me another one of his pseudo-seductive smiles. I turned my eyes back to much more pleasant viewing.

"Do you have a question in mind?" I asked.

"I do," Raphael nodded.

"Good God, he's already saying his wedding vows and they haven't even been to bed together," Roxy muttered sotto voce, but not nearly sotto enough.

Raphael quirked his lips at me. I glared at Roxy. "If we could do this without comments from the peanut gallery? Thank you. OK now, Raphael, I want you to concentrate on your question while I draw the stones for you."

"No!" Tanya inadvertently shouted directly into Dominic's ear. He swore and jumped up, rubbing his ear and firing obscenities at Tanya. She didn't even apologize, she just stalked forward, saying, "That is not equitable! He must first tell someone his question, so it can be determined how accurate your reading is."

I looked at Raphael. "You have any objections to telling your question to someone?"

He hesitated for a fraction of a second. "None at all."

"OK. You can tell two people who are neutral in all this mess—Arielle and Milos."

Raphael held a momentary confab with them, then returned to his chair. "Concentrate on the question. Oooh, interesting. I haven't seen that stone in that position before. Have you had a history of spontaneous combustion in your family?"

His eyes widened in surprise.

I grinned. "Just kidding. Let's see what we have here. Mmm. The past influences say that you have several unresolved mysteries that you desperately seek solutions for. Upheaval is prominent in relationship to your question; you suffered a veritable firestorm of anguish trying to ride it out, but in the end you did not find the answer you sought."

I glanced up from the stones to find him watching me with narrow-eyed intensity. I was tempted to ask him just whether the traumatic experience he had recently survived was connected to his secret, but figured it was a question better left for later.

"Influences on the present—hmmm. This stone, Mannaz, says you should be looking for help from those closest around you." I glanced up at him again, met his gaze, and quickly looked back at the stones. "Coupled with this stone, Dagaz, it indicates that only by joining forces with someone else will you have the breakthrough you need to resolve the question plaguing you."

I didn't look up. I wanted to, I wanted to offer my help with whatever task the runes said he had undertaken, but I didn't. I pushed the image of his amber eyes from my mind and kept my gaze focused on the amethyst stones as I moved on to the ones indicating the future. "Influences acting on the future outcome of your question are deceit, treachery, and deliberate misdirection. In order to overcome these obstacles, you must open yourself up to a partnership that is about to be offered you. Communication is vital with your partner. Jera, the last stone, says that your hard labors will be rewarded."

I risked a glance up. He was looking thoughtful, but nothing more. "So, how did I do?"

"What was his question?" Tanya demanded to know.

Milos gave a slight shrug. "His question was whether or not he would find the solution to a problem that was perplexing him."

I shivered as Milos's gaze touched on me for a few seconds. I couldn't pin down what it was about him, but he gave me a never-ending case of the willies.

"Ha!" Tanya cried, jumping to her feet.

"Sit down," Roxy grumbled. "What are you, a jackrabbit?"

"She fails! All that talk of firestorms and upheaval is just a guess."

"Actually," Raphael said as he stood, "she's remarkably close to the situation." He glanced at Dominic. "As my employer will no doubt be happy to tell you, recent circumstances have wrongly cast me under a cloud of suspicion. The situation I hope to find a solution to stems from that origin."

"Yay!" Roxy cheered. "Our team is ahead two to nothing. Still think she's faking it, Tanya?"

Tanya curled her lip in a truly frightening smile and stalked over to the table.

"Now we shall see. You shall do a reading for me. I will not be so easy to fool as the others."

"Same rules apply for you as Raphael. You have to tell your question to two people—Arielle and Roxy."

"No!" Tanya shouted, pointing at Roxy. "Not her."

"Fine," I said, wanting to get it over with. Although I didn't hold much, if any, faith in the divination power of rune stones, I found doing readings tended to be a bit draining. "Arielle and Milos again, if neither objects."

Neither did. Once Tanya had whispered her question to them, she sat down. I scooped the stones back into the velvet bag, shook it, and started pulling stones out. "Hmm. Just look at all the reversed stones."

Tanya leaned forward to glare at the stones. "You are doing that on purpose!"

"Think so? I'm not, but I'll tell you what. I'll start over and you can watch me pull them out of the bag."

"Yes," she hissed. "I shall watch you most carefully."

I picked up the couple of stones, tossed them into the bag, shook it again, and pulled out stones one at a time, careful to let her see my fingers as each stone cleared the bag.

Almost all the stones came out reversed. I pursed my lips as I considered the stones laid out in Odin's Nine. "Mmmm. Doesn't look very good, does it? Let's see—the past influences say a cycle has been completed, that relationships you held in the past have come to an end due to neglect and abandonment. Overconfidence and relationship problems have played a major part in forming your present situation."

"Lies! You are lying! You do not see that at all in the stones; you merely say that to try to win the wager!"

"We can have Arielle interpret the stones, too, if you like."

Arielle stood up. Tanya snarled something at her, and she sat right back down.

I looked at Tanya. "Shall I go on?"

"No! You are proving nothing, you are reading nothing! You do not have the power you claim you have. You are manipulating the stones so they say what you want them to say."

I looked over her shoulder to where everyone sat. "Should I finish it or not?"

"Finish it, *mon ange*," Dominic said as he strolled over to stand next to Tanya. I hoped his presence would have a calming effect on her, although I hadn't noticed it had in the past.

"All right. Influences on the present with regard to your question—a partnership is in the offing, but it will not be what you seek. This stone, Pertho reversed, indicates an ending, so the partnership will bring you only loss, not gain. To avoid this, you should not seek to undertake any new ventures now, especially ones that would put you in a position of any vulnerability."

"This is foolishness! She does not know—"

"Let her finish," Dominic ordered, his hand on her shoulder. From the way Tanya flinched, I gathered his hold on her was not gentle.

"Last bit, then we'll be done. Influences on your future." I studied the three stones indicating the future, puzzled by the combination of stones.

"Well?" Tanya demanded. "What lies do you want to tell me now?"

I touched the stones as I thought out the best way to explain what they said. "This stone, Jera, acts as a caution. It says basically, what goes around, comes around. This stone, Fehu reversed, says you will not have the material gain you expect to have unless you take steps to alter your path. The last stone, Othala reversed, indicates that something rightfully yours will be taken from you. Read together, the runes show a strong warning that you must release the plans you have made, and instead use your natural talents to shape a happier result. If you do not . . ." I shrugged.

"If I do not, what?" she asked in that sickening sweet voice. I shrugged again. I didn't want to tell her that the combined stones predicted disaster on a catastrophic level if she didn't take her future in her hands and change it.

"The stones say you'll regret following the path you're currently on."

"Bah! You think your threats will make any difference to me? They do not!" She slammed her hand down on the table, scattering the stones. I scooped them up and tucked them safely into the bag. While I didn't necessarily hold with the belief that no one but the reader should touch the stones, the amethyst runes were pretty, and I didn't want to lose one.

"What was her question?" Roxy asked Arielle.

"She asked if she would be successful in ridding herself of a threat to her happiness."

We both looked at Tanya. She smiled at me.

"I did not find your demonstration adequate," she said. "You have lost the wager. You will pay the money you owe and never step foot here again."

"Now, hold on," I said at the same time as Roxy cried, "You big cheater! She did so win the bet," just as Raphael intervened between the two of us.

"Dominic, if you can't control your people better, I'll be happy to give you a few tips on how to keep them quiet." He waited until Tanya snatched her arm from Dominic's grasp and rubbed it up and down vigorously. "Joy won the wager. She proved she could read with a reasonable level of accuracy. End of show. Come along, little troublemaker," he said offering me his hand. "I'd like a word with you in private."

I let my lips curl into a grin at the look in his eye. It was part exasperation, part desire, and part something I couldn't read at all.

"I agree that she won the wager," Dominic said as he moved forward. "But she will come with me. It is I who wishes to have a word with her. *In private.*"

The way he said the last two words made my skin crawl.

"Sorry, Raphael asked first," I said as I took his offered hand. "Even if he didn't, I like him better. Thanks for all the fun, kids. Roxy, don't forget to collect your winnings."

I followed Raphael off the stage, my hand still in his, and down the aisle to the opening of the tent before Tanya exploded. She screamed her fury at Dominic in at least three languages, lunging at him as she yelled obscenities and threats until Dominic pulled back and slapped her. I'm certainly not one of Tanya's biggest fans, but I never think it's right when a guy feels he can slap a woman around. I started back toward Dominic.

"Leave them," Raphael warned in my ear as his fingers tightened around mine.

"He's hitting her," I whispered, tugging to free my hand. "I don't like her, but I'm not going to stand by while he beats her up."

"She was almost hysterical with rage and out of control," Raphael said. "He wasn't really trying to hurt her."

I looked back at them. I had to admit Tanya *was* over the edge. She was still ranting and raving at Dominic, but other than defending himself from her claws, he wasn't striking her. He did shoot unhappy looks our way as Raphael hustled me out of the tent, but he got full marks for staying to deal with Tanya. Christian and Roxy were close on our heels, followed by the silent but eerie-as-hell Milos.

"Hey, did you notice, no catastrophes!" Roxy called out as Raphael was about to steer me away from the tent. "I guess you'll have to tell Miranda she was wrong about that after all. Of course, most of the stuff you predicted last time didn't happen for a few days, so you know, maybe now would be a good time to take out earthquake insurance."

"Oh, hardy-har-har. Where are you guys going now?" I'd been worried about what to do with Christian. I couldn't quite wrap my mind around the fact that he had an interest in me—not in *that* way—and I was more than ready to believe that his interest was all a put-on like Dominic's, except there was something stark in his eyes that had a little part of me believing he was sincere. If that was so, I wanted to make it clear to him that we had no future together, but at the same time let him know that I wished him well and wanted him to be happy. I know it sounds trite, but I did truly want to be friends with him.

"We're going to the dungeon room," Roxy said quickly, scooting aside as Milos slipped behind her. She grabbed Christian's arm and sent him an adoring look. "What do you say, Mr. Dante, sir? You up to another romp in the dungeon with me? I might not be the woman over whom you've been glaring at Raphael all night, but I'm not smoked cheese, either."

Christian was watching me with dark, unfathomable eyes. I resisted the urge to look away and raised my chin instead, willing him to understand. He turned to Roxy and laughed despite the sting of her comment. "You are indeed not smoked cheese, although I find you utterly delectable. It would be my pleasure to accompany you to the dungeon room again, but only on two conditions."

"You want me to tie you up and do wicked things to you with my tongue?" she asked hopefully.

He laughed again. "No. You must allow me to show you the dungeons at Drahanská Castle—"

"Oooh, real dungeons," squealed Roxy.

"—and it is *my* turn to control the lash in the punishment booth."

Roxy giggled and tugged him off toward the section of

the fair with the weirder offerings. I was thankful he didn't give me another of his martyred looks as he left; I felt bad enough about being the source of unrequited romantic interest.

"I wonder if it's something in the water," I mused as I turned to Raphael, my fingers still entwined with his. "I tell you, I've never had so many guys falling at my feet before. It's heady stuff, this power I have over mere mortal men!"

"How you must suffer," he said, pulling me closer. He didn't have to pull very hard. I disentangled my fingers so I could do what I'd been waiting days to do—run them through his curls.

"So, tell me," I said, leaning into the hard length of his body, "what did you want to see me about? I can only hope you are going to suggest we go somewhere private so I can rip your clothing off and investigate that belly tattoo in detail."

"I have work to do," he replied, his eyes going molten as I slipped a hand under his sweater and stroked his chest. "The crowds are reaching the maximum number we can accommodate, and I have to make sure the crew assigned to crowd control are doing their jobs."

A nipple was the reward for my dedicated exploration. I teased it and gloried in the way his breathing suddenly went erratic. "So many men are not nipple aficionados," I commented, wiggling my hips so I brushed against him in a way I hoped would make him forget about the crowds. "I'm glad to see you are, because I've always thought that it is an extremely erotic spot on a man's body."

He closed his eyes for a moment, a groan slipping out as I licked the corners of his mouth; then suddenly both of his hands were on me. He cupped a hand around the back of my head and pulled it back at the same time as his mouth descended upon mine. He invaded, he dominated, he demanded response and would not settle for anything but utter surrender. I capitulated happily, melting into him and inhaling that wonderful Raphael scent, passion firing deep within me with every stroke of his tongue. I moaned my pleasure and was just about to slide my second hand under his sweater so I could really indulge myself when he broke off the kiss.

"Hey!" I said, extremely unhappy that he stopped.

"Later," he said with a promise in his eyes that made my knees go weak. "I can't do this now, but . . . *later.*"

"Your place or mine?" I asked, running my finger over the lush curve of his lower lip. So hot were his eyes, I thought his gaze would leave scorch marks where it touched me.

"I honestly don't care as long as you're there naked."

"I like a man who's easily accommodated," I said with a little kiss to the tip of his nose. "Have fun watching the kids play."

He stopped me as I was turning to leave, pulling a key off a key chain and handing it to me. I saluted him with it, gave him a lascivious leer just to let him know he was the sexiest man on the face of the earth, and toddled off to find Roxy and Christian.

Roxy blamed every single disaster of the evening on me, claiming my cataclysient powers were running amok.

"I knew you shouldn't have read those rune stones," she grumbled as she washed her sooty hands in a bucket of water that stood under a spigot. "I knew something like this would happen. I just *knew* it! You can't keep your catastrophes to yourself! You're not cataclysient, you're a catamaniac!"

"I am not responsible for that fire! And if you recall, you are the one who arranged for me to read the runes. You begged me, you pleaded with me, you bet every cent you had on me, so even if by some weird quirk of fate my reading was responsible for the fire at the Kirlian photo booth, the entire situation would be *your* fault, not mine."

"Ladies," Christian said with what was becoming a well-known martyred look. "I believe the source of the fire will prove to be the wires connected between the aura camera and the computer. I could not help but notice while we were extinguishing the fire that the wires were charred beyond what they should be in a simple fire."

"There's no such thing as a simple disaster where Joy's concerned," Roxy muttered, taking the towel Christian held out to dry her hands.

"I would be grateful if you would stop implying that everything that goes wrong is my doing," I said through gritted teeth. "I have had no more to do with the fire than the other happenings this evening."

"You punched the lead singer of Six Inches of Slime in the face and broke his nose!"

"I didn't punch him! Not deliberately! I tripped over a power cord and fell onto him. It just so happened that his nose was right where my fist landed. Besides, he deserved it. He was hitting on me and he wouldn't take no for an answer! What was I supposed to do, let him rape me? You know, I'm getting just a little bit tired of every man around here assuming I'm fair game."

"Ha! Talk about conceited! *Every* man? What, you think you're some sort of sex goddess that no man can resist?"

"Ladies, please—"

I ignored both Christian and Roxy. "And as for breaking that fool's nose, if he hadn't ducked, I would have hit him in the eye instead of the nose, and he could have gone on with his stupid band rather than screaming for a doctor. Who knew he'd be such a big baby over a little blood? I thought Goths were supposed to like blood and pain and suffering! My inadvertent punching him in the nose should have been right up his alley."

"Oh, I see," Roxy said with obnoxious innocence. I ground my teeth even harder. "So it *wasn't* your fault that the crowds rioted and tore up the main tent when Six Inches didn't go on because their lead singer was having his nose set? And it *wasn't* your fault that Raphael wasn't here controlling the crowds like he was supposed to be, because he was busy driving your victim to the hospital, thus leaving Dominic in charge—a man who clearly has no idea of how to keep large crowds in control?"

"It's his fair; you'd think he'd take precautions to make sure all those Goths didn't get out of control."

"Joy, Roxanne, I understand you are both angry, but this is not the—"

I finished drying my hands and shoved the towel into Christian's hands. Roxy turned and faced me, her hands on her hips. "He did take precautions; he hired Raphael, who would have been here but for you attacking that poor singer."

"Roxy, I swear, if you tell me one more time that I'm responsible for—"

"Joy!"

"Aren't you supposed to be off looking for my Dark One?" I snapped at Christian. "Aren't you supposed to be watching Milos to see if he's the walking dead?"

"Don't you yell at him," Roxy shouted, throwing herself in front of him and waving her arms in an excited fashion. "He's a famous author! You can't yell at famous authors like that! Besides, he's innocent. He's not the one who—"

"Don't say it," I warned, shaking my finger at her. "Don't you say it! I swear, between the runes and Tanya and Dominic jumping out at me all evening trying to corner me and that little twerp with the glass nose and fighting a fire with fire extinguishers that spray everything but the fire, I'm at my limit!"

"I don't care, you can't yell at Christian!"

"I'll yell at whoever I want to yell at!"

"You want to yell? Good. Yell at her!" Roxy pointed over my shoulder. I turned to see Tanya charging toward me, a look of fury and hatred on her face that was clearly visible from twenty paces.

"Oh, God!" I swore, knowing she was coming to rip a few strips off me, and helpless without Raphael to keep her from going rabid on me.

Christian was at my side in a flash. "I will take care of her," he said in that beautiful voice that was tinged with menace so threatening it sent unpleasant shivers down my back.

"No," I said quietly, trying to slap a smile on my face. I wasn't successful. "It's OK. She's all bark and no bite. She wouldn't dare do anything so foolish as to assault me in front of witnesses. I'm sure she'll throw a curse or two on me, but I can live with that. It won't hurt me to let her vent her spleen if it makes her feel better."

"You!" Tanya growled as she drew close, her eyes black as coal. Unlike earlier in the evening when she was positively frothing at the mouth with anger, now she had the appearance of calm, but it was misleading. There was a curious edginess about her, as if she was filled with tightly coiled energy that threatened to burst open at any moment. "This time you have gone too far. You will be punished, of that I am promising you. There is no escaping your fate."

"I've always believed that the concept of people being helpless against fate was a load of cow cookies," I said mildly. "I prefer to make my own future, thank you."

Tanya's lip twitched. A tremor ran through her. She fisted her hands. "I will not be in the way sorry at all for what is coming you," she ground out.

"Do you know that your English goes to pot the more upset you get?" I asked, my head tipped to the side as I tapped a finger on my lips. "There must be some sort of direct correlation between stress and the language-skills part of your brain."

She leaned forward until she was a scant few inches away from me. The wind carried her long red hair forward until it brushed against me. I stepped back, uncomfortable with any part of her touching me. Her lips curled back into a vicious, gloating smile that made me wonder about her sanity, her voice a rough whisper meant only for my ears. "You will die tonight. I hope your prayers you have said."

"You don't scare me at all, Tanya," I whispered back to her. Christian moved restlessly behind me, but I held out a hand to keep him from interfering. "Do you know, I honestly don't feel anything for you but pity? You're consumed with anger and hatred for me because you think I'm usurping your position, but the truth is, you wouldn't be happy if I left tomorrow. I think you should look within yourself for the answers to what's making you so miserable. As the runes said, blaming others for misfortunes you've brought on yourself is not the way to achieve happiness."

"I will be happy only when you are dead," she promised, this time loud enough for both Roxy and Christian to hear, as well as half a dozen other people near us. Several people turned around at her words, just in time to see her snatch up the bucket of sooty water and throw it at me.

"What the—" I bellowed, stunned by the cold water slamming me full in the face. I looked down at myself to find muddy, sooty water pouring off the front of my jacket, down over my lovely crushed velvet dress, pooling on the matching flats with the freshwater pearl ankle straps.

Tanya was already striding off by the time I finished sputtering enough to call her a few choice swear words. The people standing around us quickly turned away as if embarrassed to have witnessed such a scene. Roxy grabbed my arm and kept me from racing after Tanya and rubbing her face in the mud.

"Geez, you're a mess. Come on, Rocky, we'll get you home and into dry clothes before your next round with the Witch of the Moravian Highlands."

Christian handed me a handkerchief to clean off my face, all the while murmuring softly reassuring things.

"No, thank you," I said, mopping up and trying to brush the worst of the mud off. I smiled at Christian. "I'll have this washed before I return it to you. I think, if you don't mind, I'll go get out of these wet clothes."

"I'll come with you," Roxy selflessly offered. I gave her hand a little squeeze.

"Not necessary. I'm not going back to the hotel just yet. I'll use Raphael's trailer to dry off." I said the words to Roxy, but my eyes were on Christian. He stiffened for a moment, his inscrutable gaze searching my face.

"You sure?" Roxy asked, looking between Christian and me.

I nodded. "I'm sure. I'll see you tomorrow morning, OK? Christian, are we on for the tour of your dungeon tomorrow?"

He was silent for a moment, his eyes hooded as if he was unwilling to reveal any of himself; then he made an elegant gesture of capitulation with his hand. "I would be delighted. I have some business to attend to in the morning, but if you are free in the afternoon, I would be happy to show you around the castle."

"Great," I smiled, giving Roxy a glance warning her to behave herself. "Then I'll see you tomorrow. Thanks for all your help. I really appreciate it." Just for the hell of it I kissed him on his cheek. His hands clutched my arms for a moment before releasing me.

I started off in the direction of Raphael's trailer, skinnying in and out of the thickening crowds.

"Joy!" I turned when Roxy called my name.

She hurried up to me, glared at a couple of mohawked

teens who were staring open-mouthed at my soaked self until they turned away, and hissed, "You're OK for this evening, right?"

OK? Huh? "What?"

She pulled me out of the stream of traffic and started rooting through her purse. "This evening. Later. You and Raphael. Here, take these."

She shoved a handful of condoms in my hand.

"Roxy!" I said, shocked. "What are you doing with condoms? I thought you were saving yourself for Mr. Right?"

"Duh! Miranda said I'd be meeting him within a month, so I brought them with me just in case. But I haven't seen anyone here who's even remotely right, except Christian, and he has the hots for you."

"He doesn't have the hots for me, he's just one of those men who thinks he wants something someone else has. He's not serious."

"Mmm. Reserving judgment on that. Here—" She snatched the condoms from my hand and stuffed them in my purse. "Use them with my blessing."

I ignored her suggestive leer and headed back out into the crowd, feeling an awful lot like a salmon swimming upstream as I walked away from the fair to the line of trailers that ran in a curve around the far end of the meadow.

I figured Raphael wouldn't mind if I used his digs to dry off. He had given me his key; clearly he expected to find me in his trailer when his job was done. I'd much rather wait for him there than in my small hotel room, or wandering around the fair where I could run into Tanya again. Not to mention Dominic and his octopus hands. Or the über-creepy Milos.

A half hour later I was sitting in Raphael's trailer warm and dry in one of his sweatshirts. My dress hung over the chair, toweled clean as best I could get it. My coat was hanging over a stack of newspapers. My underwear was tucked discreetly into my bag. I had debated the "undies on/undies off" dilemma, finally deciding that although undies off might lead Raphael to believe I was the sort of loose woman who was anticipating the type of action that underwear would inhibit, it was better than lounging around in wet, soggy underwear—or worse, having him discover wet, soggy underwear on me! Gross!

That serious issue resolved, I curled up with a blanket and a book on Raphael's bed, resisting the urge to search through his belongings to see what I could find out about him. Part of the spice to our whole relationship—what there was of it so far—was the sense of mystery that wrapped around him. I was greatly looking forward to uncovering all the many interesting bits and pieces that added up to an extremely snacky man.

That thought reminded me of the condoms Roxy had shoved into my purse. Although I was sure Raphael would be equipped with his own supply, there was no sense in taking chances. I glanced around to see where I could stash a condom, hidden from view just in case things didn't turn out as I hoped they would, and yet handy if it did.

"Pillow!" I said brightly, turning around to put a condom under one of the pillows on his bed. My hand paused over the nearest, then carefully edged my hand back.

There was no gun under the pillow.

"Hmmm." I looked under the other pillow. It, too, was gun-free. I placed the condom under it and leaned back, pulling my knees up so I could rest my chin on them while I thought.

I had felt his chest, had leaned up close against him, and he didn't have a gun strapped under his armpit, so where was it? I looked through the open door down the length of the trailer, wondering if he had hidden it somewhere here, or if he had moved it elsewhere.

"And come to think of it, why does he have a gun in the

first place?" My voice was harsh as it echoed around the room, an intruder in a private little sanctuary. I scooted beneath the blankets, taking my book with me, and buried my face in his pillow as I gave myself up to the wonderful Raphael scent that never failed to make me go all girly inside.

It started the same way it had before.

Beloved, the voice echoed through my head. I fought to wake up, fought to shed the silken bonds that held me down into sleep and kept me from awareness. Once again my body seemed to be a heavy, alien thing that didn't answer my demands.

Beloved, do not fight me. He was touching me, stroking my body even though I knew he wasn't physically present. How could I fight a man whose very thoughts felt like the lightest of touches on my skin? I moaned deep in my throat as I struggled to escape the whispered strokes of his fingers. *It was wrong,* my mind shrieked at me. Every touch of his mind to mine was wrong! I had to make him understand that what he wanted was not mine to give.

I could never hurt you. You are my Beloved. You must not deny your fate any longer.

No, I screamed inside my head. He was coming closer to me, I could feel him moving through the night, graceful, powerful, a timeless hunter filled with the fury of eternal torment, calling through the night to the one person he believed could save him. Me.

I am not she, I pleaded with him. *I do not belong to you. It is wrong. We will both suffer if you do not stop now.*

I could never hurt you, Beloved.

I sobbed Raphael's name, struggling to break free of the Dark One's power, desperate to escape and regain control of my own body. My skin crawled with the thought of what would happen once he arrived. I would be damned as he was—I knew that as surely as I knew the sun rose each morning to banish the terrors of the night.

"You are more beautiful than any woman I have seen." Heat covered me, filled me, kindling desire within me, within him.

Beloved.

Raphael! I answered, fighting with every ounce of strength I had left.

A warmth, a presence I hadn't felt in the vision of the other night surrounded me. "You smell like flowers, but you taste of heaven." Flames licked up my back, burning my neck, lighting me on fire. I struggled to escape the flames, but the Dark One's hold on me was too great.

"I've thought about you all evening, thought about this. You were never once from my mind. You were meant for me. Every inch of you is perfect, perfectly made for me. You are mine."

He was coming closer. He was almost upon me.

We will be together forever, Beloved.

Nooooo!

"Say it. Say the words. I want to hear them." The fire consumed the front of me, burning down past flesh and muscle and bone, boiling my blood away until there was nothing left of the essence of me. What was left was love.

"Raphael!"

"Mmm. I thought you'd never wake up."

I opened my eyes. Raphael's amber gaze burned into me seconds before his mouth claimed mine. I gave myself to him, gave him everything there was of me and accepted him in return.

A soulless howl of agony rent the fabric of the night, bringing tears to my eyes even as I understood that there was nothing I could do for the Dark One.

"Joy?"

I opened my eyes again and smiled at the concern in Raphael's beautiful eyes. "Hello, Bob."

"You went stiff for a moment."

I allowed my smile to go naughty and rubbed up against him. "I'm not the only thing that's stiff."

"Cheeky," he grinned, dipping his head down for another taste of my lips. The feel of his warm skin touching mine, the taste of him, of his body pressing mine down into the mattress, reaffirmed the knowledge that this was right, that this was meant to be. His presence banished the nightmare that almost was. A tiny spark of guilt flared to life with the thought that I should not be celebrating life with Raphael while another was suffering, but the honest part of my mind stomped out the guilt with the acceptance that some things were beyond my control.

I sucked on Raphael's tongue as he checked my teeth, sliding my hands down the muscles of his shoulders to his back.

"You're naked," I said, pausing in our kiss to breathe.

He leaned back and looked down at me, trailing a finger across my collarbone, down the middle of my breastbone, still farther down to my belly, ending with a tickle at the gates of my own personal paradise. "Ah, baby, so are you."

I melted into one big puddle of goo. *Baby*. It wasn't the word, it was the way he said it.

"I was waiting for you. Somehow I thought you would prefer me dressed this way."

He leaned forward to nuzzle his cheek across my breast. The barest hint of stubble added a dimension of tingle that I hadn't felt before. I sucked in a delighted gulp of air.

"You are positively psychic."

"And you're only *just* discovering this?" I laughed, my laughter turning to a gasp as his mouth closed over my nipple. "OK, I like that," I admitted, wondering why my voice was an octave higher than normal.

207

Raphael laved my breast with long strokes of his tongue before he released it. "So do I," he growled, his voice deepening as he bent over my other breast. "Fancy that, a spare."

"Yes," I gasped, trying to get some air into my lungs. It was impossible to breathe while his mouth was on my flesh, so I gave up the notion and just concentrated on what he was doing. "I keep it there for emergencies. You never know when you'll need a spare breast, my mother always said. And she was right. I'm extremely happy at this moment that I had the foresight to bring my spare along with me on this trip."

"And it's in such delicious condition," Raphael said just before his teeth closed gently over my nipple. I purred and arched my back so he could feast on more of it. "Round and firm and fully packed."

"You watch . . . too much . . . television," I panted as he kissed a hot trail across my belly. I had an idea where he was headed, and although I enjoyed the little nips and kisses he was delivering along the way, I figured I'd better stop him before he went too far. "Um, Raphael? You're not going to . . . you don't plan to . . . um . . . *you know,* tongue tango down there, do you?"

He bit my hip, kissing the sting away as he parted my hesitant legs and settled between them. "I certainly am. I take it you don't have any objections?"

His dark head bent down to kiss a hot line up my thigh.

"Well, actually, I do."

He looked up. "You do?"

"Yes," I nodded. "It's nothing personal, but I don't like it. So if we could just skip the appetizer and get on with the main course, that would be fine with me." I reached under the pillow and pulled out the little plastic package. "I brought my own in case you didn't have any."

He frowned at the condom I handed him, then gave it back to me. "What do you mean, you don't like it?"

I made an indefinable shrugging gesture with the condom. "I don't like it, that's what I mean. I've tried it, and I don't like it, and since it can't be all that scenic for you down there, I'm sure you won't mind if we just skip it."

He shook his head, his curls brushing my thighs in a way that made them feel as if they'd been licked by flames. "I do mind. I don't understand how you can say you don't like it when you haven't tried it."

I frowned at him. "I have tried it!"

"Not with me!"

"Well, I don't have to, do I? I mean, it's pretty much the same with anyone, isn't it?"

Now *he* was frowning. "No, it isn't. I happen to be pretty good at this, or so I'm told, so if you'll just stop telling me you won't like it and let me do my job, you'll see for yourself."

I took a deep breath. "Look, do you think you could come up here to discuss this? I feel like I'm talking to my gynecologist with you down there face to face with all my feminine parts. I mean, that's not the very most attractive location on my body, and I'd really rather you not sit there and stare at that part of me."

He looked at the parts in question. I grabbed his head and pulled it up. "Don't LOOK at me there! I just told you not to look there, and now you are!"

He cocked one eyebrow at me and gently disengaged my hands from his head. "I've never before met a woman who had an inferiority complex about her genitals."

"I don't have an inferiority complex," I snapped, fast losing my temper with his insistence to stare at my crotch. He was doing it now, he was eyeing me like he expected Bugs Bunny to pop out and start dancing. "I just don't like people setting up camp at my crotch and admiring the view, OK?"

"Joy."

"What?"

"Lie back and close your eyes."

"No."

"Yes."

"I don't trust you. You'll just take advantage of me and look."

"I'll close my eyes too."

"Promise?"

He sighed, his breath gusting warmly on all of those delightful tingly albeit unscenic parts. "Yes, I promise. Now do as I say. I won't do anything you don't like, all right?"

"I'll hold you to that," I warned, lying down again, tense as a nun in a whorehouse.

He didn't answer me, he just rubbed his cheeks on the inside of my thighs. Just as it did on my breasts, the abrasion was just rough enough to make my skin tingle.

"Do you like the feel of that?" he asked.

"Yes. Do you have your eyes closed?"

"Yes." He rubbed his cheek against my thigh again before kissing a serpentine path upward. "I like it as well. You taste sweet, and your skin is so soft, it's like satin." He kissed the other side, licking and nibbling a path northward. My legs tensed up the closer he came to home base. "Relax, baby. You'll like this, I promise. You're so hot, I know you must be burning up inside."

I clutched large quantities of the blankets as he eased a finger inside me.

"You *are* hot. You're hot and silky and almost ready for me."

"Are you going to narrate this whole thing?" I asked, peering down over my belly at him. "Must we have the annotated version of oral sex?"

He grinned as he placed a kiss very carefully on the exact center of me. "I thought it might be more reassuring for you if you knew how much I was enjoying it, too."

"Oh. OK. That's fine. I was just checking in case there was going to be a quiz later."

He grinned again, his finger withdrawing, only to return with a buddy.

"Oh, my," I gasped, wondering how long a person could go without breathing. The feeling of his fingers stroking me, stretching me, was something I'd never felt before. It was warm and intimate and, coupled with the little kisses he was now pressing upon a very sensitive spot, thoroughly enjoyable.

"Like that, do you?" His fingers slid slowly out, then thrust back in fast. I arched up and came damn close to bursting into the national anthem.

"Ah, baby, we're only getting started. We have so much more to try. Let's see how you like this. . . ."

His head dipped down until he was pressed against the very heat of me, his tongue replacing his fingers as he stroked and teased and sucked the layers of skin aside until he reached the hot spot. "You taste like heaven," he moaned into me, his fingers sliding in and out with an increasing rhythm. His tongue matched the rhythm, making my whole body throb in time to it as he picked up the pace faster and faster, spinning me higher and higher until I was sure there was nowhere else to go, but there was, and he took me there.

"That's it, baby, let yourself go. I'm right here with you."

And he was, too. He was in my heart and my soul, in my blood, in every breath I took, in every thought and every desire. An orgasm so strong it shook me to my core swept through me, starbursts of ecstasy bursting behind my eyelids as I arched up and called his name to the heavens.

When I came back to earth, five or six hours later by my best estimate, he was propped up between my legs with an extremely smug, extremely male smile on his face. One eyebrow rose. "So, you didn't care for that, I take it?"

211

"You," I told him as he crawled up my body and stretched out next to me, "are going to suffer for that comment."

"Is that a promise or a threat?" he asked.

"Both," I told him as I pushed him onto his back and leaned over to kiss him. "Hmmm. Different."

"I like the way you taste," he grinned. "You're hot and sweet and better than an all-day lolly."

I bit the tip of his nose, my hand skimming down the planes of his chest. "I'm sure I will be able to return the compliment."

"I hope you will, but I don't think I can wait for that now." He reached over to the built-in nightstand and tugged open the drawer, pulling out a blue box.

"My treat," I told him, retrieving the condom from where it had slipped under his hip. I gave him a little love bite similar to the one he'd given me, then scooted over and gave in to the desire that had plagued me ever since I saw him naked.

"Tattoooooo," I cooed, licking it. His belly contracted. I smiled one of my special wicked smiles, and lowered my head to suck his sunburst, reveling in the way his breathing quickened as my hair brushed against his erection.

And boy, was it erect. It banged me on the ear. I stopped sucking his tattoo and gave it a good, long, critical look. Up close and personal, so to speak.

"Um," I said.

"Here," he nudged my shoulder with the box. "Would you care to do the honors, or would you prefer I do it?"

I continued my visual exploration. "Um."

"Baby, much as it turns me on to have you staring at me like that, I'm fast approaching the bursting point, and it's starting to get painful."

I gave him one last look, then started to open my condom. "Sorry. I'll just put this on and you can dive right in." I glanced back over at the part in question. "That's assuming you'll *fit.*"

"Joy, use these. Your condom will break if we try to use it."

"Huh?" I read the box that was shoved under my nose. *"L'homme Grande: for the gentleman who requires extra personal space."* I looked back at his penis, trying to measure it with my eyes. "You know, I think maybe we need to talk about this a bit. You seem to be bigger than any other guys I've been with. A lot bigger. I know I said bigger is better, but there is a limit to everything. You don't happen to have a ruler handy, do you?"

Raphael groaned and swore, his eyes tightly shut. "Joy, please, just put the condom on, or let me do it. I honestly don't think I can take much more of this."

I pulled one of his condoms out and tore open the package, then started to unroll it on him. It unrolled and unrolled and unrolled. With each roll of the condom I got more and more worried. Raphael twitched and groaned and muttered prayers to please allow him to survive the experience.

"There, it's on," I said finally. Raphael took a deep breath, then with one smooth move, flipped me over and settled between my legs, propping himself up on his elbows long enough to kiss my wits away.

"Wait a minute!" I yelled as I felt the tip of him start to push into me.

"Now? You want me to wait *now?*" he asked, a touch desperately, I thought.

"Yes, now. There's something I want to say."

"It couldn't wait?" He nudged a bit more into me. "Can't you save it for later? I'd be happy to hear you then. You can tell me anything you want *then.*"

"No! Now!" I squirmed slightly. "You're too big! I'm sorry, Raphael, I hate to do this to you since you're all dressed up and everything, but you're just too big. You have to trust me on this, I know my body, and it's not going to be able to—"

With a groan that sounded like it came straight from his soul, he slid into me.

"Holy Mary and all the saints," I squeaked as he withdrew slightly, then surged forward.

"Ah, baby, you're so tight. So hot and tight."

"Aaaaiiiiiiiiiiiieeeeeeee!" I sang as he sank in even more. His lips teased mine until I let him into my mouth, my hips thrusting up to meet his as he pushed in deeper. "Dear God, is that all of you?"

"Just a little more," he groaned, his breath hot and ragged on my lips as he nipped and teased; then he grabbed both my hips, his tongue sweeping into my mouth as he rammed forward, filling me, completing me, merging our bodies together until we were one entity.

"Baby, I can't last much longer," Raphael moaned into my mouth. "Tell me you're with me. Tell me you're almost there. Ah, Christ, you're so damned tight!"

"Now, love, now." I bit his shoulder and rocked my hips forward and he slammed into me, groaning with each forward thrust. I wrapped my legs around his hips and dragged my fingernails down his back, nipping his neck where his pulse pounded madly. "Come with me now, my love."

He arched back, his fingers digging into my hips as he pulled me upward, slamming into me again and again until I was sure I was going to black out with the wonder of our joined bodies. His head snapped back as he throbbed and pulsated his heat deep into me, his cry of conquest roared to the heavens where it mingled with my sobs of pleasure.

He collapsed onto me, both of us covered in sweat, gasping for air, our hearts beating wildly. This was the man I'd been waiting for, I thought as I pressed gentle kisses into his dark curls. I was made for him as surely as he was made for me. There could be no doubt about that. I stroked his damp back, savoring the feel of my body cushioning his. We fit together so perfectly, it was as if we were two halves of a whole.

"Am I crushing you?" he asked after a little bit, his voice muffled since he spoke into my shoulder.

"Yes," I said, stroking the wonderful curves of his behind. "But it's a good kind of crushing. I like it. I like our bodies squished together like this. It's a good thing I'm so big, though. I think you'd flatten someone tiny like Roxy."

"Let me know when I become too heavy for you," he said indistinctly. "I don't think I have the strength to move, although I do have one question."

"Mmm?" I asked, kissing his salty shoulder.

He propped himself up on one elbow and grinned a slow, lazy grin. "What was it you wanted to say about me being too big?"

"You big oaf," I said in mock anger, and pushed him backward. He moaned as he slid out of me, rolling onto his back, pulling me along with him until I was nestled up against his side. I tickled his belly tattoo, giggling when I made him growl at my touch. He kissed me back into submission, leaving me momentarily while he sat up to peel the condom off.

"Damn," he said, the word enough to make me stop rubbing my legs against his.

"What's wrong?" I sat up to look. He turned to me with a face full of consternation, embarrassment, and just a tinge of "what now?"

"I blew out the end of the condom."

I blinked. "I guess this'll teach me to be careful what I wish for."

Chapter Twelve

Even quiescent, Raphael's dangly parts were an impressive sight. I was amazed anew that he fit into me, but since he had, and we had both enjoyed the fitting process, I wasn't going to complain. I glanced up to see if my moving down on the bed had disturbed him, but he remained on his back, sprawled across the bed, one arm crooked over his head, the other outstretched toward the wall. His chest rose and fell regularly, the belly tattoo reminding me that there were hidden depths to the man who had captured my heart.

"Your owner doesn't snore, but he is most definitely a bed hog," I told his penis, stroking down the soft, velvety length of it with my fingertip. I didn't often spend the night with a man, but the few times I had, I did not find myself sleeping more or less tucked under my bed partner, his arm and a leg pinning me down and keeping me cocooned in his warmth. "It's not a bad way to sleep, mind you," I added, determined to be fair. "I certainly felt safe, protected from marauders or wolves or whatever. Still, there's no denying he's a bed hog. But then, there's so *much* of him, I suppose it's no surprise."

I patted Mr. Happy and pushed him a bit to the side so I could admire the long line of Raphael's legs, stroking the heavy thigh muscle. His skin felt like the softest velvet covering steel. I leaned forward to taste, placing a line of chaste kisses along his inner thigh, pausing when he muttered in his sleep and shifted his leg.

"Oh no you don't," I whispered as he narrowed my working space. I gently eased his leg back to where I wanted it, climbing over him until I was lying on my belly between his thighs, bobbing my feet over my behind as I contemplated the view. "Thigh one, thigh two, or Big Jim and the twins? Ha! Sounds like some sort of X-rated version of Dr. Seuss."

I decided that what worked for me would probably work for him as well, so I nuzzled my mouth against the velvet heat of his thighs, kissing and nibbling my way up his leg until I reached a dead end. Raphael said something unintelligible as he moved again in his sleep, but I kept his legs where I wanted them, smiling with wicked intent at the object facing me. I scooted up until I was sitting on my knees, one hand stroking a path up either leg as I leaned forward and gave him a little encouragement to wake up.

He did. All of him.

"Ah, baby, I thought I was dreaming," he moaned, the muscles in his legs stiffening as I rasped my tongue on the sensitive underside of his no-longer-dangling bit. He lifted his head to watch me as I moved up and down on him, applying as much negative pressure as I thought he could stand. "I *am* dreaming," he croaked, his eyes rolling back in his head as his hips thrust upward at me.

"You're not the only one who's good at this," I told him with no little amount of smugness in my voice.

"Nnnnnnnnnang!" he agreed, his body glistening with a

light sheen of perspiration as I applied myself to making him lose control.

I pointed out later just how dedicated I was to seeing a job done right.

"Very dedicated," he said from the floor of the hallway where he lay in a tangle of blankets, gasping great quantities of air.

I rolled onto my stomach and peered over the end of the bed at him. "How did you end up down there while I'm up here? Didn't we start out at the same spot?"

"Magic," he wheezed, little aftershocks rippling through him. I smiled and would have commented on just what sort of magic he worked on me, but I caught sight of the alarm clock lying on the floor next to him.

"Blast! I've got to go. I promised Roxy I'd have breakfast with her, and then we're going to visit a folk museum some-one recommended, and then we have an appointment to see Christian's dungeons."

Raphael lay with his eyes closed until that last item; then he cracked them open and pinned me back with an amber glare. "Alone?"

I smiled as I stepped carefully over him to grab my clothes. I've always maintained that a little bit of jealousy looks good on a man. "Roxy will be there with me, so stop looking like you're going to do something stupid like forbid me to go, because it won't do you the least bit of good, and we'll only end up arguing, and then we'll make up our ar-gument with more wild, untamed sex, and if we do that, I'll miss the museum. So you just go back to sleep now and get all nice and rested for later on."

"Later on?" His brows pulled together in a frown.

My reply was muffled as I spoke while pulling my dress over my head. "I thought we could get together at the bar before you go to work and Roxy and I meet Christian for dungeon viewing."

"What's wrong with you meeting me here?" he demanded, still frowning. I slipped on my shoes and stepped over him, lowering myself to sit on his stomach.

"Look at you, you're drained as dry as a rag," I said, trailing my fingers across the rippling muscles in his chest, leaning forward to tease the tip of an impudent nipple. His hands were warm as they pushed my skirt up my legs. "If you plan on being the love of my life, you're going to have to build up your strength. We'll work you into a full program of non-stop lovemaking slowly. Today you sleep, tonight you be social with me in public, and later on, after the fair's shut down for the night . . ." I gave him my best leer.

His hands tightened on my thighs as I leaned down to kiss him. He tasted like a sated man, warm and happy and utterly delicious.

"Am I?" he asked, his hands abandoning my legs to wrap around my waist, pulling me down over his chest so he could deepen the kiss. His tongue mated with mine, dancing a seductive dance that made me want to do over again everything we'd just done.

"Boy, you sure do give one hell of a goodbye kiss," I murmured, stroking my fingers through his hair. "Are you what?"

The look he gave me could have steamed open a clam. "The love of your life."

I melted onto him and gave him a kiss that should have said it all, but just in case it didn't, I added, "Yes, I very much think you are."

Smug complacency stole over his face as he let me go. "I like a woman who makes up her mind quickly."

I decided to leave his male ego inflated, and went to gather my things.

"Baby?"

From any other man, that term would rankle, irritating me enough to point out that I was neither an infant nor someone who enjoyed being treated like one, but the way Raphael said the word sparked a fire deep inside me.

"What is it, Bob?"

He rolled onto his side and propped his head up on his hand. "Remember that goodbye kiss when you're with Dante."

I let him see the desire in my eyes. "As if I could forget it?"

The morning was bright after the cloudy night of the evening past, but the wind was still sharp as it whipped leaves into doing somersaults along the ground. Birds squabbled raucously over garbage in the dustbins near the food booths, scattering with hoarse objections when I jogged through them. The lingering acrid smell of burnt canvas and wood hung in the morning air as I passed the Kirlian aura photo booth, but I was pleased to see that new wood had been hammered into the charred, blackened frame of the booth. Evidently, Raphael and his crew had been busy while I slept through the last few hours of the fair. The main tent had been restored to its former state as well, I noticed as I hurried past it, although there were a few tears in the canvas, and some spray-painted words that I thought were best left untranslated. I glanced to my right toward the tent city as I passed beyond the fair, and almost came to a halt at what I saw.

"It's a population explosion!" The half of the meadow given over to the tents was now a solid mass of bodies, tents, vehicles, tables, chairs—and all, at this time of the morning, strangely quiet. I waved at a man sitting cross-legged, wrapped in a blanket as he groggily poured dog food into a bowl for an attentive black dog, and headed out of the camp for the hotel.

An hour later I had washed off the scent of Raphael and our activities, and was dressed in jeans and my fisherman's sweater. Roxy eyed me as I smiled at the waitress, mimed my need for coffee, and sat down at a table next to the window.

"Geez, I though you'd never get here," Roxy said with a sour look. "I know I told you to have fun, but I didn't expect you to have that much fun. I'm surprised to see you can still walk."

I waited until I had ordered breakfast and took a few sips of life-restoring coffee before answering her.

"You know, I'm going to be so glad when you find Mr. Right and I can tease you for a change."

"You're grinning," she accused me, a frown wrinkling her brow. "You should have snapped my head off for that comment, but you didn't, and you're grinning to boot. Oh, Lord, don't tell me you've fallen for more than just his pretty crotch?"

I sipped my coffee and admired the view of the mountains and forest in the distance. "Isn't it lovely here? I like this area."

"Dammit, you have, haven't you? You've gone and fallen in love with him!"

"It's a little brisk this time of year, but sometimes brisk is good. I like the feel of fall in the air."

"Joy, you idiot, don't you know that you're just a fling to him? Holiday romances never last!"

"And the people are so nice here. Don't you think the people are nice here? I think the people are nice."

"Once the festival here is over, he'll be off to Italy with the rest of the fair, and you'll be flying home. Have you even *thought* about the future?"

"I thought the language would be a problem, but you know, it's really not. Everyone speaks German or French."

"You don't know anything about him! You can't just throw yourself on someone you don't know anything about. How can you think about getting serious with a man who keeps secrets from you? Doesn't it bother you in the least that you don't really *know* him?"

"It's a romantic area, too, what with all the history surrounding us."

Roxy tossed her hands up in a gesture of defeat. "I give up. You just go right ahead and head for Heartbreak Hotel. I'll try to pick up the pieces of what's left of your heart after Raphael stomps all over it. I won't say another word about the fact that you're making the greatest mistake of your life."

"Thanks. You're a doll."

"However—"

I groaned and grabbed a roll from the basket, reaching for the butter and preserves.

"—if I was to say something to you, it would probably be to point out that although you've had more experience with physical relationships than I have, you've always had worse taste in men than me."

"Mmmf mmf mmmf mweamfam moo."

"What?"

I swallowed my mouthful of roll. "La la la, I can't hear you."

"Sure you can, you're just too stubborn to admit I'm right. You two deserve each other. Hey! Do you realize that you and Raphael just took the fifth step of Joining?"

"Fifth?" I thought about it. Roxy was right, if the third step was the first passionate kiss we shared, the fourth would have been Raphael revealing his secret to me, only—

"He didn't tell me his secret," I objected. "So the fourth step is void even if we did do the fifth step. Repeatedly. With much enjoyment."

"He told you he *had* a secret! That's almost the same thing as telling you what it was."

"No, it's not."

"Sure it is! Trust me, it counts as the fourth step."

"Regardless, the point is moot. Raphael is not a Dark One."

"My point exactly! You should be thinking through this relationship a bit more before you throw away your whole life for him."

And on it went. Unfortunately, Roxy didn't keep her word, taking periodic opportunities to point out the idiocy of falling in love with a man I knew nothing about. When I reminded her that she'd been perfectly happy for me to bind myself to him when she thought he was a bloodsucking soulless wonder, she waved that point away with the statement that Dark Ones never ran off with another woman while their Beloved was left pregnant and penniless adrift in a strange land.

I had to admit that she had a point, but it didn't dim the strength of my blossoming emotions one bit. They might not be rock solid yet, but I felt strongly that Raphael and I had taken steps down the path to something a bit more serious than a holiday fling. As for the wisdom of falling in love with a man I knew little about . . . well, I squelched that niggling worry with the reminder that everything important, everything that truly mattered about Raphael—his character, his morals, the fact that he wasn't the undead—was already clear to me.

Roxy and I visited the museum, poked around two nearby towns, and returned to the hotel for an afternoon nap.

"The fair's late hours and your insistence on being a tourist are playing merry hell with my beauty sleep," Roxy grumbled an hour and a half later when I woke her.

"You don't have to stay out until two A.M. every night, you know. What did you and Christian do all that time?"

She groaned and rubbed the sleep from her eyes. "He left at about one. I hung out with a group of people from Portugal. Did you know there were Portuguese Goths? There are. They're kind of cute, too. None of them speak English, but we had a good time dancing. I think maybe we should go to Portugal before we go home."

I didn't say anything, just looked out the tiny window to the rooftops of nearby buildings.

"Joyful? I know you'll start 'la la la-ing' again if I bring it up, but have you asked Raphael what his plans are after this weekend?"

I sighed and turned around to face her. "No. It's too soon. We've only just gotten together. I can't be asking him yet if he thinks we should make the effort to stay together or if he doesn't have any room for me in his life."

"Pooh on him—how about you?" Roxy asked, smoothing out the down comforter. "Do you have room in your life for him? Would you leave everything at home for him? Would you travel around with the fair just to be with him?"

I started for the door. "Why do you always ask hard questions?"

"Someone has to. Joy, the fair is due to leave in four days. If this is as serious as you think it is, shouldn't you two be talking about the future beyond a few days of jumping each other's bones?"

I paused at the door for a minute, my hand smoothing over the cool planes of wood. "If you're asking if I've thought of what it would mean to leave everything behind, the answer is, yes, I have. If you're asking will I go through with it—well, that answer depends on Raphael. If you're done grilling me now, I'll see you down in the bar. The gentleman in question said he'd try to drop by for a few minutes before he has to get the security teams in place."

"You're not stupid, Joy," she called out as I closed the door. "If you think he's really different, if he's the one you've been looking for, make him prove it."

Our neighbor across the hall emerged from the shared bathroom, keeping me from bellowing my reply to Roxy. I smiled, murmured politely in my best German, and skipped down the stairs to the bar where I hoped Raphael would be waiting.

He was, but he sat against a wall with three tables pushed together, surrounded by seven fair employees, mostly guys who did all the grunt work around the fair. A large sheet of paper was in the center of the table, and Raphael was marking off areas that I assumed he felt were hot spots. He had told me earlier that the shape of the grounds had altered how they set up the fair, so I gathered he had called a strategy meeting to alert everyone as to how best to handle the swarm of people expected for the next few days.

Arielle sat across from the guys, a glass of untouched beer in front of her. I blew Raphael a kiss when he looked up and smiled at me, then went to sit down with Arielle.

"Good afternoon, Joy," she said in her careful English.

I scooted in the opposite side of the booth and reached across the table to pat her hand. "Hi, Arielle. What's wrong? You look like you've been crying. Are you upset about something? Is something the matter?"

She gave me a pathetic smile. "I look like I have been crying because I *have* been crying. Something is wrong, but I am not upset."

I lifted both eyebrows. "No?"

Her gaze dropped to her hands. "Perhaps just a little."

My heart went out to her. I was sure her sister had ragged on her over her decision to stick with her boyfriend. I looked around the bar to see if Tanya was lurking in a corner. It was dusk, night just beginning to take over the sky, and there was a steady stream of people coming into the bar, but thankfully no Tanya. I assumed that with the huge hordes in the tent city, all of the bars in town would be running at full capacity. A busy bar was no place for Arielle to be doing the unloading she clearly wanted to do. "Listen, if you'd like to have a good cry, you're welcome to use my room. It's not great, but it will give you a little privacy."

"No, I am not going to cry anymore," she said adamantly, giving a defiant little dab to her nose. "Paal said it is not necessary to cry since all will resolve well." She gave a big sniff and sent an adoring glance over to a prematurely balding Viking sitting at the end of Raphael's table. Paal gave her a little nod and turned his attention back to the orders Raphael was snapping out. "It is Tanya, you know? Dominic had an argue with her last night, a big argue. Much of it was about you, but once they were finished, Dominic said it was that Tanya was no longer compatible with him, and she must leave since she caused very much trouble last night."

"Trouble? You mean trouble other than the scene when I read the runes?"

Arielle nodded. "Yes. Dominic was very angry with her, and Milos said she was a *responsabilité* to the fair and that she must leave."

"*Responsabilité?* Oh, you mean she was a liability? Because she's angry over the way Dominic has been treating her? I have to say that although there's no love lost between Tanya and me, I'm in agreement with her on that issue. Dominic is a classic example of the love-'em-and-leave-'em type who should be beaten soundly by their own egos."

"No, it is not because of their affair which has ended so sadly, but of the other that Milos is so angry about."

I sat back against the high settle. "Wait a minute, you've lost me. What does Milos have to do with the history between Dominic and Tanya?"

"Milos owns the fair with Dominic, yes?"

I nodded.

"Dominic is for the customers, the . . . mmm . . . ring-leader?"

"Ringmaster? That's a circus term, but I think I know what you mean. He's the flashy bit of show for all the people

226

attending the fair, while Milos is the silent partner?"

"No, he is not silent, he speaks many languages quite well, better than me. But he is the businessman. He finds the bands and makes the arrangements for where we will stop. He is the one who pays us."

"Ah, he's the moneybags. Gotcha. So what did Tanya do that miffed Milos enough to make him angry at her?"

"She threatened to go to the local police with information about violations of the permit granted to the fair," Raphael said as he slid in next to me.

I was distracted for a moment by the warm press of his leg against mine. Raphael was a big man, but even allowing for that fact, he didn't just sit, he dominated whatever environment he was in, making spaces that previously appeared adequate suddenly seem intimate. Was I going to complain about the fact that he took over our side of the booth, squishing me up against him? I was not. I just breathed in that wonderful clean smell that always seemed to cling to him, and made a mental note to buy stock in whatever company produced the soap he used.

"She also threatened to tell the truth about Dominic to the newspapers unless he kept his promise to make her a partner in the fair. That was *after* she accused him of sleeping with you, Roxy, and approximately half the female population of Eastern Europe," Raphael drawled, signaling to the bartender.

"Truth? What sort of truth? The truth that he's not really a vampire? That's hardly worthwhile as blackmail material," I said.

He shrugged. "I don't think that's what she was talking about, but as no one chose to enlighten me as to the truth, I can only speculate what she meant to do."

I mulled that over as I watched Theresa, one of the owner's daughters who doubled as a barmaid, trot over to

Raphael, ogling him despite the fact I was plastered against his side.

"Raphael, how nice to see you again," she cooed, blatantly ignoring Arielle and me. "Will you be free later? There are many things I would like to show you." She licked her lips. I put a possessive hand on his thigh and gave her a squinty-eyed glare to let her know I didn't appreciate poachers. She gave him a look that could have steamed drapes. "Many sights around the town, of course."

Oh, right. Let's have a show of hands for those of you who believed it was sightseeing she had on her mind.

"Thank you, I'm going to be busy later," Raphael said gently.

Theresa pouted as Raphael placed our orders, curling the fingers of his hand into my hair and teasing the back of my neck. "And you thought *I* was acting territorial," he said quietly.

"You don't mind if I rubber stamp TAKEN on your forehead, do you?" I asked, pleasure shivering down my back at his touch.

He grinned in response. "Only if you promise to wear a robe and veil in return."

I slid my hand up his thigh a little just to let him know what effect he was having on me. When I turned back to Arielle, she was smiling at us delightedly, a definite twinkle in her eye.

"Don't you dare say what you want to say," I warned her, laughing as she suddenly looked chagrined. "You're as bad as Roxy."

Her smile returned. "It is just that I am so very happy to see you happy. Both of you. It is good to find someone you are matched with, yes?"

"Mmm." I turned back to Raphael. "So what happened after Tanya threatened Dominic? Milos told her to pack up her stuff and go?"

"More or less." He tossed a few coins to Theresa as she brought our beers. She sloshed some of mine onto the table in front of me, but other than giving her another glare, I didn't say anything.

"Getting information from you is like pulling teeth," I complained, mopping up my spilled beer. "By the way, are you intending to drink that one or dump it in a plant when you think no one is watching?"

He looked startled for a moment before his eyes went to a dark amber.

"That first night," I explained. "I saw you spill your beer in the plant. It was one of the reasons Roxy believed you were a"—I glanced at Arielle and gave her a toothy smile—"it's one of the reasons we thought you were someone else."

"I plan to drink this one," he said, his eyes muted. "This is a lager. The other was a dark ale and too strong."

"Too strong?"

"I don't like to drink much before the fair opens. That night the bartender was bragging to me about the strength of his local brew; I didn't want to hurt his feelings if I didn't drink it."

I gave his thigh a little squeeze to show my appreciation for his thoughtfulness toward others, and then another one just because I liked to squeeze his thigh. I was rewarded when he shifted restlessly. It didn't take a rocket scientist to figure out that my hand so near Happyland was having a predictable effect. I resisted the urge to torment him further and withdrew my hand.

"It was a very bad time last night," Arielle broke into my smutty thoughts. "I was present as well, and there is nothing to tell other than Tanya was most angry at Dominic, and when Milos told her she must leave the fair after the festival, she cried and returned to our trailer." Her gaze dropped at those last words, tears puddling up in her pretty blue eyes. "I did not go to her as I should. Paal had arranged—that is,

I was to be with Paal that evening, and I did not go back to the trailer until much later. And now she is gone!"

"Gone?" I asked, looking between her and Raphael. "She's left the fair already?"

"No," Arielle said before Raphael could answer. "Her things are still in the trailer, but she has not been seen for many hours."

I looked at Raphael.

"I think she's probably gone somewhere to lick her wounds," he answered my unasked question. "If she doesn't return by later tonight, Arielle can contact the police."

Arielle's lip quivered at the last word.

"Arielle can contact them? You're the security guy—don't you think you should do that?"

He looked away. "No. It's better if she does it."

Better for whom? I wondered. Why was Raphael so reticent to talk to the police? I was sure it had something to do with his secret. The idea of him doing something wrong, seriously wrong, was unthinkable, so I quickly cobbled together another explanation. Maybe the charges against him were false, accusing him of some illegal crime that he didn't do, but which resulted in him being on the run from the police. That would explain his desire to hide out with a small fair that never stayed in one location for any length of time. A sniff from Arielle had me leaving that avenue of thought and returning to her problem.

"You don't think . . ." I hesitated to bring it up in front of her, but I didn't like the sound of Tanya disappearing without taking her things. I pinched Raphael's thigh until he looked at me. "You don't think something could have happened to her, do you? What with the recent event in Heidelberg?"

His eyes glittered brightly, a sign he understood my unspoken question.

"Doubtful," he said with a glance to Arielle, his hand tightening on mine. Beneath both our hands his leg was tense. Clearly he was more concerned about Tanya than he was willing to let on.

"Heidelberg?" she asked. Her eyes widened in distress as she understood what I had meant. "You mean Tanya could be like that poor woman—"

"No, of course not. I'm sure she's just off somewhere pouting," I reassured her as I patted her hand again. "I'm willing to bet she's holed up with someone in the tent city. There must be at least three hundred people there now. She'll turn up tonight, you'll see. The murder in Heidelberg was just an isolated incident, one that has nothing to do with the fair. I'm sorry I mentioned it."

I looked to Raphael for support, but surprisingly, he said nothing.

"I hope you are right," Arielle said with another quick glance at her balding Viking as he sat laughing with the group of workers from the fair.

Roxy walked into the bar, waved at us, and turned to call back through the door. Raphael stiffened as Christian followed her.

"There they are. Do we have time for a beer? Hi, Raphael. You look surprisingly rested considering Joy's lustful appetites." Roxy stopped teasing as soon as she caught sight of Arielle's face. She scooted in beside her and shot me an accusatory glare. "Arielle, what's wrong? You look like you've been crying!"

"Don't look at us, *we* didn't do anything to her," I said before turning to Christian and greeting him. He pulled up a chair and sat at the end of the table, nodding to Raphael. Raphael nodded back. In a smooth Mr. Casual move that men have practiced for eons, he dropped his arm over my shoulders and hauled me even closer to his side.

Christian's eyebrows rose at the blatant show of possession.

"Subtlety is his forte," I told him.

"Would you like me to go find that veil now?" Raphael growled. I pinched his thigh.

"Oh my God," Roxy said, having got the full story from Arielle. "They're firing Tanya? Wow. Bad karma. Guess that qualifies as another one of Joy's disasters, huh?"

"No, it does not."

"Sure it does. It's right up there with that poor couple's house you washed into the ocean."

"I didn't wash their house into the ocean—the storm did!"

"Same difference."

I bit back the retort, refusing to argue with her in front of everyone. Roxy reassured Arielle that Tanya was sure to show up soon. "Bad pennies and all that," she said sagely. Luckily, Arielle didn't understand the reference.

A half hour later we headed out to our respective destinations: Roxy, Christian, and I to his castle to see the dungeons and have the grand tour, and the fair folk back to the meadow to get ready for the crowds. Raphael held the door open for me as I left the hotel, walking beside me with his hand resting possessively on my lower back as he escorted us to the parking area.

"You could place a tag in her ear and a radio collar around her neck," Christian suggested from behind us. "It might keep you from wondering where she is."

Raphael's hand tightened on my back. "But not who she's with," he snapped in return.

"Boys, if you insist on having that pissing contest, please do it downwind," I said in my best mom voice, glaring at Raphael. He glared at me in return, then suddenly pulled me close in an extremely hard, dominating kiss. His mouth was hot and demanding as his tongue got all pushy with mine, ordering it around and generally behaving as if it owned the place. I thought about asking Raphael and his tongue where they got off, then admitted to the shameful secret that I loved it when his body got bossy with me. I sighed into his mouth and allowed him to plunder at will.

"If that's how he kisses goodbye, you have to wonder how he—"

"That's enough!" I tore my mouth from the heat of Raphael's and glared at Roxy sitting in the front seat of Christian's car. She grinned back.

"I see what you mean about subtlety being one of his virtues," Christian said with just a hint of terseness in his voice. "If you're quite finished . . ." He held the rear door open for me.

Raphael gave me a look that told me to behave myself. I gave him one that informed him I always behaved myself, and that he'd better not be finding any excuses to go back to the hotel to have another beer, at least not while that man-stealing hussy Theresa was on duty, lest he find a certain portion of his anatomy severed away with a dull butter knife and two rusted spoons.

He rolled his eyes.

Drahanská's dungeon was not what I'd expected. I figured old castle dungeons were bound to be dank, dark with memories of suffering and horror, rotting torture devices lying broken and forgotten in a corner, the air tainted with the whisper of rats scurrying off into the shadows. Christian, I was just coming to realize, was a man of many surprises, and his dungeon followed true to form. The steps leading down to the lowest level of the castle were cut out of stone, but lit by electric lights on the wall. As we reached the bottom of the stairs, I braced myself for dirt and rats.

Christian flipped a switch. I stared in complete surprise as a line of lights recessed into the low stone ceiling hummed to life, illuminating a long row of marble statues, each on a matching marble pedestal.

"Statues?" Roxy asked, pushing past me to stare at the nearest statue. "You keep *statues* in your dungeon?"

"Can you think of a better place for them?" Christian asked, moving past her to turn on a spotlight for the statue she was looking at.

"They're beautiful," I said, gently touching the stone leg of a partially nude woman. They truly were stunning works of art. Museum quality, I was guessing. The lines of the woman's face were delicately rendered with exquisite detail, almost as realistic as the sweep of material sliding off her shoulders. I couldn't help but draw my fingers down the stone folds, marveling at the talent of the sculptor.

"Where are all the torture devices? Where's your rack?" Roxy asked, disappointment rife in her voice as she wandered down the line of statues.

"That is Venus," Christian told me as he flipped the light on for the figure I stood before. His voice was as smooth as the polished stone under my fingers.

"I've never seen anything like it," I said.

He stood next to me, his eyes soft with satisfaction as he looked at the statue. The woman was reclining back against a column, a seductive look on her face as she toyed with the folds of the material partially covering her. "I have one or two Italian pieces here, but the rest are patron saints of the Czech Republic."

"Where are your walls stained with the blood of thousands of men tortured over the centuries? Where are your skeletons hanging from a cage? I thought for sure there were going to be skeletons!" Roxy's plaintive voice echoed down the long room.

"She is beautiful, is she not?" Christian stroked a finger down the woman's exposed calf, ending where my hand rested on a delicately arched foot. His fingers touched mine briefly, but I knew it was no casual touch.

I withdrew my hand. "Yes, very beautiful."

"She is five hundred years old." He cocked his head and looked at me. Under the spotlight, his eyes were black and unfathomable. "I believe that you and she share a timeless quality in your beauty."

"Where are your rusty swords and shackles and cat o' nine tails? Isn't that standard equipment in a dungeon? I'm sure it is."

"Christian—" I hesitated telling him to lay off his advances to me. I felt bad enough about him without being rude to the man in his own home, but I didn't want him to think he could continue.

"You have chosen," he said calmly, his face a mask, his eyes intense and unreadable.

"Yes, I have, and I'm sorry if that hurts you in any way, but I think if you see that you really aren't interested in me, you're just into some macho game trying to one-up Raphael, you'll realize how silly this all is."

"You do not believe that you are the one meant for me."

"I know I'm not," I said gently, trying to edge away.

"You are wrong," he said simply. "Since you do not believe me, I will have to prove it to you."

"Now, wait," I protested, getting a bit worried over the stark look around his eyes. "There's no reason to prove anything—"

Blackness opened at my feet as I balanced on the edge, consumed with hunger, blasted with the hot breath of anguish so strong it stripped the air from my lungs. Memories of dark, endless, solitary nights, one after the other spanning centuries, filled my mind as unceasing despair shredded my soul until there was nothing left but the memory of a life beyond this nightmare. In the middle of the torment was a tiny flame of hope, of the salvation that one person could bring, the return of life, of an end to the eternal loneliness . . . and the long-hoped-for promise of love.

I backed away from the blackness, backed away from Christian until the icy cold of marble met my back. I stared at him, shaking my head as he watched me, unable to understand everything he was pouring into my mind.

"No," I whispered, clutching the statue and slowly working my way around it, wanting only to put distance between Christian and me. "Not you. It can't be you."

Roxy called out something from beyond the statues, but her words did not reach me. There was only Christian's beautiful voice and desperate eyes. He moved slowly toward me, using his voice to calm me. "Beloved, do not run from me. I will not harm you."

"No," I said, unable to take my eyes from him, unwilling to believe the evidence before me. I backed up another couple of steps. "How could you do this to me? I thought you were my friend—how could you do this?"

He took a step toward me, his hands held out with the palms up, as if to show he meant me no harm. "I did not intend that you should suffer, Beloved. I was not aware you had found me, I could not know you were able to read my thoughts so easily. Once I saw you, once I realized you were in distress, I blocked my mind from yours."

"Not entirely," I said, rubbing my arms and shivering with the chill that seemed to permeate me with the memory of his intimate visits. Something cold pressed into my backside as I continued to back away from him. I scooted around the statue. "You . . . *touched* me."

He took another step forward. "It is my right. You are my Beloved."

"It is *not* your right," I corrected him, clinging to the statue for support as I moved past it. "I am not your Beloved. I love Raphael, not you. Nothing you say is going to change that fact."

He waved away my objections as he glided forward another step. I let go of the statue and reached behind me to feel where the next one was. "The love you think you feel for him is an illusion," he said. "Your mind does not wish to accept your fate, and so it creates a means of escape for you. Once we have taken the fifth step of the Joining, you will realize the truth of your emotions."

"Joy? Christian? What are you guys doing over there?"

"You betrayed me. I looked to you for help, I thought you were my friend, and you betrayed me." The cold, sightless eyes of a long-dead saint peered down on me in sorrow as I moved past him.

"Hey, guys? What's going on?" Roxy's voice grew louder as she approached.

Christian suddenly lunged at me, catching me off guard, wrapping me in an embrace of inflexible intent.

"GUYS?"

"Don't do this," I pleaded with Christian. "You're wrong, I know you're wrong, I feel it in my bones. We were not meant to be together. Somehow, somewhere, something got screwed up. I'm not the woman you need."

"Joy?" Roxy appeared at my side, but Christian never spared her a glance. I was afraid to take my eyes from him, sure that if I did so, his control would snap.

"I have lived almost nine hundred years," he said quietly, his arms like steel around me. I heard Roxy gasp, but she said nothing. "I have seen countless Dark Ones give themselves over to the monster that lives within because they could no longer wait to find their Beloved. There has never been a case where a Dark One has chosen the wrong woman. It is impossible."

"Nothing is impossible," I whispered, allowing my weight to rest against his arms. "'There are more things in heaven and Earth'—Shakespeare knew that, and I know it as well. I wish I could ease your pain, but the simple truth is that I cannot be your Beloved. I love Raphael. I *need* Raphael. I want him, and only him. He is my other half. If you try to make me into something I'm not, you will only destroy us both. Do you want that, Christian? Do you want to destroy me?"

His eyes closed for a moment, but, held so close to him, I could feel the wave of pain wash over him even though he kept his mind blocked from mine. I realized at that moment that he wasn't fooling himself; he truly believed I was his Beloved, the woman who would redeem him and give his life meaning.

And with that knowledge I became very, very afraid.

"I'm not quite sure what's going on here," Roxy said, her eyes huge as she looked between the two of us. "But whatever it is, it's starting to give me the creeps, and Joy doesn't look any too happy either, so maybe we'd better give the rest of the tour a skip, huh?"

"I will not hurt you," Christian said, his voice slipping around me to whisper velvet-soft against my skin. "I will never hurt you, of that I swear."

"Thank you," I said, meaning it. I had a nasty suspicion that unless I could convince him that I was not his soul mate, I'd be called on to hold that promise up as my own salvation.

His eyes searched mine for another second before he released me from his iron hold. I started to breathe again, surprised to realize that I'd been holding my breath. Christian took a step back, then made a slight bow in Roxy's direction. "You are in possession of a truth that very few people have known over the centuries. I hope you will not abuse my trust in your discretion."

"Oh, no," Roxy assured him. Her face was pale, her eyes wary as he took her chin in his hand and stared into her eyes. "Honest, Christian. I would never tell anyone your secret."

He looked at her a bit longer, then released her chin and swept his hand toward the stairs in an elegant gesture. "As neither of you wish to see any more of the dungeon, we can return to the upper floors and continue the tour."

I wanted nothing more than to get the hell out of there

and throw myself into Raphael's arms, but the memory of Christian's anguish was strong. I gave Roxy a feeble smile in answer to her questioning look as I shook off the clinging sense of nightmare, heading up the stairs toward the bright glow of reality.

Chapter Thirteen

"So, what does it feel like when you're drinking someone's blood?" Roxy asked.

Christian glanced in the rearview mirror and gave me such a woebegone look I couldn't help laughing. It was the first time I'd laughed all evening, and it felt a bit stiff and unsure in his presence, but I gave myself full marks for being able to laugh with a man who I'd just discovered had a lifespan that could be ticked off in centuries rather than decades.

"Do blood clots get stuck in your teeth? What if someone's anemic; are you hungry again an hour later? Has anyone ever bitten you? If you run out of blood, do you shrivel up like a really old orange?"

"Roxy!"

"OK, here's an easy one. How come you can eat and drink when other Dark Ones can't?"

"What makes you think I can?" Christian asked, his eyes on the dark road ahead.

"We saw you!"

He glanced at her.

"At the hotel," Roxy added. "You had dinner with us, remember? And you were in the bar earlier. We saw you drinking then . . . didn't we?"

His eyes met mine in the mirror.

"With your sleight-of-hand abilities, you ought to be the one giving the magic show, not Dominic," I said.

He smiled.

Roxy finally figured it out. "Well, that's just not fair! If I'd realized you were only putting on a show, I'd have known right away who you were. OK, on to the next question—"

"I have no idea if you can do any of those handy mind-control things that the heroes in your books do, Christian, but if you can, I'd appreciate it if you gave Roxy the mental command to shut up."

He laughed.

"Can I help it if I have a bunch of questions?" Roxy asked with an infuriated look back at me. "This is a once-in-a-lifetime situation here and I'm not going to waste it! Besides, you got to ask all the questions when we were seeing the castle; now it's my turn."

"Questions about the origin of the Conspirators' Gallery are not *quite* as offensive as asking someone what they pick out of their teeth. Stop being so rude."

"You don't mind me asking you personal questions, do you?" she asked him.

Christian gave her a look that said yes, he did mind, but she ignored it. "See? He doesn't mind. Now, about this eternal damnation you suffer—"

"Oh, for God's sake—Roxy, lay off him!" She turned around in the seat to level me another glare before turning back to pout out the window, but both glare and pout left me unfazed. I watched the back of Christian's head as we drove the few miles back to the hotel. It was difficult reconciling the friendly, amusing Christian I'd grown to like with the tormented immortal who viewed me as his only means to salvation.

And it left me feeling guiltier than ever.

I leaned back against the soft leather seat and closed my eyes, thinking back over all the times his mind had touched mine, trying to adjust my mental picture of him with the emotional one his mind had left me. It was *him* I felt approaching the bar the first night. It was *his* hunger that filled me when he bent to kiss my hand, not Raphael's as he stood watching us. It was *his* desperate need that scared me the night Raphael came to my room. And it was *his* wordless scream of anguish that ripped through the night when I gave myself to Raphael. Christian was wrong about me, I knew he was. But how was I supposed to make him understand that?

I let my body relax into the seat, trying to clear my mind of everything but what I wanted to do, following Miranda's rules regarding meditation. I stretched and reached with my mind.

Christian?

Immediately he was there, his thoughts warm and reassuring. Or they would have been except that I felt anything but reassured with the ease he invaded my head. *Beloved? You call to me?*

Oh, no! What had I done? What if only his Beloved was supposed to be able to communicate with him mentally? My mind scurried around trying to remember what I had read from Christian's books about mental communication between a Beloved and her Dark One. What if only a Beloved was supposed to be able to communicate mentally with him? I thought I remembered reading he could talk to others that way, but what if I was wrong? My hash was really fried if that was so. I resisted the temptation to see if he was looking at me in the mirror, deciding that as of that moment, all mental communication with Christian was verboten.

"I'm sorry, I didn't mean to disturb you just then. I wanted you to know how bad I feel about how things have turned out. I know you don't believe me yet, but I'm going to prove to you somehow that I'm not the one who can save you. Better than that, I promise to help you find her. I don't want you to suffer anymore, Christian, I truly don't."

His eyes glittered blackly in the mirror. "It is, perhaps, a subject we can discuss more fully at another time."

I shook my head. "No, it isn't. You don't have to worry about Roxy, she won't repeat anything. I told her what happened in your dungeon. She understands."

He glanced at Roxy. She just smiled at him.

"Not that I have a lot left to say. I think I've pretty much said it all."

"I, however, have not said all," he replied mildly, and turned his eyes back to the road.

Glaring at his head helped a bit; so did a stringent round of mentally calling him every variation of the terms *pigheaded* and *obstinate*. For a while. By the time he dropped us off at the hotel, I was resigned to the fact that I would have to redouble my efforts to make him understand that I was not what he wanted me to be.

"Are we going to brave the crowds?" Roxy asked as we stood in the parking area of the hotel, looking at the meadow below.

"Do you have to ask?" I turned to smile at Christian. "You're welcome to join us if you've got nothing else to do. That is, if you don't mind being around a bunch of people. If we don't bother you, I mean. Having all the people . . . around . . . you . . ." My words trailed off under the knowing look he gave me, my cheeks heating up with embarrassment over what I couldn't put into words.

"She means if you've fed," Roxy chirped. "I don't suppose you'd let me watch—" He transferred his look to her. "No. You're right. It's a bad idea."

"If you will allow me, I believe I will join you later at the fair."

"Sure thing," I said brightly, trying not to acknowledge that he was off to prey on some unsuspecting victim. "Later. We'll be there. Somewhere."

"*Bon appétit*," Roxy said.

I grabbed her by the arm and hustled her down the grassy hill toward the fair. "For God's sake, Roxy, you don't tell a Dark One *bon appétit*! That's utterly tactless!"

"Why?" she asked, stumbling over a clod of dirt. "I want him to have a good meal. What if he picked someone who was born in an off year? Or someone with a blood disease? You may not have any plans for him later, but I do, so I'd like him to be in a good mood. I want to hear all about the stuff he hasn't written yet, all the dirt on the Dark Ones. And he promised me it was my turn next with the thumbscrews in the dungeon room."

I looked back over my shoulder as we reached the bottom of the hill. Christian was silhouetted against the glow from the hotel, the wind setting his long coat flapping around his legs as he stood frozen, watching us.

"Raphael can't be done soon enough for me. I sure hope nothing goes wrong at the fair tonight," I muttered under my breath.

Roxy heard me. "What could go wrong tonight? You're not reading any rune stones tonight, so the world ought to be safe from any of the disasters, catastrophes, and general acts of God that follow when you do."

There are times when Roxy isn't particularly prescient.

I found Raphael by one of the two tents that served pre-packaged food and hot beverages. Although the fair was not licensed to serve alcohol, many customers brought their own in. With the crowds gathering for the big festival a few days away, Raphael was particularly hard-pressed to weed out those who had overindulged and were making a nuisance of themselves. He was escorting two women and a tall, skinny young man off the fairgrounds, telling them they could come back later after they'd sobered up.

"From the way they're staggering—not to mention the bits of song interspersed in their condemnation of your actions— I'm betting they sleep it off rather than return later."

"That's the general idea." Raphael smiled as he turned to face me. There were lines of stress alongside his mouth, and his beautiful eyes looked troubled and distracted. I squelched my plans to tease him into a frenzy of lustful thoughts, and tried instead to smooth away the frown that creased his forehead.

"Not going well tonight?"

"No worse than what we expected." He caught my hand and pressed a warm kiss to my palm. "How did your evening with Dante go?"

I swallowed back the horrible memory of Christian's torment. "OK. I'll tell you about it later." Much later. Say, five or six years later.

A burst of static and unintelligible garble came from the radio clipped to his belt. He seemed to understand it, however, because he barked a command into the radio, and grabbed me as he started back toward the fair proper.

"Here. You take this." He pulled his trailer key out of his pocket and shoved it in my hand. "I'll be there as soon after closing as I can. Rico needs help with a fight near the main tent. Stay away from that area until we can clear it out."

"No problem. Don't worry about me. I'll go find Arielle and see how she's doing."

He started off at a trot toward the big tent, then changed his mind and pulled me into a quick, hard kiss. "Have I told you how wonderful you are today?" he growled into my mouth.

"No, but I'm willing to entertain your apologies later for so gross a negligence." I nipped his chin and felt a glow of happiness inside me at the heated look he sent before turning back toward the main tent.

"Be careful," I couldn't help but calling out.

He raised his hand in acknowledgment, and muscled his way through the thickening crowds.

Arielle was near the end of her rope.

"Joy!" she shouted as I wandered by her tent, pleased to see the huge line of people waiting to have their palms read. She stood up, excused herself to the startled client, and dashed after me, clutching my hands in hers when she reached me. "Oh, Joy, I am so happy to see you. I have sent Roxy to find you—please, you must help me. I am in a situation most desperate."

I smiled and gave her hands a little shake. "Of course I'll help you. What do you need?"

She started dragging me back toward her booth where the line of people—steadily growing with the increasing crowd—were beginning to look a bit disgruntled. "Tanya will not read. She came back earlier and refused Dominic's order to read the tarot cards."

I guessed where this was going. "I'm glad she's back safe and sound, although I'm sorry to hear she won't read, but I'm afraid I can't help you. I don't know the first thing about tarot cards—"

"No, no," she said, shaking her head vehemently as she continued dragging me past the line of people waiting. "It is all arranged. I shall read the tarot, and Renee—she is Bastian's wife, you know her? She is very much with child— she will read the palms, but you must read the runes, for Renee is a *bohémienne*, a gypsy, you see, and she does not

246

feel the runes inside her. You will read the runes most successfully, and I shall be very thankful to you."

"But, but—"

"It is all arranged," Arielle repeated, shoving me into her chair. "I will go now to Tanya's booth and read the tarot. Renee is using the tea tent for the palm readings. You give a three-stone reading for 150 koruna or five euros. You may keep the tips, of course. Here are your stones—Roxy brought them from your room. Is that all you need? Yes? Excellent." Arielle clapped her hands and shouted out over the din that a great reader of runes had come halfway across the world to read for them. No one looked particularly impressed by either that news or my appearance in faded jeans and a Bavarian sweater, but no one cried foul either, so I picked up my bag of stones and gave the woman in the chair opposite me a smile.

"You must think of a question you'd like some insight on," I told her in German, praying everyone in line would get tired of waiting and go off to another booth.

Three hours and twenty-four minutes later I wished a young Czech couple good night as I tucked the last few coins into Arielle's cash box, dumped the money from her tip jar into a cloth bag I assumed she used for that purpose and stuck that into the cash box as well, then stood up to stretch my exhausted body. Besides the steady stream of people who wanted to have the runes read for their benefit, I had other visitors too. Dominic swept in dramatically, giving me one of his seductive smiles as he thanked me for helping. I accepted his thanks, ignored his leer, and told him in an undertone to take his act elsewhere unless he wanted me to get up and walk away right that moment. He took one look at the line of people waiting, wrestled my hand away from where I was clutching the table, and made a showy bow over it, kissing my wrist and making sure everyone saw him licking his fangs.

"Ham," I growled.

"*Mon ange,*" he oozed.

Raphael was a much more welcome visitor, but although he stopped by three times, he looked distracted and did nothing more than to ask if everything was all right. Roxy and Christian waved twice as they passed while making the rounds, stopping the second time to drop off a bottle of cold water and a big pretzel.

Even Milos visited, once to express his appreciation for my helping—in a voice so low I almost couldn't hear it— and the second time to clear out the overflowing cash box. By the time I'd read the last rune for the last customer, I was sore and tired from the stress of reading runes for more than fifty people. I pulled out Raphael's key, intending to crash there, but the thought of a long, hot soak in the tub at the hotel sang a siren song to my aching body.

I creaked my way over to where Arielle was still reading tarot cards. "I finished with everyone, so I'm going to call it a night. Have you seen Roxy?"

She shook her head.

"Never mind. How about Raphael?"

"He was here a few minutes ago. He said he was checking on a problem someone had reported, but he would be back directly after that."

"Ah. Well, if you see him again, would you tell him I've gone to have a bath, but I'll be back?"

She nodded, her eyes warm with thanks. I left the cash box with her and did the salmon-spawning-upstream thing again through the crowds until I reached the edge of the fair. The noise from behind me indicated the first band was about to play, which accounted for most of the people heading in that direction. I stepped over the usual signs of people having fun—a puddle of vomit, empty wine bottles, discarded condom wrappers, and miscellaneous trash blowing across the crushed grass—and headed away from the noise and lights to the relative calmness of the outer fringes.

Voices raised loud in song made me pause as I was about to take my usual path past the tent city. Eight or nine people were dancing in various stages of undress around a burn barrel, clearly members of the intoxicated group Raphael had ushered out earlier. Rather than risk attracting their notice, I cut sharply to the left, huffed and puffed my way up a steep hill made slippery with pine needles, and plunged into a small stand of fir trees at the far end of the hotel's property. It was a dark, close area that smelled heavenly, but gave me goose bumps with its isolated location. After the experience in Christian's dungeon, I wanted the security of lights and people around me.

As I rounded a large pine tree, I stopped. Ahead of me someone was hunkered over between two trees at the fringe of the stand. Probably just a solitary drunken Goth ralphing up too much cheap wine, I told myself. But as I quietly tried to edge my way around him, I could see that the person wasn't a Goth, wasn't ralphing up anything, and wasn't alone.

The figure silhouetted against the distant hotel was large, muscular, and extremely familiar to me. But what held my gaze, and what kept me from calling out in delight, was the person at his feet.

Even in the almost dark I recognized the crimson hair that spread like a stain from her head.

If Raphael had been attempting CPR, or trying to slap Tanya awake, or even talking to her, I'd have run forward to help him, but the silence he maintained, the economical but efficient movements as he searched Tanya, kept me frozen behind the tree that partially hid me from his view. Raphael plucked something from the ground near Tanya, examined it for a moment, then tucked it in his pocket and looked out into the night, his head turning slowly as he made a scan of the area. I ducked back behind the tree, my heart pounding madly, unsure why I was hiding from him, but doing it nonetheless. When I peeked out a moment later, he was gone.

Tanya wasn't, however.

"Please just let her be sleeping. Or unconscious. Or playing possum. Or in a drugged stupor. Please oh please oh please don't let her be . . ." I couldn't even say the word, which was stupid because I knew full well she was dead. Raphael's body language screamed it, Tanya's still form screamed it, and every hair on my head that stood on end as I'd watched him looking her over screamed it.

She was dead. She lay on her side, curled up into a ball, resting on a pine-needle mattress with her hair streaming out around her like a red halo. Her eyes were closed. I didn't see any sign that she was breathing, but figured I'd better check to make sure she wasn't gravely wounded instead of dead.

I leaned forward to look at Tanya, felt a warning tickle high up in my nose, and threw myself backward, pulling out a handful of tissues from my pocket as I did so. I sat back on my heels a moment later, praying there wasn't any bad karma to be had from sneezing on a possibly dead person. She sure looked dead. I swallowed back a lump of revulsion before I reached out with a hand that shook more than I was willing to acknowledge, pushing back the collar of her jacket and touching one fingertip to her chin. It felt warmish.

"Pulse, you idiot—you can't tell anything from a person's chin. Check for a pulse," I lectured myself. I scooted forward until I was leaning over her, moving her head gently to the side so I could find her pulse point.

My hand froze.

A scream tore through the heavy night air, startling the birds nesting in the trees around me. I ignored the screaming, unable to take my eyes from the horrible sight, unable to believe I was seeing what was in front of me. A distant part of my mind wished that whoever was screaming would shut up so I could think in peace, but the rest of my mind, the part that was staring at Tanya's neck, was too stunned to do any thinking at all.

A dark form swooped out of the blackness and grabbed me, slamming me up against a brick wall of warmth and comfort, mercifully silencing the screamer. "Hush, baby. You're all right, I'm here now."

I shuddered into the warmth that called to me, clinging desperately to Raphael, pressing against him in an attempt to block out the horror of the thing behind me. "It's Tanya," I shivered into his neck.

"I know, baby."

"She's dead."

"I know."

The horrible image of her neck torn open, the blood drained from her filled my mind. I tried to wedge myself in tighter to Raphael. "I know who killed her," I whispered.

His arms tightened around me as he pressed his lips against my temple. "So do I, baby. So do I."

Chapter Fourteen

"It isn't you," I told Raphael as soon as I could pull myself from him.

"What isn't me?" he asked as he peered around us.

"The person who killed Tanya."

He slowly turned to look at me. "I'm delighted to hear you don't think I have a murderous nature."

"I didn't say that. I think you probably could kill someone if you had a reason to, but I happen to know you didn't kill Tanya."

He strode the few steps over to me, grabbing both my arms and staring intently into my eyes. "How do you know that? What did you see?"

"I didn't see who killed her, if that's what you're asking."

He sighed with relief and let go of my arms, continuing to scour the immediate area.

"But I saw her neck. I know who was the only one who could have killed her. With all the . . . *damage* that was done, and the fact that there's not a drop of blood to be seen, the only one who could have killed her is a . . ."

"Vampire?" he asked, squatting down to examine something on the ground.

I nodded, realized he wasn't looking at me, and added, "Yes. I know you don't believe in them—God knows I didn't before I came here and had my mind invaded—but even you have to admit that her death looks like just what you'd expect from a vampire."

"Yes, it is," he agreed as he examined the ground around the tree. I had no idea what he expected to find, since the soft bed of pine needles wasn't conducive to footprints or other helpful clues, but still he looked.

And suddenly that struck me as odd. "What exactly are you doing?"

He ignored my question, tapping his finger on his chin for a moment before marching over to put both hands on my shoulders, his eyes alight with concern and worry. "I know it's asking a lot of you, but could you stay here by yourself for a few minutes until the police arrive?"

I blinked at him. "The police?"

He nodded. "They should be here shortly."

"You called them?"

"Of course. I know it won't be pleasant for you to stay here by yourself, but I have to leave before the police get here. I . . . er . . . I have to let Dominic know what's going on." The words were stiff and halting. "You won't be in any danger; I will only be a few minutes."

I stared at him for a moment, then glanced over at Tanya's body. I didn't really want to be alone with her, but it was clearer than ever that Raphael wanted to avoid contact with the police. While I didn't think running from a problem was the answer, now was not the time to give him a lecture about facing up to his past. Or whatever it was that was bothering him. "OK. I'll stay."

He looked a bit surprised by my easy acquiescence. "You don't mind? You won't be frightened?"

I shook my head. "No. Tanya isn't going to do me any harm, and certainly her killer won't." After all, he'd sworn earlier that evening that he'd never hurt me. "Go ahead. I'll wait here for the police."

Raphael opened his mouth to say something, closed it, then opened it again with a little shake of his head. "You and I are going to have a very long talk just as soon as I can manage it."

"Good," I said, wrapping my arms around his waist and giving him a hug. "I have a lot of questions I'd like answered."

He shook his head again, told me what to tell the police when they arrived, and strode off into the night.

As I watched him walk away, the questions kept running through my mind. What were you doing out here instead of watching over things at the fair? What did you pick up off the ground near Tanya? What are you hiding about your past? And how did you find out about poor Christian?

Poor Christian. The words echoed in my head as I glanced over to Tanya's lifeless body. *Poor Christian* had done that to her. *Poor Christian* had viciously ripped her throat open and drained her dry. I shuddered at the thought of it, sickened by the stark reality of a Dark One's true nature. His feeding on her wasn't romantically erotic as he described it in his books—Tanya's life had been stolen from her in an act of brutal savagery, animalistic in its butchery. My stomach lurched unpleasantly as I recognized the undeniable truth: Christian was extremely dangerous, a killer without remorse.

And he was insanely jealous of the man I loved.

The police arrived before I worked out a solution of what to do about Christian. Black-and-white police cars swarmed the far end of the hotel parking lot, their lights flashing as they formed a semicircle around the area where I stood. I was surprised to see so many police there, figuring Raphael might only have left a warning that there was a body to be found; then I felt guilty for thinking so poorly of him. He might be no stranger to the police, but that didn't mean he would shirk his duty.

An older man with salt-and-pepper hair and a big mustache sauntered over to me. He asked me something in Czech. I shook my head and pointed to Tanya, answering him in German. "Raphael, the man who called you, told me to stay here with her while he went to the fair to let the owners know what is going on."

"Raphael?" the man asked in heavily accented English. He consulted the notepad one of his cohorts pushed in his hand. "Raphael Saint Johan?"

"St. John," I answered. "It's pronounced 'sinjun' actually. He's British, you see."

The man stared at me.

"They do things like that. With their names, I mean."

He stared a little more, then with deliberate movements pulled a pencil from his pocket, licked the end, and made a notation. "I am familiar with the British, madam. I attended Oxford University in my youth."

"Oh. Sorry."

He inclined his head in acceptance of my apology. "I am Inspector Jan Bartos of the Brno police. Your name?"

I told him. He took down the information that I was staying at the hotel, my home address, and what I was doing in the Czech Republic; then warned me that he would check the information against my passport.

"Fine, I have nothing to hide," I said, glancing over my shoulder to see if Raphael had returned. "I was on my way back to the hotel to take a bath when I found Tanya. Raphael ran into me after calling you guys. That's all."

"Tanya? You know the victim?"

"Just slightly. That is, I've met her, and talked to her a couple of times"—if you could call the threats and curses she tossed at me talking—"but I didn't really *know* her. She worked at the fair. I'm just here as a tourist."

He made another note. "You do not work with the fair?"

"No." As soon as I said the word, I felt the need to explain, just in case the police questioned people attending the fair who'd had me read the runes for them. "That is, I don't actually work for them, but I did read rune stones there tonight."

"You read—?"

"Rune stones. They're little stones with runic graphics on them. It's kind of like reading tarot cards, only different. Here, I have my set, I can show you." I pulled the black velvet bag out of my purse and plucked an amethyst stone out. "See? These are amethyst. I was reading these at the fair tonight, but I haven't done it there any other time. Well, except a couple of nights ago, but that was special."

"I see." He didn't look like he understood, he looked like I had a neon light over my head blazing PRIME SUSPECT for everyone to see.

"It was a wager, just a stupid bet my friend had with Tanya."

Inspector Bartos frowned at the tip of his pencil, tucked the pad of paper under his arm, and patted his pockets until he extracted a small black object. Carefully he inserted the tip of the pencil into the sharpener, rotating the pencil with exacting precision. His tongue peeked out of the corner of his mouth as he worked. I had to bite my lip to keep from giggling.

"Now," he said, having finished with the task of sharpening his pencil. I waited for him to lick the sharpened end. He looked like he was going to, then thought better of it. "You will tell me, please, about this wager you had with the victim."

I looked again over my shoulder, hoping to see a large man with beautiful amber eyes charging up the hill from the meadow, but there was nothing but the police swarming the area, roping off a large section around Tanya's body.

"It wasn't *my* wager, it was my friend Roxy's. Roxanne Benner. We're traveling together. Tanya was saying some nasty things about me, so Roxy bet all of her money that I could read runes. It's as simple as that."

"Is it?" he asked, taking notes. It was a weird feeling knowing that everything I was saying was being taken down.

"Yes."

"Tanya lost a great sum of money to your friend, no? She was angry?"

I gave him a wry smile. "Not with Roxy, no. It wasn't really between the two of them, you see, it was because of—" I closed my mouth on the word "me" and swallowed nervously.

"Yes? Who was the cause of the wager?"

"Um. Well, it really wasn't any one person; there were a bunch of us there at the reading."

"I see."

This time I truly did have the feeling he saw. I had no doubt that he could see right through my pitiful blathering to the ugly fact that Tanya hated my guts. The PRIME SUSPECT light overhead suddenly acquired flaming red arrows that pointed directly down at me.

"I will need to speak with you later," Inspector Bartos told me, making a final note before staring up at me with a cool, assessing look in his eyes. "I will be able to find you at the hotel?"

I hoped the darkness was enough to keep the blush that heated my cheeks from being seen. "Um . . . well, there or . . . uh . . . Raphael has a trailer on the far side of the fair. It's the blue one with a giant red hand painted on the side. If I'm not at the hotel, I'll be there."

He pursed his lips and pulled his notebook back out of his pocket. "You do not work for the fair but you read rune stones for them, you are the subject of wagering with members of the fair, and you are"—he flicked an unreadable look at me—"closely acquainted with a fair employee. Is that correct?"

I curled my toes up inside my shoes and wished I were anywhere else but where I was. "Well, it sounds so suspicious when you say it like that, but really, it's all quite innocent."

"You have known Mr. Raphael St. John for how long?"

"Well, maybe *that* isn't quite innocent. That is, it's innocent in that we're not doing anything wrong, but it's not innocent because we are . . . um . . . doing . . . not innocent things. Together. With each other, I mean." I cleared my throat and tried to look like I didn't just admit I was a trollop.

"How long have you been acquainted with Mr. St. John?" the inspector asked again.

My blush cranked up another couple of notches. If it got any hotter, I could fry an egg on my cheek. "About four days," I muttered to my shoes.

"I could not hear you."

"About four days," I said louder, staring at his chin. "Four long days. Very long. Action-packed, you could say."

"I see," he said again.

"Can I go now?"

He nodded and moved aside so he was no longer blocking the path to the parking area.

"No, I'll just go back the way I came," I said, pointing through the trees.

He paused in the act of putting his notebook away and shot me a martyred look as he riffled through the notebook pages until he found the notes he'd just taken. "You stated that you were on your way back to the hotel to take a bath when you found the victim."

"Yes. But I don't want a bath any more. I'd rather—" This time my brain stopped me before I admitted any more damning statements.

"I see," he said, just as I knew he would. "Your passport will be held by the police. You may not leave Bransko until it is returned to you."

I nodded that I understood and sidled around him. I'd just made my escape, giving the police a wide berth, and was starting down the slippery pine-carpeted slope when Inspector Bartos called my name. I stopped and looked back at him.

"Who won the wager?"

"I did," I answered.

"Ah. And what was the victim's response when she lost?"

I stared at him, unable to answer. He nodded his head as if I had, and waved me off. I didn't wait for him to change his mind. I hurried down the hill, and raced for the lights and people of the fair.

"Where's Christian?" I asked Roxy a short time later. She was talking with one of the fair workers who had been drafted into Raphael's security force.

"Mmm? Oh, he left a while ago. Said he didn't want to listen to the bands again. I don't blame him. That Six Inches of Slime guy doesn't sound any better for having had his nose broken."

"Damn. Have you seen Raphael?"

"Nope. Did you see Raphael, Henri?" she asked the slightly overweight man who was nervously watching the crowd.

"He was here a few minutes ago. He was looking for Dominic and Milos," Henri said.

I pulled Roxy a little way from Henri and looked around to make sure no one was within listening range. This was the last night of the fair proper, and finding breathing space, let alone somewhere one could talk in private, was difficult. "Come with me," I ordered her, and scooted through the crowds until I was behind a line of portable toilets.

"What's gotten into you? Henri was telling me all the dirt on the bands. Why do we have to stand here?" she asked, glaring at the backs of the toilets.

"Because no one else wants to come here. Listen, I have something to tell you, but you have to promise to keep it a secret, OK?"

"Again? That's two major secrets in as many days. Do you have any idea what this is going to cost you in hush money?"

"This is serious, Rox. Tanya's dead."

She stared at me, her mouth slightly ajar.

I nodded. "Raphael found her, and I found him. He's gone to tell Dominic, I guess. I've already spoken to the police, but the worst thing is"—I looked around again to make sure no one was near enough to hear—"her neck was torn out."

"Torn out? Like an animal attacked her?"

"No," I said, watching her steadily. "Like a vampire killed her. There was no blood, Roxy, nothing. Somebody ripped into her throat and drained the blood from her body."

She put her hand over her mouth as if to keep from screaming. I know I certainly felt like it. "Oh my God, you don't think—*Christian?*"

"I don't know of any other vampires around here, do you? Oh, Lord, it's all my fault, too. I had no idea he would lose control so easily. I figured if he had lasted nine hundred years, he could last a little longer until we found him his Beloved, but I guess he finally realized that I wasn't she, and he went berserk."

"Oh my God," Roxy said again, her eyes huge. "Christian—who would have thought? He's been so nice to us."

"I have to find him. I have to find him and calm him down, and make him see reason. I have to make sure he doesn't do anything like this again."

260

"How are you going to do that?"

"I don't know," I wailed, heading back around the toilets toward the mass of humanity. "But I'd better do something pretty damn quick before anyone else figures out what happened, or the famed reclusive author C. J. Dante is going to find himself on the business end of a sharp stake."

Roxy and I searched the fair but did not find Christian. We saw Raphael and Dominic in grim consultation, a silent Milos standing with them. Arielle's tarot-card booth was dark and empty, so I assumed she'd been told of her sister's death. Roxy offered to go sit with her after I borrowed a nice couple's mobile phone and had no luck getting hold of Christian at his home.

"I talked to Demeter," Roxy told me after a quick confab with the aura photography woman. "She says Paal took Arielle to her trailer, and Renee is sitting with her. All the fair employees know about what happened to Tanya."

"It was bound to come out," I said, tapping my lip. I wondered aloud where Christian had gone, and how I was to find him.

"Easy. Call him," Roxy suggested.

"I just tried. His housekeeper, who I think I woke up, said he was gone for the evening and she had no idea when would be back, and could I please not call again this late because she had to be up early to get ready for the festival."

"Not that kind of call. Use your Vulcan mind-meld, or whatever you said you can do with Christian."

A cold chill raced down my arms at the thought of such intimacy with a man who could savagely kill another person. "No, thank you."

Roxy turned to look at me. "Why? What are you afraid of? He swore never to hurt you."

I rubbed my arms. "I'm just afraid, OK?"

She gave me a weak smile. "Do you remember when we were seven and I got my head stuck between the school gym wall and the drainpipe, and I wouldn't go near the gym for months? You went all philosophical on me and told me that it was all right to be afraid of something as long as you didn't let the fear control you."

"I remember," I glared at her. "My mother used to say that to me. Damn, I hate it when you're right. All right, I'll try to see if he's got his receiver on, but it'll be on your head if he swoops down and carries me off because of it."

She held one arm, watching me.

"What?" I asked.

"Are you doing it now?"

"No!"

"Oh." She sounded disappointed. "So are you doing it *now?*"

"Roxy, it's not a circus act. I'm not going to do it with you watching me."

"Why not?"

"Because, it's something . . . intimate. I can't do it with people watching me. I have to be somewhere private to do it, where I know I'm not being stared at."

She looked around the fair. People were elbow to elbow in the long aisle leading up to the main tent where the second band was setting up for their session. The tarot-card booth and the palm-reading booth, both empty, offered no privacy. She turned back to me with a faint grin. "I guess there's only one place for you to use."

I nodded. "Raphael's trailer."

She shook her head. "Do you really want to take the chance of having Christian swoop down on you where a bed is handy for that all-important fifth step of the Joining?"

"Oy. You have a point. So what great idea do you have?"

She pointed at the lines before the portable toilets. "Voilà! Instant privacy."

I didn't like it, and spent a good fifteen minutes trying to find an alternative, but in the end I waited in line for an eon to use a toilet, Roxy at my side to keep me from being bored, or so she said. I think she was really just hoping to see me "do it."

"Good luck!" she called as I stepped into the toilet, closing the door on a bunch of startled looks. I decided I'd rather stand than sit, and closed my eyes, trying to clear my mind of everything but the thought of Christian. It was difficult to do, what with all the noise—the second band had started their set—not to mention the unpleasant and aromatic surroundings, but I made a conscious effort to block everything out.

I let my mind stretch and reach out to find him
Christian?

I caught the image of awareness, of Christian turning to look at me, but he didn't respond. That was followed by a horrible thought. Maybe he didn't know who I was. Maybe he was so far gone in his madness that he had lost his memory of me.

Christian, it's me. Joy. Are you all right?

A distant noise so faint it might have been the wind moaning through the trees swept past me.

I know you're probably hurt and angry right now, Christian, but I'm worried about you. If you could just let me know where you are and that everything is OK, it would make me feel a lot better.

My head was filled with silence.

Christian? Please let me know you're all right.

He did not answer. I tried to contact him again for the next few minutes, but he would not respond to anything I said.

"No luck," I told Roxy as I stepped out of the toilet.

"You should eat more bran," a short, magenta-haired Goth told me in perfect English as she claimed her turn at the toilet.

I ignored Roxy's giggles and headed away from the toilets, drained by my attempt to contact Christian.

"Raphael's looking for you. The police are here, although no one is supposed to know. Raphael said it was business as usual. What are you going to do about Christian?"

I shrugged and searched the crowd for my amber-eyed Romeo. He was standing in the empty tarot-card booth with Dominic and Inspector Bartos. "What can I do? He won't answer me. I know he's out there, I can feel him, but he's ignoring me for some reason. I don't have control over him, Rox. I can't demand he come to me, so there's nothing I can do but hope he's holed up somewhere away from people."

She nodded. "Raphael said the police are going to want to speak with all of us. I've never been interviewed as a witness before. It'll be one for the diary, huh?"

"That's one way of putting it," I said grimly as I headed for the tarot-card booth.

It wasn't until a few hours later that Raphael climbed wearily into his trailer. I was curled up on his bed, fully clothed this time, reading one of the many mysteries he had tucked into a tiny bookshelf.

I set the book down as he locked the door, flipped the lights out, and walked to the bedroom. "Was it bad?" I asked.

He shrugged one shoulder as he peeled his coat off, leaning out of the bedroom to toss it onto the tiny table. "They're police. It's always bad when there's been a murder." He turned back to face me. Both eyebrows lifted as he stood on one leg to pull his boot off. "I liked you better last night."

I looked down at my jeans and sweater. "So did I, but I wasn't sure if you wanted me here after you'd been grilled by the police. I know how you must have been dreading that."

He grunted as he pulled off the second boot. "Baby, the only thing that kept me going tonight was the thought of you waiting for me."

Questions? Yes, I had questions galore about what he'd been doing near Tanya's body, but first things came first, and at that exact moment, Raphael's mental and physical well-being topped my list of priorities. I pushed the book off the bed as I slid down. "Oh, well then, seems to me it's my duty as a humanitarian to render you whatever aid you require."

I got to my feet and wrapped my arms around his neck, wiggling my hips against him as I kissed a trail around his lips. He slid his hands under my sweater and teased my nipples through my bra as his mouth captured mine.

"I am going to require a lot of aid," he said between nips to my lower lip. His hands were burning my breasts, stroking and teasing until I gave in to his demand and parted my lips, welcoming that bossy tongue of his into my mouth with a hum of pleasure. "I will be needing so much aid, it's going to require multiple applications."

"Multiple, hmmm?" I slid my hands down his back, lovingly stroking the hard curves of his behind. "I like the sound of multiple."

He growled as I sucked his tongue into my mouth, tugging his shirt out of his pants. His hands tightened around my breasts as I gently raked my fingernails up his belly until I reached his chest.

"Nipples," I cried in delight. "Imagine finding them here! I must explore more fully."

"That's not fair." His breath was hot and ragged on my neck as he nuzzled me, licking and kissing and nibbling while his hands slid around to my back. "You have bare flesh in your hands. It's only right I should have some as well. I want bare flesh. I *need* bare flesh!"

I saw the reason in his argument as soon as he got my

bra unhooked and his hands had pushed that annoying bit of material away to cup my breasts, his thumbs teasing my nipples mercilessly. Tiny little rivulets of fire started in my toes and worked their way up my body as I gently scored my fingernails up his sides, throwing my head back so he would have better access to my breasts. He peeled my sweater off, tossed my bra after it, his hair brushing against my bare skin as he bent to take a breast in his mouth.

"OK, that's it, I give." The feel of his mouth on my flesh was making my bones turn to jelly. I arched my back and pushed my breast at him in a brazen, shameless sort of manner. "I was going to torment you and tease you and arouse you till you had steam coming out of your ears, but I give. You're just too much for me. I surrender."

"Baby, if you arouse me any more, I'll explode," Raphael growled, the steamy look in his eyes confirming his claim. "As I calculate it now, I have about three more seconds before that happens."

We had our clothes off in record time. Raphael hit the bed first, me following immediately thereafter. I ignored his little grunt when I landed on him rather than the bed. I straddled his waist, sitting up and running my hands over his belly and chest, thinking about all the many and varied things I wanted to do to him.

Raphael swore.

"What?" I froze, wondering what I had done wrong.

"Just a minute." He put both hands on my hips and heaved me off him, rolling over until he was sitting on the side of the bed. "Stay there. Don't move. And don't stop thinking about what you're thinking, because I like that wicked glint in your eye."

I stared at his back for a moment, then figured out what he was doing. "Would you like me to hum a little condom-donning music while you're busy over there? Something in a march, perhaps? Or a Latin beat? Or maybe you prefer skaaaaAAAAAAAA!"

Quicker than you could say "extra personal space" he was on his back again, and had me hoisted over him.

"Wait a minute," I said, looking down from where he held me about a foot and a half above his body. "I see what you're doing, Bob, don't think that I don't. You're not going to impale me with that thing until I'm good and ready to be impaled, and that's not going to be until I do some of those wicked things you saw glinting in my eyes, so let me down nice and slow and no one will get hurt."

He grinned and slowly lowered me until I was sitting on his groin. "It's like sitting on a broomstick," I said, my eyes widening as I wiggled around on him a little, sliding back and forth along his long, hard length. Raphael's hands grabbed my hips, his fingers biting hard into my flesh as his head thrashed side to side on his pillow. "Oh, my! Maybe I'm ready now. Maybe those wicked things can wait. Maybe I was a little overhasty in ruling out an immediate impaling."

"Thank God," Raphael croaked, his voice as harsh as gravel. In one smooth move he lifted me up, positioned himself, and thrust upward as I sank down. His groan of sheer pleasure rang in my ears as my body accepted his. He was heat, he was fire, a very, very hard fire that pushed and shoved and burned its way into my tender flesh, filling me, stretching me, pushing me beyond everything I'd known into some new world inhabited only by us. I ceased to be one person and happily joined myself with him.

The last thing I saw before my eyes rolled up in my head was his back arching up off the bed as I tightened every muscle I had around the hard heat of him.

"Do you know, you're almost panting in time to your heartbeat, which says a lot, considering your pulse rate must be at least in the two hundreds."

Raphael groaned beneath me. I was drawing lazy circles on his chest, enjoying the feeling of his chest hair tickling my face as I pressed occasional kisses onto his flesh. His chest rose and fell quickly beneath me, making me wonder if I was squashing him. I put my hands down onto the bed and levered myself up slightly. Immediately his hands settled onto my bare behind and held me in place. I smiled to myself. We were still physically joined, a testament to his girth that we hadn't parted ways, so to speak.

"What does it feel like when you use a condom? I mean *after*. Does it feel ooky? I can't imagine it's a terribly comfortable feeling, what with all that . . . um . . . just hanging around the end there."

Raphael's hands slid up to rest on my back, but other than that he made no response to my question. A perfectly good question, too, I thought. But perhaps he was embarrassed that he'd only lasted a couple of thrusts before blasting off. Poor man. That was all it had taken for me, too, but unlike women, men invest so much ego in their sexual prowess. I didn't want to make him feel anything less than a stud muffin, so I decided to let the subject drop and talk about something else.

"Did you have a chance to see Arielle after the police questioned her? I was going to sit with her, but that minion of Inspector Bartos . . . what was his name? . . . Detective Kovar made me go over the whole evening again. Poor, poor Arielle."

"Why is it women can work just as hard as men while they're making love, but when it's all over, they can still put words together and have them make sense?"

I smiled at his disgruntled frown. "It's called afterglow, sweetheart. Pillow talk is the best kind of talk. Do I take it you'd rather I let you recover in peace than discuss the important topics of the day?"

Raphael moaned an affirmative, his eyes closed tight. I

grinned and pushed myself into a sitting position. His eyes shot open when I wiggled just enough to remind him that my cheerleaders were still entertaining him at their home-coming dance.

"Baby, I wish I could oblige you, but I think you killed me a few minutes ago."

I raised up just a little, then sank slowly back down, gripping him as tightly as I could. He bucked beneath me and sucked in half the roomful of air.

"You don't feel dead to me," I said, leaning forward to tease the tip of his little brown nipple with my tongue. "You feel hot and hard and very, very alive. I can feel your pulse deep inside me. Here." I did my best Kegel squeeze.

"Ah, Christ," he groaned, grabbing my hips and holding on as he rolled me onto my back. He scooped my legs up until they rested on his shoulders. Slowly he pulled out of me until just the very tip of him rested inside; then just as slowly he stroked forward, filling me with so much more than just a delicious bit of flesh that tears came to my eyes with the beauty of him.

"You think I killed *you?*" I gasped, flexing my legs to pull him deeper into me. "You're going to be the death of me if you do that again, you know that, don't you?"

He smiled a wicked, wicked smile so hot it singed my eyebrows. "I'm not going to kill you, baby. Just take you to heaven and back."

Oh, Lord, did he!

Chapter Fifteen

"So, Superman, it's been a half hour. Have you recovered enough to talk now?"

Raphael, lying on his belly, lifted his head just enough to press a tender, but sated, kiss to my ankle. "I may never recover, but if you don't require anything more strenuous than me moving my mouth, I will strive to satisfy you."

"Oh, Bob," I crooned, wiggling my toes and reaching over to tickle his feet, "there is no question about my satisfaction. I'm probably the most satisfied woman in the world. I certainly should be after the heroic effort you made to curl my hair."

He rolled over onto his side, a smug smile gracing his adorable lips as he teased a finger along the line of my pubic bone. "Looks like I succeeded."

I bit his ankle.

He sighed and rolled onto his back, taking one of my legs with him, idly stroking my calf as he spoke. "I assume you want to discuss the murder."

"Amongst other things," I said, thinking of Christian. "You . . . um . . . did talk to the police, didn't you? I mean, really talk to them?"

"I did." He didn't look too upset by the experience, so they must not have questioned him about anything but the murders. I breathed a sigh of relief.

"What, if anything, did the police say to you when they questioned you? They wouldn't answer any of my questions, they just kept telling me to explain again why I was in those trees rather than taking the shorter way to the hotel."

Raphael swirled little circles on my leg. "What makes you think they told me anything?"

I sat up and looked at him. "You're a man. Men like the police always feel it's important to keep women out of the loop. They disguise it as a protection tactic, but really they just want something to feel superior about. So, what did they say to you?"

His lovely amber eyes considered me silently for a long minute; then he, too, sat up. "Joy, that's something I can't tell you."

"What? Why? Because of this secret in your past that you refuse to tell me?"

"Yes, it has to do with that. I would tell you if I could, but I can't."

I didn't like the serious mien to his face. I slid my hand up his leg. "What do you mean, you can't tell me? You can't tell me because the police asked you not to, or you can't tell me because you don't trust me?"

He watched my hand as it traced the long bulge of muscle from his knee to his hip. "It's not a matter of trusting you. There's a lot more at stake than just your feelings. The police are conducting a detailed investigation, and I can't . . . I . . . ah, Christ. I wish things were different. I wish I could just . . ."

He left the sentence unfinished, but I had no trouble filling it in. He had a secret, and he couldn't trust me with it.

I thought again of the scene I had witnessed: Raphael bending over Tanya's body. Could I have been wrong about him? Hadn't he discovered Tanya accidentally as I had? And what was he doing out there rather than staying at the fair, where he was needed? Did he have a reason to want Tanya dead?

I shook the thought away as soon as it formed. I might not have known Raphael long, but I knew I trusted him. He was not a killer. "Why weren't you at the fair?"

His eyes narrowed.

"It was only eleven. You should have been watching over the crowds as the bands changed. Why weren't you there?"

A muscle in his jaw twitched.

"OK, let's try this question on for size. What hold does Dominic have over you? What does he know about your last job that keeps you, a man who is well educated and intelligent, working an inferior job at a moderately successful little traveling fair? Why aren't you some high-powered mucky-muck at an international corporation?"

"Joy—"

He had no intention of answering me, that was plain. I didn't matter enough to him; he didn't trust me because I was nothing but an unimportant floozy who threw herself into his bed. A holiday fling, Roxy had called it. Tears started pricking behind my eyeballs.

"No good? Well, how about this: What did you pick up when you were bending over Tanya's body?"

Raphael looked shocked by what I said. "You saw me pick something up?" he asked.

"Yes. Just before you went to the hotel, you picked something up from the ground near Tanya. What was it, one of her wax voodoo dolls?"

He looked at me as if I were a stranger. "You were spying on me? Following me?"

Maybe I *was* a stranger. Maybe I didn't know him at all.

Maybe I had made the worst mistake of my life. I shook my head. "No, I wasn't following you and I wasn't spying on you. And to tell you the truth"—I brushed away a tear that rolled down my cheek—"I'm more than a little insulted that you'd think I would."

Slowly he got out of bed and grabbed his pants from where they dangled from the doorknob. "How did you know I took something from Tanya?"

Oh, God, how could things be so good one moment and so bad the next? I pulled the sheet up until it covered my now chilled flesh. "I saw you. I wasn't spying on you, I was just taking the long way to the hotel because a bunch of kids were drunk on the east side of the meadow, and I didn't want to walk through them alone. I just saw you, that's all. You were acting funny, so I just watched to see what it was you were doing. And now, if you're finished with the third degree, I think I want to go back to my hotel. I have the feeling that I'm not terribly welcome here anymore."

He reached a hand into his pants pocket and pulled out a purple stone. I stared at it, a chill skimming my spine. "It's a rune."

He nodded.

"An amethyst rune."

He said nothing.

"Just like mine."

His eyes glittered with dark emotion.

"You found it on her body?"

"Yes," he said, the word stark and bare in the warmth of his bedroom.

I shook my head. "It's not mine. It can't be mine. I was reading them earlier, before she was killed. It must be from another set."

"I asked Paal. He only had one set of amethyst stones. He sold it to you."

I was still shaking my head, hard now. "No. It can't be

273

mine. I was using them." I looked up from the stone to search his eyes. "I didn't kill her, Raphael."

He closed his fist around the stone and pulled me to his chest. "I know you didn't, baby. I didn't mean to give you the third degree, I just had to ask." His kisses were very, very sweet and apologized better than any words could. He put his mouth to my ear and growled in a low, husky voice, "I don't want you to leave. I need you."

Another tear spilled over at the pain caused by his sweet words. "But not enough to trust me with your secret?"

His arms tightened around me until we were pressed tightly together. "Ah, baby, I wish everything was different so I could explain it to you, but this is important."

I tipped my head back so he could see the pain in my eyes. "And I'm not?" I asked in a whisper.

"You're the most important thing in my life," he said softly, his eyes glowing. "It's because of my feelings for you that I need you to trust me and not ask me for answers I can't give."

"You want my trust but won't give me yours, is that it?" I asked, pushing back on his chest until we were separated.

"That's it," he answered, his gaze holding mine.

I looked at him for a long time, outwardly calm, but inside, hurt and anger were mixed up with love and the desire to give him what he wanted. I thought about what he meant to me. I weighed my love for him against a lifetime of never mattering as much to him as he did to me.

I picked up my clothes. "I'm sorry, those terms aren't acceptable to me."

"Joy—"

I turned my back to him and pulled on my clothes, tears streaming down my face as I tied my shoelaces. He didn't say a word, not one blessed word, not one word to stop me from leaving him. Once I was dressed, I paused and stared at his belly tattoo. I didn't want to look in his eyes. I didn't want to see the truth mirrored in them. I didn't want to see how unimportant I was to him.

"Thank you for a lovely evening. I hope you have fun doing whatever it is you are doing. I hope the police don't find out whatever it is you're hiding. I'm sure you'll understand if I decline any further invitations to your little love nest. If you'll excuse me, I'll be on my way now."

"Baby, look at me."

The endearment almost broke me, but I fought the desire to throw myself in his arms and swallowed back my misery. "I'm not your baby. Goodbye, Raphael. Have a nice life."

He walked me back to my hotel without saying another word.

Despite the fact that I had been up most of the night, discovered a body, and been grilled by the police for two hours, I didn't sleep. Having had my heart crushed by the man I loved more than anything else kept me wide awake. I tossed and turned in my cold, lonely, Raphael-less bed and alternated between a pity party to end all pity parties, and fury that he could treat me in such a callous fashion. In between the two extremes, the voice of reason popped up and pointed out that if I really loved Raphael, I would support him rather than damning him for whatever it was he was unable to share with me.

I told the reasonable voice to get stuffed.

I tried contacting Christian twice more before the sun crept up out of the mountains, but either he wasn't receiving me or he had chosen to ignore me. I wished there was something I could do to convince him to answer me, but if there was one thing I'd found in recent days, it was that vampires didn't like to be pushed around.

Roxy looked surprised to find me breakfasting at our usual table next to the window. The sun was out, indicating it was going to be another glorious day weather-wise.

"You look like hell," she said, sitting down and grabbing a breakfast roll from the basket, tearing off a piece, and stuffing it into her mouth. "Where's your better half? I figured you guys would be shacked up together until all hours making little Raphaels and Joys."

I grimaced. "No. That's all over with."

She stopped in mid-chew, then gave a big swallow. "What do you mean it's all over with? It can't be all over with, I just decided to give you my blessing. What happened?"

I shrugged and looked back out the window. Nothing had changed out there; it was still the same tranquil scene. Birds flew overhead, people got into cars and drove away, late-blooming flowers bowed and dipped their heads in the wind. Everything was the same. Everything but me.

"Joy?" Roxy put her hand over mine, her voice worried. "Honey, what happened? Last night Raphael looked like he couldn't wait to get back to you."

I willed myself not to cry. I'd done enough of that during the long night, too. "He wouldn't tell me his secret."

She frowned. "What secret?

"He has some secret, something to do with the police and his past. I think he was convicted of some crime and never really cleared. Dominic knows about it, and is using it to keep him with the fair. I asked Raphael about it, but he said he couldn't tell me. He could tell Dominic, but he couldn't tell me. He doesn't trust me, Roxy. I don't matter enough to him that he can trust me with some stupid secret about his last job."

"I don't believe for one minute you don't matter to him. I've got eyes, babe. I can see how he looks at you, and it is not the look of a man who's simply using the closest dipper to drink from the well. He's crazy about you. Serious crazy, too, which is why I changed my mind and decided that you two were perfect for each other."

"But his secret—"

She waved his secret away with a bit of breakfast bread product. "Have you told him every little secret in your life?"

"No, of course not, but this isn't little, this is something big, something serious, something that's affecting him now and will no doubt continue to affect him in the future. I wouldn't keep something on that level secret from him."

She nodded. "You're a woman. He's a man. Women don't mind asking for help with a problem, while men take it as a slight to their character if they can't deal with everything themselves. Besides, you both kind of jumped into this relationship quickly. Sometimes trust takes a bit of time to build. I'm sure he'll change his mind about not telling you whatever it is he's hiding if you're patient with him and don't do anything rash."

"Rash like telling him I didn't want to see him again?"

She stared at me, jam dripping off the spoon she was applying to her roll. "You didn't!"

I nodded.

"Oh, geez." She slathered the piece of roll and popped it in her mouth. "Well, we'll deal with that in good time. We'll take the most important things first."

"Raphael is the most important thing to me," I objected.

"I know that," she said indistinctly around a mouthful of roll. "I meant important things as in stuff we must accomplish in order for you to be able to get Raphael where you want him—by the short and curlies."

I pushed my cup of coffee away untasted. "Roxy, I don't understand a thing you're saying. What things are you talking about?"

She wiped her jammy hands on a napkin before ticking the items off on her fingers. "One, we find out what Raphael's secret is."

I stared at her. "Have you heard anything I said? He wouldn't tell me."

"We won't ask *him*." She smiled complacently. "Two, we determine who killed Tanya."

I rubbed my forehead. The headache I had been nursing ever since I got up was building. "Christian killed Tanya," I said very slowly, enunciating clearly just in case she couldn't hear and chew at the same time.

She waved her roll—her third roll—at me. "I don't buy that. Christian doesn't seem to me to be the type to kill someone."

I stared at her. "Roxy, he drinks people's blood to survive. He can kill people without touching them. He's lived for more than nine hundred years, and he's been turned down repeatedly by the one woman who he thinks can save him. Of course he's the type to kill! You're just letting the fact that he's Dante sway your judgment."

"Geez, you really don't have faith in anyone, do you?"

That stopped me dead.

"You don't trust Raphael when he asks you to, you believe a man who's only showed you kindness and given you information that could be used against him is a murdering bastard, and you don't give me credit for seeing a few things you're too blind to notice."

"I'm sorry, Rox, I didn't mean to imply that you aren't seeing things clearly. I just—it's just that Christian didn't share his visions with you. They weren't nice, Roxy. He's a very, very powerful man, tormented and in constant battle with himself. It's because of the blackness I've seen within him that I know he is capable of killing."

"Has he been anything but gentle with you?"

"No, but he thinks I'm his Beloved."

"Exactly. So why would he take the chance of angering or sickening you by ruthlessly killing someone, knowing full well that you'd guess he was responsible for it?"

I stared at her in surprise. I hadn't thought of that. Surely Christian must realize I'd know if he killed Tanya.

Roxy nodded as the understanding dawned in my eyes. "If you're right and he can feed on anyone he wants, it only makes sense that he'd do so away from here, somewhere you wouldn't hear about it. Killing Tanya just doesn't make sense."

I rubbed my forehead again. "All right, if that's the case, then who *did* kill her? And don't tell me it's Raphael, because I won't believe it."

"Well, he did have both the opportunity and the motive."

"What motive?" I asked, bristling against my will at the slur on his character.

"His secret, whatever it is. Which brings us back to the list. Once we find out what his secret is and clear him of murdering Tanya, we will know what to do about Dominic."

"Dominic?" I tried to follow her convoluted reasoning. "You mean about him blackmailing Raphael?"

Something occurred to me as I spoke the words. Dominic had a fight with Tanya the day before she died—he might fill the role of murderer. "Or about Tanya's murder? Or both?"

"Hmm. Dominic as murderer—I suppose it's possible." She shrugged and reached for my pot of coffee, pouring herself a cup and adding an unhealthy dollop of cream. "Doesn't matter; either way, we get Dominic off Raphael's back. If he's the murderer, he goes to jail. If he's not and we figure out Raphael's secret, we apply a little judicious blackmail pressure of our own."

"What sort of blackmail pressure?" I asked suspiciously.

"Who knows? We'll cross that bridge when we come to it. You want that last roll?"

I stared at it, not seeing it. Raphael's face loomed large in my mind. "OK. I guess. I'm game."

"Either he's worth fighting for, or he's not the one for you," Roxy said sagely, buttering the roll.

I met her gaze as her words clicked into place. "He's worth fighting for."

"I thought you'd see it that way. Let's get a little breffy under our belts, then we'll tackle item one."

"You've already eaten enough rolls for two people," I pointed out.

"A girl needs her strength when she's saving her best friend's romance, not to mention uncovering mysterious secrets and solving a murder."

"You sound like an overgrown Nancy Drew," I smiled.

"I always liked Nancy. You can be my George."

"Oh, hell," I said, looking over her shoulder.

"What? You want to be Bess instead? That's OK with me, but I always thought Bess was a bit of a wet blanket."

"No, it's not that."

"Don't tell me you want to be Hannah Gruen? Wasn't she elderly? Well, OK, you can be her, but don't be saying things like 'Lawks a-mercy, Miss Nancy' to me."

I nodded to the man in the doorway and rose from my chair. "Will you stop? Inspector Bartos and that flunky of his are here. Eat up, Nancy. I think we're about to be grilled by the coppers."

The bar was closed at this time of the morning, which evidently made it a good place for the local cops to interview people. There were four tables set up at opposite corners of the room, each occupied by a policeman. People from the fair staggered in through the outer door, lining the hall, their eyes blurred and red from being short-shifted in the sleep department.

A policewoman with a little black moustache held up a hand to stop us as she consulted a list. She said something and waved me forward, but stopped Roxy before she could enter the bar.

"Looks like you're on your own, George," she called out

to me as I entered the bar. "Don't be so stubborn that you don't call Ned Nickerson for help if you need it. I'm sure he'd help if he knew you needed it."

Calling Ned, AKA Bob the Pigheaded, was not going to be a problem, I reflected as I stepped into the bar. He was standing near one of the tables with Inspector Bartos, arguing in a low but vehement voice. Whatever he was saying did not go down well with Bartos, because the latter was shaking his head and looking like he was wishing he could shut Raphael up. I wondered whether Raphael had volunteered to speak to them or if they'd had to drag him in, then lectured myself for having so little faith in the man with whom, even if he did drive me up the wall with his refusal to dish with the truth, I was madly in love.

Inspector Bartos spotted me and managed to get a word in to Raphael. I decided the best defense was a strong offense and, raising my chin, marched over to where they both watched me. "Inspector Bartos, Raphael. You wanted to see me?" I asked Bartos. "I told you everything you could possibly want to know last night, several times, in fact. What do you want now?"

Not even Nancy Drew's brash best friend George would address a police inspector in such an arrogant tone, but I was just about at my limit, and it wasn't even lunchtime. Inspector Bartos didn't seem to be offended, however. His voice was mild as he said, "Mr. St. John was just giving me the benefit of his advice, Miss Randall. If you would wait at that table, I will be available in a very short time."

"Mr. St. John is very good at giving advice," I told him, ignoring Raphael looming over me. "It's taking it that sticks in his craw."

"Joy," Raphael growled at me in warning, taking my hand.

I took it back. "Unless you have something to confide in me, I don't believe we have anything to say to each other."

His eyes turned molten. "We damned well do." He

grabbed my head and laid his lips on me so quickly, so hard and fast and full of unspoken demand, that I just stood there and let him kiss me. "Don't give up on me," he said in a low voice, his eyes burning me as his thumb brushed a line along my jaw. He looked over my head to Inspector Bartos. "You're making a mistake, Bartos. I can prove what I've said. If you'll just contact the Heidelberg police—"

"It is my mistake to make, you agree? Contacting the German police won't be necessary," Bartos told him. "You will remain available for interview."

Raphael's jaw tightened, but he nodded, then looked back at me. His thumb teased my lower lip. "Remember what I said," he warned me, then dropped his hand from my face and left the bar.

I stood brainless, bemused, so madly in love that I could just lie down on the floor kicking my heels and having a hissy fit over the way things had turned out, but we Randalls are made of sterner stuff. Raphael gave me much to think about, but unfortunately—"I am ready for you now, Miss Randall," Bartos said behind me.

I watched through the window as Raphael strode across the parking lot, heading back to the meadow. He looked so tired and frustrated, I wanted to cradle his head against my breasts and make everything all better.

"Miss Randall?"

Two policemen passed Raphael on their way in to the hotel. He literally stood head and shoulders above them, the very embodiment of masculinity. I sighed. He certainly was perfect, if you were willing to overlook the fact that he was pigheaded and stubborn, had difficulty trusting people, and didn't want to need anyone.

"Miss Randall, the morning is passing. If it would not be too troublesome, I would like to conduct your interview now."

Raphael disappeared from view. I turned to look at Bar-

tos, not really seeing him. The conversation Raphael had
with Bartos was *very* interesting. Had he volunteered advice? About the murder in Heidelberg? Perhaps he had decided to come clean with the police regarding his past . . .
then again, the way Bartos demanded he remain available
for interview was not a sign the police viewed him as innocent.

"The chair is very comfortable, I assure you. And the table
is a fine example of local craftsmanship. If you would just
seat yourself, I believe you will agree."

What did Raphael mean about not giving up on him?
What kind of a demand was that for him to make of me?
He'd given up on me even before we had a chance, hadn't
he? And just what did *give up* mean? Ha! I knew what he
wanted. He wanted me to fawn all over him, telling him
how marvelous he was no matter how terribly he treated
me. How dare he expect me to stay devoted to him, consumed by thoughts of him, thinking of him to the exclusion
of all else?

"Miss Randall, my wife is expecting me home for dinner
this evening. Shall I tell her otherwise?"

Well, I wouldn't do it! I just wouldn't! If he wanted a devoted slave, a groupie, he could just look elsewhere. I had
too much self-respect to turn myself into a doormat just so
his manly ego could stomp all over it. Give up on him, ha!

Inspector Bartos sighed, his moustache ruffling with the
force of it. I blinked and realized I had been staring at him.
"What? Did you just ask me to dinner?"

His lips compressed to a hard line. "Have you returned to
us?"

"Returned? What are you talking about? I've been standing here waiting for you. Are you ready now?"

He looked like he wanted to sigh again, but shook his
head instead. "Yes, I am ready for you. If you will please
sit?"

The interview didn't cover any new ground. I didn't understand why they wanted me to go over my actions the night before again and again, but figured maybe they were waiting for me to suddenly crack and admit I killed Tanya, or make some glaring mistake retelling my story that would indicate I was lying through my teeth. I did neither.

Until he started asking the *hard* questions.

"Is it true that two days ago Tanya Renauld said to you"—he flipped a couple of pages in his notebook—"that she would *only be happy when you were dead?*"

My stomach wadded up into a tiny ball and rattled around my body. I wondered who had snitched on me—Roxy? Christian? It had to be Roxy; I doubted the inspector had found Christian before he disappeared for the day. I frowned at that thought, wondering why Christian had remained silent through the night if he was innocent. Could he have been wounded somehow? Restrained by some means? In light of his innocence, his silence took on a new, more worrisome meaning.

"Um . . . maybe."

Inspector Bartos looked up from his notebook. "Maybe? Could you be more specific? Did she threaten you or not?"

My palms started sweating. "Well . . . yes, she did. But she was very angry—"

"Immediately upon threatening your life, did she throw a bucket of water on you?"

There was no use denying it; too many people had seen us. I gnawed on my lower lip and nodded.

"Was it your impression that she was serious in her threats to you?"

I hesitated. I didn't want to lie, but I couldn't see what good telling him that she was in deadly earnest would do anyone. "Although I didn't really know her, it was fairly obvious that Tanya was a very volatile person. She was also extremely irate over the fact that her boyfriend was using me to make her jealous—without my permission, as I've told you a couple of times. Given all that, I would say that at the moment she threw the water on me, she wouldn't have broken out into sobs if I had dropped down dead on the spot."

His moustache ruffled a little at that. I watched it, fascinated. It was as if the thing had a life of its own. He flipped through a few more pages. "Miss Renauld made statements that could be interpreted as threatening to you at other times, did she not?"

"She was pretty much angry nonstop with me, so it's no surprise she said nasty things." I leaned forward. "Look, Inspector, I don't know what you're driving at with all these questions about Tanya threatening me. *She* was killed, not me. She held a grudge against me, not vice versa. I was more than happy to go my own way and not have anything to do with her, and I certainly didn't bear her any ill will other than disliking being used as a pawn by her and Dominic."

"A woman has been murdered, Miss Randall," Bartos said neutrally, reminding me of Christian at his peacemaking best. "It is my duty to uncover all the unpleasantness surrounding her death whether or not you believe it has a bearing on the situation."

My spirits dropped to hang around my knees with the wadded-up ball of my stomach.

"If you would go over the events of the evening one more time, beginning with your conference with Miss Arielle Renauld here in this bar. . . ."

I slumped in my chair. The day stretched before me in a perpetual loop of retelling the same thing over and over and over again.

An hour later I stumbled out of the bar, the inspector's rebuffs echoing in my ears.

"You are under a misimpression, Miss Randall. My role in this investigation is to gather information, not give it," he said in response to my question of whether or not Raphael was a suspect. Our interview was at an end, but I had figured there was no better opportunity to try and worm a few facts out about Raphael.

"I'm not asking you to tell me what he said to you, just whether or not he's on your list of suspects. I can't help but be worried, what with his history with the police . . ." I purposely let my sentence trail off in hopes he'd take the bait, but evidently he'd been hooked before.

"Mr. St. John did not inform me that you were acquainted with his past history with the police," he said, faint disapproval tingeing his voice.

I tried not to squirm under his gimlet eyes. "Raphael and I are very close, as I have told you. And we have discussed the situation, and the issue of his past." Truth—it was all the truth. Misleading, yes, intended to give a false impression that I knew everything, true, but still a form of the truth. "I'm sure it just escaped his mind to tell you that."

"I see. And what do you expect me to tell you?"

"That you don't consider him a likely suspect for killing Tanya."

Inspector Bartos just looked at me out of half-closed eyes.

"Oh, come on," I said in response to his silence. "Just because Raphael has a history involving . . . well, involving the police doesn't mean that you can pin this on him. He's no more likely to have killed Tanya than I am! If I'm not a suspect, there's no way you can rationally include Raphael on your list of supposed perpetrators."

He gave me one of his martyred looks. "Ah, but Miss Randall, when have I given the impression that you are *not* on that list?"

I stared at him open-mouthed, stunned that he could consider me capable of murder. He took advantage of my speechless state to escort me to the door of the bar, wishing me a good day.

I headed straight for the bench out front where I could sit

and breath fresh air and enjoy not being questioned. Roxy, who had been interviewed and released before me, was chatting with a group of people getting ready to go on a bike ride.

I plopped down beside her with a, "Well! How do you like that! The good inspector thinks I murdered Tanya!"

Roxy shrugged and called out a goodbye as the bike riders pedaled off.

"What do mean by that shrug?" I demanded. "Do you mean you're not surprised that your best friend in the whole wide world is a murder suspect, or do you mean that it's all too silly for words, and thus you won't even try to express your contempt for a man who could say such patently false things?"

"We need to get you some Valium or something. You're going postal."

"I am not going postal, I've just been third degreed. Bartos all but brought out the rubber hose. I'm surprised he didn't flick a few lit matches on me, just to see if I'd sing."

Roxy chuckled and got to her feet, pulling me up after her. "You've got your sense of humor back. I'm glad to see you're not depressed over Tattoo Boy any longer. Come on, we have investigating to do. While you were in there having bamboo shoved under your fingernails, I've been busy working."

"Working how?" I asked as we headed toward the meadow and the fair.

"Talking to everyone from the fair who came in to report to the police. Hurry up, we have an appointment with your favorite vampire, and we're already late."

"Christian?" I looked up. The sun, hazy behind high clouds, was midway through the sky. "Roxy, even if we knew where he was, you know he's not awake now."

"Not Christian. Dominic."

"Ugh. He's hardly my favorite vampire. He's not even

real." A fact I suddenly appreciated, especially when the image of Tanya's torn throat came to mind. I wondered what Bartos made of that wound. I wondered if he believed in Dark Ones.

"Yes, well, he's about to become your favorite vampire. I told him you wanted a little information from him, and were willing to exchange your favors for it."

"ROXY!" I stopped dead at the edge of the parking lot. "I will NOT sleep with fang face!"

"Did I say you had to? I did not! I said *favors*, such as reading rune stones."

"What? Again? I did it last night to help out in a pinch, but—"

"If you want the dirt on Raphael, you're going to have to pay with a little of your time. So make up your mind. Which do you want more—a couple of free hours during the evening, or the scoop on what Raphael's hiding?"

I kicked at a rock imbedded in the soft soil. To be honest, I was feeling a bit unhappy over the whole idea of sneaking behind Raphael's back to find out what he was hiding from me. The sane voice in my head pointed out that violating his trust was not the way to demonstrate my love for him. *If he wanted you to know,* the self-righteous voice intoned, *he'd tell you.*

I seldom listen to that voice. I much prefer the one that snorted indignantly at the idea of sitting around passively and waiting for Raphael to come to his senses. *Make him see how much he needs you,* that voice said. *Show him you are more than just a convenient casing to park his piston.*

"OK, I'll do another stint at the rune table, but just for tonight."

Roxy whapped me on the arm and started down the slope to the meadow floor. "Tonight's the big festival, remember? There is no more fair after tonight."

I followed her slowly. How could I forget? Tonight hundreds of fans would converge on the grounds of Christian's castle, drink, eat, dance, and listen to loud music all the while celebrating the cult of the vampire. Meanwhile, the head vampire, the real one, hadn't been seen or heard from and was up to who knew what. I hoped he was tucked away safely wherever it was he slept.

I finally turned my attention to the question I'd asked earlier. If Christian hadn't murdered Tanya, who did? Dominic? Creepy Milos? Arielle? Raphael? Roxy? *Me?*

I shook the phantoms from my head and picked up the pace, quickly overtaking Roxy. Today was shaping up to be a pretty hellish nightmare of a day. I might as well get as much of it over with as possible.

Chapter Sixteen

If I thought my day was a nightmare, that was because I
hadn't seen the inside of Dominic's trailer.

"Good God, it's like a really bad parody of a *Dark Shadows* set," I murmured to Roxy as I stepped around a tall
standing lamp with a shade made out of metal bats caught
in the act of flight. Dominic had blocked up all the windows,
so the only light came from the weird lamps he had scattered around the trailer.

"I think it's fascinating, in a gruesome mangled-car-
accident sort of way," Roxy replied. I stared at a painting
hanging on a divider wall. It looked like one of those sixties
gothic covers with a woman in a transparent nightgown racing away from a gloomy old mansion, only in this picture
the woman was naked and was being followed by a somewhat effeminate-looking vampire in full Bela Lugosi rig.

"I see you admire my painting." Dominic appeared at my
side, taking the head-tipped-to-the-side-considering-art pose.
"I painted it myself, naturally."

"Oh. Did you?" I reminded myself that I wanted something from him, and thus to inquire how many other paint-by-numbers paintings he had done was not a good idea. "It's very . . . unique."

"Yes," he said, baring his fangs at me.

"Um . . . you have a piece of something . . ." I tapped the front of my teeth.

Dominic looked all too human for a moment as embarrassment flickered over his face. He dashed into his bedroom area.

"Dark Ones do *not* eat broccoli," Roxy muttered before turning her attention to what looked like a little altar made up of cheap-looking black and red candles.

"Looks like he's been shopping at Vampyrs 'R' Us," I whispered.

She giggled just as Dominic reappeared with a food-particle-free leer. "*Mon ange*, if you will sit just there, and Roxsee will sit there, and I will sit here, yes! Now we are all very comfortable, eh?"

"Sure thing," I said to his earlobe approximately three centimeters away from my mouth. "I just love being held squashed up against someone like I'm a mustard plaster or something." I paused and sniffed delicately, then recoiled as much as I could with him holding me clamped to his side. My eyes started watering with the effort it took not to sneeze. "What on earth are you wearing?"

A muscle twitched in his eyelid. "For you, I am wearing the *Marcheur du Nuit* cologne. I have created it myself. I am thinking of selling it. It is very fragrant, is it not so?"

"*Potent* is the word that comes to mind," I muttered, rubbing my nose. "If you don't mind, Dominic, I'm really busy today, and I know you must be busy getting ready for the festival, so if we could get to the discussion that Roxy mentioned, I'd be grateful."

"*Mon ange* weeps with pleasure?" he asked, flicking a fingertip across a path a tear had taken. I jerked my head back.

"No. I'm allergic to perfumes and colognes. Makes my . . . my . . ." I turned my head so he wasn't in the line of sight and sneezed into my shoulder. ". . . nose itch. Sorry. Hope I didn't get any on your hand."

He withdrew his arm from where it had been wrapped around my shoulders and covertly wiped the sneeze off his hand while I discreetly blew my nose into the tissue Roxy handed me.

"So, about Raphael—"

"*Mon ange, ma belle*, always you are in such a hurry! I have so little time with you, can we not enjoy what we have together?"

I looked him dead in the eye, sniffing and mopping back tears. "No," I said, sounding like I had a pair of socks stuffed up my nose. "We cannot. Raphael?"

He sighed a dramatic, put-upon sigh and tapped his long fingers on his chin for a minute while I sneezed three more times.

"I'm sorry," I said, waving my hand at Roxy. She stood up and traded places with me. "No offense, Dominic, but I'll be sneezing my eyes out if I sit next to you any longer."

"She can do it, too," Roxy said, her nose wrinkling as his musky cologne hit her. "She once sneezed fourteen times in a row. Wet her pants doing it."

"ROXY!"

"She was only ten at the time," Roxy added, as if that made it better.

"If, for the fourth time, we could get to the subject at hand, namely Raphael's history . . ." I raised an eyebrow at Dominic. He looked peeved.

"And if I do this great thing you want of me, *mon ange*, what will you grant me in return?"

I glanced at Roxy. She was staring in horror at the painting. "Roxy said you needed help reading runes tonight. I would be happy to do another session for you."

"Your assistance would be most welcome to me," he nod-ded, his eyes hooded, but not so hooded I didn't notice the calculating gleam in them. If I had anything more than a little spending money, I'd offer to bribe the info out of him, feeling sure that monetary gain held more sway with him than my own dubious charms. "But this thing you ask of me, it is personal. You ask me to betray Raphael."

I frowned. I didn't like hearing my feelings put into words, especially not words that came out of his fake-fanged mouth. Idly I wondered what Christian did with his fangs when they weren't in use.

"Such a personal sacrifice demands a much more *intime* gesture, do you not think?"

I stopped picturing collapsible canine teeth and glared at Dominic. "No sex."

"*Mon ange,*" he said, his hands fluttering gracefully. "You stir my blood with your too vehement protestations. But no, it is not to the *danse sur le coucher* that I refer."

Roxy snorted.

"Good, because it isn't going to happen. What exactly do you want, in addition to me reading runes tonight?"

He smiled, the calculating light growing in his eyes. He steepled his fingers together and made a little pout over them. "Tonight, as you have mentioned, is the Festival of All Hallow's Eve. In celebration of this night most dear to all who live in darkness, we have arranged the Punkevní Cave to be open to those attending the festival."

"That sounds like a good idea," I admitted, wondering what the catch was. Maybe he wanted me to collect ticket money, or help out working the festival.

"We went on that tour a couple of days ago," Roxy added. "It was a bit damp and smelly, but fun. Although Joy barfed up her lunch at the end."

I would have stopped her, but I figured the less attractive

picture of me Dominic had, the better. "I get seasick easily," I said.

He looked momentarily disconcerted; then another of his smug smiles slid across his face. "You will not suffer from *mal de mer* with me, *mon ange*. I will see to it that you are otherwise occupied during our boat ride."

"Our boat ride?" I asked suspiciously. "You want me to go on the tour with you? That's all?"

"That is all," he said, spreading his hands wide.

I tried to find something objectionable about what he wanted, but couldn't. I gave in as gracefully as I could. "All right. I'll read the runes and go on the boat tour through Punkevní Cave with you tonight, but that's it. We'll be even then, right?"

He smiled and touched his fingers to his lips.

Roxy glanced at her watch. "Thank God the negotiating is over. Now you can dish with the dirt on Raphael and we can be on our way."

I looked at Dominic. He leaned back, toying with the ruffles on his poet's shirt. "There is not much to dish, I am afraid. I employed Raphael in Marseilles, where he had just been released from prison for the rape and killing of a prostitute."

My jaw hit my knees. "He *what?*"

Dominic made a moue and tsked. "It is true. He forced himself on a woman of the streets, harming her here"—he waved at his midsection—"inside. She was sent to hospital, and later died."

Roxy stared at me, true horror in her eyes. I blinked at her, then looked back to Dominic. "Raphael? My Raphael? I just don't believe it."

"Believe it, *mon ange*."

I shook my head. "No. Not him. I know him. He would never force himself on a woman. It must have been a mistake. He must have been falsely convicted."

"I myself have seen his papers, *Joie*. You see now why I sought to protect you from him. The man you have chosen as your lover is a criminal—one who does not care for the women he uses for his perversions. Because he had survived repeated assaults in prison, I knew he had brutality and ruthlessness, both skills which would help him to keep others safe. That is why I hired him to attend to our security. The police forced me to do so with their accusations. They came to us and said, 'You have been here, here, and here, and that is near where women were murdered, so we must detain you.' Bah! They did not find anything to connect us to the so tragic killings. It was all just a screen of smoke they create. But me, I have the alibis most unbreakable, and they must go away without me." He sat back and looked terribly smug.

"Do you mean to say that the police thought you had killed someone?" Roxy asked, scooting just a bit away from him.

"They called them the Vampire Murders, yes? And I," he said with an affected little flip of his hand, "am *le grand Vampyr*. It follows that they must suspect me."

He sounded like he was proud of the fact.

"I didn't know they were seriously investigating anyone with the fair," I said slowly, looking at the tips of his pointy boots as my mind turned over the facts. Was it the fair employees the police were investigating, or one amber-eyed man with a police history in particular? "Arielle told us about a woman who died, but she said the police at Heidelberg—" The words stopped as goose bumps crawled up my flesh. Raphael had told Inspector Bartos to check with the police at Heidelberg about something, about proving he was innocent. Oh, God! If the police had viewed him as some sort of suspect in previous murders, it was no wonder Bartos had him on his suspect list.

"Those pigs! They delayed us one whole week. We lost

much revenue in Prague because of them. But that is over with. They did not find any connection between the fair and that woman."

"And now Tanya is dead," Roxy said thoughtfully, her gaze on Dominic.

"Yes." He sobered up at that thought. "She was not the most amiable of women, but she did not deserve death."

I gave him full brownie points for showing what looked to be real grief over Tanya's death. "I didn't get a chance to say so last night, Dominic, but I want you to know I'm very sorry about Tanya. I know you were close to her—this must be especially difficult for you. Do you have any idea who would have wanted her dead?"

For a moment the real Dominic peeked out. He looked like he was going to be sick, his eyes filled with horror; then the mask descended again and he was back to his slick persona.

"No. It is deranged to me. She was angry, yes, but not enough to do something foolish."

I withheld judgment on that point. Roxy put a few more questions to Dominic regarding the murders of the other women, but he had nothing new to say on that subject, or on his warnings against Raphael. I tolerated those for a few more minutes, then thanked him for his help and promised him I'd be at the festival shortly after opening to take up my duties at the rune-stone booth.

"I almost feel sorry for him," Roxy said a couple of minutes later as we stood outside his trailer, taking deep breaths of fresh air. The fair people, most of whom looked tired and drawn due to interrupted sleep, were just starting to break down the tents and booths. Some would be packed away, others would be moved to Drahanská's grounds for the festival.

"I think I'll go see how Arielle is," Roxy said, watching

Paal and another man at a water spigot. "I take it you're going to tackle your jailbird?"

"I don't believe a thing Dominic said about Raphael. I may not have known him for long, Rox, but I do know him. He's gentle and loving and would never rape a woman, especially with such force as to tear her up inside. He's beefy, but he's not monstrous! No, there has to be a mistake. Raphael told me he was accused of something he didn't do, and I, for one, believe him."

"Atta girl," she said with a pat on my shoulder. "I knew you wouldn't stay all pissy at him for long. Not with that belly tattoo. And of course, there's his huge—"

"Oh, I'm still ticked off royally at him," I interrupted her. "He's got a lot of explaining to do. But that doesn't mean I believe he's capable of rape and manslaughter. I think since Christian is out of commission until it gets dark, I will have a word or two with Raphael."

A smile touched her eyes. "A word or two, eh? K. I won't expect to see you for, oh, say three hours? Is that enough time for you two to *talk?*"

"You really need to get a man, Roxy. Your mind is just obsessed with sex. Obsessed! It's a sign of mental illness, it really is. Get some help. Now if you'll excuse me, I'm off to beat Raphael soundly about the head and shoulders with a sharp dick. Imagine him not having more faith in me!"

I snorted my indignation and strode off leaving Roxy doubled up, howling with laughter. I didn't stay to inquire what set her off, I had a man to handle. The fact that I went all mushy inside just thinking about handling him was neither here nor there. I had a point to prove. I was trustworthy, I was the perfect woman for him, and it was about time he realized that.

As for his secret . . . well, it was clear to me that it wasn't what Dominic believed, just as it was clear that the police viewed Raphael in a less than innocent light. I was about to knock on his trailer door when I remembered what Roxy had said about trust coming with time. If I told him what I'd found out, he'd be forced to trust me. But was forced trust what I wanted?

No, it wasn't. It wasn't good enough. Therefore, I couldn't let him know I knew what he had told Dominic. I gnawed on my lip while I figured out what I'd say to him. My last words had an awfully *ultimatum* feel to them. Perhaps an apology would start things off nicely. Maybe if I admitted I was wrong, he would do likewise and spill his guts about what really happened in his past.

The door opened without me touching it. "Are you writing obscenities on my door, or can you not bring yourself to knock?"

"Oh, very funny, Mr. Ha Ha. I happened to be in the area, and I thought it would be polite to say hello." I mentally pinched myself for the horrible inanities emerging from my mouth. What was I thinking? I sounded all stiff-rumped and prissy.

"Hello," he said, not moving from where he blocked the door. The glare I was about to level upon him for making me beg to be let in died when I saw that his eyes were dulled with fatigue.

"I also came to apologize," I said, unable to keep from stroking my hand down his temple. "You look exhausted."

"I am," he answered, grabbing my hand and pulling me up the three stairs, slamming the door behind him. Unlike Dominic's Trailer o' Darkness, Raphael's was filled with sunlight . . . and him. "I've had a hell of a day. First the woman who makes me mad with desire left me, then the police refused to listen to me, and finally my employer informed me my services were no longer needed."

I took a step toward him. He stood in the aisle, his arms crossed over his chest, his legs in battle stance. One of the things I appreciated most about Raphael was how he made me feel feminine in comparison with all his hard maleness. I took another step until I was close enough to brush his crossed arms with my breasts. "Dominic fired you? Why would he do that? He needs you now more than ever."

"He pointed out that I was engaged to keep the peace during the fairs, and his employees safe at all other times. Obviously, I failed in that duty." He bit the end of the sentence off as if he wanted to say something else, but didn't.

I leaned into him a little. His eyes grew brighter. I tried to count how many different shades of amber were within them, but failed. "That doesn't make sense. You can't possibly be responsible for everyone all the time."

One corner of his mouth turned up in a wry grimace. "Regardless, after the festival, I will be unemployed."

"Oh." I scooted closer, putting one arm around him, my fingers stroking the nape of his neck. "I'm sorry about that. I'm also afraid I can't do anything about the police. But the first item on your list, this woman you spoke of, perhaps I can make you forget her."

"No," he said, his eyes glittering now. I froze in mid-stroke. Suddenly his arms were around me, pulling me tight against his hard body—and I do mean all of it—his mouth a breath away from mine. "I will never forget her. She's everything I want in a woman—smart, sexy, and all mine."

"Ah," I said, allowing my lips to brush his as I spoke. "Well, since I can't help you with that, I'll just have to recommend that you go to bed. Perhaps a little rest will make your future look brighter."

"Bed," he growled, grinding his hips against mine. Every bone in my body melted into gelatin. I sagged against him. He shifted and hoisted me up in his arms, turning to carry me toward the tiny bedroom. "Now why didn't I think of that?"

"You don't have the intelligence I do. I am much more

reasonable than you. You are tired, therefore you must rest. In bed. For a very long time."

"That *is* reasonable," he agreed, his voice deep with desire. He set me on my feet and had my coat off and my dress whisked up over my head before I could so much as protest. Not that I was going to, but his disrobing me still took me a bit by surprise. I stood in my bra and underwear before him.

"Very pretty," he said, eyeing the lace of my bra and matching undies. "Very nice. Very feminine. Now take them off."

"You first," I said, crossing my arms and tapping my toe, trying to look bored. I was anything but bored, though, when he complied, peeling off his shirt and baring that lovely chest and belly tattoo. I actually started to salivate at the sight of his bare flesh.

He pulled his boots off, never once taking his gaze from mine. His hands reached for the fly on his corduroy pants.

"Allow me," I said, ignoring the fact that my voice was as husky as a sled dog. I kicked off my flats and put my hands on his belt, unbuckling it as I said, "I love the way your eyes go all steamy when you look at me. You make me feel like I'm bathed by the fire inside you."

"Baby, you *are* the fire inside me."

I unbuttoned the button on his pants. "I love the way you smell. You smell like a man should smell, masculine, hard, hot . . ."

I pulled his zipper down slowly. He took a deep breath and held it as my hand deliberately stroked against the long length of his penis, his eyes positively glowing now.

"And how you make me feel when you touch me." I slipped my hands inside the waistband of his underwear, pushing them and his pants down past his hips and thighs. He kicked them off the rest of the way. I took him into both my hands, and indulged in a little tactile exploration. "You make me burn for you, Raphael. Only for you. I need your touch to feel alive. I need you."

"Ah, baby, what you're doing to me," he groaned, the cords in his neck standing out with strain.

"I haven't done anything," I said with a naughty smile as I lowered myself to my knees before him. "Yet."

"Baby, I don't think I'm going to be able to stand it if you—ah, Christ!"

He tasted just like his scent: hot, hard man. I remembered everything Dr. Ruth had ever said about the way to drive a man mad, and added a few little ideas of my own. He had both hands on my head, directing me to a rhythm that pleased him, his hips moving in time to my strokes. "Oh, God, baby, that's so good. You feel so good to me."

I added a little suction. His voice went up an octave. "You're going to kill me if you keep that up."

I lifted my head. "Do you want me to stop?"

"God, no!" he yelled, then groaned when I redoubled my efforts.

"I'm not . . . going to be able . . . oh, Lord do that again . . . aaaaiiiigggghhhhh . . . not going to be able . . . oh, sweet Christ, your mouth should be illegal . . . to last much . . . oh, God . . . much longer. Joy, stop. Stop now."

I didn't want to. I'd never really been one for oral sex before, but with Raphael it was different. It gave me immense pleasure to give him pleasure. I added a little fillip with the end of my tongue and heard him groan in response. "Baby, you have to stop now."

I wrapped my fingers around his balls, lightly raking my fingernails down them, tracing that fascinating little vein that runs forward. His hips jerked as I gave him one last stroke of my tongue.

"JOY!" he yelled, panic tingeing his voice.

I looked up. "What? Oh. Sorry. I didn't realize you were that close. Wow, no wonder you blew out the end of that condom. That's got to be at least five feet over to that wall."

"Woman," he growled, pulling me up until I was pressed against his body. "You are going to be the death of me."

His hands were busy on the hooks of my bra.

"Yeah, but what a way to die."

He smiled a smile that was filled with all sorts of wicked promises, promises I couldn't wait for him to fulfill. "Baby, you have *no* idea."

"Really?" I asked, allowing him to remove my bra. He pushed me back onto the bed, rolling on top of me for a moment to kiss my wits away. I smiled to myself as his tongue went wild ordering mine around, checking my teeth, stroking the roof of my mouth, and generally being demanding, but then it was gone as Raphael rolled off me and opened the drawer to his nightstand.

"I get to put it on you this time. I want to try doing it with my tongue. Roxy said she heard it's possible . . . what's that?"

He rolled back over until he was lying on his side next to me, a long bottle in his hand. "I'm partial to cherry. I hope you like it as well."

"Oooh," I squealed, partly in response to the idea of something a little different, partly because of the desire in his eyes. "Is that one of those slicky lotions that make you slide all over one another and heat up when you blow on them?"

"Yes," he said, flipping open the top as he bent to take my breast in his mouth. I squealed again when he tugged ever so gently with his teeth on my nipple, then moaned when the cool liquid hit the tip, oozing downward. He leaned over me and took my other breast in his mouth while his fingers teased the slick oil over my breast. The combination of the heat of his mouth and the coolness of the lotion made my mind go numb with pleasure. He teased circles around my cherry-flavored breast, gently rubbing my nipples between his slippery fingers just as he started suckling hard on my other breast.

I almost came off the bed, my back arched up so high.

"Like that, do you?" he chuckled, his voice intimate and sexy and rough with pleasure. He dribbled a little lotion on my bare breast, then switched sides and sucked all the cherry goodness off the first breast, laving my breast and nipple with long, sweeping strokes of his tongue.

"Repha*EL*," I screamed, clutching his shoulders as he burned my breasts up with the fire his hands and mouth were causing. "Oh, please, Raphael, you have to stop! My nipples are going to explode, and then what'll I do? I don't think they can do nipple transplants, can they? Oh, sweet baby Jesus, that's so goooood . . ."

He drizzled cherry down my belly, his fingers painting me with the wetness, tracing intricate paths that his mouth soon followed. While he was busy nibbling around my belly button, his hand slipped down to my underwear, rubbing the heel of his hand over me, his fingers teasing the satin into my heated core. My eyes crossed at the cool silk of his curls brushing against my skin with each stroke of his tongue on my belly. The dance of his fingers against my soft folds was driving me wild, winding the coil inside me up tighter and tighter. "Raphael!" I shrieked.

He smiled against my stomach.

"Take my underwear off!"

He cocked an eyebrow at me. "Demands? Do I hear demands?"

"Please," I begged.

"That's better," he smiled, and nuzzled the flare of one hip. "Do I take it you don't like it when I do this?"

He pulled my underwear tight against my flesh, his finger stroking out a quick tempo that had me mindless in seconds.

I whimpered. It was all I could do, I couldn't form

words—words were too much to expect when my body was being pleasured beyond any pleasure it had known.

"Baby, all you have to do is tell me what you want," he crooned, his eyes hot and wicked and full of the terrible, terrible things he wanted to do to me.

I prayed he had time to get to every last one.

"Please," I sobbed, my body bucking in time to his fingers. "Just you. I want to feel just you."

He ended one torment by pulling my underwear off, but started another when he spread my legs and went wild with the bottle of cherry.

"Dear God in heaven," I cried at the first stroke of his tongue against my heated flesh. "Raphael! Bob! Please!"

"Anything for you, baby," he said, settling my thighs on his shoulders and preparing to send me flying. His mouth sent me into a maelstrom of sensations: fire, silk, pleasure, love, desire, need . . . they were all tangled up together as he drove me higher and higher until at last I went up in a bonfire of ecstasy. He caught my shout of exultation in his mouth as he plunged into me, so deep it was impossible to tell where he ended and I started. He pulled my hips against him as he entered me again and again with quick, hard thrusts, touching my womb, touching my soul, searing himself into my heart with every hot word of love he moaned into my neck, setting me alight with the pure joy of our combined rapture.

"Each time," I told him later as I stroked my fingers down the long, damp sweep of his back to the curve of his lovely behind; "each time I think it can't get any better, and then it does."

His head raised from the crook of my neck just enough to press a kiss to my collarbone.

"You set me quite a standard to follow," I complained. "I don't know how I'm going to match you, let alone exceed you. Everything you do to me is wonderful. Do you have any idea what sort of stress that puts on me to strive for perfection? What if I fail? What if I can't ever match you?"

"You're forgetting an important fact." He pushed himself up so he could grin before swooping down to capture my lips in his. "Practice makes perfect. We'll just have to let you practice until you're perfect."

I thought about that for the scant second before I gave myself up to the hot lure of his mouth. "Works for me."

Chapter Seventeen

"Where's your gun?" I asked, stepping out of the claustrophobic shower so tiny I wondered how Raphael fit into it.

He was dressed, sitting on the bed pulling his boots on, having washed off all our cherry fun. He looked up as I toweled myself dry and reached for my clothes.

"My gun?"

"Yeah. You know, the one you pulled on us when we did our breaking and entering the other day. The big one."

"Why do you want to know?"

I unzipped my dress, stepped into it, and turned so he could zip me up. "Idle curiosity. I thought maybe since you were in charge of security you'd be wearing it, but you haven't, and it's not under your pillow, so I was just wondering what you did with it."

His hands were warm on my back as he pulled the zipper up; then he turned me around and looked at me for a minute with those amber eyes that could melt my knees. With a sigh, he bent down and reached under his bed, pulling out a small black metal box.

"Oh, it's in there?"

"Yes."

"Ah."

He pushed the box back under the bed, then grabbed my hips and pulled me onto his lap. "Joy, about what you said earlier—"

"Oh, my apology? Yeah, I know I still owe it to you."

"No, about—"

I put my hand across his mouth. "Let me do this with style, will you? I really am sorry for what I said, Raphael. You're entitled to your privacy, and if you don't feel like you can trust me with something in your past, that's fine. It hurts me, but I'll live. I just want you to know that, despite the pain I feel because I know I'm not as important to you as you are to me, I will still be here for you. I love you, and that means I'm stuck with you no matter how badly you treat me."

I pulled my hand from his mouth and smiled at him, pleased I had gotten my groveling out of the way.

There was a decidedly disgruntled look on his handsome face. "That was an apology?"

"Sure was."

"Ah. Perhaps it is the latest rage in apologies—one that backhands the person you're apologizing to."

I nudged him on the shoulder. "Stop being so argumentative. You're supposed to accept it and tell me you love me and worship me and you'll never, ever keep anything from me again."

"I'm supposed to do that, am I?"

"Yes, you are."

He tipped me over onto my back and loomed over me. I smiled and looped my hands around his neck.

"And you came all this way just to apologize to me?"

He started nibbling on my neck, his hot breath starting familiar fires that had just been put out.

"Well, not just for that. Roxy and I had to talk to Dominic."

"Why?" he asked, his hands sliding up my dress to massage my breasts.

I squirmed and lifted my jaw to give him better access to all the sensitive neck spots, my hands tracing out the muscles in his back. "Roxy set it up. Dominic had something to tell us."

"Something about what?" His tongue curled around the outer edges of my ear, his uneven breath doing more to me than the hot touch of his mouth.

"Something to help us. Oh, God, Raphael, you can't do this again, we just got cleaned up!"

"Something to help you what?" he asked, sucking my earlobe into his mouth as he gently squeezed my breasts.

I nuzzled his cheek and tried to remember what I wasn't supposed to tell him. "We're trying to find out who killed Tanya."

He froze for a moment, then released my ear to look into my eyes. "Why?"

I traced my fingers across his silky eyebrows. "Because you're a suspect. So am I, although I don't think Inspector Bartos was serious about that. I *hope* he wasn't serious. But you . . . he doesn't seem very happy about you. And, Raphael, say what I will about you being pigheaded and stubborn, you're everything to me. I can't lose you. I won't let him take you from me. So if Roxy and I have to do a little detective work to prove you're innocent, we will."

He kissed me, hot and demanding. "You're the most amazing woman. I've never known anyone as giving as you." I opened my mouth to tell him that was the sort of thing I wanted to hear, but he silenced me with another hot kiss. "Regardless, I can't let you do this. I appreciate that you want to help me, but you don't have anything to worry about."

"But Inspector Bartos—"

"Leave the detecting to the police, Joy."

I pushed him back so I could sit up. "Look, I have enough on my plate right now, what with having to deal with Christian, I do not need you locked up in jail on a trumped up murder charge simply because I didn't make the effort to prove you're innocent."

He took hold of the back of my dress and kept me from getting off the bed. "You don't have to prove I'm innocent; the police know I am. What do you mean, you have to deal with Christian?"

I gave him a look of sheer disbelief. "Oh, sure, the police know you're innocent. That's why you're heading up their suspect list."

"What has Christian done? Why do you have to deal with him?"

"I don't want to talk about Christian, I want to talk about saving you, you arrogant, maddening man! Why I want to save your annoying, if extremely dishy, hide, I don't know, but I mean to, so you can just stop being all macho and ordering me around and—"

"Joy." He took my face in his hands and leveled a look at me that shriveled the words up on my lips. "You will not investigate this murder any further. The man who killed Tanya has not been apprehended, and until he is, you are not safe. Do you understand me?"

"Of course I understand you—you're being possessive and dominating—"

Raphael rolled his eyes, muttered something that sounded like an oath, and pulled me forward, his kiss hot enough to take the curl right out of my hair. "I'm telling you I love you, you foolish woman."

"You are?" I asked, breathless from the power of his kiss.

His eyes were things of beauty, gems of the brightest quality, clear and translucent and filled with love. Somehow his declaration took the sting out of his bossiness.

"I am. I love you and worship you, and after this is over, I'll never keep anything from you."

It was exactly what I wanted to hear, what I *needed* to hear. He was acknowledging my concerns and fears, and promised to answer all my questions . . . *after* it was over? I stopped him just a hairsbreadth from my lips. "What do you mean, *after* this is over? Raphael, you could be in jail then!"

His fingers curled into my hair, teasing my nape. "Baby, I won't go to jail."

"What's to keep you out this time?"

I regretted the words as soon as they left my lips. His fingers stop stroking my neck.

"This time?" His gaze held mine. I stared at him, my heart tearing into a thousand pieces at the flicker of pain in his eyes, a layer of ice settling around me as he pushed me off his lap and cocked an eyebrow at me. "I see. *That's* the information you wanted from Dominic. Do you mind my asking how you expect to use what Dominic told you to prove who the murderer is?"

"That wasn't exactly the purpose of our meeting with him," I said miserably, tears starting at the back of my eyes. "I'm sorry, Raphael. I'm very sorry and ashamed of myself. I don't like poking into your past, I just want to help you. I want to keep you safe, and since you won't tell me what it is you are keeping from me, I thought if I knew, I'd be able to do whatever it takes to keep Inspector Bartos away from you."

He watched for a moment as tears streaked down my cheeks, then wrapped his arms around me and pulled me to his chest. I buried my face in his neck and watered his shirt. "Baby, I wish I could tell you everything," he said, his lips in my hair. "I wish I could, but it's not possible yet. You have to trust me just a little bit longer."

"I do trust you; it's you who doesn't trust me," I pointed out, sniffing and wiping the dampness of my tears off his neck.

He didn't say anything to that, just thumbed the tears off my cheeks and looked at me with eyes dark with longing, regret, and pain.

"What is the problem you're having with Christian?" he asked.

"You're changing the subject."

"I know I am. What is the problem you're having with Christian?"

"This hasn't resolved anything. Even if Roxy and I don't go after the murderer, I'll still be worried about you, and will continue to worry until Bartos has someone other than you under lock and key."

"If it will make you feel better, Joy, I will swear to you that he won't arrest me for Tanya's murder."

"How can you swear that?"

His eyes went darker.

I looked into them and saw the answer for myself. He was still keeping things from me, still hiding secrets that he wouldn't share, but that was no longer the issue it had been earlier. He loved me. I had to trust that in time, he would tell me everything.

"I should be going. I've got a lot to do, and I imagine you do as well." I got up from the bed and gathered my coat and purse.

He stopped me. "What is the problem with Christian?"

I thought about not telling him, but decided he would be safer knowing the truth. "Nothing's the problem with him, unless you count a nine-hundred-year-old vampire as a problem, unless you find the fact that your mind and body and soul can be invaded by him with the merest thought of his mind a problem. Problem? I don't know—is it a problem to have an immortal man with limitless power thinking you're the sole person in the entire history of time who can save him from eternal damnation?"

"Vampire?" Raphael couldn't have looked more surprised than if I'd stripped off all my clothes and stood on my head. "You don't mean to tell me that you actually believe he's one of those creatures he writes about?"

"Oh, I don't just believe it, buster, I *know*."

Disbelief was rampant in his eyes.

"Don't you give me that look," I warned, pointing my finger at him. "Don't you give me that 'She's mad, I'll humor her because I'm a manly sort of man and she's my woman and thus I must put up with all of her foolishness and pretend it's not foolish at all even though inside I'm laughing so hard I could break my spleen' look! I am *not* mad, and I'm *not* imagining it."

"Joy," he sighed, taking my hands in his. I tried to take them back, but he was too strong. "I know you're upset about this murder and the fact that I've got a job to do—"

"What job?" I interrupted him, suspicious. "You mean something other than just your security work? Do you have another job? A secret job? Something *else* you aren't telling me?"

"—and I know you and Roxy are enamored with Christian because he writes books you enjoy, but, no matter what he tells you, there is no such thing as a vampire."

I turned my hands so I could pinch his wrists. "I used to think that too. I thought Roxy was nuts for wanting to come here, but then the visions started, and then he started making midnight visits to me in bed—"

"WHAT?"

"—and I have to tell you, being seduced long distance by

someone's mind goes a long way into making a believer out of you."

Raphael stared at me for a minute, as though seeking the truth in my eyes, then let go of my hands so he could rub his jaw. "Joy, I don't know what you've experienced, but I do know it can't be real."

"It is real, Raphael. I didn't know it was him at first—I thought it might be Milos or someone—but then Christian admitted it when we were in his dungeon. Roxy heard him."

"He's bamming you, love."

"No, he's not. I know what I felt! He invaded my mind. He touched me, physically, only he wasn't in the same room."

Raphael's frown deepened. "Touched you how?"

I held his gaze. "As a lover might."

The muscles in his jaw flexed. "He's drugged you. He's drugged you with something to make you see visions and believe he has supernatural powers."

"Oh, God, Raphael, he hasn't drugged me—"

"Baby, there's nothing you can say to make me believe that anyone is a vampire, least of all Christian. A parasite, a psychotic madman bent on seducing you, a poor fool who's deluded himself into believing his stories are real, yes, he's all that, but not a real vampire. They just . . . don't . . . exist."

"Well, we're going to have to agree to disagree here, because I know what I know." I stuffed my arms into my coat.

"Damn it, woman, there is no such thing as a vampire!" He grabbed my coat as I stepped into my shoes. I tried to walk past him, but he caught my chin in his hand and tipped my head back so he could fire those amber eyes at me. "This is not arrogance talking, this is not jealousy, it is simply a matter of facts."

I stared at him for a few seconds, wondering if he knew the danger he was putting himself in by being so blind. So stubborn. So determined to not need anyone's help. "I don't blame you for not believing me. I didn't believe it at first either, not even when Christian invaded my head. But it is the truth, and pretending it's not won't make it go away."

"I don't need to pretend to make Christian go away," he growled, grabbing me and hauling me up against his chest. His eyes were dark with emotion, frustration and love and anger all mingled together.

"You're hurting me," I whispered against his lips. He gentled his hold on my neck, then dropped his hands from me altogether, stepping back to release me.

I looked at the man I loved with my heart and soul, and swore an oath that I would not let his stubbornness ruin our lives. He might not want me playing detective, he might not believe that Christian was who I knew he was, but I could, *and would*, do whatever it took to keep disaster from rolling over us. Slowly I gathered up my things.

"Do you understand what I'm saying, Joy? Christian is nothing to us."

I stood still for a moment, then nodded and turned to leave. Oh, I understood him. The problem was, he wouldn't believe what he couldn't see. I opened the door, curiosity forcing me to stop on the top step and ask, "You know who killed Tanya, don't you?"

He came up behind me, standing so close I could feel the heat from his chest. "Yes, I do."

I looked at my hand on the door latch. "Is it Milos?"

I felt rather than saw him stiffen.

"He's always given me the creeps. Now I know why. I'll see you tonight at the festival?"

"Joy, I don't want you to—"

I opened the door and walked down the steps. Outside the sun was still shining, the men were still breaking down the booths and tents to reassemble on Christian's land. Everything was the same, and yet everything was different.

A warm hand settled on my neck, gently this time, his

thumb rubbing away the sting of his earlier hold. I turned and slid my hands under his coat, holding him close, breathing in his wonderful smell. He wrapped his arms around me, holding me just as tightly.

"I won't go near Milos if that's what you're about to order," I whispered, kissing his ear.

"This is not a game, Joy."

I kissed his chin, his obstinate, blunt chin that I loved so much. He still thought I was upset because he wouldn't admit to me what he was really doing with the fair. Silly man. "I know it's not a game."

"If you persist in playing detective, I'll have to spend my time keeping an eye on you rather than proving the murderer's guilt to Bartos. I need this time, Joy. I'm not going to have another chance."

"And if you don't succeed?" I tipped my head back to examine his eyes. They were hard again, just as determined and stubborn as the rest of him. "What happens if you don't convince Bartos? What happens if the festival ends and the fair moves on without you? What then?"

He rubbed his thumb over my lower lip. I bit it. "Then my future is written for me."

My heart tightened painfully. "And it won't include me?"

He didn't answer me right away. "Let me do my job. Let me do it without worrying about you. I need to know you're safe, otherwise this won't end."

I nodded and started to pull away, but his arms tightened around me. "Please, baby. You wanted to help me, now I'm giving you the chance to. Stay away from Milos."

He wasn't asking, he was demanding, but now wasn't the time to argue over words. I nodded again and slipped out of his embrace, giving him one last very gentle kiss before starting off to find Roxy.

* * *

"Let's see," Roxy said, circling around me as I stood outside Arielle's trailer. "Hair: mussed. Lips: swollen with impassioned kissing. Dress: wrinkled, as if it had lain on the floor for a while. Face: blushing. Yep. All signs you had a really good *talk* with Raphael."

"You are an obnoxiously bad woman and you will be punished one day."

She grinned and fell into step as we started back to the hotel. "I take it by the sated look you're wearing that all is right in Raphael-land?"

"Relatively," I admitted. "Somewhat. Kind of. How is Arielle?"

Her grin fizzled away into nothing. "Upset, worried, and frightened. But she'll survive. Her boyfriend is hanging around, keeping an eye on her. I think he'll make sure she doesn't suffer more than she has to."

I stopped. "Maybe I should see her now rather than later?"

"No. Paal gave her a couple of sleeping pills; she'll be out until the festival tonight. Come on, it's lunchtime and I'm hungry. I'm willing to bet that man of yours didn't feed you, either." She shot me a knowing glance. "At least, not food."

"Oh, grow up!"

"So let me get this straight," she said a short time later as we sat over bowls of vegetable soup and fresh baked bread. "You've done a one-eighty on the whole 'he won't tell me his secrets' issue?"

"Right. He loves me. He'll tell me when he's ready to."

"Wow. You really have grown up, haven't you? So then, why the long face?"

"Raphael doesn't believe Christian is a Dark One. He's letting his stubbornness blind him."

"So?" Roxy stuffed a roll in her mouth, crumbs drifting onto the table as she spoke. "I admit that he's being stupid about it, but what's the big deal? You get Christian to show a little fang, and voilà! Instant believer."

I stirred my soup. "The problem is that Raphael's letting his stubbornness blind him about everything. It's not just Christian, it's the whole thing with Inspector Bartos, too."

"You're just a control freak, that's your problem. You want Raphael to admit you're right and he's wrong."

I threw my bread at her. She caught it and took a bite.

"It's not nearly as simple as that. For one thing, Raphael is in danger of being arrested again. Call me silly, but I'd like to avoid that. I really don't want to spend the rest of my life hanging around a Czech prison begging for visitation rights."

She crumbled the bread into her soup. "He says he's not in danger of being arrested."

"Yeah, well, he didn't hear Inspector Bartos say he was a suspect. You think the police are going to tell he's on the list? They don't want him to have his guard up! They want him to feel secure so he'll slip up and they can nab him and take him away from me." I took a deep breath and slammed the flat of my hand onto the table. "I'm not going to let them do that! Raphael doesn't want me getting involved with finding out who the murderer is, but he didn't say I couldn't find someone who can do it for me."

"Who's that?" she asked, her head tipped to the side.

"Christian," I said without thinking. "He can read minds, can't he? I'm sure Milos is the murderer, so all I have to do is ask Christian to read his mind and find a little tangible proof for the police."

"Oh, right, and Christian is going to help you save your lover, the man whose job he wants?"

I waved that issue away. "He'll help me, I know he will. How much time do we have before it starts to get dark?"

She glanced at her watch. "Four, maybe five hours."

"Good. That gives us time to catch a little sleep. The festival won't be starting until nine or so, so we should have a good three hours to find Christian and have him scan Milos's mind."

"We?"

"I *assumed* you were going to help me."

She sighed and dunked my bread in her soup. "I suppose I'll have to keep you in line if I want to see you and Raphael settled happily. I just wish I knew why you didn't trust him to take care of himself."

"Of course I trust him, the man's a spy. He's perfectly able to take care of himself physically."

"He's *what?*" Roxy shrieked.

I glanced around the nearly empty room, smiling wildly at the elderly couple who were giving us frowns. "Shhh! You want everyone to hear?"

She goggled for a moment, then grabbed my wrist, leaning forward to hiss at me. "What do you mean he's a spy? Raphael?"

"Yes, Raphael, a spy. Or a government agent of some sort. Honestly, Rox, I thought you would have figured it out by now."

"Did he tell you that?"

I gave her one of the many patient looks I save just for her. "No, of course he didn't, that would qualify as secret-telling. It's obvious, though. Raphael is clearly not in the least bit concerned about the police other than seeing Milos brought to justice. He carries a gun, and who knows what else he has locked away in that metal chest. Probably his spy papers or something. And that cock-and-bull story about him raping a woman and killing her is just too ridiculous for words. It's just the sort of thing those spy places would make up. Thus, he must be working undercover to figure out who the murderer is. Let go of my arm, it's starting to hurt."

"Damn, girl, you take the cake," she answered, releasing my wrist. "I just hate it when you outguess me. So now you know his secret, right? Are you going to tell him?"

"And puncture his ego? No way. Behind every good man stands an exceptional woman, and I am that woman. I'll just make sure that Inspector Bartos doesn't nab Raphael by mistake, and never tell him I helped."

"Why would Inspector Bartos want to nab Raphael if he's a spy?"

I rolled my eyes as I picked up my spoon. "He's undercover, silly. If he reveals himself to Bartos, word could get back to Milos and then the whole case will be blown. You need to read more spy books."

We spent the next half hour detailing our plans for the evening. I was heading upstairs to take a much-needed nap when Roxy—on her way to the bar to ogle the natives—stopped me with a question. "You do realize what Raphael did, don't you?"

"When?"

"Earlier. He took the sixth step to Joining by asking for your help. Now all that's left is for you two to complete a blood exchange."

I made a face as I continued up the stairs. "That, I can assure you, is not going to happen."

A few hours of nap time, and I was feeling much more optimistic that the plan we'd agreed on would actually work. I pulled out the long blue and green peasant skirt I'd bought in Brno, and added a frilly silk blouse and an oversized paisley scarf that doubled as a shawl.

"Going with the gypsy look?" Roxy asked, poking her head into my room.

"Yup. You remember everything you're supposed to do?"

"Keep an eye on Arielle, warn you whenever I see Raphael, and act as courier whenever you need a message sent to Christian."

"Right." I pulled on my underwear and the ruffled petti-coat I'd bought with the skirt.

"I have a question."

"Shoot."

"Why do I have to act as courier for you when you can just call Christian up on the mind-phone?"

I shivered. "I told you earlier, I don't want to do that. It's a very intimate thing, and the less intimacy I have with Christian, the happier I am. Besides, he's not answering me."

"You make him sound so dangerous."

"He *is* dangerous. Very dangerous. You have no idea of the torment he's in, what he's capable of, but I am."

"He'd never hurt you."

I tucked the blouse into the skirt and draped the scarf around my waist, à la gypsy, then turned to look at her. "It's not me I'm worried about him hurting."

She pursed her lips in a silent whistle and admitted I might have a point.

By the time we left the hotel, the sun was just sinking down behind the indigo mountains.

"You are going to be done in time for the magic show, aren't you?" Roxy asked as we settled back into the ancient Peugeot taxi. "Believe it or not, Dominic is really great at it. Even Christian was impressed with some of the illusions he did."

"I should be done with the readings by then. Tell me again when you and Christian parted ways last night."

"He left right after the magic show. Said he'd heard all he could take of the bands, and since you were nowhere to be found, he said he'd see us tonight, before the festival."

"Hmm."

"Why? What are you thinking?"

"I'm not sure. I just can't help wondering why he disap-peared, and didn't try to seduce me. I can't shake the feeling that something is going on with him, that something isn't right."

She didn't say anything to that, but cast me occasional worried glances. I looked out into the darkening night and wondered what Raphael was doing, and if he was thinking about me even half as much as I was thinking about him.

"Boy, do I have it bad," I muttered to myself.

"That's the understatement of the year," Roxy grinned. She gave my hand a little squeeze. "However, I have to admit I don't really blame you. Raphael's kind of cute, in an immense, overpowering sort of way."

There was nothing that could be said in response that she wouldn't interpret as the smutty imaginings of my mind, so I just looked out into the night and tried to construct convincing arguments for Christian to help nail Milos.

Chapter Eighteen

"Found him! Come on. He's in the west garden."

I looked up from the stones scattered in front of me on the casting cloth I'd bought earlier and frowned at Roxy. "The line of people standing here might have escaped your notice, but I am busy right now, Rox."

Although we had arrived a couple of hours before the festival itself was due to begin, Dominic had arranged for the more popular attractions of the fair to be open early on the grounds of Drahanská, including the tarot, rune stone, and aura photography booths, as well as a stage set up for Dominic's magic show, and later a lineup of European Goth bands. I had been reading runes nonstop since we arrived a short while earlier.

"You told me to find Christian. I found him."

"Damn." I smiled reassuringly at the woman sitting in front of me before turning back to Roxy. "Do me a favor and go find Renee. She said she'd spell me if I needed a break."

Roxy sped off to find Arielle's friend while I hurried

through as many readings as I could before she returned.

"I'm not very good at this," Renee told me in breathless French as she maneuvered her very pregnant self into the chair I vacated for her. "But I will try."

"I won't be long," I promised her. "I know you're helping Arielle with the tarot readings."

I gave her the hematite stones Arielle had been using and reiterated that I'd be back shortly, then headed off to speak with Christian. On the way, I ran into Raphael and Inspector Bartos. They were deep in discussion and didn't notice me when I made my way to them.

"—forensic report must confirm that," Raphael was saying.

"Unfortunately, the forensic examination has not yet been completed," Inspector Bartos replied, his eyes on the crowd. I had noticed several of his people mingling with the festival-goers, as well as an unusually high number of uniformed police. I gathered they were there to not only keep the peace, but to nab Milos if he turned rabid again. That is, if they weren't there to grab Raphael. "This is not Lyon, Mr. St. John. We do not have such resources at the tips of our fingers. As for your suggestion regarding—ah, Miss Randall."

Both Inspector Bartos and Raphael turned to look at me. Neither looked particularly happy with what they saw. I gave the inspector a toothy grin and latched on to Raphael's arm, a suspicion growing in my mind. "Evening, Inspector. Pardon me for interrupting what sounds like a fascinating conversation. I don't suppose you care to continue it?"

Both men just looked at me.

"No? What a shame. Raphael, if I might have a word with you?"

I pulled on his arm, but he stood firm, his eyes wary. "What about?"

"Christian," I hissed, still smiling at Inspector Bartos. His mustache looked unhappy with me. "He's in the west garden."

"I know where he is."

I stopped tugging on his arm. "How do you know?"

The corners of Raphael's lips quirked. "Baby, I told you I wasn't going to allow you to go ahead with your plan to play detective."

"You odiously arrogant man!" I immediately understood exactly what he was saying. "You're having Christian followed? Who else, Raphael? Milos, I hope, but what about Dominic? Why stop there? Why not have Arielle, Roxy, and me followed as well? Sheesh!"

A familiar exasperated expression began to form on his face. "Joy, I've explained this all before, but I'll do it one more time on the chance that this time you'll heed me and do as I ask. You are not going to poke around trying to find out who murdered Tanya."

"I have no need to poke around. I know who murdered Tanya. It's Milos," I told Inspector Bartos, just in case Raphael hadn't. He pulled out his notebook and made a note.

"You are not going to convince me that Christian Dante is a vampire."

"A Dark One," I explained to Inspector Bartos. "They're kind of benign vampires, but I expect you know all about them, having lived here."

He licked the end of his pencil and made another note.

"And furthermore," Raphael said, "you are going to do everything I ask you to do this evening, starting with staying put at your rune table."

"You really do think you're the cat's pajamas, don't you?" I asked Raphael, annoyed with his arrogance. He might be everything I ever wanted in a man, but that didn't mean I was going to let him do something stupid when I could prevent disaster.

"Cat's ..." Inspector Bartos asked, his pencil poised above his notepad.

"Pajamas. It's an expression that means Raphael thinks I'm helpless against his masculine charms, which is just ridiculous, because I'm trying to save his sorry hide. That reminds me—I want to have a little talk with you later about some misconceptions you might have about him."

"Joy." Raphael's voice sounded like that of a particularly hard-pressed saint. "Go back to your table."

"No. If you won't come with me to see Christian and let him knock off some of those blinkers you're wearing, I'll go by myself."

"You will not."

"Oh, really? And just how are you going to stop me, have me arrested?"

"If I have to."

I looked at Inspector Bartos. He smiled. I gaped at him. "You wouldn't dare!"

His moustache smiled, too.

"Ha ha ha, you guys are so funny." I started to edge away, picking up speed quickly until I called the last few words over my shoulder. "Well, I think I'll be taking a little walk now. See you both later."

I dashed off, Raphael's sexy chuckle caressing my ears. I didn't for one moment believe Inspector Bartos would arrest me on Raphael's say-so, not even if my growing suspicion about the two of them was true, but I really didn't want to leave Renee at the rune table long.

I passed Arielle's table and paused for a moment to see how she was doing, and to tell her that I'd be sending Renee back to help her as soon as I could.

"I am fine, thank you," she said with a watery smile. Her eyes still looked red and swollen, but all in all, she was holding up remarkably well. I spun around and dashed through the line of people waiting to have their cards read, almost mowing down Henri in the process.

"Sorry, Henri. I'm in a bit of a hurry." He muttered an apology and stepped back as I threw myself back into the crowds. I headed toward the west garden, but suddenly made a detour when I saw Dominic slobbering over the hand of an extremely buxom woman dressed in fishnet stockings, PVC, and fake blood running out of an equally fake wound on her neck. Considering Tanya's death, it gave me a bit of the heebie-jeebies, but I swallowed my revulsion and waved to catch Dominic's eye.

"*Mon ange,*" he said, looking a bit embarrassed about being caught fawning over another woman's hand. "I thought you were reading the runes now?"

"Just taking a little break. Renee's covering for me. I just wanted to let you know that I'll read them until nine, and then I'm calling it quits."

He smiled and reached for my hand. I snatched it back and turned around, running smack dab into Henri again.

"Sorry, Henri. Guess I'm two for two with you, huh? Did I hurt your toes? No? Great. See you later!"

Off I went again at a fast trot, or as fast a trot as I could manage in the huge horde of people that had descended upon the well-groomed grounds of Christian's castle. I veered around a maze, realized I was going in the wrong direction, turned around, and raced around the corner to head to the west.

"Damn!" I rubbed my nose where it had smacked into Henri as he barreled around the corner toward me. I blinked back the stars, and glared at him. "Oh! Henri, are you fol-lowing me?"

Henri, a nice guy with warm brown eyes and a rather shy smile, looked horrified. He stammered out a feeble excuse, which I trampled over brutally. "Tell Raphael I don't need a nursemaid." I zipped past him, heading in the right direction for the west gardens. "And stop following me!"

He followed me anyway. When I stopped to face him, my hands on my hips, he told me he didn't dare ignore Raphael's orders. "He was very adamant that I should remain with you if you left the rune table."

Henri was about my size, but he had a friendly puppy air about him that kept me from laying into him. Besides, it wasn't really him I was angry with—that delight was reserved for Raphael.

"OK," I told him. "You can come with me, but you have to stay out of my way. And no snitching to Raphael what I'm doing."

"Snitching?"

"You can come with me, but you can't report back to him where I've been or whom I've spoken with. OK?"

"OK," he nodded, obviously relieved.

Christian was overseeing the tapping of several oversized kegs of beer arranged in sort of an informal beer garden. Long trestle tables and benches had been placed within the walled garden. Due to its distance from the main stage, the garden was relatively quiet . . . for the moment. As soon as the beer garden opened its doors, I had no doubt it would be just as mad as the rest of the festival.

"Christian!" I bellowed across the garden and waved to get his notice. One of his servants, a big beefy guy with a wicked scar down one side of his face, stood blocking the entrance and wouldn't let me in. Christian turned and motioned for him to let me pass. I told Henri to wait for me, smiled at and scooted around the behemoth at the gate, trotting down a line of tables to where Christian stood directing the placement of kegs. He'd had torches set along the perimeter of the garden, the flickering light of which cast a medieval feel to the whole setting.

"Christian!"

He turned to face me, his face as pleasant as ever. I examined him closely for a minute, looking for signs that he'd suffered some sort of difficulty, but his eyes were warm, and the ever-present smile lurked just behind his lips. "Are you all right? I've been worried sick about you! Where have you been?"

Both his eyebrows went up in mock surprise. "Such passion. I have been here, readying the estate for the festival."

"You know full well what I'm talking about!" I smacked him on the shoulder, then grabbed his hand and pulled him over to an unoccupied corner. "Where were you last night? I was worried about you after . . . after Tanya's body was discovered. You heard about that, didn't you?"

He reversed my grip so he was holding my hand, raising it to his lips, his eyes holding mine as he kissed the back of my fingers. Say what you will about women's lib, I had to admit there was something about having my hand kissed that made me go all girly inside.

"You look lovely tonight, my Beloved. However, I must presume to inform you that I do not care for you to be sharing your charms with every man present." He reached to the front of my ruffled blouse. I looked down. The top button, a small faux pearl, was missing, leaving my blouse gaping open, exposing my breasts down to the edge of my very low-cut bra.

I grabbed at the material and clutched it closed. "Damn. Must have happened when I crashed into Henri."

He smiled and flashed his hand. In it was a very old-looking gold brooch of a griffin clutching a large red stone in its beak. "Allow me," he said, brushing aside my hands, pinning the brooch so it closed my blouse.

"It's lovely, Christian, thank you. I'll take very good care of it."

"Consider it a gift from one who admires you."

I didn't want to accept it since it looked valuable, but I

figured I'd return it after the festival when I could explain my feelings without insulting him.

"Thank you, but that still doesn't explain why you didn't answer me last night." I peered into his unfathomable eyes.

"My housekeeper said you called," he answered, not batting an eyelash at his obvious evasion. "Alas, I was not at home at that time."

I squinted my eyes at him. "Christian Johann Dante, you know full well what I meant, so don't try to pull that Mr. Innocent crap on me." I put my hand on his wrist and gave it a little squeeze. "I know you heard me; I could feel you out there. Why didn't you answer me?"

He didn't move a muscle, but I felt him withdraw. "I was under the impression you found such form of communication distasteful. Further, I believed from the activities that followed that you preferred your privacy to my company."

I stared at him, my mouth hanging open for a second before I realized what I was doing. "You rotter!"

I bellowed the words so loud, all his staff turned to look.

"You did it on purpose! You wanted me to be worried about you! You wanted me to think you were lying sick or injured somewhere. You great big . . . POOP!"

A smile flirted with the corners of his mouth. It just made me see red.

"Gah!" I yelled at him in frustration, then stomped off, swearing to myself about men who played mind games. I thanked God Raphael didn't do that. He might be secretive now and then, but at least he told me that he wasn't telling me everything.

"Joy," Christian called after me. I kept walking. He took my arm and walked with me. I refused to look at him. "I will not apologize for my actions, since I cannot regret anything that makes you look upon me with a favored eye, but I do lament the fact that I caused you worry."

"I can't believe you used me like that," I said, a tiny bit

mollified. I didn't know if it was the magic his voice worked, or the sincerity in his eyes, but I did at least stop thinking about torturing him. "I can't believe you deliberately let me worry all night and all day about you." Something he said suddenly penetrated the layers of irritation. I stopped and turned to face him. "Hey! What do you mean, 'the activities that followed'? How do you know what activities followed? Were you spying on Raphael and me?"

He rubbed the top of my hand with his thumb. I pulled my hand away. I liked it better when Raphael did it. "No, I was not spying on you. I hold you in more esteem than to do that. But you are my Beloved; our minds are as one. I can feel when you are subject to strong emotions, just as you can feel when I am."

A massive wave of blush washed up my chest and neck, firing my cheeks to egg-frying temperature. "You mean you can tell when I'm . . . when Raphael and I are . . . you *know?*"

Distaste flickered across his face, something a whole lot more ominous darkening his eyes. "You may rest assured that I do not savor the knowledge that my Beloved is in the arms of another, but the answer is, yes, I know. Just as you would know should I betray you."

The pain in his eyes was too much for me. I took both his hands in mine, pressing them to my bosom.

Just as I was about to speak, a throat cleared. I turned my head and glared at Henri. "Go stand over by the statue of the horse. You can watch me from there."

He looked a bit mulish about my order until Christian turned his gaze on him. Henri blinked a few times, then backed away, bumping into several people, a large potted tree, and finally colliding with a small iron table that held the cash box for the beer garden. He didn't stop by the statue, however, he kept going. I figured I had only a couple of minutes before he found Raphael and tattled.

I squeezed Christian's hands until he looked back at me. "Christian, I'm so sorry you think I'm betraying you. I truly am, but we've gone over this and over this. I don't have the same feelings for you that you have for me. I just can't be what you want me to be, pure and simple." His fingers tightened around mine. "I know that's cruel of me, and selfish and self-serving, but it's the truth. I love Raphael. I will always love Raphael, and nothing and no one will change that. If you truly can share my emotions, you must know that I'm not deluding myself."

"I know that he has bewitched you, yes. You are fascinated with him, and he arouses you sexually as I do not, but it is apparent from the fact that you have not taken the final step of Joining that deep inside you know the truth."

My blush, which had started to die, was reborn with a vengeance at his mention of the attraction Raphael held for me.

"I feel your emotions, Beloved, feel the depth of your passion and know that the source of them cannot be anyone but myself. You are my Beloved. Because I know this, because I know that ultimately you will be mine, I am allowing you time to rid yourself of the affection you feel for St. John." His eyes were as cold and hard as the hematite rune stones. "It has not been easy for me, but my belief that you will see the truth is the *only* reason I have allowed another to possess you."

In hindsight, I guess I'd been around too many men that day telling me what I could and couldn't do. There is really no other explanation for what happened next.

"You know, this macho 'I will allow you' stuff is really starting to irritate me. I'm not a possession, Christian. I have a mind. I can make decisions on my own. And I've made it! Now, I like you. I'd like to count you as my friend. I've promised to help you find your Beloved"—I held up my hand to stop the objection I could see he was about to of-

331

fer—"OK, your *other* Beloved. I know you don't think it's possible, but what's to stop there from being two women for you, huh? Me with my wires crossed, madly in love with Raphael instead of you, and some other poor woman out there who is your soul mate and doesn't know it. Regardless, as I was saying, I'd like to be your friend, but I swear to God, if you tell me ONE MORE TIME what your high-and-mighty self is *allowing* me to do, I'll belt you one right on the nose."

His eyes glinted dangerously at me for about three seconds before I was slammed up against his chest, his arms like iron around me. My mind was filled with his anger, his need to dominate and bend me to his will. I honestly don't know what might have happened if he had shown me the other side of his anguish, the desperate need for love and unbearable loneliness, but he didn't. Instead I was swamped with his belief that he had every right to take control of my life. "You . . . are . . . mine." His voice was like liquid metal, smooth and beautiful and hard with resolve. "You will always be mine."

He made his mistake then. He pushed me with his mind, actually tried to push me into admitting what he wanted to hear. The rebellious me screamed a war cry of defiance as I curled my fingers into a fist. His head leaned in to kiss me. I slammed my boot heel down on his foot, watching with satisfaction as he jerked back at the unexpected blow, his eyes opened wide with surprise. As I brought my foot up from his foot, I kneed him in the groin, then swung my fist forward and punched him in the nose as he doubled over in pain.

"Don't *ever* do that again," I yelled as he crumpled up. "My mind is my own! You are not allowed to force me to do ANYTHING!"

I stormed away from him, ignoring the stunned expressions on the faces of his staff as they watched their employer writhe on the ground, rubbing my knuckles and feeling extremely pleased with myself.

332

Until I remembered I wanted Christian to tackle reading Milos's mind for me.

"Well, hell," I snarled, shocking a white haired old man who had his arms full of tablecloths. "Sorry," I apologized, and did an about-face. I walked back to where Christian was being helped to his feet by the big burly guy. The guy looked like he might give me trouble until I made mean eyes at him; then he backed off enough so I could see Christian.

He wasn't clutching himself anymore, but he wasn't standing with his usual elegance, either.

"Are you going to strike me again?" he asked, his normally smooth voice a bit spiky around the edges. "If that is your intention, please allow me to send my staff out of the garden. I don't particularly wish to have them witness you repeatedly bringing me to my knees."

"I'm really sorry I hit you. And stomped on your foot. And kneed you. I hope everything is OK down there."

We both glanced at the abused spot in question. His hand twitched as if he wanted to double-check things, but instead he straightened up and waved the hovering hulk away. "I accept your apology. I will request, however, that in the future if you take issue with something I do, you alert me to your intentions to strike me. I did not find the experience one I wish to revisit."

I cocked a brow at him. Thanks to watching the master of eyebrow emoting, I was getting pretty good at it. "You mean that's the first time you've ever been punched?" I lowered my voice so no one else could hear me. I had no idea if his employees knew what he was or not, but I wasn't about to spill the beans if they didn't. "You're almost nine hundred years old, for heaven's sake. Are you telling me that in all that time, no one's ever socked you in the nose?"

His eyes were dark as they held mine. "It has been attempted once or twice."

The underlying menace in his voice was clearly a warning.

"You let me hit you," I pointed out, ignoring the warning. "I know the power you wield, Christian. You could have crushed me where I stood. At the very least you could have kept me from kneeing you or punching you in the nose, but you didn't. Why?"

"You are my Beloved," he said. "I cannot hurt you. If it is your desire to harm me, I must allow it."

"But I hurt you," I argued. "Doesn't this whole soul-mate thing swing both ways? If I was truly your Beloved, wouldn't it be impossible for me to deliberately harm you?"

The corners of his lips turned up in a wry smile as he gingerly felt his nose. "I had always believed so."

I smiled and gently pushed his hand away to feel the bridge of his nose. "Nothing broken, just your pride damaged. And I'm sorry about that, although if it has made you rethink what I am to you, you won't have suffered in vain."

He gave me one of his martyred looks.

"I guess I'm really going to put our friendship to the test," I added, pulling out a tissue and dabbing at a tiny trickle of blood that seeped out of his nose. He stood perfectly still, but his eyes were dilated, black with strain. I backed off and put a little distance between us. "I wanted to ask a favor of you. If you haven't scratched me off your list of friends entirely, I'd like you to help me with a little problem concerning one of the fair people."

He considered me silently for a moment, then snapped out a few orders to his staff, and held out his arm for me. I took it and we strolled out of the temporary sanctuary of the garden, back into the noise and bustle and general madness that was the All Hallow's Eve festival.

"Why do you do this every year?" I asked, momentarily forgoing my request for his help. "It looks like it's a lot of trouble for you and your employees."

"Trouble?" He looked out at the sea of faces, people in all sorts of costumes, Goth and non-Goth, families, teenagers, adults, everyone eating and laughing and dancing, a mass of humanity whose shadows flickered and shimmered upon the white stone walls of Drahanská Castle. "It is not trouble. I do it because for a very short time, I am allowed to believe I am one with humanity." His eyes turned back to me. "Just because I am who I am does not mean I shun the company of humans. On the contrary, I quite enjoy them."

My eyes opened a bit wide at that comment.

He smiled and leaned toward me to whisper, "And not always as dinner."

He laughed at the look on my face, guiding me through the crowds.

"Um," I said, trying not to wonder about who he might have fed on that night. "Is that why you write, too?"

He nodded.

"I assumed you were using the books to find your Beloved."

He laughed again. "The books brought you here to me, did they not?"

"Yes, but I'm not your Beloved."

His smile lost a bit of its wattage. "I write because it gives me pleasure to tell the tale of my people, and because I can imagine a life that has thus far eluded me."

Talk about laying a guilt trip! Uncomfortable, I changed the subject. "About you helping me—"

"I am at your service, naturally. I can do no less for you."

I stopped and turned to face him, oblivious to the fact that we were blocking traffic. "I might as well tell you right now that I'm only doing this to help Raphael. I want you to understand my ulterior motive. I don't want you to feel like you were *being used*," I said with particular emphasis on the last two words. "Or exploited. Or manipulated. Or—"

He held up his hand. "I take your point. What is it exactly you wish me to do to help St. John?"

I took a deep breath and counted to five. "I want you to get proof that Milos murdered Tanya."

His eyes drifted lazily over my face. "I find myself surprised that St. John is allowing you to assist him in tracking down the murderer. Despite the obvious differences between us, I find myself in lamentable accord with him in regard to issues of your safety. I am having difficulty believing he has solicited your help in finding proof of the murderer's identity."

"That's because I haven't."

I didn't turn around. I knew full well what the expression on Raphael's face was going to be. I did, however, look at his shadow, as I nervously shifted from foot to foot.

"Traitor," I told Henri.

"He's not the one who has gone against orders."

I turned around at that, my hands on my hips, my lips thinned with annoyance. "Who died and made you God?" I de-hipped one hand long enough to poke him in the chest. "I do *not* take orders from you. You do *not* have the right to give me orders. You do *not* have the right to dictate my actions. Got that?"

Raphael sighed and grabbed my still poking finger. "You're going to make me do this the hard way, aren't you? You're going to be stubborn and foolhardy, and make me take extreme measures to keep you safe, isn't that so?"

My blood was up now. I don't mind feeling cherished and wanted and protected, but Raphael—and Christian—were going overboard.

"What we have here is a rampant case of alpha male-itis," I announced, glaring at Raphael. He raised one sleek brow in a "Who? Me?" question. "Well, guess what? I've suddenly become an alpha female, and that means I don't have to take any crap from either of you. So you can just stand here and beat your chests at each other all night, because I'm going to go read some damn runes and then find Milos and get the truth out of him one way or another. Gentlemen, Elvis has left the building."

I tried to stalk off on that beautiful exit line, but Raphael ruined it all, blast him. He grabbed the scarf tied around my waist, twisting his hand into it so I couldn't escape. I slapped at his arm a few times, but when that did nothing, I started to pick at the knot holding the scarf closed.

"I assume that, personal history aside, I can count on your assistance in this matter?" Raphael asked Christian. I snarled at both him and the knot and bent over to try to pry the material apart with my teeth.

"Joy's safety is tantamount in my mind," Christian answered. "Given the circumstances, you have my full cooperation. There are one or two members of my staff I can put at your disposal if they are needed, and I myself will be available as soon as my duties as host are completed."

"I'm never, ever wearing this damned scarf again!"

"Thank you. I will appreciate your help," Raphael said with a polite little bow to Christian.

Roxy raced up, breathless and pink-cheeked. "There you are! Renee has been waiting for you! She has to use the little girl's room. Come on, come on, you can eat your scarf later." She grabbed my wrist and started tugging me in the direction of the tables.

"I am happy to be of service," Christian said, making Raphael an equally polite bow.

"I don't like either of you anymore," I told them.

Raphael just smiled and released his death grip on my scarf, taking me by one arm as Christian took the other. With Roxy clearing a path ahead of us like some deranged flower girl, I was frog-marched back to the rune table.

Renee happily hoisted herself to her feet when she saw me approaching, waving an expressive hand as she waddled off for the nearest portable toilet. Raphael put his hand on my shoulder and pushed me into the chair. I bit his thumb.

"Stay here until I come to fetch you," he told me.

"I no longer recognize you in the Republic of Joy," I loftily informed him. "Our diplomatic ties are severed."

"Unsever them," he growled, "or the Country of Raphael will be forced to declare your republic a protectorate."

"Dictator," I muttered.

"For life," he agreed. "Stay here."

"You sound like something's going on," I said suspiciously. "You sound like you're doing exactly what you told me not to do. You wouldn't be planning an attempt to prove Milos is the murderer and clear your name with Bartos, would you? You are! You are planning on catching him! Well, you can just let me help, buster. I'm supposed to be the one you turn to in time of trouble! We've done the sixth step; I demand that you turn to me for help!"

His gorgeous amber eyes lit with a fire from within. "You do an alpha female quite well. I expect our children will give us nightmares. *Stay . . . here.*"

With a squeeze to my shoulder and a look that left no doubt in my mind that he meant every word he said, he waved Christian ahead of him. The two stood talking together for a minute, then parted and headed off in opposite directions.

"That's so romantic," Roxy sighed, watching them. "Bitter enemies pursuing the same woman, their love for you bringing them together."

"Romantic my Aunt Fanny," I snapped, and would have said more but the woman waiting to have her runes read coughed politely. I apologized for the delay and gave her the "think of a question" spiel, using her moment of indecision to whisper to Roxy.

"I'll need you to help me a little later. Obviously, the

Bobbsey Twins are going to make a stink if I try to talk to Milos by myself, so you'll have to help me get away from them."

"Talk to him? Why do you want to talk to him? He's a killer! I have to say I'm with the guys on this, Joy. Let the police handle the situation. Let Raphael do it—if he's a spy, he'll know all about truth serums and stuff. Let Christian mind-meld with him, but there's no reason for you to talk to him by yourself."

"Raphael doesn't see the truth, he's too stubborn. He needs my help whether or not he realizes it. Besides I won't be by myself," I said, shaking the amethyst runes in the bag. "I'll have you."

There wasn't much she could say to that, not with me laying out the runes and telling the woman what they said, but she sure sent me a look that promised retribution at the earliest possible moment. I grinned back.

Sometimes silence truly is golden.

Chapter Nineteen

I read runes for another two hours, looking up periodically to find either Raphael or Christian watching me. I ignored both of them, as well as the two men Christian posted on either side of the aisle. There were just no words to adequately express my disgust with either overprotective, pigheaded, domineering man. Individually, I could have dealt with them; working together, they were almost impossible to conquer.

Almost.

"Are you done here?" Raphael asked as I was tucking away my stones.

I started to glare at him, then realized he was looking at me with a strange expression on his face. "What is it? Is something wrong?"

He sighed and waited for me to finish putting things away, then took my hand and steered me toward the long lawn. "Yes, something's wrong, something is very wrong, but unfortunately, I find myself in a position—"

I had a sudden premonition of what he was going to say.

"—of needing to ask you for help."

"Yes," I said immediately, squeezing his hand and all but jumping up and down with the warm glow of pleasure that filled me. He needed me! He wanted my help! He finally acknowledged the fact that I was the one who was put on this earth to aid him in his greatest hour of need.

"You don't even know what I want you to do," he answered, pulling me to a halt behind the aura photography booth. His lovely eyes were grim.

"I don't care, I'll do it."

"It's dangerous—" He ran a hand through his curls, then shook his head. "Hell, what am I doing? It's too dangerous for you, I can't ask you to put yourself in that sort of a situation."

"Yes, you can. Raphael, I trust you. I know you'll keep me safe no matter what I have to do."

He stared at me for a moment, then took my face in his hands. "Baby, I wish there were another way, but—"

"I'll do it, I'm happy to, honest."

"There's no time to come up with another plan—"

"I'll do it, Raphael, I'll do it! Do you hear me? I'LL DO IT!"

"—and Bartos feels that you are the key . . . I know he's right, but still—"

"I'll make a very good key," I promised. "I'll be the best damned key there ever was. Let me help you, please!"

He looked me straight in the eyes, indecision mingling with regret and love in his face. He kissed me, hard and fast, his mouth gone before I could respond. "I need you to help trap Tanya's murderer."

My legs went a bit weak at his words. "Anything, Bob, I'll do anything you need me to do. Um . . . this wouldn't involve guns, would it? Because I don't like guns, and I don't know how to shoot one."

He turned us toward the long lawn, where the main stage

was set up. "No guns. You have to do everything I say, exactly as I tell you."

I saluted him. "Aye-aye, *mon capitaine.*"

"I'm serious, Joy. If you do anything, anything that I don't instruct you to do, I'll pull you out. Do you understand?"

"I'm your woman," I reassured him. "I won't even breathe without your express permission."

He sighed again and nodded to Bartos as we passed him. "I don't like it, but . . . hell. Paal and Christian's men will stay with you until it's time to bring you to the caves."

Excitement rippled through me at the thought. Here I was, madly in love with a dashing spy and he needed my help to catch a killer. Could life get any better?

It could, as a matter of fact. Raphael stopped at one side of the stage, his thumb rubbing gently on my wrist. I smiled secretly to myself. Now he would tell me everything, now he would bare his soul and take me wholly and completely into his confidence, proving without a doubt that he trusted me with his life.

"Paal will bring you to me after the magic show," Raphael said before turning to speak a few words with Henri. Then he left—he just left, walked off without even a glance back at me.

So much for trust.

By the time I stopped glaring at Raphael's disappearing figure, the crowd was gathering to sit on the ground before the stage. It was a low wooden structure about two feet off the ground, ringed with large black speakers used later by the bands, and backed by an area of draperies hung on a metal frame. Roxy had told me how much she enjoyed Dominic's magic act, saying it was surprisingly professional, much better than the phony vampire act he put on. Since I couldn't shake the two watchdogs who stuck to me like glue, and because I wanted to tell Roxy the latest news, I searched the crowd until I spotted her, following her to the spot near the stage she had staked out earlier.

I whispered the plan to her, then spent several long minutes rehashing my feelings for Raphael until Roxy finally had enough.

"Be quiet. Dominic is going to do this really cool disappearing trick. He goes into a glass box, it fills with smoke, and when it clears, he's gone. Then they do the smoke thing again, and voilà! He reappears. It's really great. I can't figure out how he does it, since the box is made of glass and they twirl it around on stage so you can see all the sides."

"Hrmph." I sat with my arms crossed and pouted slightly. I'd much rather talk about Raphael than watch some silly magic act.

"I wonder if he's going to do what he did last night?"

"What's that?" I asked, toying with the brooch Christian had lent me.

"Dominic went into the box, and Milos came out of it. I didn't know Milos was a magician, but he did some pretty amazing things after that. You should see what he does with three eggs—"

Onstage a couple of the fair workers wheeled out a large glass cube that rested on a dolly. Dominic did a little patter about the powers gained from his time studying the black arts.

I turned to Roxy, puzzled by what she said. "What do you mean, Milos is a magician? He was on the stage with Dominic? That can't be! Raphael said Tanya was killed right before he found her—her body was still warm. I know, I touched her."

"I don't follow you," Roxy said, her attention still on Dominic as he explained the illusion to come.

"Try this: If Milos was on stage doing a magic trick, he couldn't have killed Tanya."

Slowly her head turned to look at me. "If he didn't, who did?"

A wave of gooseflesh ripped down my arms and back as I looked back at the stage. "It couldn't be . . ."

"Oh my God," she breathed, her eyes huge.

I watched as Dominic strutted across the stage, tall and elegant in stark black with a red ruffled shirt. He flashed his fangs, playing up his vampirism to the crowd. He was working them like a veteran of the stage, teasing and playing with them until they yelled out their excitement.

"Dear Lord, it must be him. I always thought he was joking when he insisted he was a vampire. I mean, it was just all too ludicrous, what with those fake teeth and all. But what if he believes it? What if he really, really believes he's a vampire?"

Another wave of chill hit me. I gathered up my skirt and stood as the crowd yelled at something Dominic said. "I have to go tell Raphael. He thinks the murderer is Milos. I'm willing to bet you he doesn't know that Milos finished the magic show last night!"

Roxy tugged at my skirt, trying to pull me back down. "Joy—"

"The perfect volunteer!" Dominic bellowed from the stage, leaping into the crowd and heading straight for me, his hand held out. "*Mon ange*, if you will assist me?"

"What?"

"He was asking for volunteers, you fool. Too late—he's got you now," Roxy muttered.

"What? What?" I stared stupidly at the hand Dominic held out for me. I didn't want to touch him—he was a murderer! The crowd started cheering.

"Come, *mon ange*," Dominic said with a full-fanged smile. "Assist me. It will be over quickly, I assure you."

I wondered if he had said the same thing to Tanya. Dominic grabbed my hand and started hauling me back through the crowd. I debated accusing him there on the spot of Tanya's murder, of screaming for help, or of kicking him until he let me go so I could run to Raphael. In the end, I decided that it was better to not make him suspicious, so I made no complaint when he jerked me onto the stage and dragged me over to the glass box.

He kept a hold on my hand while he helped me into the box, doing a spiel about his powers and how I would be sent to the underworld to await his command to return. It was a bit creepy, considering Tanya. As he turned to close the lid on the box, he hissed, "Do not fear, *mon ange*. As soon as the smoke fills the outer layer, the trap will open and you will escape. Crawl under the stage to the rear. Antonio will be waiting for you there."

"Crawl? I'm supposed to crawl?" I asked as he closed the lid, getting a little panicky at the thought of being shut into a box with a bunch of smoke. I crouched in the box, my head pressed up against the top of it, the lights and the crowd blurring a little through the thick glass. Dominic waved his arm dramatically, and the box began to fill with smoke, obscuring my vision.

That was when I realized what he was talking about. The part I was sitting in was insulated, a box within a box, made of double-paned glass. The smoke filled a thin space between the two layers of glass, no doubt making it look as if I were sitting in the middle of the smoke, when in fact I wasn't. As soon as my vision outside the box was completely obscured, the floor beneath my knees gave, and I dropped down to a small space under the stage. The skirting around the edges of the stage kept me from seeing anyone, but I could hear the crowd. They roared with laughter at something Dominic was doing, no doubt misdirecting their attention so they wouldn't notice the box wobble as I dropped. I wadded up my skirt and crawled forward on my belly when I saw a bit of light flashing at the rear, muttering to myself about ruining my lovely skirt just so Dominic could impress his audience.

345

Antonio, Dominic's assistant, helped me out from under the stage through another trap in the curtained-off area. Antonio pulled on a gruesome rubber mask, saying, "Stay here until you hear Dominic announce that he's brought back a demon from the underworld instead of you. Then you can go out into the crowd." Then he dived under the stage and headed for the box.

"Like hell I will," I muttered, and peered out of the curtained area. My watchdogs must have been waiting patiently up front for me to return, because there was no one around the back. I slipped out and started hunting for Raphael, keeping well away from the audience around the stage.

I spotted Henri on the far side of the grounds, zipping up his pants as he emerged from a portable toilet.

"Henri, where's Raphael?" I asked as I raced up to him.

He frowned. "Aren't you supposed to be at the magic show? I thought Raphael said you were there. It's not over yet, is it?"

I almost danced with impatience. "Forget the magic show. I have to find Raphael. It's very important. Where is he?"

"He won't like knowing you're not at the magic show," Henri pointed out.

"He will when he hears what I have to tell him. Where can I find him?"

"He said you were going to stay with Paal. Raphael's not going to be happy that you left without him."

Friendly puppy or no friendly puppy, I wanted to throttle him. "Henri," I said with a smile that would do a shark proud. "Do you remember what I did to Christian in the west garden?"

His hand moved protectively to his groin as he nodded vehemently.

"Good. I don't want to have to do this, but if you don't tell me where Raphael is, I'll do the same to you."

His eyes opened wide. "He's down in the cave," he answered quickly, his voice thick.

"The cave? Already? Thanks, Henri. Wish me luck."

I took off like a hound after a hare, dodging around people, heading away from the festival along the graveled path that curled around the bottom of the abyss, ending at the entrance to the cave. Since the caves were only going to be open for a couple of hours around midnight, there weren't many people on the path, and those were mostly made up of couples lip wrestling.

I raced down the path toward the cool, dark entrance of the cave, large pools of yellow from the sodium lights strung overhead eating at the blackness within. There was no one at the entrance, but I could hear voices from inside. I listened for a moment, but other than guessing one of the voices was Raphael, couldn't determine whom he was talking to, or where they were in the cave. Noises tended to carry a long distance in there. I plunged in, trotting down the path, ignoring the scenic views and signs describing the various sights.

"Thank God I was here before," I said to myself as I paused at a junction in the path. The public tour continued around a bend to the left that led to the boat dock. To the right was a dirt path that according to the sign led to a maintenance area. I held my breath and listened. The low rumble of Raphael's voice echoed from the right. I started down the path, pausing for a moment, then sprinting down the path when a woman's voice answered him.

The path was badly lit, with lights distant and far between. I stumbled over debris and rocks a couple of times, but managed to keep from falling. As I rounded a bend in the path, I almost slammed into Raphael.

"What the hell?" I yelled, staring in appalled horror at him. He stood close to a woman, his mouth almost in her hair as his rotten, stinking, cheating hands moved under the back of her sweater.

"You bastard!" I bellowed, my words echoing down the walls of the cave. Their heads snapped around at the sound, identical expressions of surprise on their faces. The woman was about six inches shorter than me, had a slight figure, and a pretty heart-shaped face with long, curly hair that I wanted to tear off and stomp all over.

Raphael had the nerve to look annoyed. "Joy! What are you doing here?"

"OH!" I screamed, fury battling with the pain of his betrayal. I doubled up my fist and punched him right in the tattoo. He grunted and let go of the hussy he was holding to grab his stomach. "You cheating, lying bastard! No wonder you didn't want me down here until later! I never want to see you again. NEVER!"

I spun on my heel and raced back the way I came, stumbling and tripping over rocks because I couldn't see through the tears. Suddenly the tears dried up as fury took the upper hand. How dare Raphael put his hands all over another woman? He was mine, dammit, and I wasn't going to let him get away with that. It was time he understood one or two things. I turned around to go back and slammed right into him.

"Dammit, woman, will you stop and let me explain?" I would have fallen but for the strong hands grabbing my arms.

"Don't you dare yell at me, you beastly man! You complete and utter rotter! You can't touch anyone else, do you hear me?" I struggled against Raphael, but knew it would do no good. He pushed me against the smooth limestone wall of the cave, his body pressed against me as I fought him. He pinned my lower half back with his legs, his hands clamping down on my head, holding me in place.

"She's a policewoman," he said, breathing heavily. "Christ, baby, did you have to hit me?"

"You're despicable," I gasped. "Using your position to corrupt an innocent woman. You should be hung by your toes. And your balls. Both. At the same time!"

"Listen to me, Joy," he said, his breath fanning around my face. God help me, I was in love with a two-timing bastard, and even when I caught him with his hands all over another woman, he could still melt me with his touch. I sobbed anew at my own body's fickleness. "Kyra is a policewoman. She's one of Bartos's people. She's here to do a job for me, that's all."

I didn't want to hear him, didn't want to listen to any of his outrageous lies. "I don't believe you," I said.

"What have I ever done to make you think I'd be interested in another woman?" he said, more calmly this time, his eyes hot with desire and love.

"I . . ." I didn't have an answer. Behind him the woman appeared, pulling her sweater down. She asked Raphael in German what was going on. Just the sight of her renewed my fury. "She's a policewoman, huh? You had your hands all over her. Under her sweater. Exactly what sort of a *job* is she doing for you?"

"Kyra, show Joy your back."

"I don't want to see her back! I am not into threesomes!" I said indignantly, wondering how I could have been so wrong about him.

He rolled his eyes and repeated his order. The woman shot me a sour look and turned around, pulling up her sweater as she did. Snaked across her back was a flesh-colored cord, leading down to a thin black box about the size of a credit card. The cord and box were taped on with white surgical tape.

"She's a policewoman," Raphael repeated. "I was wiring her so we can record anything said to her. I was *not* fondling her. She's our backup in case our suspect doesn't take the bait—namely, you."

He took his hands from my head and stepped aside as Kyra murmured that she would be checking with Inspector Bartos before taking her position outside the cave. Raphael said he'd be out shortly, then looked back at me, speculation in his eyes.

"Somehow I always had the idea that if you ever caught me straying, you'd do more than just hit me in the belly."

"I didn't happen to have a castrating knife handy." I glared at him. "But I can assure you that if I did, you'd be singing soprano now. Policewoman, Raphael? Why do you need a backup policewoman? And why aren't you wiring *me?* Just what exactly are you doing?"

"Trying to catch a murderer. You know that. I was going to wire you before we sent you out," he replied, stepping closer to me, an odd smile toying with his lips. "You're jealous."

"Well, of course I'm jealous," I frowned, poking him in the chest. "You're mine, and you're not allowed to put your hands on any other woman's back. Those are the rules, and I expect you to follow them."

"Aw, baby," he growled in that low, sexy voice that never failed to melt my bones. It did now, too. Raphael grabbed me as my legs started to give way, pressing me up against the wall again, his hands next to my head, holding me prisoner. "I'm flattered that you're jealous, but you should know by now that no other woman could begin to compare with you. You're all I want." His teeth teased my ear, his breath steaming my skin, starting the familiar inferno of desire deep inside me.

I slid my hands under his leather jacket and sweater, stroking my fingers across the muscles of his back, taking his groan into my mouth, mating it with my own moan of pleasure as he ruthlessly plundered my mouth.

"You make me so hot," he said as he kissed a wet, steaming path down my neck. "How can you think anyone else can do this to me?"

He ground his hips against me. He was aroused, very aroused. I slid my hands down to investigate, smiling to myself as he groaned again, this time louder, his groan repeating itself in an endless echo of pleasure. My fingers worked quickly to free him, so I could feel his heat, feel his need and know it was all for me. I pushed his underwear aside and sighed when I found him, hot and hard, velvet over steel. I bit his tongue and whimpered against his mouth as his hands slid into my bra, wanting to feel him deep inside me where our heartbeats would merge to one wild tempo of passion.

"Raphael," I cried desperately, stroking his hot length, driven half mad by overwhelming desire stirred by his taste and his scent and his touch, knowing he wanted me as much as I wanted him.

"I know, baby, I know. This is going to have to be quick. I'm not going to be able to last long." He pressed me against the wall, blanketing me in his heat as he wrapped his hands around my thighs and settled them around his hips. I locked my heels around him, kissing him frantically, our teeth clinking together as I nipped at his lips and tongue until he gave me what I wanted and allowed me to suck his tongue into my mouth. I tasted blood as I swirled my tongue around his, moaning as his fingers teased a fiery path up my thighs.

I pulled my mouth from his just long enough to say, "Underwear," before licking the drop of blood that welled up from his lip. His fingers stroked the satin of my underwear, then with a jerk they were gone, literally ripped off me.

"Dear God," I whispered as I felt the hot tip of him enter me. "No one's every ripped my underwear off before. That's just so . . . *mmmrowr!*"

"Baby, I can't wait," he all but sobbed into my neck as he sank into me.

"Don't wait," I answered, mindless to everything but the exquisite feeling of oneness that our joining brought.

He cupped his hands under my behind, his breath hot on my neck, then with a grunt of possession slammed into me, thrusting so deep he knocked the breath from me. The wall of the cave was cold behind me, but he made me burn so hot I came close to leaving scorch marks on it. He nibbled my ear and neck as our bodies strained against each other, craving that moment of completion when we were transported past mere physical pleasure. His hips thrust and withdrew, his pace quickening with our breath. I slid my fingers through his curls and arched forward against him, close, so close to the end of our race.

"Raphael!" I screamed just as he bit my neck, his roar of ecstasy matching my own, the two indistinguishable as they echoed around us.

We stood like that for an eon, our bodies still joined, his heartbeat deep inside me matching my own, our breaths mingled, ragged, as he held me securely in his arms, still pressed against the wall.

"Ah, baby, I hurt you," he said, his voice thick with satisfaction mixed with concern. His lips were warm on my neck, his tongue a silky caress. "I bit you too hard. You're bleeding."

I tipped my head back so I could see his beautiful face, untangling my fingers from his hair to touch a raw spot on his lip. "I bit you, too. If you were a Dark One, this would be the final step of Joining."

One sable brow rose in question.

"A blood exchange." I smiled at his look of disbelief, and allowed him to lower my legs to the ground. Raphael tucked himself away, and I was just shaking my skirt down when a sharp sound started at one end of the cave and rolled past us, building in noise.

Someone was applauding.

"Christ," Raphael snarled, turning around as he did up his pants, blocking me with his body. I sent up a silent prayer that whoever it was hadn't seen us in action as I tucked my blouse back into my skirt, making sure it wasn't bunched up anywhere before peeking over Raphael's shoulder.

"*Mon ange*, I knew you had passion, but you surpass my expectations. Such fire! Such zest! I particularly enjoyed how your body arched against Raphael's at *le petit mort*. I believe we would have been well mated."

Oh my God, it was Dominic! And he had watched us! My skin crawled with revulsion even as anger surged within me. How dare he taint something wonderful and beautiful between Raphael and me with his slimy foulness? What we did was private, between the two of us, and although we might have celebrated our love in an inappropriate place, that still gave him no right to intrude. I hit the back of Raphael's shoulder, more than a little surprised that he wasn't roaring with anger at the invasion of our privacy, but it wasn't until I stepped around him to give Dominic a piece of my mind that I saw why he was so still.

Dominic was pointing a very large gun at us. Next to him stood a silent Milos.

"What are you doing here? You were doing your magic show!" I sputtered.

"All good things, *ma chère*, must come to an end," Dominic said with one of his showy bows before waving the gun toward Raphael. "Sadly, that includes you as well as the curious Mr. St. John."

I glanced at Raphael. He looked like Dominic was boring him to death. I felt better immediately.

"You will both come with me now, Raphael in front, *mon*

ange nearest me. Milos will follow. We will proceed that way to the boats, yes?"

"Boats?" I asked, scooting closer to Raphael. He didn't move a muscle, just watched Dominic with eyes so dark they were almost brown. "You want to go for a boat ride now? I thought we were going to do that later? I'm a bit busy now, so maybe I'll take a rain check on that. Raphael and I were . . . uh . . . just . . . um . . ."

Dominic snickered. "*Mon ange*, it was quite apparent what you and Raphael were doing. Now, if you are quite finished, the boats are waiting."

Milos eyed me coldly and turned to say something to Dominic. I used the opportunity to glare at Raphael. He raised his eyebrows at me.

"Well, you could help!"

"I thought you wanted to be the one to help me," he said mildly, apparently unconcerned that we were held at gunpoint by a deranged madman who thought he was a vampire, and his equally cold-blooded accomplice.

"That was then. This is now. I'd appreciate it if you did something."

"Like what?"

I pinched his arm. "Save us!"

"Ah. How?"

I threw up my hands in disgust. "You're the one who has the gun!"

Milos and Dominic both stopped whispering and looked at us.

"I don't have it on me," Raphael told them.

They didn't believe him. Dominic waved me to the side, his gun a few feet away from my breast while Milos patted Raphael down. Once they determined he was gunless, Dominic gestured me toward the way I had come earlier.

"As to your question, our boat ride must be canceled," he said, reaching for me. I slid away and ran for Raphael. "It is

354

a shame, but you will have instead the most tragic accident when you are shot by mistake. I, of course, will be saddened that you were killed in an attempt to stop Raphael from strangling you, but what am I to do?" He shrugged. "The police will have their murderer—a dead one—and I will mourn the loss of *mon ange chéri*. All will end well."

"You're going to kill us?" I don't know why I was surprised after seeing what he'd done to Tanya. Maybe both of them did it, I certainly wouldn't put it past Milos, what with the unwholesome look of excitement in his eyes. "Why? What have we ever done to you?"

"It is so," Dominic answered my first question. "Raphael has been too diligent in his investigation into our alibis for the murders of the women Milos and I have enjoyed. We cannot allow him to interest the police in our matters. Already he has gone too far. He almost caught me last night, before I was able to dispose of dear Tanya's remains to my satisfaction. I was not able to leave the damning clues as I had wanted."

"My rune stone," I said, seeing again the image of a purple stone in Raphael's hand.

"It would have worked if St. John had not followed us," Milos said, his voice cold and emotionless.

"But . . . but . . . why? Why did you kill her?"

Milos and Dominic exchanged a small, very chilling smile. "We are Vampyr. It is what we do."

"You're no more a vampire than Raphael is," I snorted.

Milos gestured toward me, prompting Raphael to note, "Baby, never mock a man who's holding a loaded Glock on you."

I pursed my lips and edged closer to him. Milos did not look in the least bit sane. "I see your point."

Raphael's hand brushed my hip as he reached behind him.

"You will come this way now," Dominic ordered.

I hate being pushed around. "Just a second. If you're going to kill us, the least you can do is admit everything in the best detective-story manner. I think you owe us that much."

Dominic smiled; his fake fangs didn't look nearly as amusing as I'd found them in the past. The beastly things glinted wickedly in the dull sodium lights. Raphael's arm slowly moved alongside me, then stopped. I prayed he had a weapon in it. Something lethal.

"I, too, read detective stories," Dominic replied. "If you expect us to admit to our sins in hopes you will miraculously escape, you are bound to be disappointed."

"You did murder Tanya and all those other women, though."

Milos muttered to Dominic. He held up his hand and looked hard at Raphael. "Our dear Raphael knows the answer to that question."

"Yes, I do," Raphael drawled. "The French police almost had you after you killed that prostitute in Paris, but unfortunately"—his lips twisted wryly—"I was pulled from the case."

"What? You knew it was the two of them all the time? Why didn't you do something?"

Raphael ignored my question, his eyes bright as they watched Dominic. "Someone bribed a technician to destroy the forensic evidence needed to convict you, Milos. Without it, the French detectives I was assisting could not bring any charges."

"Just who *are* you?" I asked him.

"Enough talk!" Dominic snapped. "You will walk ahead of me, *mon ange*."

I couldn't believe I ever thought Milos was creepy. Dominic standing there with a gun calmly discussing our murders was by far the creepier of the two.

"Kill them now," Milos said as he turned to leave. "I will return to the festival and keep the inspector busy."

"What?" I shrieked.

"I would gag her before you shoot her," Milos tossed over his shoulder as he left. "She will struggle more that way."

"I won't!" I snarled, then quickly threw myself out of the way as I screamed, "Let him have it, Raphael!"

Dominic looked at the slim black recorder held in Raphael's hand.

"*Oui*," he said, holding out his own hand. "Let me have it, Raphael."

I glared at the love of my life. "I thought you had a knife or something, not a tape recorder."

"I seldom carry weapons," he said mildly. As Dominic approached him to grab the recorder, Raphael's foot shot out and cracked across Dominic's knee. Raphael threw himself on Dominic as the latter went down, both men struggling for possession of the gun. I danced around the pair of them, looking for something I could use to brain Dominic, and had just settled on a large rock when a hand grabbed my skirt and jerked me backward.

The sharp prick of steel through my blouse kept me from moving.

"Drop the gun," Dominic gasped behind me, his hand tightening on my arm. "Very good. Now kick it toward me."

Raphael did as he was ordered.

I glared at him. "Even Dominic has a knife, Bob!"

"Do not start with me now, woman."

I snorted. He raised a brow at me in a wordless demand for silence, then held his hands up. "Let her go, Dominic. She doesn't know anything. I haven't told her about my investigations, nor why I joined the fair."

"You can say that again," I muttered with another pointed look at him.

"Joy, this is no time to bait me," Raphael answered as Dominic released me to pick up his gun.

"Oh really?" I gestured toward Dominic. "There's a madman standing there with a gun pointed at us, explaining how he plans on murdering us, and you don't think *now* is the time to talk? When do you want to talk? While he's shooting us?"

"You will stop this discussion now and march before me," Dominic ordered in his best bossy voice.

"You know full well that I had my reasons for not telling you what I was doing—"

"Right, you're a spy."

His eyes glittered dangerously at me. "I am *not* a spy."

"Yes, you are, you're a spy, and you joined the fair because you knew Dominic and Milos were the murderers. Roxy and I figured it all out."

"You must stop now and walk in single file before me," Dominic demanded in a louder tone of voice.

"You and Roxy are not entirely right."

"But we're partially right, which means you're a spy!"

"I am not a spy."

"Well, I know that story Dominic told me isn't true. I certainly don't believe you went to prison for raping some woman!"

"Now, it is *now* we will be marching. St. John, you will proceed first." Dominic took a step nearer me and waved his gun at Raphael.

"Perhaps you would care to explain why you've been trying to protect me from the police if you knew the story was untrue?" Raphael answered me with a decidedly disgruntled look on his face.

I shook my finger at him. "I wasn't trying to protect you from that, you great lummox, I was trying to keep the police from arresting you because you were a spy and couldn't tell them who you really were."

"I AM NOT A SPY!"

"I will not be ignored! You will do as I say. *NOW!*"

"Ha!" I said, raising my chin to glare at Raphael. "If you're not a spy, what are you? You admitted you're investigating the murders. You're not a policeman because you're not Czech, and there is no international police force that works through . . . different"—the words came to a stop as I stared at him—"countries. What's in Lyon?"

Raphael's jaw tightened as his eyes closed for a moment.

"*YOU WILL STOP SPEAKING NOW AND* . . . Lyon?" Dominic stopped bellowing to approach us warily, his eyes narrowed as he held the gun on Raphael. "Lyon, *mon ange*, is where you can find the headquarters of Interpol. How very interesting I suddenly find this conversation. Interpol . . . of course. That would explain so much."

"Interpol?" I asked Raphael. "You're with Interpol? Like a detective?"

He ignored me, keeping his eyes on Dominic.

Dominic stared back at him. "The only thing I do not understand is how you knew I would hire you in Marseilles. Your record—which I assume now was false, yes?—was not one that would lend itself to employment."

"I assumed that in your case, a history of violence toward women would act as a reference rather than a deterrent," Raphael answered, his eyes boring a hole through Dominic's head. He had let go of my hand, but I could tell his muscles were tense with anticipation. I suspected he was waiting for Dominic to get close enough that he could jump him. I know that was my plan.

"You know me well," Dominic acknowledged, then waved the gun toward the entrance to the main cave. "You will please do as I say now before I am forced to shoot your kneecap."

"Ha!" I snorted, much braver than I felt, stepping carefully down the path. Raphael moved behind me, but Dominic stopped us and ordered him to go first.

"I will keep our fiery one here where she is safe, yes? With her as a hostage, I am assured that you will not try to act the hero again."

"Where *is* your gun?" I whispered to Raphael out of the side of my mouth as he moved past me to take the lead.

"In my trailer," he answered just as quietly.

I glared at him. "Some detective you are. No knife, no gun. I bet you're going to be drummed out of Interpol for this."

"I'm not a detective, I'm a liaison," he answered, giving me another warning look. "And you're closer to the truth than you know."

I followed behind him, Dominic holding one of my hands twisted behind my back.

"Should have taken care of him when I had the chance," I grumbled to myself as we entered the cool air of the main cave.

Dominic told Raphael to go to the right, toward the boat dock. I honestly think if Dominic had pointed the gun at him, Raphael would have disarmed him, but with the cold barrel of the gun resting on the back of my neck, Dominic was right—I was a hostage for Raphael's compliance.

As we passed the entrance, the sound of footsteps on the wood pathway reached us. "Stand there, against the wall," Dominic hissed, pushing me to Raphael. "Do not move from there or I'll kill her."

He backed up a few feet, one eye on us, the other watching to see who would come along the curved pathway. The footsteps were growing louder.

"This doesn't look good," I told Raphael as I hugged him tightly. His arms squeezed the breath right out of me. "I think I'm going to call for help."

"No one can hear you this deep in the cave, Joy."

"Christian will," I said, tracing a finger along his eyebrows. "I've just found you, Interpol Bob. I'm not going to lose you now."

"The police know I'm here," he said quietly. "Christian can't do anything to help us."

"He can. I know you don't believe me, but he can hear my thoughts. If I tell him we're in danger, he'll come to help us."

Raphael's arms tightened around me. "Christian wouldn't be able to help us even if he knew we were here."

"Raphael—"

"I won't let Dominic hurt you, baby."

"You have to have faith in me," I told him, deliberately repeating his words, and then turning to lean into him.

Milos popped around the corner, gesturing with a small black pistol. "Police. They're everywhere. I've locked the gates to the entrance, but it won't take them long to reach the exit. We have to go now."

Christian, I closed my eyes and called out mentally, not sure if I was reaching him. *I know you don't want to answer me, but we need you. We're in terrible trouble, and Raphael doesn't have a gun.*

Immediately he was there, filling my mind with his calm presence. *Beloved, you are distraught?*

I opened my eyes and looked at Milos and Dominic, willing Christian to see them as they gestured with their guns while discussing the best way to kill us and escape.

I will come, his beautiful voice resonated in my head.

"Christian is on his way," I told Raphael, ignoring the disbelief in his eyes. "But I've always been a person who believes in being proactive. I think we ought to try to make a break for it."

"That would not be wise, *mon ange,*" Dominic said directly behind me, the cold barrel of the gun pressed between my shoulder blades.

"Oh, what do you care? You're going to kill us in a minute or two anyway," I snapped, wiggling my shoulders in an attempt to dislodge the gun.

"We have modified our plans," Milos told me as he passed, his gun pointed on Dominic. He nodded at the nearest red and white tourist boat. "It seems we have need of you alive. For the moment. Get in."

Raphael crossed his arms and didn't move a muscle.

Dominic prodded me with the gun. "You as well, *mon ange*."

"No," I said, my eyes on Raphael. If I was going to be killed, I wanted the last thing I saw to be him.

But I really didn't want to be killed.

Dominic pressed the gun harder into my neck until I flinched with the pain. Raphael's hands tightened on his arms, and I thought sparks were going to come flying from his eyes, but he didn't move. I smiled at him and hoped he saw the love and admiration in my eyes.

"Get in the boat, *Joie*," Dominic said, grabbing my arm.

What worked once might work twice, I figured. I blew Raphael a kiss, then lunged in the direction Dominic was pulling me, throwing him off balance. His gun slid out of his fingers and bounced on the wooden dock. I slammed my foot down on his, then brought my knee up into his groin. As he screamed and doubled up, I plucked the brooch from my blouse and stabbed him in the eye with it.

"Ew!" I squealed at the sensation of soft, squishy eyeball on my fingers, and jerked my hand away. Dominic screamed as he fell to the dock, one hand clutching his eyes, the other on his groin. I spun around to help Raphael, but he had disarmed Milos in one smooth move that sent the gun flying into the water, and Milos crashing into the nearest boat. There was an ugly thud when his head cracked against one of the wooden seats. He didn't move after that.

"Are you all right?" Raphael asked as I raced over to where he was checking on Milos. "Where's the other gun?"

I looked back over my shoulder. Dominic was still writhing and wailing on the edge of the dock. "It must have gone into the water as well. Is he dead?"

"No, just unconscious. Come." He grabbed my hand and pushed me toward the nearest boat. "Get in. I'll get you out of here, then come back for the two of them. There's nowhere they can go with the police at either end."

I put on the brakes. "No."

He frowned down at me. "Joy, don't be obstinate. I know you want to help me—"

"No, it's not that. I get seasick. I didn't think I would on a quiet river like this, but I did the other day. I'll walk; you take the boat."

He sighed and grabbed my wrist again, hauling me toward the narrow path that ran the length of the river. "I have never in my life met a woman who is so contrary and argumentative," he said.

"Yes, but you love that about me," I answered, suddenly feeling incredibly happy. We had escaped! We were going to be together! We would have a deliriously happy life together—once I made Raphael understand he was never to keep anything from me again. "Go on, say it, you know you want to."

He stopped long enough to pull me up to his chest. "Yes, I love you, you maddening woman. You're stubborn and obstinate and resistant to any form of common sense, but I love you more than I had ever thought possible, and no one is going to take you away from me."

His lips were closing on mine when a noise behind us made the hair on my neck stand on end.

"How touching," Dominic rasped as he staggered toward us, blood streaming from one eye. I must have broken a toe or two when I stomped on him, because he was limping heavily. I assume the kick to his noogies hadn't done him any good, either, because he was walking hunched over like an old man. The gun he held clutched in one hand made any satisfaction in his condition moot, however.

"He must have been lying on it," I said apologetically to Raphael.

"You," Dominic spat, his mouth twisted in a snarl. The madness in his eyes was clear now. I wanted to cling to Raphael, but knew he had a better chance of disarming Dominic if I backed off a bit. I sidled away, Dominic's eyes blazing at me. "You have laughed at me, and mocked me, and spurned my attentions for those of him—" He waved the gun at Raphael, then suddenly fired.

"NO!" I screamed, lunging for Raphael, but Dominic was faster than he looked. He slammed the gun into my face, sending me flying backwards. I crashed into the wall and lay numb for a few seconds, too stunned to do anything but wait for the burst of pain to reach my brain. It hit and left me gasping and retching as I dragged myself to my knees.

"Raphael." I knew the pathetic whimper was mine, but it didn't seem to belong to me any more than the haze of pain that nearly blinded me. All that mattered was that I get to Raphael. I crawled toward Dominic as he stood above a silent and still Raphael, pointing the gun at his chest and ranting in a high, insane voice.

"No one will doubt my power now. No one can. They laughed at me just as you laughed at me, but now I will be vindicated. All will fear my power and know me to be the true master of the dark! I will take my place with the great ones, and they too will bow down before me. I will rule the dark world, become what I was meant to be. No longer will I be burdened with this mere mortal's body. I will be invincible!"

"I am afraid there can be only one way to be rid of your human body, but as you are determined to do so, I will be happy to oblige you." Christian's voice was like a cool drink of water on a hot summer day. He appeared out of the shadows, walking toward Dominic, the power and deadly menace surrounding him making the air crackle. His eyes had changed, had deepened in their blackness if that was possible, allowing a glimpse into the endless torment that held him in its eternal grip.

I used the distraction to scoot closer to Raphael, praying with all my might that he was still alive. Red stained his left side, spreading across his stomach.

"Oh my God," I sobbed, touching him gently, unsure of what I should do to stop the bleeding. I didn't want to press on the wound if it would make it worse. "Oh, God, Raphael, please don't die. I need you. Please don't die."

His eyes opened at the sound of my voice. They were dulled with pain and anger, but they were his lovely, lovely eyes and I wept all the harder to see them. I pressed his hand to my lips and started repeating every prayer I knew.

Dominic cried out and stepped backward as Christian stalked him. The hairs on the back of my arms stood on end as I watched, unable to look away, unable to tear my eyes from the terrible weapon of retribution that Christian had become.

"You wished to see the great ones? Behold! I have touched eternity. I have walked the earth in darkness only, never to know the warming touch of the sun upon my flesh, never to have a family, a lover, friends. I have lived in silent torment wishing I had the strength to end the nightmare of my existence, but failing because I am cursed to live damned and shunned, an abomination to every living thing. Do you still wish to join me, little mortal?"

"Joy." Raphael was trying to prop himself up. "Help me up, baby."

"Don't move," I told him. "You'll make the bleeding worse. Should I be pressing on it? Will it hurt you if I do? Oh, God, Raphael, you've been shot!"

He pulled himself up into a sitting position, panting with

the effort, his beautiful eyes glazed with pain. "Have to protect you."

"No, my darling, you don't have to. Don't move anymore, you're making it worse! Just sit still. Christian is here. He'll take care of Dominic."

"That's who . . . have to . . . protect you," he gasped, his face pale with the strain.

Dominic screamed something in a language I didn't understand. I put my hands on Raphael's shoulders to keep him from moving, and glanced over to where Christian was backing Dominic against the wall. Teeth, long and sharp, flashed in Christian's mouth. He stalked his victim as a panther would an insignificant rodent, slowly, without wavering, sure of the outcome.

Evidently, Dominic was sure as well, for he suddenly raised his gun and began firing at Christian. The noise of the gun being fired in the large open chamber was deafening, each gunshot echoing until I had to cover my ears to keep from screaming.

A terrible, high-pitched shriek ripped through the echoes, setting new ones bouncing off the walls, rippling through the air in one long, endless cry of death. When the noise stopped, I opened my eyes. Christian held Dominic a good two feet off the ground, one hand closed around his neck, his head tilted at an unnatural angle. With a flick of his wrist Christian sent Dominic flying. He hit the wall and slid down it like a soggy rag doll.

I gagged. Raphael tried to move, but I held him down.

"Don't move, my love. Oh, God, the stain is getting bigger. How long will it take the police to come around the other end? Raphael, please don't try to move!"

His hands were tight on my waist as he tried to shove me aside. A shadow fell over the two of us.

I looked up, tears streaking my cheeks. "Christian, can you help him? Please, will you help him? He's been shot, and I don't know what to do. Please help us."

Christian held his hand out for me, his face closed and impassive. I thought he wanted me out of the way so he could help Raphael, but when he pulled me to my feet, he didn't take my place. He just stood holding me.

Raphael snarled and tried to shift himself. "She's mine, Dante."

"No! Stop him! Raphael, you're going to kill yourself if you keep trying to move!" I struggled against Christian, but the arm he had around my waist was like steel. He looked from Raphael to me, his eyes deep wells of suffering. One finger traced the welt on the side of my face where Dominic had struck me with the gun, a drop of blood clinging to his finger. He looked at it for a moment, then brought it to his lips.

"I have allowed this to go on long enough. It is at an end."

I looked in his eyes and knew he would do nothing to help Raphael.

Unless I bargained for that help.

"Please help him," I cried, my lips trembling as more tears spilled down my cheeks. Raphael grunted with pain as he tried to get to his feet. I held my hands out to him, but Christian would not let me move. "Please," I begged. "I love him so much, Christian. Don't do this to me; please don't make Raphael suffer."

By some miracle of willpower, Raphael dragged himself to his feet, one hand clutching his side as he panted, leaning drunkenly against the cave wall. "You can't have her," he said, his voice low and rough. "She's mine."

Blood seeped up from between his fingers. I moaned at the sight of it, and willed Raphael to look at me.

"I love you," I told him. "I always will. Nothing will ever change that."

He lurched away from the wall toward us, but was slammed backward when Christian lifted his hand.

"Leave him alone, God damn you!" I shrieked, and turned to pummel Christian.

"He already has, Beloved."

I looked back at Raphael. He was slumped against the wall, bright red smeared against the light-colored stone behind him, his body shaking with the effort to stay upright.

"She's . . . my . . . love," he said, his eyes on me. "Not yours. Never."

"Come with me, Beloved." Christian's voice was like velvet sliding on my skin. "I will make you forget him. I will give you everything you want. I will be everything to you."

Raphael took a step away from the wall. With a flick of his eyes, Christian sent him flying across the room.

"NOOOOO!" I screamed. Raphael lay halfway across a bench, his belly and chest bright with blood. He raised himself up on one arm, his head hanging, blood dripping from a cut on his temple.

I closed my eyes, unable to bear seeing him hurt, then turned in Christian's arms. "I will come with you."

"No, baby."

I ignored Raphael's low cry, watching as Christian's eyes flared to life.

"I will come with you and live with you for however long you want me to, but you have to save Raphael first. You have to save him and let him go and promise never to harm him."

Christian's eyes searched mine.

"You have to save him now, and swear to me that you won't ever do anything to hurt him. Ever."

"Baby, don't leave me," Raphael called hoarsely to me, sliding down the bench to the floor. I sobbed while my heart shattered into little pieces, my nails biting into my palms as I watched the man that I loved die.

"You would do this for him?" Christian asked. "You would give him up?"

"So that he might live? Yes. I would do anything for that."

"I won't let you go." Raphael's words were the merest whisper, but they cut through my heart like a razor. I didn't look at him. I *couldn't* look at him. There was no way I could save him unless I gave myself to Christian, unless I bartered myself for Raphael's life.

Christian's eyes narrowed. "Everything you've said, every protestation and objection you've made—you say to Join with me will damn you; you would risk damnation for him? Would you sell yourself for his life?"

"In a heartbeat," I answered. "He is more precious to me than life. Please, Christian. Help him before it's too late."

Christian stood silent for a moment, then released me and walked over to where Raphael lay. When Raphael tried to raise his hands, Christian squatted next to him, placing a hand on Raphael's side.

"He is dying."

A moan slipped out of my lips, fresh tears burning down my cheeks. "Save him," I begged.

He placed both hands on Raphael's side for a few moments, then brushed his thumb across Raphael's forehead, leaving a long bloody smear. Raphael twitched, then slid the rest of the way off the bench, onto the floor.

I watched, a silent scream of anguish so deep there was no end to it building inside me. He was dead.

With him died my heart.

"I feel your pain, Joy, but you allow yourself to suffer needlessly. He is not dead, simply resting. I sent him to sleep so his heart would slow down. I cannot correct all of his injuries, but I have repaired enough of the damage that he will recover with medical attention."

My relief at his words was so great that I dropped to my knees, my arms wrapped around my waist.

"Thank you," I said, my eyes on Raphael's still form, unable to say anything else. "Thank you."

He walked over to me and held out a hand. I looked up

at him, unwilling to take it, but knowing I had to keep my part of the bargain. "Do we have to go now? Can't I stay with him just a little longer? Just until an ambulance comes for him?"

Christian took hold of each arm and hoisted me to my feet. He held one of my hands in his, rubbing Raphael's blood off my fingers. "With you as my Beloved, I would see to it that you lived in eternal happiness, untouched by any of the emotions which trouble mortal man." He glanced over to Raphael, then raised my hand to his lips. "Tell him for me, please, that for the first time in a very long life, I truly find myself envying a human."

I stared at him for a moment as the full meaning of his words sank in. He wasn't going to take me. He was sacrificing himself for us. I knew that Christian honestly believed he was giving up all hope of his salvation. I blinked back more tears, then pressed my lips to his in a gentle promise. "I swear to you that I will find her. I will find your true Beloved. You won't have to spend the rest of eternity alone."

He set me aside gently, a faint mocking smile curving his lips. "This once I will not object to help from a human." He looked at me intently before making a courtly bow. "Be happy, Beloved."

I met his dark gaze, filled with longing and resignation and despair.

"I'll find her," I promised, then turned and ran to Raphael.

I didn't see Christian melt into the shadows of the cave, but heard his beautiful voice as it echoed back to me. "I will hold you to your promise. I, too, wish to know what it is like to be loved above all else."

The words reached me as I knelt over Raphael, one hand holding his, the other stroking his face. His skin was warm, his pulse was slow but steady, his long brown lashes resting peacefully on the taut skin of his cheeks.

"I love you, Bob," I whispered to him.

His fingers tightened around mine as voices from the far side of the cave echoed down to us, calling to find out if we were all right. The police had finally arrived.

"Love you, baby," he murmured.

High in the night sky a beautiful voice etched into the heavens the song of a brave warrior and a beautiful maiden, and their love so true it could not be destroyed, not even by death itself.

I smiled at my warrior as I waited for help to arrive.

Epilogue

To: Joyful <JoyRandall@btinternet.net>
From: Roxanne Benner <RoxyB@oregontechlib.com>
Date: November 5, 2003
Subject: I'm baaaaaaaaaack!

Hi Joy (and Raphael)! I'm back home, and boy do I have
a lot to tell you! You're not going to believe what happened
to me after I left Germany . . . but I'm going to tease you and
make you wait for it. Are you waiting? Am I driving you nuts?
Good. Now you know how it feels. Hahahahahah!

I'm glad to hear you guys made it to London OK. What's
Raphael's apartment . . . sorry, FLAT look like? 'Roomy and
near a big park' doesn't tell me much. Take pictures.

And speaking of him, I'm happy the tattoo wasn't touched
when they dug that bullet out of his gut. A scar you can live
with, but if that tattoo was ruined . . . well, I'm just glad it's
not. How long will it be before you know if Interpol is going
to throw him out of the organization for going off on his

own to find the vampire murderers? I can't believe they yanked him off the case in the first place. I mean, didn't he have Dominic and Milos pegged all along? It wasn't his fault if someone messed up the evidence; he knew it was Dominic, they should have listened to him, not forced him to take a leave of absence. Is he still in denial about Christian, or has he finally given in and admitted that there are Dark Ones? Must be tough living with an infidel unbeliever. Still, all's well that ends well, eh? You got your man, Inspector Bartos has Milos locked up safe and sound, and I got . . . heee! Nope. Not going to tell you yet. Waiting, waiting, waiting . . .

OH! I got an e-mail from Christian! Who knew Dark Ones were Internet savvy? He said he was going to send me a sneak peak at Book Thirteen, and was even going to name a heroine after me. Too cool, huh? I hope you're doing everything you can to find his Beloved, although I don't have a clue how you're going to go about it. Maybe you should put an ad in a London paper asking to interview single women? Or how about this—write a book about vampires so steamy that it will bring Christian's Beloved out of the woodwork. I even have a title for you: *A Girl's Guide to Vampires*. Brilliant, huh? Yeah, I know. I should be in marketing.

Work is the same old same old, no fun without you, but I'm not crying in my coffee. Want to know why? Ha! I just bet you do. Keep waiting. That's a hoot what your mom said about Bradley, BTW. I always said he was no good. I hope they take his license away. There's just no excuse for drunk drivers! Can we say LOSER? Sure we can!

Rats, it's after five. I have to go. I'm flying out to Rio tonight. RIO! As in, de Janeiro! You're dying to know why, aren't you? OK, I'll spill, but only because you're my best friend, even if you did leave me to shack up with a guy halfway around the world. You'll notice I'm not screaming about this. Why, you must be asking yourself, would dear sweet old Rox be so calm and collected?

I'll tell you why—Captain Richard Blaine. That's captain as in airline captain. Richard was deadheading on the flight home from Frankfurt, and sat next to me, and we talked, and I spilled my screwdriver on him, and one thing led to another, and . . . well . . . let's just put it this way: Miranda is two for two, Joyful.

Can I have my condoms back, please?

Will e-mail you when I get back from the land of sun and samba. Kisses and hugs to the big guy!

Roxy the no longer pure

Turn the page for a sneak peek at two more

Katie MacAlister Dark Ones novels

SEX AND THE SINGLE VAMPIRE

On sale April 2011

and

SEX, LIES, AND VAMPIRES

On sale Summer 2012

From Avon Books

Sex and the Single Vampire

The message waiting for me at the hotel desk was short and concise: *Either you come back from England with bona fide proof of a spiritual entity, or you needn't bother returning to the office. There's no room in UPRA for crackpots and never-beens.*

It was signed by my boss, and the head of the western U.S. division of the United Psychical Research Association, Anton Melrose II.

"Well, isn't that just Jim Dandy fine," I muttered to the message as I crumpled it up and tossed it into the appropriate receptacle, situated at the end of the reception desk, wishing as I did that I could Summon up a demon or two, minor ones, just bad enough to scare the bejeepers out of my employer. "I'd pay good money to see him eat his words."

The woman at the desk smiled as she passed me the key to my room. "I'm sorry, Miss Telford; we're not responsible for the quality of the messages. We have to deliver them no matter what they say."

I smiled back, secure behind the sunglasses I wore everywhere. "That's okay; it's just my life falling apart, nothing to worry about. Is there a computer free now, do you know? I'll only need fifteen minutes."

Tina, the receptionist at the St. Aloysius Hotel in jolly old London, checked the log for the two computers kept in a small, dark room for the use of those businesspeople who couldn't live without an Internet connection. "It's all yours."

I gathered up my bag, ignoring the clinking that came from within, and mumbled my thanks as I limped down the short hallway that led to the computer room. One of the two computers was taken up by a skanky-haired young man of about twenty, who raised one pierced eyebrow as I carefully set my bag down next to the chair of the second computer. The clink of glass bottles was loudly evident.

"It's holy water," I told him when his pierced eyebrow rose even higher. "For the ghosts. Nothing drinkable. That is, you *could* drink it, but I've had it on the best authority that holy water tastes like tap water that's oxidized for a couple of days."

He blinked at me.

"Bland," I explained, then turned my attention to the computer. I waited until he was busy with his own screen before pushing my sunglasses up so I could better see the computer screen, logging quickly into the e-mail account I'd set up for those rare times UPRA had seen fit to send me outside of the Sacramento area (which is to say, twice), just as quickly scanning the six messages collected. "Spam about an herbal product guaranteeing to make my penis grow larger, spam about low mortgage rates, e-mail from Mom, spam about something to do with furry barnyard friends that I'm not even going to open, e-mail from Corrine, and spam asking me if I'm single. Well, it's nice to know I'm missed."

The young man snickered and logged off his computer, pulling up a briefcase that had the name of a major software company embossed on the side. "Do you see lots of ghosts, then?" he asked as he stood and shoved in the chair.

I pushed my sunglasses into their normal position and gave him a little moue of regret. "So many I hardly have a moment to myself. They're very simpleminded, you know. Really no different from a puppy. Just a kind word or two, a little pat on the head, and they follow you around forever."

He stood staring at me for a moment, as if he couldn't decide whether I was serious or not.

I held up both hands to show him there was nothing up my sleeves. "I'm joking. No ghosts to date."

He looked relieved, then managed to twist his relief into a familiar sneer common to all young twenty-somethings. I ignored him as he left, pulling my glasses off as I scanned my mother's e-mail, filing it to be answered later before I clicked on Corrine's.

Allie: This is just a reminder in case you've forgotten—the Dante book signing is at the new Hartwell's store in Covent Garden tomorrow night, 7 p.m. London time. Be there or I'll do something so horrible to you, I legally cannot put it into writing.

Hope you're having fun! I don't suppose you took my advice and left the shades at home?

Corrine

P.S.: Don't forget to give Dante the key chain I made him. Be sure to tell him how long it took me to embroider his name into the warding pattern. And don't forget to ward it! I doubt if I will ever live down the embarrassment of the time you handed over an unwarded key chain to Russell Crowe!

"Mmm. What a shame. The C. J. Dante key chain was mysteriously left at home," I told the computer as I logged off and popped my sunglasses back on just in case I ran into anyone in the hallway. For a moment I just sat, exhausted, listening to the sounds of the hotel and the noise outside the window of London on a busy winter afternoon. Anton's message did nothing but add to my exhaustion. I had seen the handwriting on the wall for the last six months— "Produce or else" was his motto, and I was lamentably lacking in the proof department.

"This is it, Allie," I said aloud to the empty room. "Put up or shut up time, and I have to tell you, the job openings for an unproven Summoner are pretty slim."

My voice echoed in the room as I continued to sit and dwell on my grim future. It almost seemed like too much trouble to push myself out of the chair and haul my bag of tricks upstairs to the small corner room that had been allotted to me, but a glance at my watch got me up and heading to the bed that promised a few hours of much-needed blissful nothingness before I had to go off to a haunted inn and hunt ghosts.

The dream started even before I felt myself relax fully into sleep. It was dark, nighttime, the air damp and musty-smelling. I walked through an empty house, its walls stained with mold and age and unsavory things that my mind shied away from identifying, my footsteps echoing loudly as I moved from room to room, searching for something, a place, somewhere I was supposed to be. Small black shapes skittered just beyond my range of vision in every room I entered, faint, soft phantom noises trailing behind me like a wake. Mice, or something more disturbing? I wondered as I let my fingers trail over a dusty banister that led me downstairs into a dark pool of inky blackness. Fearless as I never was in real life, I pushed open the door at the foot of the stairs and saw a man stretched out on a table.

A man? Even in my dream I modified that word. He was no mortal man; he was a god, a perfect specimen of masculinity created just for my pleasure. Long black hair spilled onto the table, a halo of ebony against the light wood. His eyes were open, dark, but not as dark as his hair, almost mahogany in color, rich with browns and reds and even a bit of gold flaring around the edges of his irises. The long, chiseled lines of his jaw and squared chin were still, as if he were sleeping, but his eyes followed me as I moved into the room. He was naked but for a piece of cloth covering his groin, his body striped with what looked to be hundreds of small cuts, blood dripping slowly from the wounds onto the floor beneath the table.

I approached him, wanting to touch his wounds, wanting to heal them, but his voice caught and held me in a net of immobility when he spoke my name.

"Allegra," he said, his eyes dark with torment. "Help me. You are my only hope."

I reached out to touch him, to push a lock of his hair off his forehead, to reassure him that whatever it was he needed, I would do, that I wouldn't let him suffer any longer. I would send him on to eternal rest. As my fingers touched his heated skin, I woke up, gasping for air, sitting bolt upright in the bed in my hotel room, shivering despite the fact that I had cranked up the heat just before I settled down for my nap.

Sex, Lies, and Vampires

I kept telling myself that he was a vampire, a man whose prey tendencies didn't stop at wanting a date. I could be his dinner, for Pete's sake! I tried pointing that out to my libido, but all it saw was one extremely dishy guy. He was tall, taller than me and I'm no slouch, with lovely broad shoulders and a chest that had my Inner Nell doing a girlish swoon. His hair, a thick, heavy auburn, brushed the top of his collar. Reddish stubble grazed his lower cheeks and chin, turning my girlish swoon into a full-fledged strumpet-attack. His eyes changed from a light sky blue to a blue-black that was almost indistinguishable from his pupils. But it was something else, something more profound, that kept me from fighting him or trying to escape. Somewhere deep within this man, this vampire, I sensed a need, a cry for help that struck an answering chord inside me. I looked into his beautiful eyes and for a moment, for a breathless moment of time between seconds, I glimpsed the true nature of the darkness within him.

Life as I knew it ceased to be.

"Take slow breaths and keep your head down."

The words, rough and abrasive, were oddly calming as awareness returned to me. I was sitting on the floor, my head between my knees. All I could see were two booted feet swimming in a nauseating spinning pattern until slowly they settled into unmoving solidity. I lifted my head and looked at the vampire. "You don't have a soul."

"No," he said dryly. "Are you better now?"

"Yeah. I've never fainted before. Then again, I've never looked into a man's eyes and seen nothing but hell, either, so I guess this is a first all around. Since I don't hurt anywhere, I take it you caught me when I passed out?"

"Yes. Can you stand?" He held out his hand for me to take.

I beat down the warm thought of what it must be like to be held in his arms, and got to my feet. "Yep. A little wobbly in the knee department, but other than that, everything is OK. Listen, I'm sorry about the soulless thing. I'm sure it's nothing you care to be reminded of."

"Come," was all he said to my apology, holding open the door to the library.

"Sure. Oh, just let me grab the notes. I think they say something about where her nephew is being held." The torn sheets of paper lay scattered on the floor. I had no idea how they had fallen out of my pocket, but my brain, jet-lagged and paranormaled within an inch of insanity, decided it wasn't important.

The vamp glanced at the window. Through a crack in the heavy curtain I could see that the sky was starting to lighten. "Leave them. I don't need the notes. I know where Damian is being kept."

"You do? Great! You can tell Melissande. She's outside, waiting for me. Uh . . . we're going the wrong way. Her car is behind the castle, by a big crypt thingy."

"We're not going to Melissande."

I put the brakes on. The vampire snared my wrist in one of his steely grips and tugged me forward. "Wait a minute! Melissande is desperately trying to find her nephew and her brother. If you know where Damian is, you have to tell her so she can rescue them."

"Saer needs no help." His eyes were ice blue now, so cold I felt as if I'd been burned where his gaze touched me. I tried fighting his hold on my wrist, but he pulled me through the empty hall like I was a sack of potatoes. I *hate* pushy vampires!

"You know Saer?"

"Yes. Stop fighting me. You cannot escape."

"Ha! Just watch me," I yelled, grabbing at a nearby suit of armor.

The vamp spun around and scooped me up in one move. The breath slammed out of my lungs as he stalked off with me slung over his shoulder.

"Hey!" I yelled, dragging my gaze off the fascinating sight of his upside-down butt. I pounded my hand on his back. "Let me down! All the blood is rushing to my head!"

"Perhaps it'll do a little good there," he muttered as he flung open a wooden door, my body bouncing painfully as he raced down a long flight of stone stairs.

"I heard that! Now put me down and we can discuss this kidnapping plan you have."

"No. Stop struggling or I will be forced to subdue you."

"Subdue me?" I asked his butt, which, I'm ashamed to admit, I couldn't seem to stop ogling. Encased in snug-fitting black jeans, it was a thing of joy to behold as it moved. "Oh, right. Like what, you're going to bite my leg?"

He didn't even pause. One minute I was bouncing on his back as he trotted down the stairs, the next minute a sharp sting burned the back of my thigh.

I rose up as far as I could, shocked (and strangely thrilled) to my very core. "Oh, my God! You bit me on the leg! You drank my blood! *I am not an appetizer!*"

You are much more than an appetizer. You are a twelve-course banquet.

"Oh!" I yelled, pounding his back again. "Stop it! Stop it right now! Stop whispering into my mind, and stop biting my leg. Let me down!"

"No."

Without the least sign of gentleness or concern for me, he continued down the stairs. He didn't even pause when he reached the floor, he just headed straight into the inky-black abyss of what must have been a very large basement. Looming up in the faint light coming from the stairwell I could see stone statues, statues that seemed oddly lifelike in the shadows that embraced them.

Worry began to well up inside me. It was one thing to banter with a vampire, but if he had plans of dragging me into his crypt with him . . . my breath stuck in my throat at the thought of being buried alive. It was my worst nightmare. "You're squishing my stomach! I'm going to barf if you don't let me down."

That did the trick. He came to a halt, lowering me to the ground, his fingers encircling my wrist as I took my first full breath since he'd picked me up. "Whew! That's better. Now, about this—"

"We have no time to waste in conversation. The sun is rising. Come."

"You know, I can walk and talk at the same time. I bet if you put your vampy mind to it, you could do the same. Now, I know you've got some sort of a bee up your"—incredibly attractive—"butt, but I'm not leaving without letting Melissande know where her nephew is. She's worried sick about him."

"Regardless, you will not return to her," he said grimly, pulling me after him as he entered a narrow stone passage. There was a metallic *clink* as he flipped open a lighter, the blue flame set high. It did little to illuminate the tunnel, however. All I could tell was that it was damp, seemed to go

386

on forever, and smelled earthy. As I was dragged down the passage after the vampire, the floor changed from rock to sand, then to root-riddled dirt.

My worry turned to anger as he dragged me deep into the bowels of the castle. How dare he leave poor Melissande to worry and fret when a simple word from him could help? "You heartless bloodsucker! How can you be so selfish?"

"Selfish?" The vamp cast me a disdainful glance.

"Yes, selfish. I'm not an idiot, you know. I saw the way your ears pricked up when you found out I am a Charmer—not that I am, but Melissande thinks I am. You want me to unmake the curse I saw on you, don't you?" I asked, stumbling over a tree root that poked up out of the ground. He caught me, wrapping one arm around my waist. I ignored the voice inside me that was screaming to enjoy the embrace, realizing he was simply trying to keep me on my feet. "You think you can use me to charm away your troubles!"

"Yes."

The word was spoken with a coldness that left me shivering.

"Well, you can just think again. I can't charm anything. I'm just here to help Melissande . . . which is what you should be doing, as well. There's a boy's life at stake, and even if you aren't particularly kind or even polite, surely you're not so much of a monster that you don't care."

"How do you know I'm not a monster?"

Something flickered deep in his eyes, and once again I felt a warmth within me answering his silent call. "Don't be silly. If you were a monster, you would have ripped out my throat or made me your queen of eternal night or something like that. You're just a man, not a monster. Yes, a man with really sharp, pointy teeth and hands like a steel trap, but you're still a man, and because of that, you're bound by the constraints of humanity to help Melissande."

He marched onward, not even pausing at my plea. "She wouldn't welcome my help."

"But—"

"No!" The word was spoken with a finality that was just shy of chipped into stone. I glared at him and promised myself that the first chance I had, I'd pry the information from him about the kid and pass it on to Melissande.

"This way." He veered off into a yawning black opening, releasing me in order to throw his weight against a root-bound stone door. It squealed its protest, a nasty stone-grinding-on-stone noise filling the small chamber as the vampire slowly pushed the door closed. I stumbled backward over a large rock, the dim flame of the lighter not doing much along illumination lines.

"Who are you?" As I spoke, a dull, solid rumble shook the room, stopping with a horribly final sound. The vampire turned from the now-closed stone door. "Who are you, and where are we, and just exactly why have you kidnapped me?"

The vamp searched until he found an arm-sized piece of wood. It must have been dry, because it flamed pretty quickly when he applied the lighter to it. He held the burning wood high like a torch, his shadow massive as it flickered on the rough-hewn stone walls behind him.

"My name is Adrian Tomas, this is a small room off the tunnel leading from the castle's bolt hole, and I have taken you so that you will unmake a curse created by the demon lord Asmodeus."

"Adrian?" I whispered, my brain reeling. "Adrian the Betrayer? The one who turns his people over to Asmodeus for endless torture and horrible deaths? *That* Adrian?"

"Yes," the vampire answered, the light from the burning wood glinting on his fangs as he smiled a grim smile. "I am the Betrayer, and you, Charmer, are my prisoner."

At Avon Books, we know your passion for romance—once you finish one of our novels, you find yourself wanting more.

May we tempt you with . . .

- **Excerpts** from our upcoming releases.

- Entertaining **extras**, including authors' personal photo albums and book lists.

- Behind-the-scenes **scoop** on your favorite characters and series.

- **Sweepstakes** for the chance to win free books, romantic getaways, and other fun prizes.

- Writing **tips** from our authors and editors.

- **Blog** with our authors and find out why they love to write romance.

- **Exclusive content** that's not contained within the pages of our novels.

Join us at
www.avonbooks.com

AVON

An Imprint of HarperCollinsPublishers
www.avonromance.com